NIGHT SONGS

BEDFORD COUNTY BOOK ONE

JENNIFER SIENES

ISBN: 978-1-951839-56-7

Celebrate Lit Publishing

304 S. Jones Blvd #754

Las Vegas, NV, 89107

http://www.celebratelitpublishing.com/

This book is dedicated to my husband Chris. I am so blessed by your adventurous, God-loving heart. Thank you for always encouraging and supporting my dreams, taking on menial tasks so I can write, and loving me unconditionally.

PROLOGUE

Charlie

No amount of makeup could hide my red-rimmed eyes, and there wasn't a pill known to man to mend a broken marriage. Mine had melted away like homemade ice cream in the hot Tennessee sun the moment I caught Nick in bed with another one of his groupies.

As cold air blasted from the car vents, I dared one last look at my image in the visor. I'd concealed as much pain as possible behind a mask of foundation and mascara, and not a strand of blonde hair out of place. If the good Lord was with me, no one would see past the artifice. Then again, if the good Lord was with me, I wouldn't have been in this position to begin with. If I could just get through the day, I'd have time to fall apart later. What was Scarlett O'Hara's famous line? *I'll think about it tomorrow.*

I climbed from the Lexus and smoothed the wrinkles from my yellow linen dress before heading toward the back door of Nashville's Downtown Decor. The humidity and bass-drum-beat of my heart made breathing a chore, and, for once, I welcomed the air-conditioned chill of the showroom.

"You're late." Patrice clamped a hand around my bare upper arm and dragged me into her office.

With gritted teeth, I stepped out of her grasp. "I apologize. It couldn't be helped." Confessing that the only thing holding me together was web-thin determination would be pointless. She wasn't that kind of a boss.

"Juliette Delacroix is here. Again."

And the hits just kept coming.

Patrice, hands planted on generous hips, leaned toward me. "She's *your* client, Charlotte. No more changes. She's going to run my business into the ground if she keeps this up."

Your client. *My* business. Patrice couldn't have it both ways. "What do you want me to do?"

"I don't have a clue, but if she costs me any more money, it's coming out of your commission. Do you hear me?"

Two minutes later, I faced Juliette, Patrice's bone of contention. She was a challenge, I'd have to agree. But stuck in the middle of Patrice's mantra, "Give the client what she wants", and a client who couldn't make a decision to save her soul left me more confused than a turtle on a center stripe.

I didn't have a chance to utter a greeting before Juliette jumped in. "I know what you're thinking." She held her hands up like a traffic cop stuck in downtown commute. "But if we can make this one little adjustment, I think I'll be golden. It's a matter of moving a bank of cabinets from one wall to another. Easy, peasy, right?"

I couldn't say for sure what made me snap. Could be it was her dark, wavy hair so much like the groupie's wrapped around Nick's body the night before. Or maybe it was being bounced back and forth between Patrice and Juliette like I was just a means to an end. But most likely, I was looking for a target, and Juliette was available.

The end result was Patrice's promise that my career as an interior designer was finished. I might not have put myself in the coffin, but I sure as heck nailed it closed.

CHAPTER ONE

Charlie

The drama in my life could be captured in the lyrics of a country-western song—the only thing missing was a dog. If Nick wasn't all hat and no cattle, he could make it into a chart hit. After all my support and encouragement, the downfall of our marriage could be the catalyst his music career needed. Wouldn't that just be the icing on a cow pie?

Everything I'd put my faith in had dissipated like summer fog in a holler. It left me standing in front of Nana and Pawpaw's house with despair deep in my soul, much like I'd done twenty years ago. Except I was no longer a twelve-year-old girl, Nana and Pawpaw were gone, and the house would be more at home in a Flannery O'Connor story than on a quiet road just outside Shelbyville, Tennessee.

Nashville might only have been an hour's drive away, but the gap between success and failure couldn't be so easily traversed.

Climbing from my car, I tugged at the sweaty tank top stuck to my back and stared at the dilapidated house that sat in the middle of five acres. The sun was just starting to set, and its glow was a kindness. Nana always said ladies look much better in candlelight—and this old lady was no exception. The once-white exterior had blistered and peeled to expose gray weathered wood beneath. Termites must have feasted for years on the small balcony above the door, and it was now held together by spit and a prayer. The tall, narrow windows, upstairs and down, peered at me with suspicion, and goose-bumps skittered up my arms.

Pawpaw would've said a goose just walked on my grave.

Well, what had I expected? That the only thing left in my name, other than a car payment and a useless wardrobe, would prove to be a blessing instead of a curse?

Fingering away a trickle of sweat from my temple, I moved up the pathway, my sandals crunching in the weed-infested gravel. A low growl halted my progress, and I squinted in the waning light toward the wrap-around porch. Was that a dog hunched beneath the cock-eyed swing? I looked up toward heaven as if God was actually watching. "You've got a sense of humor, I'll say that much for You." Was it a stray, or did it belong to a neighbor? Either way, it didn't make much difference. I didn't do dogs. Especially the big, ill-tempered variety. Wouldn't it be just peachy if I was mauled by a rabid animal?

With a sudden whimper, the surly canine ambled down the wide steps, his bushy black tail swinging like the pendulum in a Grandfather clock. Wagging was a good thing, right? I mean, a dog didn't generally wag its tail if it had nefarious intentions, did it? Still, when it plopped on its hindquarters in front of me and gave me a pitiful gaze, I wasn't moved.

"Go home." I waved a hand in the general direction of

anywhere but here, hoping he knew where home was. "Go on, now." As if it could be that easy.

Ignore him. The more attention he got, the longer he'd hang about. I continued down the path, patchy grass tickling my bare ankles, and pulled the key from the front pocket of my jean shorts. My heart about thumped out of my chest when something thicker than cudweed brushed my bare leg, and I jumped aside to find the dog only inches from me. Well, heck. He'd get the message sooner or later—or die from starvation and thirst. Despite myself, I sighed. Even in my pathetic state, I wasn't cold-hearted enough to let that happen.

"Let's see if we can find you some water." We moved up the steps in tandem as if we'd been doing it forever. I laid a hand against the royal-blue double doors, faded with time and years of early morning sun. Nana believed the superstition that the color blue kept haints away. She didn't hold with Mama and Daddy's theory that all she needed was Jesus. Of course, the fact they both died young didn't give much credence to their beliefs.

A mourning dove lamented from high in the cottonwood that loomed over the house as I took a deep breath and unlocked the door. It seemed every step I took of late led me into deeper despair. Would Nana's house be an exception?

The dog pushed his way in ahead of me. The house had been vacant since Nana died, but I didn't have the time or inclination to check it. I knew there was work needing to be done, which is the reason I gave Nicky for not selling it, as he'd wanted to do. I'd hired some teen boys to store the furniture in the basement, too heartbroken to face the chore myself.

Dog and I moved through the foyer where the hardwood floors were covered in dust and scratches, and interestingly, the impression of shoe tread. A flashback of *Goldie Locks and the Three Bears* flitted through my memory. *Who's been walking through my house, said Mama bear.* Surely, this couldn't have been left over from two years ago. The windows I'd seen as yet were whole, but maybe the back door had been left open and curiosity got the better of a neighbor. Might be best to keep Dog close by until morning.

I bypassed the wide staircase and made a slow trek through the family room. Someone had stripped paint from around the window trim and left their chemicals behind. A can of Jasco sat on the floor along with a pile of rags and paint spatulas. Honey-gold tones shone through the bare wood like the glimmer of hope.

Dog sat at my side and peered up at me. I couldn't help but pat him on the head. Although a puff of dust rose from his fur, he was soft and warm to the touch. "You're more loyal than my husband, and that's a fact," I said. "Let's see what we can find in the kitchen."

Derek

If the dull throb of my low back wasn't enough to keep me awake, the quintessential question of my life's purpose was. I dragged my body from bed and stumbled through the dark room to snag the rolled-up mat behind the door. Wouldn't my Special Forces comrades get a kick in the ribs to see I've resorted to yoga? They could laugh all they wanted, but better to perfect the child's pose than let some surgeon do a hatchet job on my back.

At first the pain intensified, as it always did—like knife blades twisting in my spine. Time to schedule another round with the decompression unit. God had a plan and purpose in this. Leastways, that's what I kept telling myself. One helicopter accident, and everything had changed. Definitely put a hitch in my faith walk. Me and God were working it out, though.

With effort, I rose from the floor, stepped to the window, and raised it a bit more. The night air was warm and moist—summer in the South—and I drew it deep into my lungs. Cicadas were loud as rock music but with the smoothness of jazz. Being away all these years, I'd missed it. Didn't know how much until my first night back when the sounds of wildlife washed over me.

Mama had wanted me to stay with her in the big house—said it was more comfortable. The guest house did me fine, though. My address might've been the same, but it wasn't a lie to tell my buddies I wasn't living with my mama. A man could only take so much humiliation.

If luck was with me, I could still grab a few hours of shut eye before another day was upon us. I wandered into the kitchen to down a glass of water first. A flash of light caught my attention through the window above the sink. Was it coming from the Van Cleave house? Drink forgotten, I stepped out the back door to get a clearer view. Sure enough, a light shone through a second-story window. There wasn't anything worth stealing, but that wouldn't stop squatters from taking advantage.

After retrieving my Glock from under the bed and my shoes from the back porch, I set out for the trail that connected Mama's property to the Van Cleave's. It'd been busy as a bypass once Charlie had moved in—until about ten years ago. Had it really been that long since she and Nick married? Time was a funny thing.

The scurry of nocturnal animals rattled the brush alongside the path as I made my way by moonlight. Could be raccoons, a fox, or armadillos. The only animals that concerned me were skunks. But I arrived at the back porch without mishap and found the key I'd left under a cracked terra cotta pot alongside the door. The screen creaked like an old man's bones and gave me pause. A house this old wouldn't make it easy to sneak around, but unless I could sprout wings and fly, there was nothing left to do.

I toed my shoes off and left them in the kitchen. Glock at the ready, I snuck through the house on bare feet like I was on a deep-cover rescue mission. The stairs were solid, and I gave myself a figurative pat on the back for my stealth. How pathetic was I? Maybe I should rethink the desk job offered to me. There were worse things.

The deep growl of a canine came from the end of the hall—Charlie's bedroom from what I remembered. It was one thing to hold a squatter at bay with a gun, but a dog?

"What is it, boy?" The low words coming from the other side of the closed door were unexpected. Definitely a woman. Didn't matter—a girl was just as capable of discharging a weapon as a man.

Raising the Glock, I clicked off the safety. "You're trespassing on private property," I called out. "Slowly open the door and come out with your hands raised."

There was a rustling sound from within the room and then the definite snick of a lock. "I called the sheriff," she yelled. "You better leave before they get here."

That voice sounded familiar. "Charlie?" I reset the safety and let the gun drop to my side. "Is that you?"

"Who's there?"

"Derek." I took a few strides and reached the door just as it flew open. A ball of snarling black fur stood between me and the girl formerly known as Charlotte Van Cleave. Gone was the poised and polished woman I'd last seen at her nana's funeral.

Instead, she looked like the lost waif I first laid eyes on twenty years before.

I itched to reach out and touch her to be sure she was real, but I expected her canine protector would extract a limb if I did. “What’re you doing here?”

Her eyes widened as she folded her arms, chin jutted. “What am *I* doing here? What are *you* doing here? Aren’t you supposed to be overseas saving the world from communism, or socialism, or something?”

Stepping forward, I was stopped short by another low growl. “Nice dog you have there. Want to call him off?”

“He isn’t mine.”

I quirked an eyebrow at her.

“I swear. He was here when I showed up a couple hours ago. I don’t even like dogs.” The softening of her eyes when she patted his head told a different story.

“So, is my brother here with you?”

The scowl she threw me would’ve had more impact if it weren’t for the tear that slid down her cheek.

Why was I not surprised? Didn’t I warn her all those years ago? Hadn’t I reinforced it with every meeting since? But saying I told you so would only rile her. Practicality was the best course. “Think you should call the sheriff’s office back and let them know there isn’t a prowler?”

“I was bluffing. I left my phone downstairs.” Her face crumpled, and I took my chances with the dog to pull her in for a hug.

CHAPTER TWO

July—2002
Charlie

Charlie snuck out of her bedroom and down the wood stairs on bare feet, carrying her shoes to keep the floors quiet. She'd been to the house before, but its size still confounded her. Why would two people live in such a grand place when there were others who lived in shacks? This was the house her Daddy grew up in, but he and her Mama chose to do things different. Not better, for dang sure, but different.

Even though the sun wasn't full up yet, bugs and butterflies darted about. She stopped on the back porch and slipped her shoes on before running across the yard to the pathway she remembered from her last visit. The moisture in the air smelled sweet. Could be the blossoms on the magnolia tree that towered over the house in the back. They were white and fat and looked to be out of a storybook like *Alice and Wonderland*, with waxy green leaves as big as her hand. She'd not seen the likes of it in Africa.

She picked her way through red maples, hackberries, and birch so thick the sky didn't poke through. It was the perfect place to hide out, where Nana and Pawpaw wouldn't hear her screams or rants at God. The heat and humidity were familiar. The forest of trees between her grandparents' home and the Daniels' farm next door brought with it the flavor of the Congo, and her heart ached a touch just to think on it.

She missed Mama and Daddy the most, especially since she'd never see them again—at least not on Earth. But they weren't the only ones she wouldn't see again. There was Mose and the other girls who were trying to teach her Swahili while she helped them with their English. And, of course, the other missionaries in the village.

She plopped on a giant rock—there were plenty of them around—and tipped her head back to get a glimpse of dark clouds between the foliage of trees. Birds sang out as if they hadn't a care in the world and she spotted red and brown cardinals flitting from branch to branch. The only birdsong she could identify was the coo of doves and that of the mocking-bird. Daddy explained to her last summer when they visited Tennessee that the mockingbird didn't have its own song but gave a jumbled rendition of other birds' greatest hits. "Like a classic rock medley," he'd said.

The memory of Daddy shaking his head and laughing at the constant chatter of a mockingbird brought a fresh onslaught of tears. She'd been crying almost non-stop for a week now. Her eyes should be as dry as the Sahara Desert.

With fists clenched and sobs choking her, she cried out, "How could You?" The tree limbs shook with the sudden flutter of dozens of birds hightailing it for safety. There were no more songs being sung above, and the humid heat that was familiar before now felt heavy as Nana's piano sitting on her chest. "Mama and Daddy didn't do nothing but serve You, God. They gave up everything for You." Even me, she thought. All those years in the Congo, she knew she didn't fit in—even with Mose. But she didn't fit in here, either. Especially with Mama and Daddy gone.

"Hey there."

Charlie snapped her head around. Who was infringing on her grief? Two boys. Well, one boy and one almost-man, so tall he'd dwarf her daddy. Maybe she'd wandered off her grandparents' property, and she was the one in the wrong.

"You're Charlie, ain't you?" the almost-man said. "I'm Derek and this here is my brother, Nicky." He hitched a thumb at the other one. Derek's hair was so short, Charlie could almost see his scalp beneath. They each had a cane pole resting on their shoulders, and Derek carried a small bucket. "We met last summer when you came to visit. Do you remember?"

They must think she was a cry baby. She hopped off the rock and swiped the tears from her cheeks with the back of a hand. "I remember. Didn't mean to trespass."

"You ain't." Nicky smiled as he pushed a hank of dark hair off his forehead. "We're crossing your granddaddy's property to get to our fishing hole. So, we're the ones trespassing."

Derek's dark eyes focused on something above her head, and he shrugged. "We're sorry as we can be about your mama and daddy."

Heat flooded Charlie's face while a fist-sized knot set in her throat, and she dropped her gaze to the ground. A black caterpillar with a yellow stripe inched its way across a weedy patch of dirt. What would it be like to change from one thing to another? Charlie would give anything to hide away in a cocoon only to wake up a butterfly. She'd fly from niche to nook until she found a place that felt like home—if there was such a thing.

"I didn't mean to upset you."

Clenching her hands, she swallowed hard and lifted her head. "You didn't."

Silence sat like an unwelcome guest, and she didn't know where to look. Why didn't they just go on and fish?

Nicky squirmed. "What grade are you gonna be in?"

That was an easy enough question. "Seventh." It only took a second or two to remember her manners. "You?"

His grin was so wide, she could see one of his front teeth was crooked. "I'm starting high school." He nudged his brother. "Derek here is going into the army."

Charlie guessed he wasn't an almost-man if he was leaving home. "The army?" What in the Sam Hill was he thinking? "Why?" The question popped out before she could filter it through common sense.

Derek flashed a smile and shrugged like he wasn't the least bit perturbed by her question. "Best way to pay for college."

Nicky snorted. "Yeah, right." He leaned in close to Charlie like he was going to share a secret. "He wants to save the world. College is just an excuse."

August—2002

Derek

Derek hadn't recognized Charlie when he first laid eyes on her crying her heart out to God. It'd taken him a moment to connect the news his mama had shared the week before to the skinny, pigtailed waif. He couldn't imagine losing one of his parents, let alone both at the same time. Of course, he'd seen her before. She and her mama had been out a few Christmases before, and both her parents were with her when they visited last summer. But Derek didn't pay her no mind. She had been just a kid.

Still was.

But there was something in her eyes that latched onto his soul and made him question his reasons for deploying. Maybe she was a messenger from God, like the prophets in the Old Testament, staying his decision. It seemed like every time he turned around, there she was. A few weeks passed, and the days were drawing close for him to leave.

Mid-August was hot as Hades with enough humidity to fill a bucket. He promised Daddy he'd get the John Deere Taskmaster running or die trying, which was a real possibility. The old tractor was twenty-five years old—still in her prime—but she resisted all his attempts. He praised God for the cloud cover because there was no way he was going to wrangle her into the barn. Then a breeze kicked up taking the temperature down a notch or two. Still, sweat poured down his face as he tucked back into the engine.

"Watcha doing?"

Derek jumped at the unexpectedness of the voice and cracked his temple on the cover. "What's it look like?" Pain put sharpness to his tone, and regret was quick to follow. He'd learn to curb his tongue one of these days. He might could memorize a few verses from James to start.

"Well, ain't you in a mood." The grin that flirted at the corners of her mouth told him she took no offense to his outburst.

She wore faded jean-shorts that her long legs had outgrown. Water dripped from her braid, leaving wet spots on her ratty pink t-shirt. Her skin was the color of his coffee when he laced it with a good dose of cream. No doubt she been swimming down at the pond while Nicky sat on the bank picking at his old guitar. It didn't make no difference to him—he was just relieved to see the old-soul pain in her eyes subsiding a smidge.

"Let's trade places, and we'll see how it sits with you."

"Nah. I wouldn't know the first thing about fixing an engine." She sidled up close to him, and he caught a whiff of Coppertone and pond water. "Another two weeks before you leave for the army, huh?"

Derek grabbed a rag off the tractor seat and swiped the sweat from his eyes. "Yep. Just about the time you'll be getting ready to start school."

She wrinkled her nose and ran a thumbnail along a spot of chipped green paint.

"You don't look too excited about it."

She drew her shoulders up to her ears and let them drop again. "My mama home-schooled me from the time I was four. Sitting in a classroom doesn't sound like much fun."

What little he'd learned in history about civil wars in the Congo, and what he'd researched since Charlie showed up last month, made him grateful that she'd be tucked away in a boring classroom. If he ever became a daddy, he'd sure not want his kid in that kind of danger.

"Once you make friends—"

"I had friends."

He craned his neck in time to see her bat the tears from her eyes and swallow a couple times. Arms folded across her skinny chest, she looked down and kicked at a pebble. She seemed so feisty and independent he could sometimes forget her life had just been hit with the force of a tornado.

"I'm sorry, Charlie."

Her lips twitched despite her tears. "You sound like the tuna commercial."

Derek conjured up a grin. Poor kid. "Well, knowing you, I'm sure you'll make all kinds of new friends."

She plopped onto the tractor's running board. "So, what Nicky says about you wanting to save the world. Is it true?"

Her question played right into his own recent thoughts, and he wanted to ignore it. But Charlie wasn't easily put off. "I told you already. If I give four years to the army, I can go to college on the G.I. Bill."

"My mama and daddy thought they could save the world," she mumbled. "Look where that got them. Why can't you do something safe, like Nicky's going to do?"

"I do declare, Charlie Van Cleave, you sound like you're worried about me."

She reached down to nab a small rock from the ground. "I don't want nothing to happen to you is all."

He didn't think she'd feel any better if he reminded her that he could just as easily die in a car accident or get hit by a bus crossing the street. Instead, he infused a little humor in his words. "Yeah? And what would you have me do? Sing backup for Nicky's county-western band?" He laughed. "Afraid I'd starve to death."

"You think Nicky will really be a star someday?"

"I think if Nicky learns to get out of his own way, he can do anything he sets his mind to."

Lines formed between her eyebrows. "I don't know what that means."

"Mark my words, sweet Charlie, the day'll come when you will."

He ruffled her head, reached into the cooler at his feet, and offered her a Coke.

CHAPTER THREE

Charlie

A raucous mockingbird pierced through my dream—confused, my mind searched for a tangible place to land. Where was I? What day was it? Then dread and dismay grappled for position as it all flooded back, quick as a lick. Nick's betrayal, my colossal meltdown at work, and Derek's strong arms holding me up while I drenched his shirt with my sobs. Even with eyes squeezed shut, I knew the sun was full up—there was a pinkness filtering through my lids. I wanted the escape of sleep, or, better yet, a deep coma that could hold me in place until my world had righted itself.

Nana's words whispered to my spirit as if she were floating over me. *The quickest way out of a problem is through it.* It might be, Nana acquired her wisdom from the book of Proverbs and Psalms.

With a groan, I cracked my eyes open a smidge. My childhood bedroom was in a sad and worn-out state, much like me, with its faded pink walls, grungy baseboards, and grime-covered windows. There was little resemblance to the first time I saw it when Nana had been trying to assuage my little-girl grief with a princess-pink palace.

The mockingbird continued its concert, flitting from one birdsong to another like an indecisive gossip. The warm breeze that touched my face brought with it the tang of fresh-cut grass, and I caught the sound of a lawn tractor nearby. I rolled onto my side, stiff back kicking up a protest, to squint through one of the three floor-to-ceiling windows along the east wall. A hundred-year-old cottonwood filled the view, which is where I assumed Mr. Mockingbird's stage was set.

Where had that mutt gone off to? I propped myself up on my side, Derek's thin sleeping bag the only thing between my aching bones and the hardwood floor. Dog was sprawled in the doorway, my knight in shaggy fur. Before I could call him over, he leapt into attack mode and stared down the hall, a rumble deep in his throat. Was it my imagination, or did the fur on the back of his neck stand up?

Before concern could wrap itself around my muddled brain, Derek called from downstairs. "Charlie, you up? I brought coffee and donuts. Just want to make sure you survived the night."

My stomach competed with Dog's growl, and I tried to remember when I last ate. Could be my problems wouldn't look so bleak with something in my belly. "I'll be right down."

I pushed off the floor with the speed of an eighty-year-old, every muscle in my body screaming while Dog abandoned me. Maybe I should've taken Derek up on the offer of his couch, after all. Instead, I allowed him to bless me with a sleeping bag for a mattress, a sheet for a blanket, washcloth, hand towel and a roll of toilet paper. It clearly wasn't my finest moment when I showed up yesterday with only the clothes on my back.

Without a change of clothes, I resembled a bag lady without a bag. But it was just Derek.

When I got downstairs, Derek was in the kitchen placing a bowl of food in front of my canine hero—which he didn't hesitate to devour. A bag of Purina Dog Chow sat next to a couple travel mugs on the chipped and yellowed Formica counter, along with a paper sack.

"Sorry I can't offer you a seat at the table." I leaned my backside against the chipped sink and accepted the mug stamped with "Go Army" Derek offered. "I'm suddenly very aware of how unprepared I was to come here."

He hopped onto the counter, his legs so long, his toes nearly touched the floor. I'd have to be dead not to notice the muscles bunching in his arms or the width of his shoulders. He definitely wasn't a 17-year-old, almost-man anymore. "Panic mode'll do that. Course, I'm only making assumptions here since you haven't divulged any details."

I'd been able to divert his questions with my pathetic sobs, too tired and distraught to relive the drama. But today was another day, and the truth would have to come out sooner or later. I voted for later. "Thanks for taking care of me last night." I saluted him with my mug. "And this morning."

"Should I assume you and Nicky are having marital problems?"

I choked on the coffee as it was halfway down my throat. After coughing it clear, I tested my voice with an answer. "Assume away." It came out more croak than substance.

"Anything that can't be repaired?"

Oh, how I wished I could blurt it all out. I hadn't seen Derek in two years—not since Nana's funeral. He'd made some crack about three funerals and a wedding, and it had taken me a moment to realize it was a play on the movie *Four Weddings and a Funeral.* His daddy's, Pawpaw's, Nana's, and my wedding. As sure as I was sitting there, once I told Derek the truth about Nicky, he'd play the hero to my damsel-in-distress. It was his nature.

"I don't want you involved, Derek." My stomach gurgled, and I slid the paper sack toward me. Even before I opened it, I knew what I'd find. Homemade donuts. Bless Mama G's heart.

"You worried I might challenge him to a duel?"

I broke off a piece of dough and popped it into my mouth. Sugar and cinnamon melted on my tongue and, for the moment it took to chew it, I was in heaven. "At the very least."

"Does my mama know what's going on with you two?"

I shook my head. "I visit Mama G every month or so, but I only share the stuff that'll make her smile. It's not fair to put her in the middle, either."

He scowled. "Heck, Charlie, we're the only kin you got."

Hearing I was considered family eased my distress, though not by much. There were fewer than five people I could count on in a crisis. "That's not strictly true. I have my cousin, Jenna. And don't forget her parents." Of course, I couldn't quite remember the last time I'd seen my aunt and uncle. They weren't two of the favored five.

"What about close friends? Anyone you can confide in?"

"Jenna's got that covered, too."

His eyes caught mine, the sympathy in them rich as cream. "Let me help."

There was one thing he could do. The idea of driving back to Nashville to collect my things didn't sit well. Nicky wouldn't be around, I was sure. Still with his groupie, or sleeping off a party at a bandmate's, most likely. But just walking into our apartment would do me in.

"Would you be willing to pick up a few things from my place? If not, no problem, it's just—"

"Done." He reached into the bag and pulled out a donut. "Give me a list, some clue where to find things, and a key."

Guilt sliced through me. "Are you sure? I mean, I don't even know why you're home. Are you on leave? When do you report back?"

He froze for an instant, his eyes wide, before he shook his head. "Reckon things are worse than I thought."

"What d'you mean?"

"Nicky's known I was home for the last couple weeks, and he hasn't bothered to tell you?"

Why wasn't I surprised? Neither kin nor communication was much of a priority for my husband.

Derek

Downtown Nashville was a sweltering 93 degrees with heat radiating from the concrete buildings and streets. My shirt stuck to the small of my back the moment I climbed out of Charlie's car. The windshield of the Lexus sported a parking permit—necessary if I didn't want to hike a mile or pay a hefty fee.

I'd only ever been to Nicky and Charlie's once before when I'd come home for another funeral. Charlie's nana's. I figured with Charlie in the midst of grieving, yet again, we'd have a quiet evening to talk. But I should've known better—Nicky didn't do quiet evenings. Everything with him was an event, and that night was no different. Safety in numbers and all that. Was he so insecure with himself, he needed the buffer of a crowd? There must've been twenty people crammed into the small apartment. The music was loud and the drinking hard. Charlie wasn't there, and I didn't bother to stay. I hadn't seen or heard from her again until the night before.

The apartment building on 2nd Avenue, with a view of the Cumberland River, was convenient to Broadway where Nicky spent much of his time playing bars. There was nothing unique about the place, which made it difficult to imagine Charlie being at home there. I found it impossible to reconcile the child-Charlie who'd cried on my shoulder twelve hours ago with the grown-up Charlotte who drove a Lexus. One was pond water and lightening bugs and the other was expensive perfume and pearls.

Will the real Charlotte please stand up?

The two-story interior atrium was enclosed by brick walls with rows of concrete planters lined up along the sides. Each ivy-filled planter had a metal arch behind it, and the vines grew to meet in the center. At the far end of the atrium was a spiral staircase. The faint of heart could take the elevator, but I was made of sturdier stuff—at least in that moment. Aside from traffic, I hadn't seen anyone on the street, and the building was quiet, as well. Most people were probably at work or locked away in their air-conditioned apartment.

With a large empty duffel bag slung over one shoulder, I climbed to the second floor. My footsteps echoed on the metal steps, each one increasing my discomfort. What did I know about women's stuff? Going through Charlie's drawers didn't sit well with me, but what was a guy to do? A promise was a promise. Get the bag filled and get out. Easy, right? I pulled the keys she'd given me from the pocket of my jeans and found the right one. Charlie didn't think Nicky would be there, but I wasn't taking any chances. If some guy came into my place uninvited, I wouldn't take it too kindly. I knocked loud enough to wake the dead before unlocking the door.

Empty beer bottles and overflowing ashtrays littered the family room. My nose wrinkled at the lingering smell of alcohol and stale cigarette smoke. The exterior wall was brick with three tall, arched windows overlooking the river. The light pouring in only highlighted the mess. Charlie's interior design skills were wasted on this place. Colorful artwork and creative Knick knacks looked incongruous among the remnants of party central. How had she lived in this environment for ten years?

"Charlie? That you?" Nicky called out before a fit of coughing took his voice.

Staring down the hallway, I dropped the duffel bag on the floor and pocketed the keys. "It's not Charlie. It's Derek."

Wearing only a pair of black boxers, he stepped into the hallway scratching his bare chest. Dark hair fell into his bloodshot eyes, and he sported about a week's worth of scraggly beard. "What the—what're you doing here?" He sounded as welcoming as a skunk at a hen party.

"Charming as usual." I waved a hand around the room. "Love what you've done with the place."

He threw me a scowl on his way to the kitchen. "Should've called first, Derek, and I might have cleaned up a bit."

I leaned against the kitchen door jam and watched him fill a glass with water at the sink, his back to me. "I'm not here to see you. I came for Charlie's things."

That got his attention. He rounded on me, eyes wide. "Where is she?" The concern in his voice soured my gut.

"You going to tell me you're worried about her?"

"Of course, I'm worried. She didn't come home last night."

"Yeah, looks like you really missed her."

He glared at me. "What d'you know? You haven't been around for years and suddenly you're an expert?"

"Not an expert." I turned to retrieve the duffel bag. "Just

the guy whose shoulder she cried on last night. I don't know what you did, but—"

"It was one time, and it didn't mean squat."

It took a beat for me to make sense of his words. I snatched up the bag and turned on him. "You piece of... you cheated on her?" I'd hoped there would be a chance for them to reconcile, but after his confession, I wasn't so sure.

He jabbed a hand in the air. "I'm telling you, Derek, it didn't mean nothing. She was some groupie, is all."

Red-hot rage shot through me, and I slammed him up against the wall, the duffel bag now between our bodies. My fist shook with the effort it took not to plant it into his face. His eyes widened. With shock or fear? Never had I lost control like this. What was wrong with me? I pushed him away like he was nothing more than yesterday's trash.

Nick slid to the floor. "This is none of your business. You ain't her pa or even her brother, so it don't concern you."

With shaking fingers, I pulled Charlie's list from my pocket as I headed down the hall. "You don't really believe that do you?"

Nick's voice followed me. "You should be thanking me, big brother. You've always had it bad for Charlie, and now's your chance. You can swoop in and be her hero." His voice cracked on the last word.

I swallowed the emotion that sat like a fist in my throat. I couldn't deny what Nicky said. But the way he said it made it sound like a joke...and it didn't make me feel one whit better.

CHAPTER FOUR

Charlie

Loss was a hard row to hoe, and there'd been plenty to go around. When Mama and Daddy passed, and I was sent back to the states, I thought I'd live the rest of my days grieving it. I had Nana and Pawpaw, sure, but it was Mama G who pulled me from the mire. That woman had a way about her—could lay eyes on a patch of chickweed and see only their minuscule flowers. Unless they dared to encroach on her yard.

There wasn't a stray blade to be seen between the bricks laid out in a path leading up to her front porch. Boxwoods stood like sentinels in the flowerbed along the front of the railing, their starkness softened by yarrow, purple coneflower, and red day lilies. A magnolia, older than Moses, shaded the east side of the house, the faint scent of its blooms blanketing me with memories.

The only time this haven was less than its Southern best was right after Nicky and Derek's Daddy died a little over six years before. He was vibrant one day and—lickety-split—had gone home to Jesus the next. Mama G told me that a heart attack could do that to a body. Aside from the unkempt look about the yard and the dullness in her eyes, I wouldn't have known she was suffering a loss far deeper than my own.

I shook off the memory with a sigh. There was more than enough gloom attached to this visit, and it wouldn't do to add to it with the past.

I couldn't step onto Mama G's porch without the sense of being wrapped in a Southern hug, the likes of which could snatch the breath clear from my lungs. A porch swing nestled the railing at one end. At the other, two wing-back rattan chairs with chintz-covered cushions invited passersby to sit a spell. No doubt, Mama G would offer a plate of homemade chocolate chip cookies or Moon Pies and sweet tea.

The moment I stepped onto the first tread of the painted-wood steps, the cicadas began to sing. Dog nudged my hand with his wet nose as if asking permission to join me. Short of tying him up at Nana's house, I couldn't have stopped him. Why he chose manners at this time confounded me. It might be he sensed he'd soon be in the company of a fine lady.

The front door was open, and I peered through the screen. It could be Mama G was out back in the vegetable garden or elbows-deep into canning in the kitchen. Although I strained my ears to listen, there was no sound to be heard. Maybe I should have called first, but it was hard enough to face her with the news I had to share without being caught up with questions ahead of time.

"Land sakes alive. Charlie, is that you?"

I spun around at Mama G's voice. She stood at the bottom of the stairs with a bouquet of sunflowers cradled in her arms like a newborn babe.

Before I could answer, Dog abandoned me to sit at her feet

like she was a queen, and he one of her loyal subjects. She shifted the flowers and scratched his ear. His eyes drifted shut while he groaned. I couldn't blame him; she had the same effect on me.

"Sorry to just drop in." I crossed my arms and descended the steps.

"Pshaw. Child, you know better than that." She stepped around Dog and pulled me in for a hug. "A visit from my daughter is of highest importance. I don't suppose you brought that husband of yours."

Her words were bittersweet. Once I told her about leaving Nicky, would she be so quick to bless me with the endearment? Then again, I'd received that honor long before I married him.

"We need to talk."

Her mouth tightened into a hard line like she knew my news would be unpleasant.

"Let me take those in for you." I gathered the flowers from her arms and turned to move up the steps.

"When did you get a dog?" There was a lilt to her words as if she wouldn't allow any unseemly business to mar her good graces.

"I didn't. He just appeared."

Mama G reached past me to open the screen door, and I stepped into the house where it was cooler by degrees. If only this was like any other visit. A pit sat in my stomach at the notion of disappointing her. She'd been a mama to me longer than my own, and to lose that might be more than I could survive.

"I wonder where he came from," Mama G said as she held the door open for Dog to enter. "He doesn't look like a stray."

"He can stay outside." It was one thing for him to leave dog prints and hair in Nana's house, but it was altogether another thing for him to track it into Mama G's. I shooed Dog out onto the porch and closed the screen behind him. It wouldn't be the worst thing if he wandered back to wherever he came from before I got attached.

I followed Mama G into the kitchen, and she filled a large glass vase at the sink. "Do you want to clip the ends of the stems before we put them in water?"

She hefted the now heavy vase onto the counter and swiped a strand of gray hair from her face. "What's my boy done now?" Her piercing blue eyes, so much like Nicky's, caught mine and held.

"How'd you know?"

She cupped my cheek with a work-worn hand. "Sweet Charlotte, of all the people I know and love, none have eyes that reveal the soul more than yours." She gave me a weak smile. "And although I love my Nicky more than my own life, I'm not blind to his faults. The boy's always been his own worst enemy."

Relief had tears pricking at the back of my eyes and choking off my voice.

"Why don't I fix us a glass of sweet tea and we can sit here in the kitchen for a spell? It's too hot to be outside. You can get a bowl of water for that dog of yours."

"He's not my dog."

"Try telling him that. And you might could come up with a more creative name for him."

As I retrieved a metal bowl from the cabinet, Mama G collected the tea things and dug into the cookie jar. Chocolate chip, just like I expected.

Derek

Charlie's house sat quiet as the air preceding a tornado, which seemed a precursor to what was to come. Life was a balancing act between the quiet and the chaos, but it seemed as if Charlie'd had a bigger slice of misfortune than most. Nicky's words pecked at my head like an accusation—*you can swoop in and be her hero*. As if after all the years that had passed, it could be so easy.

The front door was open, so I slipped the duffel bag full of Charlie's things into the foyer, traded the fancy Lexus for my Ford pickup, and headed back to Mama's. As I pulled the truck around the back of the house, I spotted the mutt who'd adopted Charlie laying on the front porch. Where Dog was, Charlie was sure to be. I was grateful as could be for the warning.

Sure enough, Mama's laughter met my ears as I stepped up to the back door. Charlie sat across from her at the kitchen table. The two of them together were like peanuts and Coke—different as night is to day, but still a sweet combination.

When I stepped through the door, Mama beamed at me. "There he is. Charlie and I was just talkin' about you."

Charlie's face twisted up like she'd bit into a lemon. What got her tail up? Hadn't I just drove to Nashville and back to save her the hassle and humiliation?

"Derek Lucius Daniels," Charlie said like she was getting ready to lay down the law. "Why didn't you tell me you'd been in a helicopter crash?" She stood to her full height and pierced me with a hard stare which lost its punch when her eyes swam with tears.

I'd rather face a platoon of combatants than a crying Charlie. "Probably for the same reason you didn't tell me Nicky cheated on you." Charlie's cheeks turned pink as she crossed her arms and glared at me before turning to Mama.

"What?" Mama slowly rose, reaching a hand toward

Charlie as if to soothe. "You said y'all was having a difference of opinion."

She huffed out a breath. "I'm of the opinion he shouldn't sleep around, and he's of the opinion he should."

"Goodness gracious." Mama sighed. "That's quite a kettle of fish he got himself into, isn't it?"

Charlie reached down to snag a bucket on the floor filled with cleaning products, paper towels, and rags. "It's nothing for you to worry about, Mama G. This is between Nicky and me." She gave Mama a quick hug and trounced out of the room like she had a right to turn her nose up at me.

"I left your things inside your front door," I called out after her.

No response other than the sound of her footsteps marching through the sitting room.

"You're welcome, Charlie."

The front screen slammed. A grin itched to grow, and I shook it off. She might act all high and mighty, but I knew her anger was born of worry over me which would dissipate the second she remembered I was still walking upright.

Mama clucked her tongue and gathered up the dishes on the table. "It sounds like neither of you were very forthcoming when you talked."

"I figured Nicky told her I was home. Guess that bit of news wasn't all that important to him." Of course, why should that have surprised me? "Did she tell you she lost her job?"

Mama's mouth tightened, and she shook her head. "I didn't even think to ask why she was coming by on a weekday."

"She had a meltdown at work, and now I know what precipitated it."

"Did you see your brother?"

"Yes'm. I went by their apartment to collect some things

for Charlie. Didn't expect him to be there. Looked as if he was sleeping off quite a night. I don't know how she's lived with it this long." Maybe it was for the best, Nicky showing his true colors.

She rummaged in the refrigerator and pulled out the fixings for sandwiches. "I do declare, some days that boy's only got one oar in the water."

"He's not a boy anymore, Mama. He's a grown man with little sense. If Daddy were here, he'd box his ears."

She frowned. "Tell me you didn't do it for him, Derek."

"Came close. Don't reckon I can understand how he could just throw away the best thing going for him."

She pursed her lips. "You know what else your daddy would do if he was here?"

A sermon was sure to follow. "I'm afraid you're going to tell me." I took a couple plates from the cupboard.

"He'd help him get back on the narrow road, son. He's lost his way, and just needs a little guidance. I'm sure if you talk to him, he might could turn things around."

"Oh, Mama, you do tend toward optimism. If he's not willing to bend an ear to Jesus, I don't think he's likely to listen to any wisdom I might impart. For reasons I can't figure, he always seems ripe for a battle with me. The least little thing I say gets him riled."

Mama lined four slices of white bread on a cutting board and unscrewed the lid off a jar of Duke's. "He's jealous of you, Derek. You're Abel to his Cain, is all."

I froze in the process of uncovering a plate of meat loaf. "That's ludicrous. What's he got to be jealous of me for? He has it all. Pursuing a career he loves with the girl of his dreams by his side."

"You mean *had* it all." She touched my arm. "Don't you see that everything he does is a cry to be noticed?"

I let that stew for a moment. "Okay, yeah. I get that. But what's it got to do with me?"

"Let's just say your offering is much more pleasing to God than his. You've always had a mind to serve others in some way. You were born with it, son. But Nicky, he's been scrambling for a way to one-up you from the moment he could walk, and it seemed to get worse once Charlie was in the picture."

I've no doubt Mama meant her observation to be a compliment, but it didn't lay on my heart as such. It's like I'd failed my little brother by merely being me. What was I supposed to do with that?

CHAPTER FIVE

Charlie

Sweat trickled into my eyes as I attacked the linoleum floor in Nana and Pawpaw's kitchen with a bucket of Spic & Span and a scrub brush. How the heck could I be back here, twenty years later, in such a deplorable condition? At least when I was a child, I had Nana and Pawpaw. What did I have now?

"A worthless cur for a husband, no job, no dignity, and no family to speak of," I muttered to no one in particular. It was doubtful even God heard me these days since I hadn't seen fit to set foot in a church since my wedding day. If I was of a mind to think on it for long, there could be a correlation.

A low whine shifted my attention to Dog, who lay in the kitchen doorway, head cocked as if to remind me that I had him. Since my arrival two days ago, the mutt hadn't left my side for more than the time it took him to do his business. And though a softness tugged at my insides at his loyalty, reality was a wet slap in the face—he wasn't my dog, and even if he was, I could barely afford to feed myself, let alone a seventy-five-pound bodyguard.

"Yoo-hoo. Anybody home?"

Dog's feet spun on the linoleum to get traction as he scrambled out of the kitchen to head off the interloper. I just hoped he didn't see fit to take a bite out of the woman, whoever she was.

I dropped the scrub brush into the bucket, peeled off the rubber gloves, and followed in Dog's wake, albeit at a much slower pace. I wasn't keen on seeing anyone, even if I'd been wearing something more presentable than ripped jeans and a stained tank top. I swiped at a strand of hair that escaped my ponytail and was stuck to the side of my face.

Dog's growl came from the foyer, low and threatening, and I was grateful for his protection. Again. Once I got used to having him around, he'd probably abandon me, just like everyone else in my life.

"Charlie?" The voice, now familiar, had an edge to it. "That's a good doggie," she said in a softer tone.

Jenna stood with her back against the wall, hands held up like a traffic cop as if that would stop Dog if he lit into her. Despite feeling tetchy, my lips twitched. She shook so hard, the pile of dark blond hair on top of her head looked close to toppling.

"Come on, Dog, let her go." I tapped his shoulder, and he sat on his haunches. Someone trained him well.

Jenna pressed a hand to her chest and laid her hazel eyes on me. "Lordy mercy, Charlie. That animal took ten years off my life."

"That's what you get when you sneak into someone's house." I folded my arms suddenly aware of the picture I must've made—and it wasn't a pretty one. Last time I saw Jenna, we had grabbed a quick bite during my lunch hour. I was dressed to dazzle then. "I'd give you a hug, but I don't want to muss you."

Jenna waved a dismissive hand, closed the space between us, and wrapped her pudgy arms around me. "Bless your heart, Charlie. I'm as sorry as I can be about Nicky. He certainly made a fist of things, didn't he? A course, I have a feeling it ain't the first time. I was jus' gonna drop off a care package for you. Left it in my van."

"Are you kidding me? How in blue blazes did you know?"

She twisted her mouth, eyes staring past me like the answer materialized on the wall. "Well, let's see. Cal told me, a course, and he heard it from one of the guys on his crew who's the brother of one of the boys who plays bass for Nicky." She turned her gaze on me. "I'd a much rather heard it from you, though."

"Sounds like I would've had to tell you before it happened to beat your efficient communication system." I led the way to the kitchen. The least I could do was offer her some sweet tea and Mama G's homemade cookies for her trouble.

She kept a safe distance from Dog as he crossed the kitchen and plopped onto the floor with a sigh. "When'd ya get a dog?"

I sighed. Maybe I should carry a sign. "He's not mine. He was here when I showed up the other day. You want some tea?" I caught the extra twang in my voice, which happened every time I was around my cousin. As a kid, it had taken me a full year to learn to decipher her drawl.

Jenna twisted this way and that as if trying to find a place to sit. There wasn't a stick of furniture, and unless she upended my Spic & Span bucket, she'd have to stand or cop a squat on the floor. She chose to stand. "Charlie, what're you doing here? How come you ain't at work?"

I rinsed out the only two glasses I had and set them on the counter. "It seems your gossip chain is a little flawed after all."

I retrieved the pitcher of tea and an ice cube tray from the Frigidaire. “I got fired.”

Her mouth dropped open. “Whatever for? You all but built that woman’s business.”

“It’s a long story. Suffice it to say, she didn’t take too kindly to me attacking a client. Fortunately for me, this place is empty.”

“If you say so. You ain’t thinking of livin’ here, are you?”

“No, of course not.” I handed her a full glass. “I’ll just jet over to my condo on the Gulf and set up shop there.”

She scowled. “There’s no call to be ugly.”

Shame birthed tears at the back of my eyes. “You’re right. I’m sorry.” I blew out a breath. “I don’t know what to do, Jenna. Everything’s gone sideways.”

“You don’t need that ol’ shop in Nashville to be a successful designer. Just start your own.”

As if it were that easy. “It took me ten years to build up a clientele.”

“So? I’m sure anyone you worked with would be loyal to you.”

I shook my head. “I signed a non-compete agreement. Whatever clients I got working there are theirs.”

Jenna sighed. “Well, boogers. You’re the hardest working person I know, Charlie. You’ll figure something out. In the meantime, you can’t live here like some kind of vagrant. You’re welcome to stay with me and Cal.”

And her four kids? Not likely. “That’s a sweet offer, but I’m fine here. Besides, I have all Nana and Pawpaw’s furniture and things stored in the basement. Once I get them up here, it’ll be more like home.”

“Are you gonna sell the place?”

The house may have looked like something out of a Rebecca James novel, but it was all I had left. “Not if I can help it." I chewed my lip and glanced around, trying to see it through Jenna's eyes. For certain, it didn't resemble any of the uppity places I'd designed in Nashville. "I know it needs some work."

"That's an understatement. If the rest of the house looks like this, it'd cost a pretty penny just to fix the cosmetic issues, as you'd know that better than anyone."

I tapped a broken nail against my glass. "I'm not afraid of hard work, and I wield a mighty fine paint brush."

"You're plumb crazy, Charlie. The second-story balcony looks like it's about to collapse, which surely means the structure ain't all that safe. Then, you got the roofing and foundation to take into consideration. It's a wonder this place hasn't been condemned yet."

Just what I needed—the voice of doom and gloom. "When did Cal put you on the payroll?" But being snarky about it didn't change the fact Jenna wasn't saying anything I hadn't already thought of.

My cell trilled from the other side of the kitchen. It was probably Nicky—he'd left five messages in the last two days, but I wasn't ready to talk to him. I went to check the caller ID. Derek. I was none too happy with him either but answered it anyway. "Hey, Derek."

"Oh, good, you're talking to me again. I have an appointment in Columbia. Need a change of scenery?"

If I'd had my druthers, as Nana would say, I'd hole up in my nearly condemned burrow like a woodchuck in winter until Jesus returned. Derek would have none of it, though, and used a good dose of guilt to motivate me to accompany him to Columbia. The truth of it was I owed him an apology. It wasn't like I'd even bothered to ask why he was home before I'd jumped all up in his business. I said my goodbyes to Jenna, took a quick shower and was ready by the time he landed on my doorstep.

"We're going where?" I was sure I'd heard him wrong. It didn't occur to me to ask why the trek to Columbia until we were halfway there. We were driving Highway 99 past fields of soybeans, corn, and rolled hay bales. Cold air blew through the vents, sufficiently cooling my cheeks. The air conditioner at Nana's was on the fritz. Of course.

"My chiropractor's." He sat so tall in the truck cab his head nearly touched the roof. What would he need a chiropractor for?

"There aren't any in Shelbyville?"

"None with the ability to take care of my needs."

There hadn't been any mention of my blowup the day before at Mama G's, but I wasn't about to let his cryptic response pass without comment. "This have anything to do with your helicopter incident?"

He nodded, eyes straight ahead, but I noted his grip on the steering wheel tightened.

"Are you going tell me about it, or do I have to dig my way to China to get the answers?" If it'd been Nicky, I'd have more details than my brain could hold. But Derek never was one to talk much.

"Not a whole lot to tell. The helicopter came down hard and compressed some of the vertebrae in my low back. I get some relief with a session on the decompression unit."

"Are you disabled?" I nearly choked on the word. If there was a specimen of health and vitality, Derek was it. I couldn't imagine him any other way.

"Depends on who's doing the asking." He glanced at me. "Special Forces says I am. To my way of thinking, I'm just a little stoved up. Nothing for you to be throwing a hissy fit about, that's for sure."

I was tempted to stick my tongue out at him as if that would prove I was more mature than a hissy-fit-throwing woman but figured that would be counter-productive. "I'm sorry for acting so churlish yesterday. You being in an accident caught me by surprise." No need to tell him the thought of losing him young, like Mama and Daddy, was harder to reconcile than losing Nicky.

"You wanna tell me about you and Nicky?" Derek said as if reading my thoughts.

A fist closed over my throat making it a chore to breathe. "Not yet, if you don't mind." I kept my gaze on the view out the windshield but could still feel his eyes probing for more. How unfair was it to expect answers from him when I wasn't willing to give any of my own?

"Whenever you're ready, sweet Charlie."

Derek always did have the patience of Job. It was just too bad I didn't recognize it in him before I made a mess of things. It did no good to wish the years away where I could've made the better choice.

I scrambled for a safe topic of conversation. "So, you've been home for a few weeks. What have you been doing to stay busy?" I couldn't imagine him sitting still for long, back issues or not.

"This and that."

"You do go on."

He turned to me with a grin. "Been working Daddy's land some. Mama let it go fallow after he died, as you know. Helping out where I can."

A thought occurred to me, and it was a wonder it took this long. "By any chance have you been doing a little of this and that at Nana's place? I noticed the old paint's been stripped off the woodwork in places."

"Depends."

"On what?"

"Whether it'll set you to fussing at me or not."

"That's what I thought."

Ten minutes later, we pulled off the highway and drove down a busy four-lane road heading for town square. I thought getting out of the house would clear the cobwebs from my brain, but they were too thick and tangled that something so simple could wipe them away. I was in a tight spot for sure, and what I was going to do about it confounded me.

Derek's deep voice cut into my wonderings. "I can drop you off at the courthouse if you'd like to walk around while I'm at the doc's."

I weighed my choices. "How long will you be?"

"About an hour. Worse case, you can always go into Hattie Jane's and get an ice cream."

Nana always said there was nothing in this world that couldn't be made better with an ice cream cone. "Sounds good."

After Derek dropped me at the courthouse, I crossed to the shady side of the square. There was a slight breeze, which made the heat tolerable, and my shoulders eased as I walked. Window shopping had a way of opening my imagination. I was satisfied to stay on the sidewalk—until I came to a unique-looking place with a blue awning over its doorway.

What drew me in, I couldn't say. Some might call it an antique store, but I quickly assessed the eclectic array of goods and realized many weren't technically antiques.

"Welcome." The woman behind the counter smiled at me. "Have you been here before?"

"First time," I said.

"Be sure to look upstairs."

There was everything from cloth napkins and placemats to antique single-pane windows. Clothing and milk paint. Fence posts and old doors. Upstairs, among record collections and 50's-era cameras, was custom-made dining room furniture. I'd never seen such an array of junk juxtaposed with treasures. Pieces I would've trashed carried hefty price tags while others I could have repurposed were a steal.

Maybe I needed to reassess the things stored in Nana and Pawpaw's basement.

I got lost in the world of possibilities until my cell phone trilled. Derek. "Are you done already?"

"Done and ready for an ice cream. Did you get one yet?"

"Nope. Meet you at Hattie Jane's in five."

I slipped the phone into my back pocket and made my way through the maze of goods. For the brief time I'd been here, not once did I get muddled by my distressing situation.

CHAPTER SIX

Derek

I didn't buy Mama's theory about Nicky and me being like Cain and Abel, but I couldn't discount it, either. Truth was, I at least owed my little brother the chance to speak his mind, even if it was hard to hear. I offered him an olive branch by way of lunch at Stillery's on Broadway. Close enough for him to walk from his apartment so he had little reason to turn me down. I'd rather parachute from a plane than park in downtown Nashville, but I chalked it up as my good deed for the day.

Nicky was sitting at a corner table, halfway through a beer, when I arrived. It was a toss-up if he was just starting to drink or continuing from the night before. He spotted me and hitched his chin in acknowledgement.

"Nicky." I pulled out the chair across from him and sat. "Thanks for meeting me."

"Didn't figure you'd give me a choice." His crooked grin took the edge off his words.

A waitress showed up and slid a menu in front of me. "What can I get you to drink? We got a pale ale or IPA on tap."

"Sweet tea will be fine. Thanks." I threw her a quick smile and opened the menu. "What're you having little brother?"

"Ale." He took a sip from the tall glass and eyed me over the rim as if baiting me.

"I meant to eat. You look at the menu already?"

"Yeah. Firehouse pie sounds good."

We continued with aimless chitchat until our food arrived. I'd prayed my way to an opening, but the good Lord hadn't seen fit to intervene. I was about as smooth with words as a prickly porcupine and was hoping for a Moses moment.

"Can I assume we have Charlie to thank for this little visit?" Nicky folded up a slice of pizza and bit off a chunk. A can of worms didn't deter him any.

"Indirectly, I suppose. I don't guess you care one way or the other what I think, but Mama's worried about you."

His eyebrows shot up. "You mean she's worried about Charlie."

"I won't deny it. What did you expect, Nicky?"

"For starters, a little support. You ever hear the saying blood's thicker than water?"

I shook my head. "How long you been waiting to use that cryptic quote? And just so you know, the original proverb meant the opposite—blood of the covenant is thicker than water of the womb."

He scowled. "You're missing the point. Why is it y'all are so quick to take up for Charlie?"

That's Nicky. Everything's a competition. "This goes deeper than some misguided idea of family loyalty. It's about what's right and wrong. Don't you see that? In what universe is it okay to sleep around?"

"It's not that simple." He shoved his plate aside and leaned his elbows on the table. "It's not like I woke up one day and said, 'Hmmm, think I'll give that groupie who's been hanging around a whirl.' This whole thing started long ago, but you show up out of the blue and play judge and jury without having all the facts."

"Fine." I spread my arms wide. "Enlighten me."

Elbows on the table, he fisted his hands together. "You and I both know Charlie wasn't too keen on marrying me in the first place."

I waited a moment, but he didn't continue. "I sure hope you have more facts than that."

"What's it to you, anyway, Derek?" A muscle in his jaw clenched. Grinding his teeth, most likely. "Mama says jump and you say how high. Learn that in the military, did you?"

I would have taken his attack on my manhood personal, but he was striking out wherever he could, hoping for contact. I wasn't playing the game. "Maybe if you moseyed on down to Shelbyville and saw Mama, you could get your marching orders directly. Until you're ready to walk that road, this'll have to do."

He glanced past me and waved his hand to the waitress. When she stood at our table, he said, "Another pale ale."

The order took me by surprise. I expected he'd call for the check and bail. How many beers did that make so far? Wouldn't do no good to ask. He already thought I was a pious holy roller. "You want to share any more facts before the jury deliberates?" I grinned at him. Maybe it would lighten the mood some.

"It's like Charlie and me aren't living on the same planet sometimes."

"You're from Mars and she's from Venus," I said. "Or maybe it's the other way around."

He looked at me like I was speaking in tongues. "Huh?"

"Never mind. Bad joke."

The waitress slid his beer in front of him. "Can I get y'all anything else?"

"We're good." I glanced at Nicky as she left. "You were saying?"

"Her job's more important to her than I am."

"You mean the one she lost because she had a meltdown at work after catching you in bed with someone else? That job?"

He blew out a breath. "I didn't know."

"And what about you? Unless I'm mistaken, she's been the one supporting you while you been waiting on your big break. You can't have it both ways."

"Sounds like y'all been having a grand reunion, picking apart our marriage and such." He acted like a surly teen who lost driving privileges.

"Take it easy, little brother. We haven't discussed you at all."

"Then where'd you get your information from?"

"Reading between the lines."

"Come again?"

"Email."

His expression remained blank.

"You know. It's that way people have of communicating through the Internet."

His expression soured. "I know what it is, I just didn't know you two were doing it."

"Only a couple here and there over the years, but enough to know what's what."

"You accuse me of playing loose, and you been carrying on with Charlie all this time."

Heat zinged up my spine. "Give me a break, Nick. You know better than that."

"Do I?" He tapped the table with a finger. "Then how come

she's not answering my phone calls, huh? It seems to me she's perfectly happy that I'm out of the picture."

"You're good at jumping to conclusions, but that don't make them true. You wanna play this game, you'll come out the loser for sure. If you want a chance at fixin' your marriage, you need to take the first step."

"I did. Five, in fact. I been calling and calling, but she's not picking up. It's her move."

Charlie

It was the middle of the night, dark as pitch, when realization jolted me upright. I left my computer at Downtown Decor. I'd slunk away like a common criminal the day Patrice fired me and forgot to grab it. She may claim my designs as intellectual property, but the computer and the programs I'd installed on it were mine. Bought and paid for by me—not the company.

I tossed and turned on the slippery sleeping bag for the rest of the night. It wasn't the heat that made me restless, but the idea of confronting Patrice. Finally, the sun slowly washed the sky in shades of pink and blue, reminding me to choose gratitude. *His mercies never come to an end; they are new every morning. Great is your faithfulness.*

How odd I could recall random Bible verses from my childhood but had no recollection of Mama and Daddy's passing—just what I'd been told. A fog hovered over me when I thought about it too long, like a nightmare that dissipated in the light of day. The not-remembering used to plague me, but with each passing year, it settled into a vague sort of uneasiness.

Once the sun was full up, I called Jenna. "Are you game for a little adventure?" It was a rhetorical question, because Jenna was not only the first in line when God handed out nerve, but she went back for seconds.

"What've you got in mind, Cuz?"

Three hours later, I pulled my Lexus into her driveway. She was out of the house before my foot hit the first brick step.

"Whooee," she said with a grin. "Aren't you dressed to the nines. Lookin' like the old Charlie I know and love."

I smoothed the purple-on-white sundress and struck a pose. "That's Charlotte to you," I said in a prim voice before collapsing into a fit of giggles. When was the last time I'd laughed?

Jenna walked in a circle around me, head bobbing. "You wouldn't look at home like this in the Piggly Wiggly, that's for darn sure."

"Don't be too impressed. It's my armor. If I'm going to confront Patrice, I need to appear successful, even if that boat's long gone."

"Don't talk like that, girl. You just hit a rough patch."

"From your lips to God's ears."

We took Highway 231 north, and I cranked up the air conditioner. I had to get my fill while I could, because God knew, there was no getting away from the heat in Nana's house.

"I can't believe it took you this long to miss your computer," Jenna said.

"I've been preoccupied with a few trivial things, like how I'm going to make my car payment or buy food." I had a little money set aside, but it wouldn't last long. "Before we head back, I need to close out one of my bank accounts. I doubt Nicky has a clue it exists, but I'm not taking any chances."

"How'd things go with Derek the other day?"

I gave her a quick glance. "Fine. He had a doctor's appointment, and I walked around the square. You ever been to that cute vintage store there?"

"In Columbia? No."

"It was kind of cool."

"Yeah? I was more interested in how you got on with Derek."

"We got on fine. Why?"

She clucked her tongue. "Don't be actin' so coy. You ain't foolin' me."

I snorted. "Talk about coy. Say what you mean, Jenna."

"Fine," She huffed. "If Derek weren't Nicky's brother, would you see him different?"

I should have known. Jenna had a romantic streak that could stretch from Kentucky to Louisiana. "We're just friends."

"I know. But have you ever considered how things mighta played out?"

Her question hit a little too close to my heart for comfort. "It doesn't matter, Jenna. You can't go back and change the past. If I could, I wouldn't have gotten fired. Better yet, I wouldn't have hooked up with Nicky in the first place. The last ten years have been a total waste."

"That's not true, Charlie. You are a talented designer—"

"Without a job."

"So, you get another job. Or better yet, start over on your own like I suggested before."

"I already told you that takes time."

"I got me an idea." She touched my arm. "We'll trade labor."

"What kind of labor?"

"Cal can do some fixin' up at your place, and you can do some prettying up in ours. I'll be the first client in your new business."

"I'm happy to do some design plans for you, Jenna. No

trading necessary. Besides, I'm not sure Cal would appreciate you sacrificing him this way."

"It's what family does, Charlie. I know if I was in a world of hurt, you'd be there for me."

Her kindness was like honey to my heart. "Still, I think you should make sure Cal's okay with it first." I didn't want to burst her bubble by pointing out that getting paid in trade wouldn't give me cash for bills.

When I pulled into Downtown Decor's parking lot, I had to take a deep breath to slow my heart rate.

Jenna unlatched her seatbelt. "You want I should come in with you or wait out here?"

I tapped the steering wheel. Jenna's presence would bolster my confidence, but if Patrice was going to be difficult, I didn't want an audience for my humiliation. "Why don't you wait here? I should be back in a flash."

She nodded.

I opened the door and turned to her. "If you've a mind to, say a little prayer for me, would you?" I figured God wasn't feeling too kindly toward me these days.

"Will do."

My legs felt thick as cement pillars as I walked through the doors of the shop I'd designed. The place my dreams took root and grew. My home away from home, where I was no longer welcome. What was the worst that could happen? It wasn't as if Patrice could fire me all over again. But that didn't make it any easier to draw breath when she spotted me across the showroom and her gaze narrowed.

A woman stood to her left, a palette of marble samples spread out on the counter in front of them. Patrice touched the client's arm and said something to her before crossing the room to meet me. Her thick hips swayed with each step as the warmth in her eyes cooled by degrees.

"What can I do for you, Charlotte?"

A loaded question, for sure. My stomach dropped clear to my purple pump-encased toes. *Just breathe.* "I came for my computer. It's in my office unless you moved it."

She pursed her lips. "You're aware of our agreement, I'm sure. Just so you know, I'm going to hold you to it."

If I wasn't mistaken, it was fear that flashed in her eyes, and not the disdain I expected. My stomach settled. "No worries, Patrice. I wouldn't dare encroach on your territory. This job was only a stepping-stone for me. I have bigger things in mind."

Now I only had to figure out what.

CHAPTER SEVEN

Charlie

The weak light from the 60-watt bulb revealed Halloween-worthy cobwebs that dangled above the narrow stairway into the basement. Just knowing they were there made my skin crawl. Had they been abandoned, or did spiders still reside in the mass?

"What's the hold up?" Jenna poked me in the back.

A shiver ran up my spine. "Spider webs."

"So, knock them aside. I have to be home in an hour."

"I hate spiders."

She barked out a laugh. "Then you're living in the wrong state. I'll be right back."

I stepped away from the door and rubbed my arms as if I could erase the apprehension that filled me. It wasn't only the cobwebs that made me uneasy. When Nana died, it was too difficult to go through her things. She had not only her and Pawpaw's worldly belongings, but all of Mama and Daddy's, too. Things she'd stored away when I returned home from

Africa. I'd intended to lease the house but couldn't reconcile anyone else living here. And truth be told, there was a fear born from the shadow of dreams that kept me from exploring the past.

Jenna reappeared with an old broom. "Use this to brush 'em out of the way."

I wrinkled my nose at Jenna's offering. The basement seemed like the perfect environment for brown recluse and black widows. Did I really want to disturb them?

"Seriously? Don't be such a sissy." Jenna pulled me away from the door and stormed through it, swinging the broom above her head. Dog sat on my feet and leaned against me as if drawing comfort from my presence. He didn't think it was such a good idea, either.

"It's all clear."

I peered down the stairs to see Jenna at the bottom, flicking on another set of lights.

"Would you look at all the stuff down here. Goodness gracious, Charlie, your nana was a hoarder."

As my gaze darted back and forth along the wall on the lookout for creepy crawlies, I descended the creaking, wooden stairs with Dog at my heels. The basement, which was a good ten degrees cooler, spanned the entire breadth of the house, and was packed from end-to-end. Boxes were stacked along the perimeter with only a few narrow passages. I spotted at least three bed sets, dressers, a roll-top desk, and lamps. But it was the things I couldn't see that gave me the willies—those items covered with white sheets like odd-shaped ghosts that held the key to secrets left best alone.

"What're you gonna do with all this stuff?" Jenna turned in a tight circle, her eyes wide as supper plates. "You might could have a yard sale and make a little money."

Not nearly enough to pull me out of debt. "I can't do much of anything until I get a good look at it all."

"How in the world did you wrangle this stuff down those stairs?"

"I didn't. I hired some young guys to do it for me. They used the cellar doors on the far end of the basement. The opening's wider."

"Well, we ain't gonna get much done in the time I got left, I can tell you that."

I ran my hand over a dusty dresser top. It was a wonder it wasn't warped from moisture. Most of the furniture was old enough to be called antique, but I had no idea of their quality or shape.

"Derek is supposed to drop by this afternoon." Then again, how could I ask him to help knowing he had a bad back?

"You have a plan, don't you?"

"Hmm?"

"As long as I can remember, Charlie, you were always working on a plan. I know things is hard right now, but as sure as I'm standing here, you're thinking up a way out."

A plan? No. An inkling of an idea? Maybe. "It's too early to say."

Jenna crossed her arms and jutted out her chin. "You ain't fooling me. Come on, spit it out. If you can't tell me of all people, then who *can* you tell?"

"That's for darn sure," I said with a grin. Her loyalty managed to send the ghosts scattering—at least for the moment. "Okay, but remember, I'm still thinking on it."

"Does it have anything to do with that vintage store you were telling me about?" How did she do that? No doubt, Cal found it impossible to plan a surprise for her. Always one step ahead.

"Actually, it does." I tapped my knuckles on the dresser. "I don't know what all is down here, but what I have in mind is far more interesting than a yard sale. A spin on my interior-design skills mixed with antiques or vintage or whatever they're calling it now."

"You mean open up a store?"

"I don't know yet. I told you, I'm still working it out in my mind. It's just a thought."

"You'd still need money, Charlie. Are you back to the idea of selling the house?"

I chewed the inside of my lip. Every cent I had to my name was sitting in a spanking new bank account. That and a little elbow grease wouldn't get me far. The answers hadn't come, but I had to trust they would. Didn't they always? Whenever I started on a new design, there was a tad bit of fear at the outset. Would a great idea come? Would I disappoint the client? Would I be revealed as a fraud?

But this was different. Someone else wasn't bank-rolling my plan, and I sure as heck couldn't count on any kind of spousal support. In fact, it wouldn't surprise me if Nicky demanded I throw a little support his way. After all, I was the only one bringing in a decent income. Now that was gone, and I was back to square one.

"Before I can do anything, I have to assess the inventory. Let's start with the boxes."

I hesitated to move forward and prayed none of them would turn out to be synonymous with the mythical jar Pandora unleashed.

Derek

Charlie saying she had a few things to move from the basement was like calling Hurricane Sally a smidgeon of rain. Fortunately for me and my stoved-up back, the military taught me the art of delegating. One phone call and three of my long-time friends showed up. All it took for them good old boys to answer the call to help was the promise of unhealthy food and drink.

Three hours later, the basement was empty, but the house was full to bursting. The boys had polished off three pizzas and a couple six packs and were lounging around the kitchen like a bunch of fat cats napping after a feast. It had more to do with the heat than the work. Dog discovered his loyalty to Clint got him a couple smuggled bites of pepperoni, so he stretched out next to him.

I tipped the kitchen chair back on two legs and watched as Charlie finished off a bottle of water. “What else you need done?”

“Are you kidding?” She offered a tired smile around the room. “Y’all did so much. I’m not sure what I’ll do with everything yet, but at least it’s accessible now.”

Don, who was slumped against the wall, opened his eyes to slits. “You sure everything that was supposed to go upstairs got there? I seen a bedroom set sitting in the room next to the parlor. Don’t reckon anyone’s gonna want to sleep there.”

“It’s all good,” Charlie said.

I pushed up from the chair and stifled a groan. Shouldn’t have moved as much as I did, but I’d be danged if I asked the boys over and stood back like an invalid. “Why don’t we go look everything over, Charlie? Just to be sure.”

“Yeah.” Clint roused himself. “Whatever you need done, Charlie. ’Cause once we’re gone, we ain’t coming back.”

“Oh, I don’t know,” Don said with a grin. “I could see my

way to being at your beck and call, Miss Charlie. You smell a might better than Clint here."

"Well, that ain't hard to do," a sleepy-eyed Mark said. "But I'm pretty sure Charlie could do better than a washed-out plumber like yourself, Don."

"Who you calling washed out?"

I motioned for Charlie to follow me out before we got sucked into the bantering. The foyer walls were lined four boxes high, as was nearly every other room on the first floor. "You got your work cut out for you."

Her mouth twisted in a grimace. "Good thing I don't have a job to take up my time."

Did I detect a little self-pity? Not that I'd blame her. "Thought you should know I saw Nicky yesterday." I kept my gaze on her face to gauge her reaction. But aside from her mouth tightening a might, I didn't notice any. "What are you going to do, Charlie?"

She sighed and closed her eyes. "About what? Nicky? My unemployment? Nana's house? The ceiling-high mess piled here? You'll have to be a little more specific, Derek. There's so much to choose from."

"Take your pick. We'll knock 'em down one at a time."

She ambled to the wide staircase and plopped onto a step. "I can't tell you how much I appreciate your help. Truly." She had dark circles under her eyes and her shoulders drooped like they carried a fifty-pound sack. "But let's talk about you for a change, shall we?"

This didn't bode well. "What about me?"

"Any plans?" She flicked her hand at me.

"For?"

"Work, to start with. You've been career military from the time I met you. I can't imagine it's easy for you to be home again."

Ain't that the truth. "I'm analyzing my options."

Her lips twitched. "Analyzing? Sounds exhausting."

I sat next to her, and my back about spasmed. Jaw clenched against the pain, it took a moment to answer. "Don't want to rush into anything."

"Must be nice to have the gift of time." She rested her chin in one hand, and her eyes drifted shut. "Do you miss it?"

"What?"

"Being in Special Forces. It must be strange not to have your routine set."

I nodded even though she couldn't see me. "It is. But it's good for me to learn to trust."

"Trust in what?"

"Not what. Who."

"Okay, I'll bite. Who?"

"God."

She wrinkled her nose. "Good luck with that. I'm sure whatever you decide, it'll be a success. I'm sure Mama G loves having you around again. I kind of like it, too." She opened her eyes and smiled at me.

"Is it possible for you and Nicky to patch things up? He said he's tried to call, but you aren't picking up."

"He's probably worried about losing his cash cow." She pushed off the step and fingered one of the boxes piled near the door. "He's real good at spending what he doesn't have." She spun around. "Do you know how I ended up with the Lexus?"

I shook my head.

"He brought it home. Said it was a gift for me. Only thing is, I'm the one who's been paying for it. Now I have to return it, and it's going to cost me money I don't have."

"If it's money you need, let me—"

"Absolutely not." She turned away and swiped at her eyes.

"I'm tired of coming across as the little orphan girl, Derek. You've been here for me more than Nicky, even when you weren't around."

I stood and moved behind her. "We're kin, Charlie. It's what we do." Maybe if I kept reminding myself that she was like a sister to me, it would make it so.

She kept her back to me but shook her head. "I've got to figure things out here, Derek. I've made such a colossal mess of things, and I can't go on blaming Nicky for it. But I also can't let you clean it up for me, either."

I clenched my fists to keep from pulling her into my arms. "At least let me lend you Daddy's old Ford pickup. It won't win any beauty contests, and the gas mileage will put you in the poor house, but it runs."

She turned to me, a smile wavering on her lips. "That's not a problem. I'm already in the poor house."

What would I give to go back twenty years and choose a different path?

CHAPTER EIGHT

Derek

The few weeks I'd been back home felt more like months—maybe even years. Never in my life had I been at loose ends, not knowing where I was going or what I was meant to do. Since I'd sought the good Lord's guidance and He didn't see fit to show me another way, I figured this was where I was supposed to be. Could be it was a period of waiting, which wasn't something I took to very well.

Of course, the timing couldn't have been more perfect, Charlie and me landing in the same place like we did. Coincidence wasn't a concept I took much stock in. Figured it was God's plan. The why of it confounded me, though. Charlie was a married woman, and whether she and Nicky split or not, she was off-limits. I'd had my chance.

Conflicted, I watched the back end of Daddy's truck disappear down the road. Charlie said she didn't want me tagging along, but if I had pushed a little harder, I might could've changed her mind. Truth was, I needed her gone to implement my plan.

I pulled my phone from the back pocket of my jeans and shot off a text—*She's gone. Let's get it done*—then retrieved the key underneath the cracked terra cotta pot on her back porch. Dirt as dry as the Sahara sat in it, yellowed weeds gasping their last breath. I hoped it wasn't symbolic.

Less than ten minutes later, Mark showed up on her front steps with a large toolbox. He raked a hand through a shaggy head of blond hair and glanced behind me. "How long before she comes back?"

"Least a couple hours." I opened the door wide to let him in, and Dog followed in his wake, circled a crowded corner, and plopped onto the floor with a groan. He must've been sleeping on the front porch.

"What's with all the sneaking around?" The metal box *clanked* as Mark shifted it from one side of his paunch to the other. "Can't you just tell her I'm checking her H-VAC system?"

"The girl's got her pride."

"You don't think she'll catch on when her air conditioner makes a miraculous recovery?"

I shrugged. "One step at a time. Let's check it out and see what's what." I led him through the house, unopened boxes and out-of-place furniture still crowding the pathway, and out the kitchen door where the unit sat. If more than an adjustment or two was needed to get it up and running, I'd be sure to tell her. She wouldn't take too kindly to me lying—she got enough of that from Nicky.

Mark descended the few steps, eyeing the unit. "It looks about as old as the house, although that can't be." He put the toolbox down before rounding the hunk of sheet metal to inspect it. After a moment, he rummaged through his toolbox and got to work. "So, when you gonna take me up on my offer? You ain't getting any younger."

I scowled at his back. "And you are?"

He turned a grin on me. "Not so's you'd notice. But I got me a job. What've you got?"

"A military pension and hefty savings account. Gives me the luxury of being picky." I scratched the stubble on my chin. "I'm not so sure the security business is for me."

"No? What else you got to do?"

His question hit a tad too close for comfort. "Aside from straightening out my little brother? Not much. Still." I shrugged. "Going into business with a friend can be tricky. What if we don't get on together?"

"Won't know until we try."

"You have any idea how many security companies are already established here, Mark? It's not like you got a unique business venture."

"Maybe not, but there's plenty of business to go around. We start slow, build up, and expand outward. Nashville's one of the largest growing cities in the U.S. Besides, I got you to come up with something unique-like. You got the special training."

I wasn't sold, but he was right. What else did I have to do?

He stood and eyed the H-VAC unit. "Let's see if we can find the breaker panel. As old as this girl is, I think she might have a little life in 'er yet."

If I were a breaker panel in an old house, where would I be? "Let's check under the stairs." We lumbered back through the house. Boxes were stacked against the closet door, and I pushed them aside. Once opened, the interior revealed more stuff shoved into its recesses, as if long forgotten. Could be treasure stashed here for all I knew. A single bulb with a thin chain hanging from it was tucked next to the door jamb, a metal panel box beneath it.

"See, this here is why I need you on my team. You've got good instincts."

I snorted. "Because I can find a panel box? That's weak."

"You'd do good with the Rapid Response Team, too. We're always looking for ex-military or law enforcement." He flipped the panel door open. "It takes a special kind to respond to a school or church shooting."

"Doubtful I'd make a decent volunteer chaplain. Can't even get my own brother to listen to me."

Mark flicked switches back and forth. "Family's the hardest. If Nicky were in a bad way, it might be he'd be more open to the saving grace of Jesus."

"He's headed that way, let me tell you."

"Yeah, I kinda figured there was problems in paradise what with Charlie moving back here. Rock bottom, my friend, that's where Nicky'll start rethinking things. Even so, you have lots of skills that could be useful outside of farming your daddy's land."

"Why is it you're so hard pressed to find me a job?"

"More 'n a job, Derek. A mission. Isn't that what your military career was all about?" He turned keen eyes on me, as if offering a challenge. "You spent the better part of two decades serving your country. That don't just go by the wayside 'cause you got hurt."

Hadn't I just been praying for divine guidance? Was Mark feeding me the answers I'd been asking for? He wasn't any more unlikely than a donkey set on a course to change Balaam's direction.

"How 'bout we find a time to work up a business plan, and I'll give it some serious thought. Until then, what can you do about Charlie's air conditioner?"

"I 'spect it's a matter of some wiring that's gotten chewed up some. If we're lucky, I can have 'er fixed in two shakes."

If only all of life's pesky problems were so easily resolved.

Charlie

When Derek said his daddy's truck was old, he wasn't fooling. I remembered driving in it with Nicky when we were in high school and figured it was long gone. It didn't escape my notice since it was sixty years old, it was considered vintage. But it didn't matter, because the bench seat, sturdy controls, and weight of it made me feel safe. I wouldn't be setting any speed records, but it was better than a slap in the belly with a wet fish, as Nana would say.

Driving up I-65 with the windows down, I let the breeze whip my long hair into a frenzy. What did I care what I looked like, anyway? There wasn't anyone I wanted to impress. I was fixing to pick up the rest of my things from the apartment, so the truck was perfect. Turning my car back into the dealer cost me half of what I had, but it was better than someone showing up in the dead of night to tow it away. I didn't have much left, but I still had my dignity, even if Nicky had done his best to snatch it from me.

Just the thought of him soured my stomach. I should've called to be sure he wasn't going to be around. Pride kept me from doing so, pure and simple. He'd called over and over again, and I wasn't about to give him the satisfaction of responding. I knew it was childish, but I'd spent most of my life being anything but, so I had a right to a little immaturity. If he was there, I'd just ignore him and do what had to be done. I hadn't seen or talked to Nicky since the night I caught him in bed with that bimbo. Why I was angry with her didn't make much sense. Nicky was the one who promised to love, honor, and cherish me until the day we died. He must've missed the part where it was supposed to be *only* me.

Parking the Ford took a little more finesse than my Lexus and two open spaces. I never did take to parallel parking. I had to maneuver the tank a few times before I was satisfied. Once the truck was locked, I dropped the keys in my purse and eyed the complex. I'd hold off carting empty boxes up until I was sure Nicky was gone. With each step I took toward the apartment, my heart kicked up another beat or two and my stomach soured. Did I want Nicky to be there? If he was, could I express myself without coming across like a woman bent on throwing a hissy fit, as Derek had accused me of doing in the past?

The key hovered in front of the lock when a thought struck me with the force of a tree branch to the brain—what if Nicky had someone in there with him? Images of the last time swam through my mind, and I gritted my teeth in preparation for the worst. Again.

I pushed the door open, stepped inside, and waited with my head cocked to catch the slightest hint of occupants. There was no one in the living room, but the sound of dishes clinking came from the direction of the kitchen. No voices. That was a good sign. I closed the door and drew in a deep breath.

Let the games begin.

"Nicky?"

The noises ceased and Nicky appeared at the entrance. His dark hair fell over one steel-blue eye, giving him the appearance of a young Clark Gable. Nana always loved Clark. This one looked a bit on the cranky side. "Charlie. For crying out loud, it's about time. You know how many times I've called you?"

I dropped my purse on the red, leather recliner next to a

pile of what appeared to be laundry. "Eight, if I remember correctly."

He crossed his arms and jutted out his chin like a petulant child. Nicky didn't like being ignored. When I was younger, I thought the attitude oozed artistic temperament. Now it was just dang annoying. "You ready to finally talk through this mess?" Did I detect accusation in his tone? How could he think any part of this was my fault?

"There's nothing to talk about, unless you're going to try and convince me I didn't see what we both know I did."

He uncrossed his arms and pointed to the sofa. "Let's sit for a minute, okay? You wanna Coke or a glass of sweet tea?"

"What I want is to collect the rest of my things. I didn't come here to try and patch things up, Nicky. There's just nowhere to go from here."

"I screwed up one time, Charlie, and you're—"

"One time?" I stared him down until he dropped his gaze. "I might not have caught you before, but we both know that girl you had here wasn't your first. I'll admit to being naïve, but I'm not stupid." If I could just grab the rest of my clothes and a few kitchen necessities—it was impossible with Nicky hovering.

"You can't lay the blame of all our troubles on me, Charlie. You changed." He shoved his hand into the front pockets of his jeans, head down. "It was like you blamed me for losing the baby."

Heat coursed through my body. I focused on the feel of my hands clenching and unclenching, the bite of my nails in the palms. Anything to distract me from the ache of loss. So much loss. *Don't cry. Don't cry.* "I didn't blame you because I—" I had to swallow back the rock that sat in my throat— "miscarried. I blamed you for not wanting her in the first place." I grabbed my purse with one hand and latched onto the doorknob with the other.

"Where're you going?" He wrapped his hand around my upper arm. "Can't we at least talk about it? I mean, are you just going to ignore me for the rest of your life?"

"No. Just the rest of yours." I yanked my arm away from him and took measured breaths. It was stupid of me to think I could ignore his presence. The apartment wasn't big enough for all the emotion roiling around between us. "I can't do this with you right now. I need to get my things, and I need you to be gone when I do."

"What about us? Do you want a divorce?" His eyes widened as if he just caught a clue to the seriousness of the situation. "You can't just end things like this, Charlie. Give me another chance."

Tears burned at the back of my eyes, and I blinked them away. Our marriage had been a series of second chances. And third. And fourth. "I don't have anything left to give you, Nick. You've taken every ounce of grace I had and threw it back in my face." I opened the door, eyes focused down the hallway. "I'll be back tomorrow afternoon for my things. Find somewhere else to be. And I suggest you look at our lease and see if there are any loopholes, otherwise you'll have to find a way to make rent on your own."

I left the apartment without another glance, but the image of him staring at me, slack-jawed, stayed with me all the way back to Shelbyville.

CHAPTER NINE

June 2006
Charlie

Morning sun poured through Charlie's bedroom window and shone like a spotlight on Justin Timberlake's image tacked to her wall. She lifted the heavy sash to allow fresh air and the song of mockingbirds to serenade her as giddiness worked its way up her throat and split a grin on her face. "Good morning, birds," she shouted. "Isn't this the best day ever?" With a commotion, the leaves of the cottonwood that stood guard over her room rustled as the birds took flight.

School was out for the summer, and that wasn't even the best thing. Derek flew in on the red-eye last night for Nicky's graduation. Better still, he'd finished up his four-year deployment, which meant he was back for good.

Charlie slipped on a pair of shorts and a t-shirt, pulled her hair into a ponytail, and clattered down the stairs.

"Land sakes alive, child." Nana stood at the kitchen doorway, hands on hips. "What's got you in such a tizzy this mornin'?"

"Derek got home last night. I'm going over and—"

"Nonsense." She waved a hand at Charlie. "You come on in here and have yourself some breakfast. Let the poor boy have some time with his family before all the hoopla begins. Besides, he's probably still sleepin'. That's a luxury he don't get too much of bein' in the service."

"Oh, Nana. Do I have to?" Her foot itched with the need to stomp it like a two-year-old. There was no way she could eat anything while she was all but bursting with curiosity. Did Derek look older? Would he see how much she'd changed since she last saw him? She wasn't the skinny girl he'd have remembered, but full grown.

Before she could answer, there was a pounding on the kitchen door.

Nana clucked her tongue, her head swinging from side to side. "I 'spect that would be your Nicky," she said, disappearing into the kitchen.

"He's not *my* Nicky." Charlie followed her. Sure enough, Nicky's face appeared through the glass-topped back door. He might be graduating high school, but compared to Derek, he was a kid.

"Might want to tell him that, child." She swung the door wide. "Good morning, young man."

"Mornin' ma'am." He peered around her, his dark hair nearly covering his eyes. "Hey Charlie. I gotta go into town to pick up a few things for Mama. Wanna come?"

"Did Derek get in okay? Is he up?"

Nicky frowned. "Yeah, he's home. Come with me to town, and I'll take you over after."

Charlie looked at Nana who was pulling biscuits from the

oven. "Can I, Nana? I surely couldn't eat a thing right now anyway."

With a sigh, she wrapped a couple biscuits in a flour sack towel and handed it to her. "Be home for lunch, you hear?"

"Yes'm." Charlie threw her arms around Nana before following Nicky to his daddy's truck.

With the windows full open, she closed her eyes and breathed in the early summer air. A hint of hyacinth mixed with cut grass and damp soil was like a balm. Life was just about as perfect as could be.

"Hey Charlie." Nicky's voice cut into her thoughts. "Can I ask you a question?"

Like she could stop him. "Yeah."

"You know Mama and Daddy are throwing a party for me tonight."

"Of course, I know. You invited me weeks ago."

"Well, I was thinking maybe you could be my girl. You know, my date." He shook the hair from his eyes and glanced at her. "Wha'd'ya say?"

His date? They'd hung out together, sure, but like friends. He and Sissy'd been a couple since junior year. "What happened to Sissy? She break up with you?"

He shrugged. "Not exactly. We decided to go our separate ways is all."

Yeah, right. "Dating you would be like going out with my brother."

He jerked his chin up and stared out the windshield. "As a favor. It'd be a little embarrassing to go stag at my own party."

Charlie could see that. "Okay, fine. Just as a favor." She pinched off a bite of biscuit and popped it into her mouth. The buttery warmth melted on her tongue and her stomach rumbled. Maybe she was hungry after all. "Tell me about Derek."

"What's to tell?"

"Is he finished with his tour of duty? Is he coming home for good?"

"I don't know. Maybe. He got in late and wasn't up yet when I left. Ask him yourself when you see him."

Charlie popped another bite into her mouth and settled back on the bench seat. "Okay, I will."

Nicky took his sweet time collecting the things on Mama G's list, and by the time they got back to his house, she was ready to bust. She had a gazillion questions all lined up for Derek, but when she finally saw him sitting in Mama G's kitchen, it was like something had snatched her tongue clear off. She couldn't seem to form a sentence.

"Hey Charlie." He grinned at her and stood. "Look at you, all grown up." He tugged at her ponytail as her face must've turned ten shades of red. Leastways, that's how it felt. His hair was military short, just like when she'd seen him last, but that's where the similarities ended. He must've sprouted a full three inches in height and was as wide as a defensive back for Crimson Tide.

"Hey Derek," Charlie finally managed to croak. She gave him an awkward hug—not at all like she'd pictured it in her mind at least a dozen times over the last month. She was going to be smooth and sophisticated, and he was going to fall hard for her. Instead, she bumbled it like she was twelve again.

"What're you and Nicky up to?"

"Just running errands for Mama G." Why did all the questions Charlie wanted to ask him get stuck inside her like a tangled ball of yarn?

Nicky moved up close to Charlie and put an arm around her shoulders. It felt heavy and foreign, and she tried to shrug it off. "Charlie's my date tonight." He said it like Derek might challenge him.

Derek nodded, his smile slipping. “Isn’t that sweet. I’ll see y’all later then. I’m on my way out to meet some friends.” He tugged on her ponytail one more time as he passed.

Charlie pushed Nicky’s arm off her and watched as Derek disappeared down the hall. All the joy that’d bubbled up this morning slipped away like the sand in Nana’s three-minute egg timer.

Derek—2006

The sun was setting over the back patio, and Nicky’s graduation party was heating up. Toby Keith’s voice belted out a tune from the boom box hanging from the patio cover. Not surprising, the place was packed with kids bent on celebrating the end of childhood. As if moving a tassel from one side of a cap to the other changed anything. Derek sat in the corner nursing a beer, feeling old as Methuselah in this crowd of starry-eyed teens. Was he ever that young? It didn’t seem possible.

Charlie was dazzling in white. She wore a strapless sundress and, even early in the season, her skin was a golden bronze tone. Derek thought about how she looked that day four years ago when she approached him as he’d worked on his daddy’s tractor. All arms and legs and possibilities. She’d grown into them well.

Derek watched as she threw her head back and laughed at something Nicky said. He seemed to take every opportunity to touch her, as if it were his right. Maybe it was. Derek felt like a deviant, unable to take his eyes off her.

Her gaze caught his, and she said something to Nicky before making her way across the crowded patio. She smoothed the back of her dress before sitting down next to him. “Hey Derek.” She plucked at the filmy material of her dress and cleared her throat. “How come you’re sitting all alone over here?”

“Just staying out of the way. You having a good time?”

She shrugged. “It’s okay. I’m surprised your mama and daddy aren’t out here keeping watch over us.”

“They passed that chore onto me, I suppose.”

“Ah.” She crossed her arms and cleared her throat. “I been wanting to ask you something.”

He figured as much. “Ask away.”

“You’re tour’s up, right?” Her eyes lock on his for a split second then slid away.

“I suppose the simple answer is yes.”

She dropped her hands to her lap and fidgeted with the folds of her dress. “And the not-so-simple?”

That one had been plaguing him all day. “Truth is, sweet Charlie, I’m at a crossroads.”

She wrinkled her nose. “What’s that mean?”

“I’ve been offered a position in Special Forces.”

Eyes wide, her mouth flew open. “But you said you were only joining up to be able to pay for college. I thought you were coming home.”

“So did I. But there’s nothing here for me.” Nothing he had a right to, anyhow.

Her eyes darted away again. “How d’ya know? You’ve been gone ever since you graduated high school. What about college?”

“The beauty of technology is that I can get a degree while still serving.”

“So, Nicky was right all those years ago.” It came out like an accusation. “You didn’t join up to go to college like you said.

You joined up 'cause you think you have to save the world." Her voice caught on the last word.

Even in the weak light, he could see the shine of tears. Was she taking this personal? "Hey, what's this all about? Why're you getting so het up?"

She swiped at her eyes with trembling fingers. "I just don't get it. Why do people feel the need to put themselves in danger all the time?"

"People? What people are you referring to?" As if he had to ask.

"First Mama and Daddy and now you." Dierks Bentley crooned about how every mile was a memory, background to Charlie's emotion.

Derek bit back an automatic response and took a deep breath. "I don't think your parents had the notion they were going to save the world, and I sure as heck don't."

"They cared more about the Congo than me, and it got them killed."

With a sigh, he touched her hand. "Your parents were killed in a car accident, Charlie. That could've happened as easily on I-65 as on the missionary field."

"But it didn't, did it?" She said it like it was a challenge. Her eyes met his. "Why put yourself in danger? Why can't you just go to college here and get a normal job?"

He rubbed his temple with a sigh. "What would that look like, Charlie? Normal. What's that mean, anyway? I need something with a purpose. A mission."

Her mouth twisted. "Yeah, like Mama and Daddy. If I ever have a kid, they'll be purpose enough for me, I can tell you that." Fists clenched in her lap, her mouth thinned. "They'll be enough."

Derek understood her anger. He even agreed with it to some extent. "You ever read the book *To Kill a Mockingbird*?"

She looked at him like he'd gone plumb crazy. "Yeah. So?"

"Something Atticus Finch said comes to mind. You remember when he tells Scout that she couldn't know how someone else felt until she walked in their shoes?"

She cocked her head.

"Seems you might be seeing this thing with your parents all wrong."

Her gaze slipped into a full-blown glare as she crossed her arms. "You think I'm being unfair to them."

"Your mama and daddy are gone, Charlie. Nothing you do can affect them. It's you I'm thinking of. You carry bitterness around long enough, it starts to eat you alive. Changes how you see things, and maybe pushes you to make wrong choices."

"Like what?"

He shrugged, his eyes on Nicky across the yard basking in the attention. "Like looking for what you don't have somewhere you can't rightly find it."

She followed his gaze. "Nicky and me are just friends, Derek. He asked me to be his date tonight 'cause he and Sissy broke up. That's all there is to it."

"If I know my little brother, once he's got his mind set on something, nothing'll slow him down."

"You don't believe me?"

He sighed. "There might not be anything on your end, but sure as I'm sitting here, Nicky's got his eye on you. Just you be careful."

She snorted. "You got it all wrong."

"Maybe. Maybe not. You best be sure about who you are and what you want. Find a purpose, Charlie. One that keeps you on the straight and narrow. Otherwise, you'll be swayed by sweet words and empty promises."

She arched a brow. "You don't think much of Nicky, do you?"

"Nicky thinks enough of himself for the both of us. He doesn't need me to bolster his ego—he does a good enough job of it on his own."

"Well, maybe you should rethink Special Forces and stick around so's you can keep me out of trouble."

He grinned. "As tempting as that is, it's not really a mission I can get behind. We all make choices we have to live with, one way or another."

She looked down. "Are you looking to make the military your career then? You're not ever going to come back for good?"

"I can't say for sure. Might be I'll give it four more years and see where things sit."

A smile trembled on her lips. "A lot can happen in four years."

CHAPTER TEN

Charlie

It took a full week to set the kitchen to rights, but the effort was well worth it. I'd poured over every detail until my vision became a reality. Blood, sweat, and plenty of tears later, I stood at the entrance with Jenna and tried to see it with new eyes.

"What d'you think?" I held my breath and waited for her reaction.

Jenna stepped over to the refurbished dinette table and trailed her fingers across the top of it then turned in a slow circle. Finally, she squealed like a teeny bopper at her first rock concert. "Well, butter my butt and call me a biscuit." She spun around to look at me, mouth open, eyes lit up like a kid on Christmas morning. "This is amazing, Charlie. This is what I'm talkin' about. You really done it up right."

I let out a long breath and held my hand against my chest. "You really think so?"

She crossed to the counter, her gaze pinging from one thing to another. "It's like you've transformed the entire room, but I ain't rightly sure how. There's nothing new in here, is there?"

"Nope."

"Where'd you get these sweet ceramic canisters? And how'd you make the cabinets look like they're supposed to be all banged up?"

"Not banged up, Jenna. Distressed. That's the difference between old and retro. It took milk paint, clear wax, and a lot of elbow grease."

"And will you jus' look at this buffet? Was that the same one your Nana had in the parlor before?"

"Yep."

"I can't get over it, Charlie. You fixed yourself up a beautiful kitchen. These old appliances actually look good in here."

"That's what matters. It's all about the look. Doesn't matter much if it's not all that functional."

She frowned. "What d'ya mean? What good's a kitchen you can't cook nothing in?"

"I created this as a display."

"A display? For what? Or should I say, for who?"

"Clients, I hope."

"Clients?" She clapped her hands and grinned. "You're gonna do it, ain't ya? You're gonna go into business for yourself?"

"We'll see. I'm really just testing the waters, but I like how you took to it."

She pulled one of the four eclectic chairs from the table and dropped into it. "Tell me more. I wanna hear the whole plan."

With a grin bursting from me, I joined her. "What if I could combine the idea of a vintage store along with a home decor business? That shop on the Columbia square gave me the idea.

They have different vendors who create their own space with whatever goods they're selling. But what if I create different spaces based on the rooms? I use my skills as an interior designer to showcase that part of the business, but at the same time, everything used to decorate the rooms is for sale."

Jenna didn't say a word, which was a first. She leaned forward and opened her mouth as if to speak, then sat back with a sigh.

"Okay, Cuz, you're making me nervous." I dropped clasped hands into my lap. "Say something. Anything."

"I think it's a brilliant idea."

"Then why doesn't your face show it?" I chewed on my bottom lip.

She waved a dismissive hand. "I'm just thinkin' on a couple things, is all. Like, what happens when people start buying up all your cute doodads? I mean, is everything for sale?"

"Well, yeah. That's the point."

She slapped the tabletop. "So, this here table's for sale? An' the chairs?"

"Everything." Jenna might not sound like she had much in the brains department, but I knew different. Why was this simple concept throwing her off?

"I know your Nana was a bit of a packrat, but the well's gonna run dry at some point."

I tapped her hand. "Silly. Of course, it will. I'll just get more stuff."

"You'll have time for all this? I mean, it seems like you're startin' two new businesses, plus doin' all the design work to boot."

"It'll be a stretch, for sure. But I have my computer back, so the design programs will help a lot. And even though Patrice laid down the law about the non-compete clause, I still have my design portfolio. I might not be able to work with those clients again, but it doesn't mean I can't show off the work I've done in the past."

"And your inventory? How you plan on handling that?"

"Come here." I hopped up and waved my hand for her to follow. Although the kitchen was a sight for sore eyes, the rest of the house was still in utter chaos. Not only all of Nana and Pawpaw's boxes, but there was all the furniture crowding the rooms, as well. And since my successful visit back to my apartment, I'd added several of my own boxes.

"Where're we goin'?" Jenna followed me through the foyer and into the parlor. "Hey, I just now realized it's not as hot in here as usual. You get the air fixed?"

"Believe it or not, it was working when I got home from Nashville last week." I didn't believe it myself. I had a sneaking suspicion Derek had struck again but telling that to Jenna would just reactivate her need to matchmake.

"Well, it ain't working too well, 'cause it's still a touch too warm." Jenna swiped at her brow as if to make a point.

"For what it costs to cool a place this size, I can live with 'a touch too warm,'" I said.

"Ain't that the truth." She looked this way and that and shrugged. "So?"

"I just wanted you to see how much is here." I opened my arms like Vanna White showcasing a big win. "Every room down here has just as much as this. Then there's more in the bedrooms upstairs."

"Okay, so you got a surplus."

"I do. And it's not a bunch of junk, either. Nana didn't keep stuff that was in disrepair. Either Pawpaw fixed it, or she got rid of it. There're things here handed down for generations."

Jenna winced. "You'll just sell off all your family stuff?"

I threw open a drawer in Nana's old desk. "I'm going to do whatever it takes to get back on my feet, Jenna. I've no use for material things." The drawer was empty, as expected, and I leaned down to close it again when I saw something wedged in the back. When it didn't come loose, I maneuvered the drawer from its tracks, took it out and placed it on a round, marble-topped table.

"What's that?" Jenna moved closer and peered in to see what I was messing with.

"I don't know." I got a finger and thumb around the edges of it. Some kind of metal about a half inch wide. I wiggled the object until it came loose from the drawer back and bottom.

"It's a cross," she said. "Looks to be right old, too."

Her words were drowned out by the sudden whoosh that washed through my body, deafening in its intensity. My heart thumped clear to my toes as I gasped for air.

Derek

I figured if I gave Charlie enough time and space, she'd become an afterthought. But the more I tried to ignore the fact that she was only a couple acres away, the more it stuck in my mind. The conversation we'd had the night of Nicky's high-school graduation plagued me. We'd been at a crossroads, her and I. Maybe if she'd have been twenty-three to my twenty-eight or even twenty to my twenty-five, things might have been different. But she'd been only sixteen. Only sixteen. The lyrics from that old 50's song came to mind—too young to fall in love.

That past couldn't be changed, and the future might be out of my hands, but I could focus on the present. Fact was, she needed a friend, and guilt could be a powerful motivator. I should've known that to leave a girl slightly heart-broken with nothing more than a mere warning was like setting the barn on fire and walking away. I all but pushed her into Nicky's waiting arms.

After hours spent looking over Mark's business plans and researching security businesses on the computer, I needed a break. I didn't have to think on it too hard to land on Charlie's back steps. I peered through the window in the kitchen door and did a double take. Then a third. What all had transpired in the week I'd made myself scarce?

The kitchen looked fit to be on the cover of a fancy farm and country magazine what with its refinished cabinet doors, dining table and gewgaws. Never gave much thought about what Charlie actually did in her career. It seemed like a whole lot of money spent on creating facades. But this was different.

I tapped on the glass with a knuckle as I opened the door. "Anyone home? Charlie?" I stepped just over the threshold and waited. It was one thing to come in uninvited when I thought someone had broken in. Or maybe when I knew no one was home so I could perform a neighborly act of service. This was a horse of a different color altogether.

Muffled voices came from the recesses of the house. Both female if my hearing was correct. "Charlie, you home?" I took a sec to admire the changes in the kitchen as I stepped through it.

"You okay, Charlie?" Sounded like Jenna's voice. "You best sit a spell. You're white as a ghost. Put your head between your knees."

I twisted and turned to get through the maze of packing boxes and followed the voice to the parlor. Jenna stood over Charlie who was plunked down on the ridiculous velvet loveseat of her nana's, leaning over so that her head was clear down between her knees.

"What's wrong?" I rushed to Charlie's side and squatted. "Charlie, you sick?"

"No," she said, her voice muffled. "Just got dizzy for a minute."

When I glanced over her flat back, Jenna was staring at me and mouthed something I couldn't make out.

"I'm fine." Charlie sat up, her ponytail flipping behind her. "Must be the heat."

It was rather warm. Maybe Mark's repair was more temporary than we'd hoped. "You got a fan around here?" I stood to do her bidding.

"She don't need a fan," Jenna said. "She just needs to turn the air up a touch."

"Will the both of you stop fussing?" Charlie swiped a hand over her sweaty face. "I tell you, I'm fine."

Jenna glanced at her watch. "I need to scoot, Charlie. I promised Mama I'd pick the kids up right after lunch, and it's gettin' to be that time now."

"You go ahead, Jenna. We'll talk later." Charlie stood and gave her a quick hug.

"It might be you oughta get this girl to eat a bite," Jenna said as she placed an old cross into my hand.

"I don't need anything to eat," Charlie said. "Don't you have enough mothering to do without adding me to your list?"

"What's this?" I held up the cross.

"That's what got to turning Charlie white as a Clorox sheet." She raised her eyebrows at me as she headed out.

I held the cross up to get a better look. Bronze or brass, maybe, turning green in places, intricately carved.

Charlie held out a hand. "Do you mind?"

Frowning, I placed it gently in her palm. "Is what Jenna said true? Is there something about this cross that upset you?"

She closed her fingers around it and held it to her chest.

"I'm not ready to talk about it, Derek. There's just too much crowding my brain right now for me to give it the proper attention."

"Look, Charlie, if there's—"

"Stop talking." She pressed warm fingers against my mouth, and heat shot clear to my toes. "If and when I'm ready to discuss it, you'll be the first to know. I'm going to fix a sandwich. You want something?"

She pushed past me and fled the room.

Well, ain't that just perfect. With a shake of my head, I followed her into the kitchen. "You must be the most close-mouthed woman I know, Charlie Daniels."

Her lips twitched. "It's Van Cleave. You know that. No disrespect to the late southern rocker, but I never did take to being called Charlie Daniels." She opened the Frigidaire. "I got turkey or peanut butter. Pick your poison."

"I'd rather we talk about that cross you got clutched in your hand. What about it had you swooning?"

She snorted. "I do not swoon, Mr. Daniels. That's for antebellum ladies with corsets tied too tight. And what I prefer to discuss is how my air conditioner miraculously resuscitated itself. You know anything about that?"

"I was sort of hoping you wouldn't notice."

She pulled a jar of Duke's from the fridge and placed it on the counter. "I may be blonde, but I'm not dumb."

I rubbed my nose. "Never thought you were. But a man can hope."

"How much do I owe you for the repair work?"

"The labor was free, and the part cost about a buck-fifty. You might want to consider hiring a pest control service to get rid of rats, though."

She slid a plate of lunchmeat next to the Duke's and shuddered. "Rats? You're kidding, right?"

"'Fraid not. Just one of the perks of country living."

She looked at the cross once more, a frown marring her face, before tucking it into the front pocket of her jeans. I'd bet my military training the bantering was a cover-up for whatever darkness plagued her mind.

CHAPTER ELEVEN

Charlie

The cross haunted me in my sleep that night. Images of it danced in the light that blazed through the windshield of Daddy's Jeep. It had hung on the rearview mirror—a token of faith and blessing. I awoke in the pre-dawn morning, a heavy weight on my chest and I struggled to breathe, until I realized it was Dog. It didn't matter I'd told him he couldn't sleep on the bed; he was there anyway. A surprising comfort.

I scratched his ears, nudged him off my legs, and climbed from the bed. There wasn't much more in the room but an antique maple chest of drawers that was probably worth more than it appeared. Everything had a price tag in my mind now, which Nana wouldn't have condoned. But a girl's gotta do what a girl's gotta do.

Dog followed me down the stairs and into the kitchen. The cross sat on the counter where I'd left it last night. Just seeing it again snatched the breath from my lungs. I flicked on the coffee maker and filled Dog's food bowl. I wanted to ignore it, but it called to me like a siren's song.

I rubbed my eyes and picked it up. Maybe this wasn't the one that hung in Daddy's Jeep. Was it possible there were two of them? Or could my memory be faulty? I closed my eyes and willed my mind to return to that time so long ago.

It was a hot day, but that wasn't so unusual in the Congo. Daddy was driving to a nearby village to drop off medical supplies, and I'd asked to go with him. The golden-colored cross swung with the movement of the Jeep. Every bump and hole had it dancing on its chain. We stopped along the way to stretch our legs—that's what Daddy liked to call a walk—and down a bottle of water.

We climbed back into the Jeep, and I touched what looked to me an ancient relic. "Why d'you have this here, Daddy?"

He unhooked it from the mirror and handed it to me. "May seem a tad superstitious, but I think of it as good luck."

"Why's that superstitious?" I hesitated to trace the delicate swirls with my dirty finger. It seemed something so good oughtn't be touched by anything that wasn't clean.

"You remember the first commandment, Charlie?"

I looked into his eyes so blue Mama used to say she got lost in them sometimes. "Do unto others as you'd have them do unto you?"

He chuckled. "That's the golden rule. It's a good one, too. I'm talking about the commandments God gave to Moses for the Israelites. The same ones that apply to us today." He paused, and I knew he was giving me a chance to get it right.

"I remember them but not the order." I took a deep breath. "Don't kill anyone, don't steal anything, honor your mama and daddy."

He nodded real slow, a glisten of sweat on his upper lip. "You got them right. But the first one is you shall have no other gods besides me. You know what that means?"

"I'm not sure."

"We have to put all our trust in God alone. He must be our first love—before our love of anything else. We don't bow to statues or believe in things other than him. So, hanging a cross on the rearview mirror might look a little like trusting in the cross instead of God. The cross is then an idol. We don't worship the cross, we worship the Lord. And believing that He's only keeping us safe because of that cross is what you'd call a superstition. An irrational belief."

The more he talked, the more confused I became. "Couldn't the cross just be a reminder that Jesus is always with us?"

He ruffled my hair. "You're surely one smart little girl, Charlie Van Cleave."

I hung the cross back on the mirror feeling right proud of myself. "Where'd you get it?"

"Your mama got it from her nana when she graduated from high school."

"It looks old."

"That it is. It's what you'd call a family heirloom. I think it's been passed down from generation to generation. And when you graduate high school, your mama will give it to you."

I tapped the cross to get it swinging again.

"Until then, we're going to keep it here to remind us that Jesus is our first love."

Dog brushed against me, bringing me back to the present. Tears I hadn't been aware of rolled down my cheeks. The grief of missing Mama and Daddy never seemed to lessen. It'd been twenty years since they'd passed, but the pain of it felt as real as if it were yesterday. And God had never felt more distant.

I stared at the cross with its delicate carvings. If it was a family heirloom, like Daddy had said, then there couldn't be two of them. And even if there was, how would Daddy's mama get ahold of it when it came from Mama's side?

I'd been told that Mama and Daddy were driving on the edge of a steep embankment when their vehicle was hit head-on, causing them to go off the road. The Jeep exploded and nothing was salvageable—including Mama and Daddy. Although I had no memory of the incident, it never did sit right with me. It didn't fully make sense.

How did a cross that burned along with everything else in the Jeep end up back here?

The uneasiness I'd felt my entire adult life over the death of Mama and Daddy didn't seem so ridiculous anymore. Why would Nana and Pawpaw lie to me? Was it because the truth was too horrendous to fathom? Or was it as I'd always feared—it was somehow my fault that they were killed?

Dog pressed his big head against my thigh and sighed.

"We got us a mystery here, Dog," I said, scratching his soft ear. "And there isn't anyone alive with the answers."

I thought about how Daddy always said the enemy shouted lies over the whispers of God's truth. It was just possible the apprehension that came on whenever I tried to remember the day of the accident was His still, small voice prodding me to do something about it.

The sky became ominously dark as clouds rolled in from the south. Hurricanes in Louisiana meant refreshing breezes and rain for us Tennesseans. It was the perfect afternoon for a drive. It didn't matter I could little afford to do so in a truck that got less than fifteen miles to the gallon. I needed the distraction. Too many hours stripping paint, scrubbing floors, and unpacking endless boxes.

I rolled the window down and took pleasure in the plop of fat raindrops on my bare arm as the moist air blew into the cab. *Please let it clear my head, Lord.* With the tip of one finger, I touched the cross, which now hung from the rearview mirror of Mr. Daniels' truck. A reminder that Jesus was with me, even if I couldn't feel His presence.

Dog sat in the passenger seat, a canine smile on his scruffy face.

I leaned across him to roll his window down, too. "You ready for an adventure, Dog?"

He didn't see fit to answer. Just stuck his head out to catch the drizzle.

There was no destination in mind, unless getting lost was my goal. If a road looked good, I turned down it. Worst case, I could pull up the GPS on my phone to find my way home again. Until then, I willed all the negative stuff to blow away with the wind. My confrontation with Nicky. The dwindling bank account. The painful non-memories of Mama and Daddy's passing. The end of my career. The fear of starting over again. Nana's house in such disrepair. Gone.

Driving off a cliff wouldn't be the worst thing.

The clouds opened a touch and rays of sunlight poured down onto the emerald-green pasture. I gasped aloud as the beauty of it filled me with unspeakable joy. I half expected to spot an angel hovering over the field. "Is that You, Lord?"

The truck stalled, coughed, and stopped. *You have got to be kidding me.* I shifted into park as the cross, glinting in the sun, all but mocked me. "First time I talk to God in ages, and this is what I get," I said to Dog. He didn't seem to be put out one bit by this unfortunate turn of events.

After three attempts to start the engine, I thought to look at the gauges then groaned. “We’re out of gas.”

Dog whined. Maybe he was now starting to understand the seriousness of our situation.

I retrieved my purse from the floor and rummaged through it until I found my phone. No service. Great. Just great. Turning this way and that, I spotted a house set back about a hundred yards down the road.

“Okay, Dog.” I held his big face in my hands. “I need you to stay here. Can’t have you going after loose dogs or farm animals.” I ruffled his ears and rolled the windows up enough so he couldn’t jump out. Flashers would have been good, but the truck didn’t appear to have any.

The trek to the house took no more than a couple of minutes. As I came closer, apprehension slowed my steps. The siding had been white at one time, but where the vinyl was still intact, mold grew in abundance giving the house a sickly green tone. The porch was missing boards and a filthy, chintz-covered sofa sat front and center like a king’s pathetic throne.

I turned in a complete circle hoping to find some other option, but farmland and trees were all I could see. Maybe I had better reception here. But when I raised my phone, *No Service* continued to mock me.

“Are ya lost?” The female voice had come from within the recesses of the house, raspy and sharp.

I squinted at the front door which was now open a crack. “I’m sorry to bother you, but my truck broke down. I wondered if you have a phone I can borrow.”

“You already got one, ain’t ya?” The words were ended with a wheezy cough.

“I don’t have any service out here.”

No response.

“If I could just make one call.”

The door opened wider, and a woman appeared. She had short, blondish-gray hair scraped back from her face. Deep parallel lines ran down her cheeks and above her mouth. Heavy-set, she wore knit shorts and a sleeveless shirt that covered her bulge.

"It will only take a minute," I said, nearing the bottom step.

"Suit yourself." She left the door ajar and disappeared inside the house.

I took ginger steps up the treads, fearful I'd fall through one. As I pushed the door open, a wet, thick cough met me inside. The place reeked of cigarettes. There wasn't a clean space in the room. Stacks of books, soda bottles—both empty and partially full—newspapers, dirty dishes and what not. Nana's house, even with all the boxes and supplies, was pristine in comparison. I just might need a tetanus shot after this.

"The phone's over yonder by the recliner," she called from the other room. The kitchen, maybe?

I spotted a side table with an overflowing ashtray and a rumpled crossword magazine. Maybe her cell was under the mess. With two fingers, I lifted the magazine and peered beneath. It wasn't a cell but a handset. Who used cordless phones these days? I hesitated to hold the receiver to my face but had little choice. Then it struck me—I didn't know where I was.

I called out toward the direction the woman had gone. "Excuse me, ma'am?"

She showed up with a cigarette hanging from her mouth, squinting through the smoke that rose in a film around her face. "The name's Darlene, hon." The cigarette bounced like a little seesaw when she talked.

"Darlene." I nodded then pointed to myself. "Name's Charlotte, but most everyone calls me Charlie."

"Good to meetcha Charlie. What's it you need?"

"Your address, please."

She blew out a stream of smoke. "Thirteen, eighty-six."

I grimaced. Why didn't I pay more attention to where I was? "And the road?"

A smile broke through. "You really have got yourself turned around, ain't ya?"

"Yes, ma'am."

"You're on Orchard. Where is it you was heading?"

"No destination in mind. I just wanted to clear my head."

"Too bad your truck broke down. It's all that technology they have in 'em now. Have to pay some mechanic a fortune jus' to tell you what's wrong."

"Actually, it's a 1960 Ford."

She squinted at me. "You don't strike me as the old truck type."

What could I say to that?

"You have any idea what's wrong with it?" She smashed her cigarette into the pile of butts in the ashtray.

If I was good at lying, I'd tell her it was the alternator or carburetor. Not that I knew what they were. "Yeah. It seems I ran out of gas."

She threw her head back and cackled until another cough doubled her over. Served her right for amusing herself at my expense.

I turned away slightly to afford myself even a speck of privacy and punched in Derek's cell number. No doubt he'd find my predicament just as hilarious at Darlene. This day certainly had gone to seed. It was then I noticed a picture hanging on the wall. It reminded me of a high school graduation shot, and the girl could've been Darlene or maybe a daughter. The frame wasn't one of those cheap, Walmart jobs, either.

Derek's voicemail cut through my musings, and I cleared

my throat before speaking. "Hey Derek, I got myself in a bit of a pickle. Ran out of gas and could really use your help." I recited the address. "I don't have any cell service, so I guess I'll just wait for you at the truck. I might try and reach Jenna."

I ended the call and replaced the receiver before facing Darlene who'd plopped into a saggy faux leather recliner. "I appreciate your hospitality."

"Sure nuff, Charlie." She slid a pack of Camels from under the crossword magazine and shook one out. "You must be new in these parts to not know where you are."

I crossed my arms and stood like an awkward schoolgirl when what I wanted to do was hightail it out of there. But the least I could do after she helped me was show a little common courtesy. "Not new, exactly. Just haven't been back for a while."

She lit the cigarette while eyeing me up and down. "Where you been?"

"After college, Nashville."

"Music?"

"Interior design."

Her eyes widened slightly. "Used to be in that line of work myself."

She was pulling my leg. Had to be.

"You don't believe me."

I held my hands up in a defensive move. "I didn't say that."

"Don't have to. It's okay. I halfway don't believe it myself, and I lived it." She flicked ash in the already over-flowing ashtray.

"What happened?" The question popped out before I could filter my tone. Did I sound as incredulous to her as I did to myself?

"Long story, princess. I'm sure your fella's on his way to rescue you."

As I stepped onto the front porch, I glanced once more at the photo hanging askew on the wall. It could be we had something in common and stopping here wasn't coincidence. The truck didn't just happen to run out of gas at this location. What was it Daddy always said about coincidence? *Coincidences are what those who believe in God call providence.*

CHAPTER TWELVE

Derek

The loft seating at the Coffee Break was empty except for Mark and me. We'd spread out charts, graphs, and the business plan for Security Works on a large corner table then got lost in possibilities.

"What've you got to lose?" Mark asked for the third time since we sat down. Don't know if he was trying to convince me or himself.

"Just my savings and pension." I tapped a finger on the profit and loss projection. "You really think you're going to find office space for this price in the Franklin area? I'm telling you, Mark, it's not possible."

He shrugged. "I got a couple contacts working on it for me. If you think—"

"Hate to break up the party, y'all." Coraline appeared at the top of the stairs. "We're closing in five."

I glanced at my watch. How'd it get to be almost 2:00 already? "Sorry to keep you. Didn't realize the time."

"Not a problem," she said then headed back down the stairs.

Mark gathered the papers into a messy stack. "Well, what d'ya think? Are you in?"

I nabbed the phone and keys I'd left on the chair beside me. "Give me a couple more days."

"What are you waiting on, Derek?"

I glanced at the phone. Somehow, I'd missed a call. "A little divine guidance."

"God?" He snorted.

"He's never led me wrong yet." If I'd only obeyed every time in the past, things might've been different today. I clicked into voicemail and raised the phone to listen as I followed Mark down the steps. It was Charlie. *Hey Derek, I got myself in a bit of a pickle. Ran out of gas and could really use your help.*

"Something wrong?" Mark asked as I swept past him.

"Gotta run. You get the check today and next time it's on me."

"You got it. Hey, Derek?"

Halfway out the door, I turned back to him. "Yeah?"

"I really want to get this started if we're gonna do it."

It wasn't fair to keep putting him off. "I'll let you know by Saturday, okay?"

"I'll hold you to it."

The military taught me to be prepared for any situation, so I had a gas can bungeed in the bed of my truck. Half hour after Charlie had called, I pulled up alongside Daddy's truck. Fortunately for her, the road was wide open, so being stuck in the middle of it wasn't too fool hardy. It'd been raining steady, but the clouds now started to clear, and the heavy moisture left behind made it feel I was breathing through a wet rag.

I jumped out of the truck and landed in a soggy ditch. A

twinge kicked up in my low back as water seeped into my shoes. I unhooked the gas can and hauled it from the bed.

Charlie's door swung open, and she climbed out, Dog nosing her backside to escape. "You're my hero. Again." She moved aside for Dog who made a beeline for the shoulder to relieve himself.

"Kind of an amateur move." I grinned and unscrewed her gas cap. "You're supposed to save those for when you're looking to manipulate a romantic interlude."

She crossed her arms, and I couldn't help but notice the golden sleekness that formed her biceps. "Not my proudest moment, I'll admit. Just kind of lost track of things." She flipped her braid back. Reminded me of the summer I left for the service. She'd watched me work then, too, with pond water staining her tank and the smell of sunscreen permeating the summer air. Twenty years dissipated in an instant.

Best to stick to the here and now.

"What're you doing all the way out here, anyway?" It was a pretty road, all green fields and trees, but not much for people. If this had happened at night, it might have turned out different.

"Needed to clear my head."

I set the can down and moved past her to the cab. The key sat in the ignition, and I cranked it to be sure the truck would start. It took a couple stutters to get her going before the engine smoothed out. "I'm just going to pull off the road."

Charlie nodded.

As I parked in front of my truck, my gaze caught the dangle of a cross hanging from the rearview mirror. It was the one I'd seen at the house the day before. I caught the chain with a finger, unhooked it from the mirror, and palmed it.

Rounding the vehicle, I met her on the other side. "You

want to tell me what's with this cross, Charlie?" I let it slip until it was hanging from my finger.

She snatched it like I'd held up one of her unmentionables and curled her fingers around it. "It's nothing."

"We both know that isn't true. Something had you driving out here in the middle of nowhere to, what'd you call it? Clear your head?"

She looked at her red-painted toes peeking out from her sandals and sighed.

And they say guys are poor communicators. There were days talking to Charlie was like plucking a chicken, one stubborn feather at a time. "Where'd it come from?"

Opening her palm, she stared at the cross for a moment before touching it with what appeared to be reverence. "I'm not sure, and it's haunting me."

A car engine sounded from down the road, and Charlie whipped her head around. "Dog?" She seemed frantic for a moment before spotting him. "Come." She patted her thigh with her free hand, and the shepherd immediately responded. Someone trained him well, and it was a wonder they weren't looking for him.

I held Dog's collar as the car sped by, the driver's arm out the window waving. Charlie and me both lifted our hands in response. Once it was clear again, I let loose of Dog. "This isn't the best place to talk."

Charlie pocketed the cross. "There isn't much to talk about. I appreciate you coming all this way. What do I owe you for the gas?" She turned away.

"How 'bout the truth?"

My challenge halted her steps, and she spun around to face me again. Her blue eyes spit fire like she was fit for battle. The girl had spunk, that's for darn sure. "I never lie to you, Derek. It's just sometimes there're things too hard to talk about.

You're not exactly tripping all over yourself to shine a light on *your* past."

"You want to know something, sweet Charlie, all you gotta do is ask. Right now, I'm asking you what's with the cross."

Charlie

Sweet Charlie. Every time Derek used that endearment, it landed me in a puddle of bittersweet yearning. A reminder that he'd always been on my side. He wasn't going to be put off, and I was tired of carrying the burden alone. I flicked a finger at the backend of the truck. "You win. Lower the tailgate and we'll sit." He didn't argue but moved to do my bidding. Probably figured I'd clam up if we waited until we were back at the house. Which I would've.

Before I could leverage myself onto the tailgate, his big hands wrapped around my waist, and he lifted me. Shocked and lightheaded, I clutched his shoulders to keep my balance. He was so close, I saw the flecks of green in his blue eyes and the musk of his shampoo or aftershave tickled my nose. A zing of awareness shot through my body, but before it could truly register, he plopped me onto the tailgate and stepped away.

I was still trying to find my voice when he landed next to me. "Looks to be the perfect place to have a private conversation."

Dog settled beneath our feet with a sigh as I grappled for a response. What had just happened? I'd always had feelings for Derek, but I'd thought of them as a childish girl's fantasy. Like having a crush on a movie star. There was safety in distance. Derek's career. My marriage.

He braced himself on the tailgate, one hand by each thigh. "Back to what we were talking about."

Oh, yeah. The cross. I leaned back to pull it from my pocket. "This?" Just the sight of it sobered me.

"You found it in your nana's things?"

"Yes." I closed my fingers around it. "I'm almost positive it's the same one that hung from Daddy's Jeep when we were in the Congo." I looked up at him to gauge his reaction.

He frowned. "I don't get why that would haunt you."

I surely couldn't expect him to understand something I didn't, but if I could share the burden, maybe it wouldn't feel so heavy. "My parents, the Jeep, and everything in it burned in the crash. So, how could it be here?"

"I never heard the details of your parents' death—only that they'd been in a car accident of some kind. Maybe your memory's faulty."

I blew out a breath. "That's the problem. I don't have any memories. Only what Nana and Pawpaw told me. Mama and Daddy were driving along the edge of a steep embankment when another car came around the corner and hit them head-on. They went over the edge. The Jeep caught fire, and nothing was salvageable."

"You never saw where it happened?"

I wrapped my arms around my stomach. "If I did, I don't remember. Not what led up to it, not the weeks that followed. But I do remember this cross hanging from Daddy's rearview mirror." I flicked my eyes to his. "Something's not right, Derek. And I'm not sure if I'm more afraid of the truth or the lie."

"Why would they lie to you, Charlie?"

I chewed my lower lip. Once I said it, I couldn't take it back. "What if my parents didn't die in a car accident?"

No response.

"I mean, I'm not saying I think they're alive or anything."

"That's good, 'cause that would reek of some kind of conspiracy theory. So, what *are* you saying?"

"Have you ever woken up in the middle of a dream?"

He shifted to face me, eyebrows drawn together. "Yeah."

"And then once you're awake for a while, you can't remember anything except random images?"

"What's that got to do with your parents?"

I scrubbed a hand over my face. He's going to think I'm nuttier than a pecan pie. "There are times, even when I'm awake, that I get these fog-like images. Like maybe memories sitting on the edge of my consciousness. It leaves me feeling empty and desolate."

"That's understandable, Charlie. It was a great loss, and since you can't remember, your mind is trying to make sense of what you don't know."

"Derek, the truth is, I've always had this feeling it was my fault Mama and Daddy were killed."

He flinched as if I'd slapped him. "That's ridiculous. It was an accident, and—"

"No." I jumped off the tailgate and nearly stumbled over Dog. "Don't you see? I don't think that's how they died. Deep down, I never thought it was. Maybe I can't remember because the truth is too hard for me to grasp. You hear about people having amnesia to protect them from what they can't face."

Derek slid off the tailgate and stood in front of me. He raised a hand, as if he was going to touch me, then let it drop. "You were a child, Charlie. How could you possibly be blamed for their deaths?"

I shook my head. "I don't know." A fist of emotion sat in my throat making it hard to breathe. "But I can't shake the images, and I don't think they're a figment of my imagination, either." I held up the cross. "And now this." It swung between us, as if taunting me. "The only reason I can think they'd lie to me is to protect me from the truth."

He pushed a hand through his military-short hair. "Let's say you're right. There's something about how your Mama and Daddy died that they hid from you. Why would you want to dig it all up? They had their reasons, Charlie."

"Maybe, but don't you think I have a right to know? To be set free? Isn't that what the Bible says? The truth will set you free?"

He scowled. "You're taking it out of context. Jesus's words were referring to Himself. He was the truth. There are some truths better left alone. And I have a sneaking suspicion this is one of them."

His words chilled me as if a cold storm had blown down from the north. I'd lived with lies for most of my life, and if he was going to stand there and tell me it was better to accept it, then he was no better than Nicky. That was enough to cool whatever feelings had burned in me at his touch only moments before.

CHAPTER THIRTEEN

Charlie

It didn't take but four or five days to regret my immature response to Derek. I should have let things be. He meant well. What got under my skin, like a blood-sucking leech, was how he could always be so calm and controlled about everything. It was enough to make me spit. He'd have said it was his faith in God—the whole fruit of the Spirit thing. Still, it was too bad some of it hadn't rubbed off on Nicky.

Add that to my spitting-mad list. Nicky. I'd avoided Mama G for days so as to not have to answer the inevitable question about what my plans were regarding him. The divorce papers sat on my dresser ready to be served, but it just didn't sit right to do so until I could tell her. Her unexpected visit gave me the perfect opportunity, if not the necessary backbone.

"Goodness, Charlie." Mama G walked around the parlor touching this and that. "I can see why I haven't seen much of you. This room is a picture. Just like the kitchen. Almost too pretty to be real."

Nerves had a way of dampening the warmth of her praise. My heart was beating clear into my throat just thinking about what needed to be said. “Thank you, ma’am. It’s been a lot of work, but I think the results are well worth it.”

She flashed me a brilliant smile. “I should say so.” She ran a hand over the intricate woodwork that framed the large windows. “When did y’all find time to strip off that ol’ paint?”

“Derek started it. He’s not taking credit, but I don’t believe anyone else would’ve broken in before I returned to do so. I finished it up mostly in the evenings.”

“I surely hope you wore a mask. The fumes alone could do damage something fierce.” I noticed she didn’t discount my assertion that Derek had been working here on the sly.

“Yes, ma’am, I did.”

She waved a dismissive hand. “Who do I think I’m talking to? You surely know what you’re doing when it comes to remodel and design work.”

“Never can be too careful.”

She perched on the edge of Nana’s hot-pink velvet settee. Not the most practical piece of furniture, and a true challenge to incorporate into the decor. “What’re you fixin’ to do with the rest of the house?”

I felt awkward standing over her, so I eased into a wing-back chair to be at eye level once again. “Same as this, I suppose. One room at a time.”

Her smile didn’t waver a speck as she nodded. “What’s your endgame?”

Endgame? Never would I have expected to hear Mama G use that word. We were moving into murky territory here, inch by painful inch. “I’m working at building up a clientele. Each room will have a different decor so I can showcase my talent. If all goes well, I’ll be self-sufficient.”

The smile slipped slightly. "You've always been self-sufficient, Charlie. Needed to be, from what I gather."

"I can't depend on anyone else." I laid the words down like a challenge.

She looked at her hands folded in her lap. "Where does that leave Nicky?"

"Mama G," I sighed, moving to kneel down at her feet. I put my hand over hers. "I know you want things to work out between Nicky and me, but I just don't see how they can. He's taking no responsibility, nor has he made any move to make amends."

She tugged one of her hands free and placed it against my cheek. "I know that, sweetheart. If I thought it'd do any good, I'd take him by the ear and give him a talking-to myself. Don't you be fretting over how I'm takin' it, either. You've been a pure joy to me, Charlie. That's not about to change." She pinched my chin before dropping her hand.

"Now," she said, "let's take another looksee at that kitchen of yours."

Before she could move, I wrapped my arms around her and held tight for a moment, relief birthing tears at the back of my eyes. There weren't many who'd offer unconditional love, so to lose Mama G's would've been more than I could bear.

Walking through the house to the kitchen, my attention was drawn to all the work that still needed doing. Where would I find the time, energy, and money? Daddy would've said I needed to pray, but my faith was just fickle enough to keep me from testing it. If I prayed with nothing to show for it but disappointment, then wouldn't that leave me worse off than before?

We stepped into the kitchen and it was like I was wrapped in a warm hug. What was it about a roomful of appliances and knickknacks that could elevate a mood? This was where most of my memories had been made, sitting at the kitchen table while Nana stood over the stove. More often than not, Pawpaw would do his personal best to tease a smile from her. She'd fight it just to be contrary, but underneath it all, she'd glow like a teenage girl with her first big crush.

"Your nana's stove looks to be original."

"Works like it, too." I grimaced. "If not for the microwave I have squirreled away in the cabinet, I'd be living off cold cereal and crackers."

Mama G threw her hands in the air. "Land sakes, Charlie. Why didn't you say something before? You're always welcome to eat with me and Derek."

"Thank you, ma'am, but I'm getting by." A thought suddenly occurred to me. "I would like to borrow your oven, though, to whip up a batch of cookies. I met this woman last week, and I can't seem to get her off my mind. I was trying to think of an excuse to drop in on her, and I think cookies might pave the way for me."

She nodded. "You never can tell what God'll do with a batch of cookies, Charlie."

"Maybe." I slid into a chair at the kitchen table and Mama G sat across from me. "I don't know what it is about her that draws me." As repulsed as I'd been by her lifestyle, it made no sense.

"There's no accounting for how the Holy Spirit works."

I started to argue that the Holy Spirit had nothing to do with my interaction with Darlene, but who was I to contradict Mama G?

Derek

The moment I pulled my truck into the lot, I knew Mark and me were going to have a problem. No start-up business could afford office space in an upscale community like downtown Franklin. And even if we could, we'd be foolish to waste the resources on it. I wasn't a hundred percent sold on the idea of working security as it was, but I didn't want to be in conflict before we even got out the gate.

It wasn't five minutes later Mark parked next to me and climbed out of his car with a grin big enough for the both of us. "Well, what d'ya think?"

I leaned my backside against the truck grill and shook my head. "I think you're under the impression Daddy Warbucks is financing this venture. Where in the Sam Hill do you think we're going to get the money to pay the lease on a place like this?"

His grin melted into a frown. "It takes money to make money, my friend."

"Yeah? Well, you got to have it first, which we don't." Truth was, I could easily afford it myself, but it didn't seem fitting given the situation. I flicked my hand toward the multi-office complex. Three stories high, all brick and gleaming windows. "What's it cost? Thirty a square foot? If all we get is a hundred square feet, we might could afford it. But then, it wouldn't be any use to us."

"You gotta better suggestion?"

I took a deep breath to get control of my tongue. I'd already shared my suggestions ad nauseam. "I appreciate your enthusiasm, Mark. But when we discussed office space, I told you it wasn't necessary at the outset. We could start online, and once things begin to take off, then we look to expand."

He scowled. "And what about the equipment? We gonna store it at your mama's place? 'Cause let me remind you, I live in a double-wide with a wife and two kids. There ain't room for me to have a thought let alone store security equipment or set up a business computer."

He had a point. The idea of anything long-term at Mama's was on par with offering up myself as a human sacrifice. Dignity was hard enough to come by when I'd convinced myself the situation was only temporary. But an office? That reeked of permanence I wasn't ready to claim.

"I don't know." I scratched my head as if it would release some brain waves. "But twelve hundred square feet's going to cost us a few thousand a month. I'm not comfortable spending that kind of change, and I suspect, if you were, you wouldn't be living in a double-wide."

"You got that right."

"Why here?"

"What d'ya mean?"

"Why Franklin? We could do a whole lot better in Shelbyville. No one's going to care where our office is set up when all the work we're doing is in their place of business."

His sigh told me he was resigned. Mark's problem was he had visions of grandeur beyond his pocketbook. Me, I didn't much care about material things or what other people thought of me. Except staying at Mama's. No thirty-seven-year-old man worth spit lived with his mama. Nicky would milk it for all it's worth, that was for sure.

"It'd be easy enough for me set up a temporary computer in the guest house," I said. "No need to keep equipment stocked since we're just starting out. We'll order as needed."

"Fine." Mark sounded like I'd just squashed his grandiose vision. "I suppose that makes the most sense. Can we at least get some business cards made?"

I grinned and patted him on the back. "Sure. We'll get some real nice business cards. First, though, we might want to find someone to design our webpage." Don't know why I bothered creating a business plan with him when he wanted to jump the gun at every turn. Keeping him on track was like herding kittens.

"You have that covered, right?"

Before I could respond, my cell vibrated in my back pocket. Nicky's name flashed on my cellphone screen. "Give me a minute, will you Mark?"

Stepping away, I connected the call. "Hey Nicky. Everything okay?" Couldn't remember the last time he'd phoned.

"Sure. Why wouldn't it be?" He sounded upbeat, which raised my suspicions.

"No reason, I suppose." I nearly bit my tongue in two to keep from asking why he'd called. But if he needed something, he'd get to it eventually.

"You gonna be up Nashville way anytime in the next day or two?" The question was casual-like, as if he was asking how the weather was in my neck of the woods.

"Not planning on it." Wasn't about to tell him I was less than thirty minutes from him. Nicky'd had it too easy his whole life. Maybe working at something would give him a new perspective.

"Oh." A sigh blew over the line, and I allowed myself a grin at his expense.

"What d'you need?"

"I just thought maybe we could talk."

"Isn't that what we're doing now?"

"Rather it be in person. Thought maybe we could meet for lunch again. Or maybe supper."

"That's a great idea," I said as I held up a finger to Mark to indicate I'd only be a minute more. "I'm sure Mama would love to see you."

"I was just thinking the two of us, Derek. I have something personal to run by you."

"That's fine. But first you take the time to have supper with Mama. How long's it been since you made an effort to see her? A couple months?"

He grumbled a response, but I couldn't catch it.

"Give her a call, Nicky. Tell her you'd like to come down for supper, and I'll make a point of being there, too. Then we can talk."

After disconnecting, I stared at my phone for a moment. Nicky wanting to talk could only be about one thing.

Charlie.

My stomach tightened.

CHAPTER FOURTEEN

Charlie

Armed with a plate of Mama G's chocolate chip cookies, I set out for Darlene's place once again. Only this time, I made sure my gas tank was full and left Dog behind. I'd woken to a rainstorm that didn't look to be letting up, and when Dog got wet, he stunk to high heaven. A bath would do him good, but that was just one more step toward ownership that wasn't mine to claim.

I'd intended to bake the cookies myself, but Mama G took pity on me, which I'd half hoped from the outset. If my intention was to impress Darlene with baking skills, my own wouldn't cut it. A foil-wrapped plate sat on the passenger seat, and the scent of chocolate and vanilla filled the truck cab. Breakfast had been a banana dipped in peanut butter, and I'd skipped lunch, which was most likely why the sweet scent nauseated me some.

I rolled down the window, drew in a few deep breaths, and let the rain-cooled breeze wash over me. After a few moments, my stomach settled. With all the paint and stripping fumes I'd been subjected to over the last couple weeks, it was a wonder the scent of cookies would unsettle me.

I pulled the truck onto Darlene's rutted drive where the gravel had washed away, leaving dips big enough to birth a whale. The dilapidated porch looked sadder today than last week if that was even possible. How could a woman who claimed interior design skills think an old couch set front and center was a good decor choice?

Before climbing from the truck, I hooked my purse onto my shoulder and collected the plate. Darlene may not be pleased to see me, so the least I could do was have a consolation prize handy. I'd gotten halfway up the weed-patched walk when the door flew open.

"Your tank run dry ag'in, Charlie?" Darlene cackled at her own joke. "Or mebe this time you blew a tire."

I took her banter as a sign of welcome. "Glad to add a little amusement to your day." Readjusting my purse, I balanced the plate in one hand and climbed the stairs.

"Couldn't stay away, could ya?" She pushed the screen wide and stepped aside for me to enter.

"I wanted to thank you for your hospitality with a little gift." The house looked much the same as before except it was noticeably less pungent.

Darlene let the screen slap shut and pointed at my offering. "Wha'd ya bring me?" She peeled back the covering and inhaled. "You make 'em?"

I chuckled. "Fortunately for you, I did not. My mother-in-law bakes the best cookies this side of the Mississippi, and she did it as a favor for me." I offered them to her. "Enjoy."

"Mama-in-law, huh?" She glanced at my left hand as she took the plate. "You ain't wearin' no weddin' ring."

"Long story."

She nodded as if she understood. "Sit a spell, and I'll fix us some sweet tea." She cleared a spot on the coffee table before putting the plate down.

As she disappeared into the kitchen, I looked around for a place to sit. There was the couch that appeared to match the one on the porch, except it wasn't faded and water stained. One cushion was junk-free, and I perched on the edge of it. How did she live in this mess?

"Here we go." Darlene bustled out with paper towels tucked under one arm and two glasses filled with amber liquid and no ice. She handed one to me. "There's coasters under that there newspaper."

Coasters? Was she serious? I lifted the rumpled paper, and sure enough, there were a couple mismatched coasters stacked beneath. I carefully set my glass on one, biting the inside of my cheek to keep from laughing.

"What's got you grinnin' like a possum?" She collected the second coaster and set her own tea down on the table by her recliner.

"Nothing." But I couldn't get control of the grin. Much as I tried, my lips twitched with it.

"I git it." She snatched a cookie and plopped into her chair. "Ya think it's funny, me protectin' my furniture when I live in a pigsty."

I waved a hand in the air as if I could erase her words. "No, of course not."

"Some things stick from birth." She bit into the cookie and chewed. "I know what y'all must think about the way I live."

Heat crawled up my neck, and I dropped my gaze. "I'm sorry, Darlene. It was rude of me to make fun—"

"Forget it. It ain't like I want to live this away."

I leaned forward and spoke before thinking on it. "Then why do it? Are you compelled to keep everything?"

"Ya mean like a hoarder?" She barked out a laugh and shook her head. "Went through a rough patch is all. It's been hard, but I'm workin' my way out. Took the first step after you was here. Quit smokin'."

I glanced at her side table where the overflowing ashtray was conspicuously absent. It occurred to me just then that I hadn't heard Darlene hack once in the few minutes I'd been there. "How's it going?"

She shrugged. "We'll see. Tried before, but it ain't never took. I'm givin' it another go. 'Cause of you."

My mouth dropped clear to my toes. "Me? Why?"

Darlene pushed out of the chair, lifted the plate of cookies, and offered me one. "Lost my daughter near 'bout ten years ago. You remind me a little of her. She'd a been 'bout your age now. Jus' seein' you here t'other day brought to mind the way it used to be."

Her words struck a sensitive chord. I'd been judging her by my own set of warped standards. It was hard enough to miscarry a baby, but to lose a grown child? I'd imagine I'd be in worse shape than her.

I snagged a cookie and pointed it to the photo I'd noticed the last time I was there. "Is that her?"

Darlene's gaze hung on it for a moment as if caught in a memory. "That's her." Her voice hitched, and she cleared her throat. "Been wallerin' for ten years now. Reckon it's time to move on."

"I'm so sorry." With no idea what else to say, I took a bite of the cookie and chewed a moment. "Is there anything I can do to help?"

Derek

Three years isn't much of an age difference, but from what I'd recalled, it'd always seemed like Nicky was eons younger. Or maybe I was just born old. Either way, we never did ride the same range. He was on one side of the fence, and I was clear on the other. Getting older only expanded the distance.

If it weren't for the delight that lit Mama's face whenever we were all together, I'd have caved into Nicky's plan to meet alone. At least then I wouldn't have had to plaster a smile on my face like a fool rodeo clown and pretend everything was good.

The kitchen table was near to busting with food Mama had prepared, like she was welcoming home the prodigal son. Roasted pork butt, baked beans, green beans with bacon, corn on the cob, potato casserole, and a congealed salad, just for starters. Dessert was sure to be homemade ice cream and a berry cobbler or something of the sort.

"You boys get enough to eat?" Mama hopped up and started clearing the table.

"We'll get the dishes, Mama. You did all the cooking." I stood and glared at Nicky until he did the same. What was wrong with him? He usually had better manners.

"Nonsense. Cooking for you boys is pure joy. You go out back and visit a spell while I do a little clean up. Then I'll bring out some dessert."

I'd have argued with her but knew it'd do no good. "It sure was a great meal, as usual." I pecked her on the cheek before following Nicky to the back patio where he started pacing.

"What's eating you, Nicky? You hardly said two words during supper."

"Yeah, I know. Sorry." He crammed his hands into the front pockets of his jeans.

I eased onto the edge of the brick planter box that bordered the backside of the patio where hydrangeas and azaleas were bursting with color. Maybe it would've been better to meet him elsewhere like he'd wanted.

"What's going on? You in trouble?"

He grunted. "Aside from my marriage falling apart, you mean?"

"Is that what you wanted to talk about? 'Cause I'm probably the last person to give you marital advice."

"Maybe. But seems to me you know Charlie better'n anyone else. What with your emails and all." His upper lip curled slightly as if he smelled something rotten.

I shook my head but held my tongue. I'd already told him there'd only been a couple. Once he'd gotten into his head that he was the injured party, there was no changing his mind. "Whatever," I muttered.

"She's gonna leave me, Derek." His gaze caught mine then slipped away when he started pacing again. "Sure as we're sitting here, she's gonna file for divorce."

Can't say the idea didn't lighten my mood some. "What'd you expect?"

"I don't know." He pulled a hand from his pocket and shoved it through his hair. "That maybe she'd give me another chance."

"And why should she?"

Mouth open, he stared at me like I'd betrayed him. "Why shouldn't she? I can't be the first husband who messed up. Is it so much to ask?"

Crossing my arms, I bit back an automatic response and gave his question serious thought. If I could be so bold to think like Charlie might, what would it take to give Nicky a second chance? Just the thought of it caused my dinner to sit like a rock in my gut.

"Be honest with me, Nicky. How many times you stepped out on her?"

He opened his mouth to answer then snapped it shut. If I knew my little brother, he'd take the low road whenever possible. Owning up to his part in things didn't come naturally. "A couple times," he finally said. I'd bet half my pension he was lying.

"If you want my help, you'll have to come clean."

With a sigh, he dropped onto a patio chair. "Maybe four or five," he mumbled. "I've heard it said that cheating is just a symptom."

"Yeah?" I snorted. "Of what?"

"Deeper issues."

"Well, I'd have to agree with that." I held up one hand and ticked them off finger by finger. "Immaturity, narcissism, lack of control, inability to commit, godlessness. You want I should go on, 'cause I still have a handful of fingers left?"

He scowled at me. "I can see you're of no mind to help."

"What would be the point? Say Charlie takes you back. What guarantees would she have you won't just step out again?"

"My word."

I stared him down, eyebrows raised. "You'll have to do better than that. You might want to hone up your Bible knowledge."

He winced like I'd struck him in the face. "How's that gonna help?"

"Gives you a pretty good idea of what a husband's supposed be like. First off, you should be the one providing for Charlie. She shouldn't be the one providing for you."

"Next thing you'll tell me is a woman shouldn't work."

"Didn't say that." I waited until he looked at me. "But she's been supporting y'all since you've been married. She's competed with your music, your time, and every groupie who tempts you to stray."

"So, I should just give it all up and quit? Then what? How will that support us?"

"Find yourself a day job, little brother. One that allows you to be home at night and doesn't include temptation. Charlie needs to be enough for you. If not, you'll just keep on making the same mistakes over and over again."

"I don't know," he said. "I've been working on it more'n twelve years now. I'm this close." He held up a hand, forefinger and thumb only an inch apart.

"You're closer than that to losing your wife. No one can make the choice for you, Nicky." I waited for his eyes to meet mine. "If I were you, I'd think long and hard before making any decisions. That's if you can even get Charlie to agree to give you another chance. That in itself would require a miracle."

"About that." He rested his elbows on his knees. "I was hoping you'd maybe pave the way some for me."

"Pave the way?" I scowled. "What'd be the point?"

"She'd listen to you, Derek. I know she would."

Nicky may not have the sense God gave a goat, but he was a long way from being stupid. Calling on me to champion him was a surefire way to keep me honor-bound to his wishes and at arm's length from Charlie. He had no idea I'd never of crossed that line, anyway. Still, the manipulation stung.

CHAPTER FIFTEEN

June—2012
Charlie

Every girl dreams of her wedding day. White dress, handsome groom, and her daddy walking her down a long church aisle. At least that'd been Charlie's plan from the time she could remember. When her parents died, she'd realized dreams and reality didn't ever mesh. They were just a fantasy born of a desire for perfection. Still, Pawpaw would be a decent stand-in for her daddy, and he'd look dashing in a tux—like Sean Connery with a southern twang—escorting her down the aisle.

Funny that in her fantasy wedding, she didn't give a whole lot of thought to who the groom would be. Or if he'd truly love her. She'd heard the jokes about shotgun weddings. They weren't so funny when you were the one staring down the barrel of such an affair. But hers wouldn't truly be a shotgun wedding because no one was forcing her to marry. Aside from Nicky, no one even knew she was pregnant. He'd said all the right things when he found out, and yet even as she stood facing him at the rehearsal, red flags were waving like crazy.

She'd considered her options, none of which included getting rid of the baby. There was no way she could live with herself if she did. But every choice that didn't include getting married required her to tell Nana and Pawpaw. She thought about running off for a year then giving the baby up for adoption, but her parents dying felt enough like abandonment, she couldn't do the same to her own child. And she did love Nicky. Maybe not as much as she'd like, but she would in time. He needed to grow up a little, but he'd make a good daddy.

Charlie felt it was the right decision until Derek arrived. She'd half-hoped he couldn't get leave just so she wouldn't have to see the disappointment in his eyes. But as they finished with the rehearsal, he walked through the church door looking like a combination of G.I. Joe and Tim Tebow. Talk about fantasy.

Everyone rushed to greet him except Nicky and Charlie. Her stomach flipped, and she wasn't sure if it was the baby making her sick or being in Derek's presence for the first time in six years. He'd been home a time or two since Nicky's high school graduation, but she'd found excuses to be absent, as if she could escape his disapproval of her relationship with his brother. The awkwardness of time held her back.

Nicky finally hooked his arm in Charlie's and tugged her forward as their families stepped away to give Derek some breathing room. "Hey, Big Brother," he said. "You missed the rehearsal."

Derek's steel-blue gaze shot from Nicky to Charlie and back again, his mouth tilted slightly. "Couldn't be helped. I think if I can field strip an M-16 in under a minute, I can manage to hand Charlie's ring to you without screwing up."

"Good deal," Nicky said, patting Derek on the back. "We're heading over to Legends for dinner. You coming?"

Derek's gaze met Charlie's. "I'm all yours."

Charlie managed to choke some food down, though she had no recollection of what she ate. She was awkward and twitchy and knew it wouldn't change until she could come clean with Derek. Nicky swore he hadn't told anyone she was pregnant, but the way Derek kept looking across the table at her—reproachful-like—made her wonder if Nicky had lied.

As they all left the restaurant to head back home, Derek stepped up behind her. "I need to talk to you, Charlie." He was so close, his breath tickled her ear. "Meet me out by the old magnolia tree in an hour?"

She started to tell him no, that it wouldn't be appropriate, but instead she nodded her agreement. Confession could be the only thing that might calm the roiling sea in her stomach.

A little over an hour later, Charlie stepped out onto the back porch where the twinkle of fireflies in the trees and bushes that bordered her grandparents' property put on quite a show. She'd been counting off the minutes from the moment they'd arrived home, but she waited a few past the agreed upon time so as not to appear too anxious. She wasn't fooling herself, but it might give Derek pause.

Her heart skittered up a notch or two when she spotted his shadow in the light of the moon dwarfed by the magnificence of the magnolia tree as she crossed the backyard. The conversation they'd had the night of Nicky's graduation chose that moment to replay in her mind. She'd sworn Nicky and she were just friends. And at the time, it was true. But things changed, and there was nothing she could do to change them back.

"Hey, Derek." Even at a whisper, her voice seemed to boom over that of the cicadas and crickets.

Derek leaned against the tree, arms crossed. Heart-shaped

waxy leaves danced above his head making it appear he was Caesar reincarnated. "Hey, Charlie. Thanks for agreeing to this. Wasn't sure you would since I didn't hear back from the emails I sent."

"I've been a little busy, what with finishing up college and all." She plopped onto the ground and the moisture from the grass seeped into her jeans. She figured he'd see through the excuse but offered it anyway.

He nodded and sat down beside her. "Was kind of surprised to get a wedding invitation."

"Nicky tell you himself?" And if he did, what else did he reveal?

"Nah. I hear less from him than I do you. Mama told me. Kind of last minute, isn't it? What's the big rush?"

"Why not?" Charlie focused on the fireflies that flickered over Derek's left shoulder. "Why wait when you know it's right?" The words were such a load of malarkey, they nearly stuck in her throat. Another month, and she'd begin to show.

"What's going on, Charlie? You can't honestly tell me you really wanna get hitched."

Tears burned at the back of Charlie's eyes as she clenched her teeth. She wanted to blame Derek for this whole mess.

She focused on breathing until she could speak without blubbering. "What d'you care, anyway? You couldn't even bother to come home after your second tour." She might as well just admit she'd been waiting for him.

"What was the point? You'd already made your choice by then."

She shook her head. "What Nicky and I had then wasn't serious."

"But you were dating. He told me so."

"Doesn't matter anymore, though, does it?"

"No, Charlie, it doesn't matter. Leastways, not if you're happy. Are you?"

Rather than lie, which never turned out well, she hedged. "He's different than you. You're so serious all the time, and duty-bound. Nicky, he's fun. Every day is an adventure with him."

"I don't doubt it, Charlie." He reached out a hand as if he was going to touch her then dropped it. "Is he the one the Lord pressed on your heart to marry?"

Charlie twisted up her mouth. "At this point, I have no doubt it's what God would have me do." She ducked her head. "I'm pregnant, Derek."

Derek—2012

The few accounts he'd heard about near-death experiences all said the same thing. It was like their lives had flashed before their eyes. Scene after scene to remind them of all they'd miss once they left this earth. It was the same for Derek as Charlie's confession registered. He'd been a fool to think that offering a few platitudes here and there over the years would keep her from making poor choices. Or moving on without him.

"Why didn't you come back when you said you would, Derek?" There was more than a hint of accusation in Charlie's tone. Was she blaming him for her taking up with Nicky?

He had to make an effort to unclench his jaw in order to speak. "A few reasons. I was in the middle of an assignment for one. By the time I was ready to resign, I heard tell that you and Nicky were together. Didn't realize it was all that serious." Hoped it wasn't.

"It just sort of happened." She plucked at the dew-wet

grass. "Honestly, it started out all fun and games. And then you didn't come home."

Derek choked back a humorless laugh.. "You're gonna tell me it's my fault? You takin' up with Nicky and getting yourself knocked up is all some kind of hissy fit you were throwing to get at me?" The moment the words were out, he wished he could reel them back. Even in the darkness, he could feel the glare she threw his way, but it was her eyes brimming with tears that sucker punched him in the gut.

"Yeah. I decided the best revenge was to get myself pregnant so I could marry a man I don't even love." What started as a sarcastic retort ended with an admission that hung in the air between them with nowhere safe to land.

Derek scrubbed his face with a hand. He wanted to tell her marriage was hard enough without starting out the gate with a lame horse, but what would be the point? She didn't need him to remind her of what she faced. Saying it would only hurt her more, and he'd rather cut off a limb.

"I messed up, Derek." The whispered words floated through the dark and settled on his heart. "I'm not saying it's your fault, it's just..."

"What?" He wanted to pull her into his arms and assure her everything would be okay, but he didn't have the right.

"It felt good that someone put me first for a change."

He blew out a breath. "You been struggling with the loss of your parents for so long, Charlie, it's made you a little hard around the edges. Your mama and daddy might be gone, but you've always had a Daddy that loves you like no one else in this world can."

She blew out an exaggerated sigh. "Are you talking about God again?"

He nodded. "You know I am. All you got to do is open your heart and eyes and let Him in."

She shrugged. "You make it sound so simple, Derek. Except I don't feel it. I've prayed and prayed, but all that comes back is a whole lot of quiet. How do you know He loves you?"

Derek pondered the question for a spell. It was too important to respond with a glib answer, but he didn't rightly know how to explain what he just knew. "We all got to figure it out for ourselves. I think when we grow up with it, it sometimes makes it harder to see Him working."

"What d'you mean?"

Derek shifted so he was leaning back on the palms of his hands and stretched out his legs. "There's this guy in my unit who grew up pretty rough. His daddy abandoned the family when he was young, and his mama worked a couple jobs just to keep them fed. Scotty started getting into trouble in high school and joined up 'cause his only other choice was jail." He chuckled. "He and I didn't hit it off so well at first. He thought I was a Jesus freak—"

"Because you are." Charlie smirked.

Derek nodded a concession. "Fair point. Anyway, we had lots of come-to-Jesus' meetings, and when he made the decision to surrender his life, things noticeably shifted for him. He'd been stuck in the mire, so to speak, so every step out felt miraculous to him."

"You're telling me if I'd started off slopping with the pigs, I'd be more aware of God's grace in my life?"

"Something like that."

"Well then it appears I'm heading in the right direction." She pushed off the ground with a sigh and slapped at the back end of her jeans. "It's not like I wasn't taught right from wrong. It's not like I didn't know God was looking down on me with disappointment in His eyes, just like you're doing now—"

"I'm not disappointed in you, Charlie, and neither is God."

"No?"

"No. Disappointed *for* you, maybe. But He takes even our missteps and uses them." He rose and stood next to her. "What d'you want to do?"

"It doesn't matter what I want to do, Derek. I made my bed, as Nana would say."

He touched her arm. "You don't have to marry Nicky. We're not living in the Dark Ages."

"I already thought it through, and this is what I've decided. I can't give my baby away, and I don't want to raise it alone."

"I can help." Derek took to the idea the moment it was out of his mouth. "Whatever you need, Charlie."

She shook her head. "This is between Nicky and me, Derek. I appreciate you offering to help, truly I do. But I don't want to shame or burden anyone else because of my mistake. Besides, we'll be okay." She reached up and planted a kiss on his cheek before disappearing into the darkness.

Derek stayed put and watched the house until he saw the light go out in Charlie's room. An ache touched his heart, the likes of which he'd never known before, but there was nothing to be done about it. He'd not made a move without enlisting the Lord's favor until he'd offered to help Charlie raise her baby. So, it was no surprise that she'd rejected the offer. He had to trust that there was a plan beyond what he could imagine, and trust in it.

CHAPTER SIXTEEN

Charlie

With temperatures predicted to get into the nineties, and humidity hovering around the same, it took all my wheedling and calling in of favors to get Jenna on board with my mission. Some might not see clearing out the junk from Darlene's house as such, but I didn't know what else to call it.

Even after she'd agreed, Jenna grumbled the entire drive to Darlene's house. "It's not like I ain't spent enough time as it is cleaning up after my own brood of slobs, now I'm cleaning some woman's I don't rightly know."

"There's a special place in heaven for you, Jenna." The words might have sounded more sincere if a grin hadn't slipped out with them.

"Whatever." She peered through the windshield as I parked the truck on Darlene's rutted drive. "Don'tcha think you have enough on your plate without addin' to it? You only got but three of the rooms put to rights and still ain't figured out how to get repairs done."

The reminder melted the grin clear off my face. "When in distress, I adopt Scarlett O'Hara's M.O."

She turned a wrinkled nose my way. "Huh?"

"I'll think about it tomorrow," I said, feigning a swoon with the back of a hand to my forehead.

She made a rude noise in her throat. "We'll see how far that gets you." She touched the cross that still hung from the rearview mirror. "This the one you found in your nana's desk drawer?"

"Yeah." I opened my door and hopped out of the truck before she could ask more questions I didn't have answers for.

"Hey, Charlie." Darlene stood on the front porch in cut-off shorts and t-shirt. "You sure a glutton for punishment. And you brought help."

With a wave of her hand, Jenna rounded the front end of the truck. "Hey. I'm Jenna."

Darlene came down the steps, one hand on the rickety railing to balance her precarious descent. "Darlene. Good to meetcha." She glanced my way. "How'd you talk Jenna into slave labor?"

"With four kids at home, she's used to it," I said. "Besides, Jenna's more than a friend. She's my only living relative, so she's duty-bound to go along with my crazy notions."

"Well, I sure do 'preciate it." Squinting against the sun, she motioned at the house. "Got started inside. Separated garbage from recyclables, like you said. Forgot to mention I got me a storage shed full to the brim with junk. Pro'bly haul the whole shebang to the dump."

Jenna's groan reflected the one I stifled. More stuff? Maybe I jumped in where I should've tip-toed. "Why don't you show us. At least then, we can get a full picture of what needs to get done."

Jenna gave me an eye roll as we followed Darlene around to the back of the weed and gravel lot. Sure enough, there was a storage shed that looked as if it was held together by duct tape and popsicle sticks. The padlock that connected the swinging doors was so rusty, pieces of it had begun to peel.

As Darlene pulled a key from her front pocket, I choked and swallowed back a bark of laughter. Like her insisting on using coasters to protect furniture in deplorable condition, the idea that the padlock could keep intruders out was ludicrous. And if all of it was junk anyway, why bother with a lock? Once it was removed, she eased open the doors as if expecting the hinges to disintegrate.

"Would you lookit that?" Jenna planted hands on her hips and whistled.

The shed was so packed it appeared as if each piece was fit together as tightly as a jigsaw puzzle. At first glance, it was just a mishmash of junk, but as I allowed my eyes to focus, treasures began to reveal themselves. Old doors and windows, pieces of furniture in need of refurbishing, farm tools, and cabinets.

"Don't know why I kept it. Too plumb lazy to clean it out, I s'pose." Darlene sighed. "Garbage."

"But it's not." I hesitated to remove even one item for fear the entire collection would fall like a house of cards. "At least from what I can see here, you've got some valuable pieces." Some could be antiques, or at the very least, vintage. A few repairs, a little sandpaper, and paint.

"This is just what y'all need for your new shop, Charlie," Jenna said. She eased out what appeared to be a century's-old farming implement from the pile.

"Huh." Darlene grunted. "Didn't know you was openin' a shop, Charlie."

"Working on it," I said.

"Had some strangers snoopin' around here a way's back. Said they was from some T.V. show or other about pickers. Wanted to take a gander."

Jenna's mouth dropped open. "You mean *American Pickers*?"

Darlene slowly nodded. "That might could be the one. Told 'em to get lost a'fore I called the law."

"Are you kiddin' me?" Jenna said.

"Didn't want no strangers pokin' around my stuff, even if it is garbage."

"A lot of this could be worth something, Darlene," I said. "We can't just take it all to the dump."

"Then you keep it." She turned to leave. "Don't have no need of it, but if'n you do, it's all yours."

We watched as she disappeared around the front of the house, then I turned to Jenna. "Can you believe this?"

"One man's trash." Jenna shook her head. "It's like your nana's basement on steroids."

"What d'you mean?" Nana's basement looked nothing like this monstrous mess.

"I don't know." She frowned. "Seems your nana kept just about ever'thing. She just didn't have as much as Darlene. Makes you wonder what treasures are hidden in all the secret hidey-holes of her house. Take that cross, for instance. Did you ever expect to find it tucked into a random drawer?"

"I never expected to find it, period. Unless my memory is skewed, which it could be, that cross was hanging from Daddy's Jeep when he and Mama were in the accident." The minute the words were out of my mouth, I wanted to shove them back in. Derek was probably right. It was best left alone.

If I knew my cousin, she'd push and prod until there was nothing left but to face it. And maybe that's just what I needed.

Jenna's eyes went wide. "Is that why you went all weird when you saw it?"

"Forget I said anything. I've got my memories crossed, is all." I folded my arms and turned back to the storage shed.

"Well, we'll table it for now. You got enough on your plate figurin' what to do with all this here collection."

But as we picked through Darlene's storehouse of treasures, my thoughts kept returning to the cross and the idea that Jenna was right. There just might be all manner of things hidden in the hidey-holes of Nana's house. If only I knew where to find them.

Derek

I hadn't seen Charlie since the day she ran out of gas. It didn't end well what with her getting all riled over me suggesting she let the past go. It wasn't her way to hold a grudge, but I'd given her some space anyway. Given myself some, too. Things were just too conflicted with Nicky pushing me to talk to her for him. I'd rather she stayed mad at me. Better I give some attention to my own future.

With that in mind, I bit the bullet and got a computer set up in Mama's guest house for Security Services before my next meeting with Mark. When he appeared at my door, it took near a full ten seconds to recognize him. All the shaggy blond hair was gone. Instead, his head was shaved down to near nothing, revealing a scalp that would've been better left covered some.

"What'd you do? Let Cassie near you with the clippers?"

He ran a hand over the stubble. Doubt he had so little of it since the day he was born. "Thought I should look the part."

A chuckle got loose, and I quickly turned it into a cough. "Is that what I look like?" I pointed to his head.

"Naw. Cassie forgot to put the guard on. She'll get it right next time." He stepped past me into the kitchen. "I figured if clients think we're both ex-military, it'll make 'em feel more confident about hiring us."

I nodded. "I can see you're committed to this venture. At least until your hair grows out."

"In for a penny, if you know what I mean." His eyes caught on the computer. "You download the software yet?"

"Yep. We can take a look at the website template the designer sent and see if we want to tweak it here and there."

"Sounds good." He moved to the doorway that led to the small sitting room situated between the kitchen and bedroom. "I don't rightly know why you don't just settle in here. Sure a lot nicer than my doublewide."

"At least your trailer isn't sitting on your mama's lot."

"What difference does it make, you ain't going to—"

"Yoo hoo." The call came as the kitchen door eased open and Mama stuck her head through the gap. "Thought I'd bring over some fresh baked cookies and milk." She stepped inside, a tray balanced on one arm—two full glasses of milk and a plate of her famous cookies.

Before I could respond, Mark stepped around the small kitchen table and met her at the door. "Let me help you with that, Miss Daniels." He took the tray from her and deposited it on the table.

"I'm not going to stay. I know you boys have work to do."

It was middle school all over again. Who in their right mind would want to relive that time in their life? "We appreciate it, Mama." With an arm around her shoulder, I herded her out the door. "Thanks."

When I turned back, Mark had half a cookie in his mouth.

"Now you understand why I can't live here?"

He swallowed and reached for a glass of milk. "Not really."

"So, you'd be okay living with your mama?"

"A course not. But she can't bake like yours." He wiggled his eyebrows and grinned. "Naw. I get it. You can't get a date with anyone as long as they know you're living here. A course, that might not be of interest to you with Charlie back."

"What's she got to do with anything?" I stepped around him and booted up the computer.

"Come on, Derek. You can't tell me you don't have it bad for her. I saw how you was looking at her the day we cleared her basement. And you were hoping for points when you asked me to fix her air conditioner. Now that she and Nicky's split, you got a chance."

"Only two problems with that."

He frowned. "What?"

"He's my brother, so that puts her off limits."

He scoffed. "That's ridiculous."

"Yeah? You'd think different if you had a brother."

He waved a dismissive hand. "What's the other?"

"Nicky wants me to convince her to give him another chance."

"You're kidding?"

I shook my head.

"Well don't that beat all." He grunted. "So, to your way of thinking, not only is Charlie off limits, because she had the bad judgment to marry him in the first place, he expects you to help patch things up between them."

"You got the gist of it."

He reached for another cookie. "You gonna do it?"

"Not sure." I blew out a breath. "Told him it wouldn't do any good unless he was willing to get a real job."

"Ouch. That must a gone over real good."

I yanked a chair from the table and sat. "Not so much. That brings me to something I've been aiming to talk to you about."

He dropped into a chair across from me. "What's that?"

"When we get this business up and running, we'll need to hire a couple people to help out."

His eyebrows shot up. "You're not thinking of hiring Nicky, are you?"

I didn't even have to ask how he felt about the idea. I raised my hands in surrender. "Just feeling things out here, Mark. Not asking for any favors."

"It's not that." He rested his elbows on the table. "I couldn't do this without you, so if you want to bring Nicky in, I'm all for it. But consider this. If someone asked you to give him a job reference, could you do it? I mean, how far does loyalty go?"

He had a point.

Scratching my chin, I said, "I don't know." It was the whole Cain and Abel story all over again. Mama expected me to keep watch over Nicky even though Nicky resented the idea—until he thought I could influence things in his favor.

CHAPTER SEVENTEEN

Charlie

Dark clouds hovered in the sky and thunder rumbled in the distance like the threat of doom. Tornado weather. When I was little, Pawpaw would tell me to not fret over them—God was just rearranging things in the sky. If one was to come our way, we'd hightail it into the basement where'd we be safe. I never did tell him the idea of being buried alive in the basement was more terrifying than the tornado itself.

But it wasn't the threat of a tornado, or what I'd do if one touched down, that had me standing on the front porch wringing my hands like an indecisive old woman. The truck sat in the gravel drive with another load weighing it down. Wind touched on the tarp that covered it, sending it flapping, giving me the occasional glimpse of the haul I'd taken from Darlene's. It seemed like such a good idea when Jenna suggested it. She'd reminded me I needed inventory. But now the house was so packed, I was back to filling up the basement.

After three loads to the dump and three more back home, I was worn slap out, as Nana would say. But the truck wouldn't unpack itself. Ever since the day I married Nicky, life had been a series of backward steps. Now here I stood with no money, no energy, and little direction. Maybe it was time I put my faith in something other than myself. Give the good Lord another chance. *If You're not done with me, Father, maybe You could send something good my way.*

Dog crawled out from under the porch swing—which hung like a drunk on a Saturday night—— and went on alert. Ears perked, eyes forward, and the hair on the back of his neck bristling.

I cut my gaze to the road as the sound of an engine reached my ears. "Good boy." I ruffled his head. "No one's going to bother me with you around." I'd gotten so used to his presence, I never even questioned it anymore. It might be time I found a title for him more endearing than Dog.

He plopped back down with a sigh, no longer on guard. He must've recognized Derek's truck when it turned into the drive. As he parked behind his daddy's vehicle, the skies opened up, the likes of which could rival Niagara Falls. A bolt of lightning lit up the dark sky only a second or two before the crack of thunder shook the house. That had been a close one.

"Get inside," Derek yelled as he zigzagged across the yard to avoid puddles as if they were land mines.

Dog and I made our escape, and once inside, I held the door open for Derek. Southern hospitality had been ingrained in me for twenty years, so what else could I do? The last time I saw him was when he rescued me. I'd been angry at him for dismissing my concerns over Mama and Daddy's death, but I'd also felt a jolt of attraction stronger than any I'd experienced before. I stood on the precipice of indecision, too common an occurrence to my liking.

Derek halted on the porch and toed off his sneakers. "You got a towel?" Water slid down his face and dripped onto his soaked t-shirt. It was plastered to his skin leaving little to the imagination.

I dragged my gaze from sleek, wet muscle. "Sure." Decision made, I left the door ajar and took the stairs two at a time, my legs burning and heart beating a hard staccato by the time I reached the top tread. Was I getting soft, despite all my activity, or was I reacting to Derek's unexpected presence? I snatched a towel from the open shelves in my bathroom and headed back down.

Derek stood on the threshold, a hand braced on each side of the door jamb, as he peered into the foyer where I'd housed the first load from Darlene's storage shed. "What in the Sam Hill have you been up to since I was here last?"

I tossed the towel at him a little harder than necessary, hoping to wipe the smirk off his handsome face. "It's called inventory."

"Ah. Mama said something about you opening up a junk shop." He scrubbed the towel over his head and face then took a quick swipe down each arm.

I knew better than to think Mama G would be so unkind as to name my upcoming business as such. Derek was wheedling his way under my skin, and I wasn't about to allow him the luxury. I straightened my shoulders and jutted out my chin a touch. "You come by to belittle my new career venture?" It might be generous of me to think of my latest escapade in such terms, but he didn't need to know it.

"No." He stepped inside and spread the towel over a piece of farm equipment I hadn't yet identified. Might be a vintage plow attachment, but it just as well could be a hunk of metal worth spit. "Came by to apologize."

Couldn't hardly turn him away if he was repentant. "Let's go into the kitchen. Can I get you some coffee or sweet tea?"

"Tea sounds good."

As I crossed the kitchen to retrieve a couple glasses from the cabinet, Derek sat at the table. "All joshing aside, are you really planning to open some kind of shop?"

"Hoping to." I pulled ice cube trays from the fridge, cracked the ice free, and filled the glasses. "I'll admit to being slightly overwhelmed."

"I know the feeling," he said.

I threw him a look over my shoulder. "Do I detect a little insecurity?"

He grimaced. "Didn't come by to talk about me, Charlie. Just wanted you to know I'm sorry as I can be that I upset you. It's not my place to tell you how to feel about losing your mama and daddy."

"I appreciate it." I filled the glasses with sweet tea and crossed to the table with them. "I know you didn't mean any harm, Derek. You never do."

He slid a finger along the condensation on the glass but didn't move to pick it up. He had something to say, I had no doubt, and my stomach clenched in response. Derek wasn't one to mince words, so why was he hesitating now?

"You want to share what's on your mind?" I kept a close watch on his face to gauge a reaction.

He shifted in the chair and leaned his elbows on the table. "Nicky came by the house for dinner the other night."

Such an innocent comment. So, why did unease blossom inside of me like a fast-growing cancer? I took a gulp of tea and waited for what was sure to come. An apology was just an excuse for the true reason Derek stopped by, which was a shade too close to manipulation. It had me on the defensive right from the get-go.

"He doesn't want to lose you, Charlie." His gaze flicked to mine then slid away like he was embarrassed. Well, he should be.

"That's between him and me." I thought he would be on my side, brother or not, and his taking up for Nicky felt like a betrayal.

"I agree. That's what I told him when he asked me to talk to you."

Heat filled my face. "Just like I thought. You didn't come to apologize." I pushed away from the table, sloshing our tea in the process. "You're here because Nicky doesn't have the backbone to talk to me himself."

Derek sighed. "You're right, but that doesn't change the sincerity of my apology. I'm also here 'cause Nicky asked me to play mediator. I'd do the same for you, Charlie."

I paced the small kitchen, letting anger fuel my steps. "Really? You'd do the same for me?"

"Course. I'm not taking sides." He leaned against the chair back and crossed his arms. "Nicky thought you'd be more of a mind to listen to me than him." He snorted. "If that were true, I suppose you wouldn't have married him in the first place." The edge in his tone proved there was a chink in his calm.

"If you're as neutral as you say, maybe you'd be willing to do me a favor."

His eyebrows drew together, and he went still like he was preparing for a strike. "What's that?"

"Be my process server. I got the divorce papers signed and ready to go. They just need to be delivered to Nicky. Two birds, one stone. Get an answer to Nicky's question and help me out at the same time."

I'd not been around Derek enough to read his mind, but if his face was any indication, he looked fit to be tied.

Derek

The rain had let up some by the time I parked my truck behind Mama's guest house. The sun was starting to peek back out between thunderclouds which hitched up the heat and humidity to suffocating proportions. I snatched the manilla envelope, jumped out of the truck, and paid the price for a hard landing when pain shot through my low back. It barely registered, though, because I was spitting mad. At Nicky. At Charlie. At myself. Near everyone was fair game.

Should have known better to show up at Charlie's with ulterior motives. It was true I owed her an apology, but I shouldn't have used it as a reason for the visit. Started out with a mind to manage her some and got the tables turned on me so fast, I didn't see it coming.

I entered the guest house, dropped the envelope on the kitchen table, and turned right around and left again. If there was one perk to living close by to Mama, it was that she always had a listening ear. The pebble pathway from the guesthouse to the main house glistened from the rain, and the smell of clean, wet earth was more soothing than anything manmade.

Crossing the back patio, I took note of the bright pink azalea blooms that lay scattered in the flowerbeds after the downpour. No doubt, Mama would have them cleared away by nightfall, and the plants would look no worse for wear.

Stepping into the kitchen, I caught a whiff of fried bacon and noticed a cutting board filled with sliced tomatoes. Could only mean one thing.

"Mama?" I snatched a piece of tomato, popped it into my mouth, and moved into the family room. Might be she was upstairs, or maybe out front gardening. "Mama, you here?"

"I'll be down in two shakes, Derek," she called from upstairs.

Too restless to sit, I stepped out onto the front porch and let the screen slap shut behind me. The sound of it brought back memories of Mama hollering at us to close it gently. It was a daily summer ritual that never seemed to change, along with admonitions to wipe our feet and pick up our laundry.

I ruminated on those memories some as I stared out across the yard. Daddy on his mower while Mama tended her garden. They always worked in tandem, even if their chores didn't intersect. If there was ever two people who belonged together, it was them. I envied them that connection even if it was cut short. Seemed like it was forever ago since Daddy had died.

The creak of the screen door preceded Mama's voice. "Everything okay, Derek? It's not like you to stomp and holler through the house like you was still a teenager."

"A little riled, is all. Nothing serious. You fixin' to make tomato bacon pie for supper tonight?"

She eased into a wicker chair with a smile. "Along with fried chicken and banana pudding for dessert."

"It's a wonder you aren't three hundred pounds, the way you cook."

"The secret is to not eat it all." She chuckled. "Why don't you sit a spell and tell me what's got your feathers ruffled."

Maybe this wasn't my best idea. The only thing worse than a thirty-seven-year-old living with his mama was one who went crying to her with his problems. But aside from Nicky, she was the only one who knew Charlie better than I did. Maybe a little perspective would be helpful.

"Just got into it with Charlie, is all." I wasn't about to tell her that Charlie was wanting me to serve Nicky divorce papers. Mama might not even know she was moving in that direction. It wasn't my place to tell.

"That's too bad. What'd you do to upset her?"

I leaned against the porch post and crossed my arms. "What makes you think it's my doing that we had a row?"

She settled against the chair back with a sigh. "Isn't it?"

"Not completely. I went over to apologize for something I'd said last week, and the conversation got away from me."

"Oh? Care to share what you said that needed an apology?"

I shrugged. "She'd gotten it into her head her parents didn't die in some car accident like she'd been told. She got so worked up over it, I innocently suggested she might think about letting it go. Chances are, she's mistaken about the cross."

The color drained from Mama's face, and her gaze slid away from mine. "What's this you say about a cross?"

It didn't take my psychological training in Special Forces to detect Mama's sudden distress over the subject. Anyone with half a brain would have noticed. "She didn't tell you about the cross?"

Eyes still averted, she shook her head. She knew something, all right.

"Seems she found it tucked inside her nana's desk drawer. Claims it was the same one that hung in her daddy's Jeep when they were in the accident."

"Could be she was mistaken, like you said. Or maybe there was a pair of them." She folded and unfolded her hands as if not sure what to do with them.

"What's going on, Mama?" I stepped across the porch and sat in the chair next to hers. Leaning in, I tried to make eye contact, but she was having none of it. "What do you know about it?"

She shook her head. "You were right to tell Charlie to let it go. No call to raise a ruckus over it."

An anvil landed on my chest. "Charlie's right? Her parents didn't die in a car accident like she'd been told?"

She waved her hands at me as if she could erase my presence. "Let it go, Derek. It'd be best if you can convince Charlie to do the same. Don't ask me to break a confidence."

"Even for Charlie?" I knew Mama loved her as if she were her own.

"Especially for Charlie." She rose from the chair and scuttled into the house.

I slumped back in the chair, my mind racing. If Charlie felt betrayed because I mediated between her and Nicky, what would this do to her? How could I know she was right to question the details of her parents' death and keep it to myself? Then again, how could I flat out ignore Mama's request to let it go?

It was choice to die by fire or drowning. Either one left me dead.

CHAPTER EIGHTEEN

Charlie

Decorating the interior of a house that desperately needed shoring up on the exterior was like plastering a smile on a broken heart and calling it good. It made no sense, but it was better to do something than sit around and lament over things I couldn't change. Instead, I had to focus on what I could. Rather than jumping willy nilly from one project to the next, I laid out a tentative schedule. My bank account was dwindling away, and I had visions of crawling back to Patrice on my knees. Better humble than dead.

Jenna showed up in a pair of ratty cutoffs and a t-shirt, hair pulled back and clipped. She handed me the portfolio she'd borrowed while petting Dog's head. "So, what's the plan today?" If only her energy was contagious.

Hugging it to my chest, I led her into the kitchen where I'd set up my laptop. "I spent most of the night working out a schedule." I opened the Word doc and stepped out of her way.

Fatigue seemed to be my ever-present companion lately—a byproduct of stress and panic over my precarious future.

She bent down, her eyes tracking line after line of detail. "Goodness, Charlie, is this here a ten-year plan?"

"Only if I want to starve to death. I know it appears to be a lot, but—"

"You ain't kidding." She stood straight. "But that's okay. It'll be like eatin' an elephant."

I tapped the portfolio. "You didn't tell me what you thought. Get any ideas for your house?"

Her mouth twisted "Nothin' that I could afford, even if your part is free. There's some expensive-looking stuff in those jobs you did. Cal'd have my head if I even gave a notion to buyin' furniture that cost near what he makes in a month."

"I told you when you asked to look at it, it wouldn't be for you." I folded my arms. "It's not my style, either." At least not anymore.

"Lots of pretty stuff, but this is more to my liking." Jenna waved a hand to encompass the kitchen. "I don't rightly know many people who could afford all that highfalutin' stuff, anyway."

"That's the whole point of mixing my decorating skills with vintage-like furniture. It's more economical and unique."

"So, we surely got our work cut out for us."

"I don't know what I'd do without you." I had to admit it was only by God's grace Jenna was so generous with her time.

"Let's not find out." She clapped her hands together. "Now, what do we got cookin' for today?"

"We need to start in the foyer. Should have done that before anything else. If I can get a handful of the downstairs rooms set up for business, then I can add the others as time and money permits." I pushed my concerns about the outdoor repairs aside. Scarlett O'Hara had nothing on me when it came to procrastinating.

"Alrighty then. What's first?"

"You want to haul the smaller items down to the basement while I clean out the closet under the stairs? Once I get that cleared, I'll help you move the bigger stuff down."

"You got it. I have to be home in time to make supper, but until then, I'm all yours."

It had been years since I explored the many hidden recesses of the house. When I opened the stair closet, Jenna's comments about Nana tucking things away in the hidey-holes flitted through my mind. I'd seen a movie about a real mansion in California called the Winchester Mystery House. A crazy woman built room after room in this old mansion for ghosts or some such nonsense.

I knew Nana and Pawpaw weren't nuts, and the nooks and crannies of the house were no more unusual than any other old house, but the thought of exploring the depths of it gave me chills just the same. Just like when I first went down into the basement. And it was only reinforced when I found the cross.

When I'd moved back to Nana's, I'd only given the closet under the stairs a cursory glance. The boys I'd hired to haul everything to the basement missed it, which made me wonder how many other spaces went unnoticed. A true purging would require me to get over my skittish sensibilities.

There was a mishmash of boxes tucked under the treads, the masking tape that once held them closed were now curled and useless. A layer of dust covered everything, which had me sneezing when I removed an old shoe box that sat atop the pile. One after another, I moved them from the closet to the foyer floor, climbing over a slumbering Dog in the process.

Jenna appeared, hands planted on her hips. "I swear, Charlie, once we get a clear spot in this house, you go and fill it with more stuff. Do you realize there's almost no room left in the basement?"

I pushed a wayward strand of hair off my sweaty face with the back of a hand. "You got a lot of nerve, cousin. You were the one who talked me into taking all Darlene's stuff."

"Didn't seem like all that much piled in the shed like it was."

"Don't I know it. Guess she was gifted at packing things away." I gazed into the nearly empty closet. "There's a couple metal boxes in back left to pull out, then I'll help you."

"You ain't gonna look through these first?" She flicked a hand at the sorrowful collection spread across the foyer and looked at me like I'd just turned down a ten-day spa vacation. "Aren't you curious?"

An old saying about curiosity and a dead cat came to mind. "It's probably just junk."

"Then let's get a dump pile started. Isn't that what you told Darlene to do at her place?"

I sighed. "I don't know, Jenna. We start going through old photos and such, we won't get anything else done."

"We'll be quick about it. I'm gonna grab some garbage bags, and you pull the rest of the stuff out from beneath the stairs."

Once we'd emptied the first few boxes, I was feeling pretty good about myself. There were some pictures, as I'd predicted, and those we set aside for another time. One shoe box was full of Daddy's old schoolwork, which brought a lump of sentimentality to my throat. It also contained Daddy's well-worn Bible, with notes written in the margins in his handwriting. The last cardboard box was full of bank records for accounts that'd been closed years before. Within an hour, all that was left were the two metal boxes.

"I think it's locked," Jenna said, wrestling with the lid of one as whatever it contained rattled against the sides.

"What's that written on the top?"

Jenna squinted at the faded label stuck in one corner. "Can't rightly say for sure, but it looks like 'safety deposit'." She slid it over to me. "Might be some important papers."

"Doubtful." Aside from the memorabilia of Daddy's childhood, I'd been a little disappointed in our find so far. I had visions of discovering long-forgotten treasure. "Probably a deed to the house, maybe Nana and Pawpaw's social security cards."

"Could be some old bonds." Jenna's eyes went wide, and she looked just like her five-year-old. "They could be worth a fortune now."

"You're such a dreamer." I shook my head. I wasn't about to admit I'd been hoping for some such thing myself. "I'll go get a knife and see if we can pick the lock." I pushed off the floor and felt the blood drain from my face. Lightheaded, I grabbed for a stair spindle to keep from keeling over.

"You okay?" Jenna's voice seemed as if it came from another room. "Charlie?"

"I'm fine." I took a deep breath as the world righted itself once again. "Just a little dizzy."

"I'll get you some water. When was the last time you ate anything?"

"Don't fret, Jenna. Maybe bring me a banana along with that water, okay?"

"Sure. And the knife to pick the lock."

As Jenna disappeared, I slid back onto the floor. My stomach rumbled, and I realized it had been some time since I'd had a proper meal.

"Here we are." Jenna handed me a glass of water, dropped a banana in my lap, and plopped back onto the floor. "I'll bust this lock open and see what's what. Then, before we do anything more, I'll fix us something to eat."

She went to work on the lock while I replenished myself with a little food and water.

"Got it," she said, dropping the paring knife onto the floor. "Why don't you do the honors?" She slid the box to me.

I flicked the catch and lifted the lid. Inside, I found the expected deed for the house, Nana and Pawpaw's marriage license, a copy of Pawpaw's death certificate, and a couple golden rings.

"See, just like I expected."

"What was rattling around in there."

I hooked a finger into the rings and held them up. "Nana and Pawpaw's wedding bands, I suppose."

She tilted her head. "Your pawpaw's maybe, but how would your nana's get in there?"

How could I have not made the connection on my own? Nana's wedding band sat in my own jewelry box where I put it the day she passed. I looked at the rings nestled in the palm of my hand. Where had they come from? They were familiar, one larger than the other. I took the smaller one and tilted it so I could see if there was an inscription inside. Initials and a date. SV—6-11-88. It couldn't be.

"You okay, Charlie? You look like you've seen a ghost."

My heart thumped clear to my throat as I held the larger ring up. CV—6-11-88. "It's not possible," I whispered.

"What?" Jenna grabbed my knee and shook. "What's not possible?"

"These are Mama and Daddy's wedding bands." I could've almost been convinced the cross meant nothing—that the one in Daddy's Jeep was different. But if nothing was salvageable from their car accident, how did these get here? Who would've gone through the rubble of the fire in order to retrieve two worthless rings?

Derek

Rock and a hard place. It wasn't the first time I'd found myself in such a spot, but it was the first it was so personal-like. I'd learned a lesson or two about loyalty during my time in the service. But what's a body to do when those loyalties conflict? I was being tugged this way and that without a care about how I felt about it. Made me feel like I should've been hightailing it for safer ground—like Beirut.

My stomach turned sour as I approached Nicky sitting at the corner table in the Stillery nursing a beer. It was a struggle to figure which was best—meet in public or private? I opted for private so whatever response he had to me serving him divorce papers would remain behind closed doors. Nicky had other ideas. Even offered to pay for my lunch as a thank you for going to bat for him with Charlie. Wouldn't be so appreciative once he heard her response.

I slid into the booth across from Nicky and slapped the manilla envelope onto the table. Best to get it over with. The longer I talked around it, the harder it'd be. "Hey, Nick."

Nicky had never been the sharpest knife in the drawer, but there must've been something in my expression that clued him in, because the welcoming smile slid from his mouth. "Derek." He flicked his hand toward the envelope. "What's that?"

"I went to see Charlie, just like you asked." I blew out a breath. "Just so you know, I'm done being the mediator here. Tired of being used for the go-between when the two of you are competent adults with the ability to communicate on your own."

A line formed between his brows as he threw me a scowl. "Don't think asking my big brother for a little help was out of line."

Of course, he wouldn't. "Sorry to say, bro, things didn't go like you'd hoped. Charlie turned the tables on you." Except I wasn't really all that sorry. Should be, but I wasn't.

"What d'you mean? What's in the envelope?"

A waitress appeared. "What can I get y'all to drink?"

I ordered a sweet tea, and as she left, I slid the envelope to Nicky. "You've been served."

He narrowed his eyes and frowned. "You're joking, right?"

"Do I look like I'm playing here?"

He picked up the envelope like it was a bomb about to detonate and pulled the stack of papers from it. "So, she's not going to even give me a chance?" His mouth dropped, and he shook his head. "I thought for sure..." As he shuffled through the pages, his shoulders slumped.

It didn't matter that he had it coming, compassion had me leaning forward anyway. "You can't send someone else to do what you ought to do for yourself, Nicky. You want another chance and expecting me to get it for you is foolhardy."

His eyes glued to the page in front of him, he shook his head. "It's too late. She already had the papers drawn up. Signed them, too."

"It takes two signatures to make it real." A war raged within me. Nicky and Charlie were married, whether I liked it or not. She didn't pay me any mind when I advised her against getting involved with him. She made her choice, and God didn't cotton to divorce. If Nicky was willing to fight for her, the least I could do was give him a foot up. "Listen, Nicky."

He lifted glassy eyes to me.

"The only way to get Charlie to change her mind is to change your ways. Mark and me are starting up a security business, and we'll need to hire a few people to work it with us."

"Security?" His mouth twisted. "What d'you know about security?"

"More than you can imagine." Never in all the years I'd been in the service did Nicky ask what I did. It was like nothing existed outside his own little world.

"What're we talking here? Event security?"

"No." I erase his words with a wave of my hands. "That's not using my skill set. There're enough firms doing that kind of work in the area already."

Nicky's eyebrows went up. "You're skill set? What's that exactly?"

"Cyber security and demonstrating holes in building security protocols for starters."

He frowned. "You're talking a language I don't even understand. Don't see how I'd be any good at it."

"Just takes a little training. Have to start from the ground up, of course."

"I don't know," he said. "What's it pay?"

I barked out a humorless laugh. He had a lot of nerve. "I'd bet odds it's more than you make working the bar scenes at night. Besides, what difference does it make if you can make a go of it with Charlie?"

He shoved the papers back into the envelope. "Why're you doing this for me?"

"I'm your brother, as you seem to constantly point out."

He snorted. "We both know you got feelings for her."

I opened my mouth to deny it, but snapped it closed again. It was true. Had been for as long as I could remember. But there were lines that couldn't be crossed, and me with Charlie would've been one of them. "It doesn't matter how I feel, Nicky. She chose you. Maybe if you'd offer to go to marriage counseling or something."

"Here you go." The waitress plopped a glass of tea in front of me. "Y'all know what you want to order?"

I tilted my head to look at her. "Give us a few minutes, will you?"

"Sure thing."

I moved my tea aside and leaned my elbows on the table. "You need to talk to her yourself, Nicky. If you want a chance, you need to fight for her. If, and only if, you're willing to put her first in your life. Because if you think you're going to hand her a line of bull, she'll see right through it."

He peered at me with a furrowed brow. "I don't get you, Derek. You and me is as different as night and day, but it still don't make any sense. Why wouldn't you just move in while you have the chance?"

I opened a menu that'd been left on the edge of the table. "It's like you said, we're different."

CHAPTER NINETEEN

Charlie

The cluttered kitchen table was the perfect metaphor for my discombobulated state of mind. I wasn't sure how long I'd sat cross-legged on the chair at the edge of the mess, but I came out of my hazy thoughts to a late evening light, which had given way to an encore performance of fireflies. They flitted across the lawn and danced among the dense tree line along the backside of Nana's yard like magical Christmas lights come to life. The sweet smell of honeysuckle and magnolia wafted through the open back door and window, but it didn't have the power to lift me from the quicksand that seemed to pull me deeper and deeper into despair.

My laptop screen glowed, the interior design program I'd booted up ignored. A mangled Pop-tart sat incongruously on one of Nana's blue willow plates. I'd been slipping bites of it to Dog, whose chin rested on my thigh. Alongside the sugar-and-carb-loaded snack, all my carefully formulated plans for the new shop were spread out. They'd received as much attention as the computer.

I'd even laid out Daddy's Bible, hoping for some Spirit-led inspiration. It had been too many years since I'd turned to the Word of God expecting to be fed, and after flipping through a few random pages, I abandoned the book, much like God had abandoned me.

It was the three pieces of jewelry lined up on the table that drew my focus. The cross and Mama and Daddy's wedding bands. How could such small items wreak colossal havoc in my mind? They defied everything I'd been told since childhood.

"What should I do about this, Dog?" I whispered. Although a sudden cicada recital drowned out my voice, Dog raised his head and perked up his ears as if preparing to give me a prophetic word.

A growl started low in his throat as he moved into guard mode. I couldn't hear anything beyond the night songs, but Dog hadn't been wrong yet. He dashed out the kitchen and into the foyer, his growl giving way to a ferocious bark.

I unfolded my legs and followed. Rather than turning on the lights, I peered through the leaded-glass sidelight expecting to see Derek in the shadows. Although he'd made himself scarce as hens' teeth lately, I couldn't imagine who else would stop by unannounced. When I recognized the vehicle coming down the gravel drive, my heart dropped clear to my cherry red-painted toes.

"Great." I looked down at Dog who stood by me like a high-priced bodyguard, barking his head off. For a split second, I considered letting him loose on the intruder then hiding away in my bedroom. That would be the easiest solution. But before the idea took root, I could hear Nana admonishing me. *Southern ladies are kind and hospitable, even when entertaining the devil himself.* Nicky ran a close second to Satan these days.

"That's enough, Dog." Even though my reprimand was half-hearted, the canine immediately quieted and sat at my side. Too bad men weren't so easily controlled.

When Nicky reached the bottom of the treads, I flicked on the porch light and pulled the door open to let Dog out, who rushed down the steps and commenced the sniff-test.

Nicky stepped back, eyes wide. "Didn't know you had a guard dog, Charlie."

I leaned against the door jamb and crossed my arms. "A woman living alone can't be too careful. You never know what manner of vermin will come crawling around."

He screwed up his mouth but didn't twitch a muscle otherwise until Dog stepped away.

"What're you doing here, Nicky?" As if I didn't know. I'd wondered how long it would take after Derek served the divorce papers for him to come crawling back. There was no way he'd let his cash cow go without a fight.

"We need to talk."

Round two. "You should've called first."

He shook his head and slowly moved up the steps, his attention divided between Dog and me. He was probably worried Dog might take a hunk out of him yet. "Like that's worked so well for me in the past."

Touché. "This isn't a good time."

"It never is." He'd reached the porch and stopped in front of me. "I gave up a gig to come out here tonight, Charlie."

I licked a finger and drew a mark in the air. "One for you, three thousand and ten for me."

He scowled. "What's that supposed to mean?"

"Just thought you were keeping score is all." I was too tired to fight, so I stepped aside for Nicky to enter.

He gave the foyer a cursory glance and waited for me to take the lead.

"This way," I said, moving toward the parlor. The kitchen was more Nicky's style, but my life was laid out on the table like a living sacrifice. Too vulnerable. Too lost. Too real.

"You got anything to drink?"

I glanced at him over my shoulder. "You won't be here long enough."

"You ain't gonna make this easy, are you?"

We entered the parlor, and I indicated he should sit with a flick of a hand.

His eyebrows shot up as he took in the room, but he only said, "I saw Derek today."

"I figured as much." I perched on the edge of a wingback chair I'd positioned in the corner. It was the perfect place to cozy up with a good book if only I could find the time. Dog sidled up next to me and leaned against my legs. "I've made up my mind, Nicky. If you drove all the way out here to try and talk me out of it, then—"

"Here me out, will you?" The tone of his voice drew a growl from Dog, who stood at attention. Nicky licked his lips and put his hands up like a traffic cop, as if commanding Dog to back off. "Didn't mean to raise my voice."

I rested a hand on Dog's head, and he relaxed against me again. "I don't need to hear you out, Nicky. I know what you want, and it's not going to happen. What's changed between now and two months ago? Did you suddenly find Jesus or something?"

"No. Have you?" The well-aimed accusation hit its mark. "I don't see you strutting off to church on Sundays or spending time reading the Bible. I know I messed up, Charlie, but so have you."

I rubbed my temple with a sigh. "You come all this way to point out my sins, Nicky? You don't think you have enough of your own to attend to?"

He shook his head. "I got plenty. I ain't saying different." He pinned me with a steady gaze. "But I've been fighting Derek's ghost since you and me got together. You wanna know why I stray like I do?"

Heat suffused my face and my heart raced. I wanted to cover my ears, close my eyes, and chant like a lunatic to drown out his words.

"'Cause I've never been good enough for you, Charlie." There was a sheen in his eyes, and if I didn't know better, I'd think they were tears. But Nicky didn't cry. Not ever.

"I don't want to talk about this." I jumped up from the chair, my head spinning.

"You know it's true." He stepped in front of me to thwart my escape. "You went out with me to get back at Derek for choosing the military over you."

We'd had some form of this conversation more times than I could count. "I married you," I said through gritted teeth.

"Only 'cause you got pregnant." There was no mistaking the tears now. "Ten years, Charlie, I been playing second fiddle to Derek. How was I supposed to compete with that?"

A trickle of tears dampened my cheek, and I batted them away while dropping back into the chair. Nicky was right. I'd always denied it before, but I couldn't do so now. Dog brushed against me, and I took comfort in his presence. "Then you should be thrilled that I filed for divorce. Now you'll be free of me."

Nicky resumed his seat, arms resting on his knees. "That's just it, Charlie. I don't want to be free of you. This whole thing has made me realize I love you, and I'm willing to fight for you."

I choked out a humorless laugh. "Don't you think it's too little, too late?"

He shook his head. "It's never too late. Whatever it takes.

I'll even quit playing gigs and get a day job." He scooted to the edge of his chair as if too excited to sit still. "Derek offered me a job."

"A job? Doing what? Working your daddy's land?" I couldn't picture him on a tractor much less mucking around in the soil.

"No, a course not. In his new security business. I gotta start at the ground floor, but I know I can make a go of it, Charlie. If you could just see your way to giving me another chance. Heck, I'll even give marriage counseling a go."

I rubbed my face too weary to think straight. Security business? Since when? As lost as I'd been in the last month or so, the only thing I knew for sure was that Derek had been right all along—marrying Nicky had been a grave mistake. Why, when I was ready to break away, did he seem to have a change of heart?

Derek

An early evening thunderstorm left the air smelling sweet and moist. I had every window of the guest house opened, as well as the kitchen door. Crickets and cicadas were putting on a show—backdrop to the fireflies that, to my way of thinking, never shifted from miraculous to mundane. Years situated in desert climes made me grateful for living in the south.

My low back was growing stiff after hours in a hard chair staring at my computer. I'd finally gotten around to following Mark's suggestion that I give the Billy Graham Rapid Response Team a look. I'd been home only a month and was itching to do something productive.

A shuffle beyond the screen door drew my attention, but

even with the full moon out now, it was too dark to see anything past the shadows created by the kitchen light. Could be a raccoon or skunk. A ground hog or armadillo wasn't entirely out of the realm of possibility either. But the last thing I expected to materialize was a grown woman with a hairy sidekick.

"Charlie? That you?" My gaze flickered to the wall clock to confirm it was late.

She pulled the screen open and looked at me with fire in her eyes. "I don't get you, Derek." She and Dog stepped through the door and let it slap shut behind them. "They say women are hard to figure out, but you take the cake. You know that?" Fatigue was evident beyond her scowl, with dark circles bruising the delicate skin under her eyes.

I stood as Dog crossed the room to greet me. At least *he* had manners. "You'll have to give me a hint." Seemed there were a few mysteries floating around, and I didn't know which one she was referring to. Did she somehow find out Mama was keeping something from her, and that I had been sworn to secrecy?

She leaned her backside against the counter and crossed her arms. "Whatever happened to staying neutral in this thing between Nicky and me? And since when did you start up a security business, anyway?"

I stifled a sigh. Life was much simpler when I juggled threats to national security. "Don't stand on ceremony, Charlie, come on in and make yourself comfortable."

She didn't seem to catch the sarcasm, because she pulled a chair from beneath the kitchen table and dropped into it. "How many times have we talked, and not a word about your own business?"

If I didn't know better, I'd say she was pouting. Did she

take it as a personal affront that I didn't consult her? "It's still in the planning stages."

Her eyes focused on something behind me. "I see you got yourself a new computer. Is that piddly little corner your office?"

"For the time being."

"It sure doesn't look like much."

Now she was just being ornery. "We're looking for rental space, but in the meanwhile, this'll have to do."

She scraped a thumbnail along a ridge in the table, eyes not meeting mine. "Did the planning stages have to include a job offer to Nicky?"

"He's my brother, Charlie. What was I supposed to do?"

Her head snapped up. "I suppose marriage counseling was your idea, too."

What got her knickers in a knot? "You set me up to serve the divorce papers. He asked for my advice." I threw my hands in the air. "What d'ya want from me, Charlie?"

"I want to not feel guilty for divorcing my cheating husband." Her voice rose on every word until she was yelling at me.

I yanked a chair out from under the table and sat across from her. "How am I causing you to feel guilty? Y'all stuck me smack in the middle of your marital mess. I got Nicky making charges on one end and you making them on the other."

She slumped against the chair and blew out a breath. "I know. I'm sorry. I guess I thought—" She snapped her mouth shut as if aware that she was about to reveal something better left unsaid.

"What?"

She shook her head. "I'm tired, is all. I don't want to fight, Derek. Not with you, not with Nicky. But whatever feelings I had for him are long gone. Have been for a while now. I thought you understood that. Instead, you're giving him false hope, and it makes it all the harder on both of us. There's nothing worse than false hope."

She was talking about something more than her marriage to Nicky. The only other false hope I could think she'd been holding onto was about her parents. "This about the cross?" I laid the words down with the care I'd give a time bomb, praying she'd deny it.

She glanced up at me. "It's more than the cross. I found Mama and Daddy's wedding bands, too. Just one more piece of evidence that I'd been lied to by Nana and Pawpaw."

I thought about how upset Mama got the other day. "Maybe they had good reason, Charlie."

She continued like I hadn't said a word. "I about had myself convinced that the cross was different from the one in Daddy's truck, or that maybe there were two of them. But the rings?" She pinned me with a hard stare. "They were engraved."

I reached a hand across the table, but Charlie pulled back.

"I'm starting to wonder if anything in my life has been true, Derek. You warned me about getting involved with Nicky from the beginning, and you were right. I regret not listening to you back then. You also told me I should let this thing with Mama and Daddy go. Could be you're right about that, too. Maybe, when I'm on the other side of this, I'll regret not taking your advice. But I can't shake the deep-down feeling that knowing the truth about it is better than the wondering."

It was bad enough being stuck in the middle of the drama between Charlie and Nicky, given the choice between love and duty. But being stuck between Mama's secrets and Charlie's needs? How could I protect and honor the two women I loved most in the world when they stood on opposing sides?

CHAPTER TWENTY

Charlie

I crouched in a crevice made by the roots of a lombi tree, Mose close by my side. Terror had us locking hands, mine stark white against the mahogany hue of her own. Gunfire cracked like thunder and shook the branches. I stifled a scream as we huddled close in an attempt to draw comfort in each other's arms. Another staccato of gunfire blasted closer still, followed by an odd strident ring that pulled me out of the clutches of certain death.

My heart raced, and I swallowed the terror that lingered in the aftermath of the nightmare. Or was it? I was in my own bedroom, bathed in the light of a full moon, not trembling in the folds of a tree root deep in the Congo rainforest. Dog stood alert at my head, and my phone trilled from the nightstand.

"What now, Lord?" I whispered. Plucking at the sweat-soaked t-shirt plastered to my body with one hand, I reached for the cell with the other. A phone call at three in the morning couldn't be good.

I didn't recognize the number, but just in case it wasn't a prank call, I drew in a deep breath, willed my heart to slow, and connected it. "Hello?"

"I'm so sorry." A woman's sobbing voice. Must be a prank, but a shiver ran up my spine in response. "I know it's late, but I ain't got no one else to call."

"Who is this?"

"Darlene." Her sniffle was cut short by the blast of a deep horn followed by the whoop of a siren. Emergency vehicles.

"What's wrong? What happened?"

"It's my house, Charlie. Burnt near to the ground."

It took a moment for her words to make sense as I was still crouched in the Congo fearing for my life. It meant something, that nightmare, but in that moment, the present was more pressing than the past. I flicked on the nightstand lamp and climbed out of bed. "Are you hurt?"

"No. Jest scared outta my wits. They offered to call Red Cross, but—"

"I'll be there as soon as I can, Darlene. Just hang on."

Dog circled my legs as if he was protecting my perimeter while I gathered up a pair of jeans and a dry t-shirt. "It's okay, Dog." I took a quick moment to rub his ears. "It's not me you need to worry about right now."

I locked Dog up so he wouldn't try to follow and stepped out into the clear, humid night where a lone mockingbird chattered from above. Its night song slowed my steps as it ministered to my soul. *Deep calls to deep in the roar of your waterfall; all your waves and breakers have swept over me.* Where the verse had come from or why the Lord put it on my heart, I couldn't have said. How long had it been since I'd heard my Father's voice? And why now?

I looked up at the star-studded sky. *I hear You, Lord. I've no idea what You're trying to say, but I'm ready to listen.*

It was a miracle I made it Darlene's unscathed, what with all the clamoring in my mind. In the past, my dreams dissipated only moments upon waking, but not this one. It'd felt too real, like a memory I could've blocked. And although the Lord and I might have been at odds of late, I had no doubt the scripture He brought to mind was perfectly orchestrated. I just didn't know what it meant yet.

A fire truck and two emergency vehicles dwarfed Darlene's property while firemen in full gear wandered about or doused smoldering timber and ash with a firehose. The storage building, which Jenna and I had emptied only a few days before, was nothing more than cinder.

I parked the truck near the street and scanned the property for Darlene. Blanket around her shoulders, she was slumped against a tree as if it was all that held her upright. Lights from the working vehicles left nothing hidden of her stark features beneath the spiky gray-blond hair. Did she have no friends or neighbors who'd come to her aid?

As I approached her, she must have heard or sensed me, because she turned and greeted me with a quivery smile. "Thanks for comin'." Her eyes shone with tears, and she brushed them away, leaving a smudge of soot on her cheek.

I put an arm around her shoulders, made bulkier with the blanket, and held tight. A memory of myself, fearful and huddled in Mose's arms, slithered across my mind. I pushed the dream, or memory, aside to focus on Darlene. "Do you know what caused the fire?"

With a shrug, she stared at the rubble that no longer resembled a home. "It was me, I'm 'shamed to admit."

"What d'you mean? Like a grease fire or something?"

With a slow shake of her head, she swiped at her eyes again. "Smokin' in bed and fell asleep. Ain't that a cliché?" The tenuous control she appeared to have crumpled into tears.

"Been livin' in that there house goin' on ten years like a hoarder and finally got 'er cleaned out only to burn 'er down."

I rubbed her back and fought my own tears. It was impossible, in that moment, to separate Darlene's plight from my own childhood trauma. "It'll be okay, Darlene. Your insurance should cover it fine, and you'll have a clean slate."

"'Fraid not." She sniffled. "Ain't got no insurance."

I closed my eyes as heat filled my cheeks. All the griping I'd done about losing everything when I had an abundance compared to Darlene. Including a basement filled to the brim with inventory from her shed.

"It's a good thing we got the stuff from your storage shed all safe and sound at my place then. Maybe you can get ahold of whoever it was had interest in it. Might be enough to get you a a leg up."

"No ma'am." She pulled out of my arms to look me full in the face. "I gave you that stuff for your new shop, and I ain't about to renege. I'd venture a guess that wouldn't set well with God."

Her response shocked me speechless for a moment. She, who was left devastated, feared God's retribution when He all but left her destitute? "You're not reneging, Darlene. I'm giving it back to you. You need it more than I do. Besides, I have enough to atone for without adding to it."

She snorted. "You ain't got nothing on me. I'll figure somethin' out, but I ain't gonna take that stuff back. 'Sides"—she waved her hands to encompass the devastated property— "I got nowhere to put it, anyway."

Although I had no intention of holding Darlene to her generous donation to my cause, it would do no good to argue with her when emotions were running high. We'd just have to take it one step at a time.

"You come on home with me. I have plenty of room."

"Jest till I can figure somethin' else out," Darlene said, sliding the blanket off her shoulders and gathering it against her chest. It was then I noticed she clutched a framed photo to her chest. Must be her daughter.

For a brief moment in time, twenty years before, I knew what it felt to be bereft. But this was Darlene's everyday reality. No friends or family, and now, not even a change of underwear. Maybe it was time I stopped lamenting over what I didn't have or couldn't change and took a lesson from Darlene. "I've got some of Nana's clothes packed away you can have. She was about your size." I guided Darlene to the truck.

"I'll tell you one thing."

"What's that?"

With a last look at the rubble, she sighed. "I ain't never gonna smoke again."

Derek

It was a sleepless night that followed Charlie's impromptu visit. Guilt has a way of keeping a body too fidgety to lay claim to rest. Charlie might not have known it, but she had every right to feel betrayed. Not because of Nicky, but because of the secret Mama asked me to keep. I'd have been able to brush off Mama's discomfort over Charlie's past if the only evidence to a coverup was the cross. Charlie's nana suffered dementia near the end and saw shadows where none existed, which made her an unreliable witness. But now that the wedding bands had surfaced, it put a whole new slant on things.

I couldn't rightly go back on my word to Mama, at least without her permission, but that didn't mean I couldn't support Charlie in finding the truth. What better way than to insert myself into the house where the evidence was stashed?

Mid-morning, I pulled into Charlie's gravel drive and parked behind Daddy's truck. The temperature was cool for early August, with another thunderstorm predicted for the afternoon. I climbed out of the vehicle and took a moment to observe the front of the house. A couple mockingbirds chattered from the tall cottonwood that stood guard over the front porch. It was a wonder what Charlie had done inside, but the outside was in pretty sad shape.

The white paint was peeling in places like the aftermath of a bad case of sunburn. The beams that held the overhang high above the porch looked to be in decent shape, but the metal roof itself sagged something fierce without proper support. A strong wind could rip the second-story balcony above the front door clear off, with the wood of the floor rotting like the teeth of a meth addict.

Didn't matter how much Charlie gussied up the interior rooms, the outside would take a might more than refurbished woodwork and repurposed furniture. That was my path back into her good graces.

I took a slow climb up the steps, testing the viability of each plank as I went. Crossing the large porch, I stopped at the haint-blue door and knocked. The leaded-glass sidelights were in better shape than the door. Updated more recently, would be my guess.

Dog's deep bark and snuffling noises came through the door a moment before it was flung open. Charlie stood veiled behind the screen in a tank top and ripped jeans, her blond hair in a messy knot on top of her head. When she pushed the screen open, I couldn't help but notice the bruising beneath her eyes appeared darker than the night before. Might could be she didn't sleep any better than I did.

"Hey Derek," she greeted in a hushed tone. A wrinkle formed between her eyebrows. "Was I expecting you?"

"I don't think so." Dog nudged my hand, and I rubbed his ear. "I have an idea I want to run by you."

She tilted her head. "If this has anything to do with Nicky, then you just march yourself right out of here." The words would have more power if she hadn't near whispered them.

I held up a hand. "Learned my lesson, believe me. Fight your own battles from here on out. I'm Switzerland."

Pushing the screen door wider, she stepped back to let me in. "Fine. Just keep it down. I have a houseguest."

"Wondered what all the whispering was about."

"Y'all don't have to be quiet on my account. I been up for a while now."

A stout middle-aged woman moved down the stairs on bare feet, hand gripping the railing, as if she was unsure of her steps. My guess was foot pain or balance issues. She wore a light blue robe over a t-shirt and shorts.

"This is Darlene," Charlie said, waving a hand toward the woman. "Darlene, meet Derek."

Darlene reached the bottom of the stairs and gave me the once-over, much like Dog did the first time we met. "So, you the ex or the young man that rescued her when she ran outta gas out my way?" Her voice was raspy but confident.

"I'm not the ex, so I suppose that makes me her rescuer." I held out my hand to shake hers. "And with all the stuff she hauled from your place, that'd make you her benefactor."

Darlene barked out a laugh and patted Charlie's arm with her free hand. "'Fraid it's the other way 'round. I'll just carry myself to the kitchen for coffee and leave y'all to visit."

Charlie hooked her arm in mine and tugged me across the foyer. "Let's go into the parlor, and you can share this idea of yours with me."

I shifted to see Darlene disappear into the kitchen with Dog close behind. "What's she doing here?" Not that it was any of my business, as I was sure Charlie would remind me.

"She's in a bind, and I offered to let her stay here until we can figure out a few things." Charlie crossed the parlor and dropped onto the loveseat.

Sweet trusting Charlie. Was she out of her mind? "Do you think that's wise?"

She arched a brow. "What happened to you being Switzerland?"

I sat on the coffee table in front of her, our knees inches apart, and spoke in low tones. "Can't be neutral when it comes to your safety. You've talked to the woman, what? Twice? Three times? What do you know about her, anyway?"

Charlie narrowed her eyes and her mouth flattened. "You have some nerve, Derek. Aren't you the one always going on about a mission? A purpose? It's okay for you to sacrifice years of your life to serve our country but let me offer one kind and generous woman help when she's fallen on hard times, and you go all neanderthal on me. What's your problem, anyway?"

"Forget it." The woman could start an argument in an empty house. "I didn't come here to get into it with you again. I came with an offer." Now more than ever I had a reason to hang around. Someone needed to look after her.

"So, offer." How was it her snippy attitude made her more attractive?

I slid off the coffee table and moved to a chair across the room where I could breathe without smelling her shampoo. "I thought we could do a trade."

She arched a brow, but for once, said nothing.

"I need office space, and you need exterior repairs."

Folding her arms, she squinted. "Keep talking."

CHAPTER TWENTY-ONE

Charlie

For the first time since I dreamt up the idea of the home decor and vintage shop, a glimmer of hope shone through my mountain of doubt. However, there were layers too tentative for comfort that went beyond a business venture and gave me pause. Derek moving his office into Nana's house would force us in constant and direct contact, which would either draw us closer or put us at a crossroads. Relationships were bound to be tested and stretched—maybe to the breaking point. Derek was keen enough to know this, wasn't he? After all, being in Special Forces as a security specialist made him a master at seeing things from all sides. Or maybe that was a skill he reserved for work. His ability to compartmentalize confounded me.

I pushed the questions aside to think about later—the list was growing longer by the day—while Jenna and I wandered through the unfinished first-floor rooms. Which area would work best for Derek and Mark, without sacrificing the space I needed to showcase my design ideas?

"Why don't y'all jus' let Derek decide?" Jenna asked when we walked through the formal dining room for the third time. "It's gonna be his office."

"He told me it doesn't matter to him. 'Just pick something,' he said." I could easily picture the dining room as an office. "This could work, but I hate to give up the fireplace. Just imagine what it'd look like in here decorated for Christmas."

Darlene appeared with a full mug in each hand. "It's too early to be thinking with no caffeine. Jus' the way you ordered it." She handed one mug to Jenna.

"Aw. Thanks, Darlene."

Darlene offered the other to me. "I know you said you didn't want none, but in case you changed your mind. I saw you had a container of that hazelnut creamer in the fridge, so I put a splash in it."

The scent of coffee and sweet creamer hit my nose, and my stomach flipped—just like the times Nana boiled up a pot of chitlins. Rude or not, I backed away from Darlene and the offending scents. "I appreciate the thought, but I think I'm fighting a stomach bug. Coffee doesn't sit right with me lately."

Jenna took a sip from her mug and frowned. "Last week you was havin' a spell of dizziness, and now your stomach's ailing?"

"Lovesick's my guess." Darlene took a slurp of my rejected coffee. "Didn't spend more'n five minutes in the same room with you and Derek last night, and it was clear y'all's sweet on each other."

"How many times I said the same thing?" Jenna saluted me with her mug and liquid sloshed over the side. "It's him you shoulda married in the first place."

Leave it to Jenna to simplify things. As if Derek's disinterest in me and six thousand miles between his life and mine had never existed. "Y'all let me know when you're done matchmaking," I said. "We got work to do."

Jenna smirked. "I dare you to deny it."

I took a deep breath and hugged my nauseous stomach. "It doesn't matter. I'm knee-deep in the middle of a divorce, my ex-husband's gotten it into his head that we're not finished, thanks to Derek's interference, and I'm dealing with all manner of other issues. Not the least of which is being broke."

"Honey," Darlene said, "you ain't got no idea what broke is. I for sure don't have a pot to piss in or a window to throw it out of, but if a fine-lookin' man was practically throwin' himself at me, I wouldn't squander the opportunity."

"Did I mention Derek's the one who encouraged Nicky to win me back? That's the opposite of throwing himself at me." Fatigue made me grumpy. "Y'all can sit here and spin fantasies all day long, but I need to sit for a few minutes. Maybe see if I can scrounge up some ginger or chamomile."

I didn't miss the look Jenna and Darlene exchanged. "We'll go with you." Jenna hooked my arm with hers as if I was an invalid.

"Don't be silly. I'm fine."

Jenna didn't listen but instead matched her steps to mine. "Just a thought, Charlie." She cleared her throat. "Any chance you could be pregnant?"

I barked out a laugh. "Of course not. Nicky and I have barely spoken the last couple months."

"Talkin' ain't what gets you knocked up," Darlene said from behind me.

"You got the symptoms," Jenna pointed out.

"You mean morning sickness?" My steps halted in the foyer, and Darlene bumped into me. I turned to include her in the conversation. “I never experienced nausea with my pregnancies.”

“Pregnancies?” Darlene’s eyebrows shot up, but her mouth went tight like she was fighting the urge to ask.

“Miscarriages,” I said. “Two of them. And I never got sick from them.”

Jenna rubbed my back. “You know, Charlie, I didn’t get sick with ever’ one of my pregnancies, either. Is it at all possible?” She arched a brow.

“No. Absolutely not.” Wasn’t I just assuring myself the night before that God’s timing was always perfect? This would be the antitheses of that.

“When did ya have your last cycle?” Jenna tugged on my hand. “’Cause if it’s been since y’all moved back here, then you’re probably good.”

I tried to count the weeks in my mind, but just the idea of being pregnant had me as lost as last year’s easter eggs. “I don’t remember. Not since I’ve been here, though.”

“It’s been near two months, Charlie.”

“I know.” I rubbed my temple where John Bonham was playing a solo. “I’ve been under a lot of stress. Besides, I’ve never been all that regular anyway.”

“If I was you, I’d be peeing on a stick,” Darlene said. “Just in case.”

Wouldn’t that be my luck? The one thing I wanted more than anything could be presented at the worst possible time. I didn’t know whether to hope for it or hope against it. Either way, I was sure God’s hand was all over it, which didn’t provide me with a whole lot of comfort.

Derek

Charlie's house, set back about a hundred feet off the main road, looked to be in decent shape from a distance, especially tucked as it was behind a couple trees that had been around longer than the Civil War. But upon closer inspection, one might wonder if it would turn out to be a money pit.

The look on Mark's face as we stood in front of it gave the impression he was of that mind. "Explain again how this is going to work. 'Cause from where I'm standing, this don't appear to be the cheapest solution. It's in even worse shape than I remembered."

"I already told you I'd cover any costs that go over our office budget."

Mark barked out a laugh and shook his head. "I'm sure it'll be considerable, too. That won't even pay for a paint job. How'd Charlie like it if she knew you was bankrolling the repairs on her house?"

"How'd you like it if I bailed out as your business partner?"

"Don't you worry, I've no intention getting in the middle of things with you two. But that don't mean she won't find out. Women have a sense about things beyond my understanding. Leastways, Cassie does. She can sniff out a lie better than a coon dog tracking a varmint."

"You let me worry about that."

He held up both hands, palms out, in surrender. "That's fine with me. Just thought you might could use a little advice seeing as to how inexperienced you are with women."

My pride took a hit, and I scowled at him. "What makes you think I'm inexperienced?"

He arched a brow. "You ain't been married, have you?"

I shrugged. "So?"

"I bet you never even took the same woman out more than a couple times."

"What's that got to do with anything?"

He crossed his arms and shook his head. "You ain't even got a sister. Boy, you are surely wading in the deep end without a lifejacket. Just don't say I didn't warn you."

I could bluster with the best of them, but uneasiness settled in the pit of my belly. He wasn't wrong. Always waiting for the right one to come along, I'd never had a long-term relationship. No one quite fit what I'd been looking for. A bright, beautiful, unavailable blonde. Only one of those existed, and she had me about ready to bang my head against a wall every time we tangled.

"So, what's the plan? Swing a hammer or drum up some security business?"

"A little of both is my guess. Cal should be here any minute to look the job over, and we'll figure it out from there."

"How 'bout you show me our new office space?"

I shrugged. "Not sure Charlie's figured it out yet, but we can knock on the door and ask."

As we climbed the steps to the front porch, I tried to see the place through Mark's eyes. Might be I offered to bite off a chunk I'd have a hard time swallowing. It was a habit of mine to pray before leaping into anything, but not this time. All my experience in Special Forces and years of chewing on the Word of God went out the window with this one. Seemed to be a habit when dealing with Charlie.

"At least we know the place is air conditioned," Mark said, peering through the screen door.

The woman from the night before, Darlene I believe her name was, appeared in the foyer. I could hear voices beyond—sounded like Charlie and Jenna—tinged with hysterics that put my fight or flight instincts on alert. "Charlie said y'all was coming by." She pulled the screen open and stepped aside. "She's in the kitchen."

"Everything okay?"

"Hey," Mark said, tapping me on the shoulder. "Looks like Cal's here."

I glanced at Darlene. "Sorry, but this can't wait."

Sure I'd just escaped something, I was only too happy to hightail it back outside with Mark.

Cal's truck pulled up behind mine in the gravel drive as we crossed the weed-infested yard.

Mark glanced at me. "If we'd gotten office space in Franklin, you wouldn't have to run like a sissy girl every time Charlie or her friends have some kind of emotional meltdown."

"You couldn't even hear what they were talking about," I said as we approached Cal. "No way you know that's what was going on."

"Inexperienced," Mark said shaking his head. "Just like I said."

I ignored him and held out a hand to Cal. He was tall and lanky but could probably out-bench anyone I knew. "Thanks for coming, buddy. I know how busy you are this time of year."

"No worries." He pointed to a mini van parked on the grass. "Jenna here?"

I nodded. "Appears to be. You need to see her? We can wait for you out here."

Mark clucked like a chicken low in his throat.

Cal glanced at Mark and grinned. "Couldn't hurt to have her two cents worth. She was driving nails and pulling wire right along beside me when we built our place. Licensed or not, the girl's a decent contractor."

"I'll go get her," Mark said. "I ain't afraid of female hormones."

While Mark went inside, Cal and I walked around the perimeter of the house. He pointed out areas of concern, not the least of which was the front porch and balcony above it. No surprise there. The exterior was wood, not unlike many of the historic homes in Tennessee, and needed to be scraped and repainted.

"Termites are a real problem," Cal said as Mark reappeared without Jenna. "Might call a pest control place sooner than later."

Mark stopped next to Cal and scratched his eyebrow with a thumbnail. "Jenna asked if you could catch her up on everything tonight."

"Sure," Cal said. "Is something wrong?"

"I don't know. Probably." He looked at me. "Charlie showed me where she'd like us to set up our office. She said to give her a couple days and she'll have the room ready."

"Okay. What makes you think there's a problem with the girls?"

"Call it a hunch. Been married fifteen years, and I'm rarely wrong."

CHAPTER TWENTY-TWO

Charlie

Once Jenna opened the door on the possibility that I might be pregnant, I could think of nothing else. Every symptom, every twinge, every sensitivity became one more piece of evidence that might prove or disprove her theory. But this wasn't just some random science experiment—it could shift the trajectory of my entire life. It seemed to be the season of such.

After the men left, Darlene insisted on fixing supper. "It don't matter what y'all have here, I can make a meal from nothin'," she said, shooing Jenna and me out of the kitchen.

The sun was setting at the back of the house, so we slipped out front where it was a touch cooler and sat on the top step. The worn wood was rough on the back of my thighs, but its warmth seeped into my skin and comforted me some, along with Dog, who settled close by my side. I buried my hand in the soft fur between his ears and closed my eyes. A breeze rustled through the leaves of the cottonwood, harmonizing with the chatter of mockingbirds.

"I suspect it's about time you went home, Jenna," I said. "It's getting close to supper."

"Cal's pickin' up take-out after he collects the kids from his mama's. I thought maybe you and me could go on down to McGee's and pick up a pregnancy test before I head off."

Pregnancy test. My heart fluttered like a swarm of moths intent on eating a hole in my insides.

"You didn't tell Cal, did you?" Why the idea of it set my heart racing, I couldn't say. Maybe the more people who knew about it, the more real it'd become.

"A course not. I wouldn't do that unless you said it was okay." She nudged my knee with hers. "So, you wanna go on over to McGee's?"

What I wanted was to bury my head in a pile of comfort food and pretend everything was fine. It'd just come right back up again and wouldn't change anything. "My daddy used to tell me that truth is power." I cut a glance at Jenna. "Do you believe that?"

She patted my knee. "I'll take Dog inside and tell Darlene we're runnin' down to the pharmacy."

"Grab my purse off the table, will you?"

"Sure thing. I'm parked behind you, so might as well take my van."

The trip to McGee's and back didn't take but a half hour, every one of those minutes expanded exponentially by fear. Only thing was, I didn't know what I feared the most—that I was pregnant or that I wasn't.

A vague memory of Mama telling me once that if I had enough faith, I wouldn't fear anything that came to mind. I couldn't remember what led up to the conversation, but in the Congo, there were all manner of things that set a little girl's heart to quivering. People that looked to be as different from me as day was to night; evidence of poverty and disease; the sound of wild animals hidden in the depths of the tree line; even strange foods such as grasshoppers and caterpillars.

I'd allowed my faith to trifle away year after year until there was no more substance to it than a ghost from the past. My prayers were weak because my faith was weak. It wasn't that I didn't believe God could do anything, but that He wouldn't.

When we arrived home, Jenna and I snuck up the stairs like a couple middle school girls hiding makeup shop-lifted from the drugstore. We sat on my bed, and I upended the white paper sack from McGee's between us. A First Responder Pregnancy Test box slid out and lay on my quilt like an omen.

"Well?" Jenna said. "You gonna do it or not?"

I picked up the box and thumbed the tab on the end. "You read the bible much, Jenna?"

She shrugged. "I suppose as much as the next person. Why?"

"When I was little, before Mama and Daddy died, they read the Bible every day." I sighed. "It was kind of their job."

"Sure. The whole point of them serving in Africa was to share the gospel, right?"

I nodded. "When they died, I sort of shut God out of my life. I figured if He didn't love them enough to keep them safe when they were doing His work...well, I just didn't want anything much to do with Him."

"I don't think it works that way, Charlie."

I slid the tab open and peered into the depths of box. How could one skinny piece of plastic hold so much power? "I made so many mistakes, Jenna." An unexpected sob rose and my voice cracked. "Of course, you know that already." I swiped at a tear that slipped down my cheek. "It seems like all my past choices were made out of anger or hurt."

Jenna took my hand and squeezed. "Well, shame on you for bein' human."

I drew in a deep breath to get my emotions under control. "I've never told anyone this before, but I always felt as if God took my babies from me on account of my sins. I slept with Nicky as if it would somehow punish Derek for rejecting me. I thought the pregnancy was the punishment. But losing that baby?" I caught Jenna's sympathetic look. "That was like what God did to punish David for the sins he committed in his lust for Bathsheba."

"Oh, Charlie. Y'all know better than that." She wrapped an arm around my shoulders. "Don'tcha?"

"I know it in my head, Jenna. It's just my heart's having a hard time believing it. I never really loved Nicky, not the way I should have, and he knew it. Losing baby number two seemed like more of God's wrath."

"Girl, you got some of the beatenist theology jangling around in your brain, ya know that?"

Tears flooded my eyes. "It's just so many hard things got all jumbled together, I don't know how to separate them out."

Jenna hopped up and disappeared into the bathroom. When she came back, she held a wad of toilet paper, which she pressed into my hand.

I swiped my eyes and nose and tried to swallow the sobs that had gotten stuck in my throat. "I can't take care of myself right now," I said. "What am I supposed to do with a baby?" If I was even able to carry it to term. "And what about Nicky?"

Jenna frowned. "What about him?"

"He'll have something to say about it, I'm sure." I balled the tissue in my hand. "After all, he is the daddy."

"He never wanted a baby to start with. It ain't like he's

gonna want to fight you for custody or anything."

"Still, it's bound to complicate things, as if my life doesn't already resemble a reality show."

"You're gettin' yourself all riled up before you even know if you're pregnant, Charlie." She slid the test out of its box. "Are we gonna do this thing?"

Derek

Sixteen years in Special Services may not have clued me into how a woman thinks, but body language communicated a whole lot more than words. Mark's assessment about the female emotions between Jenna and Charlie had been spot on, although I wasn't of a mind to tell him that. His head was big enough as it was. But when we'd gone back inside to figure out the office space, Charlie had been as twitchy as all get out, and Jenna watched her like she feared Charlie was about to crack.

Back at Mama's guesthouse, I played the scene over and over again to see if I could decipher a clue to what was going on, not that it was my concern. Unease gripped me as I packed up my computer for the big move. Maybe Charlie had rethought the plan to exchange space for repairs. That wouldn't explain the heightened emotions, though. And Charlie was never one to hold back if she had a say.

My gut told me it was more. Something that couldn't be fixed with a flat-out honest conversation. One where everything was laid out on the table and picked over until things were put back to rights. Of course, there hadn't been a whole lot of that going on lately. Not between me and Mama, Charlie and Nicky, or me and Charlie for that matter. I hadn't been completely honest with her since Nicky's graduation party, and even then, I'd hedged. Maybe if I'd have asked her to wait for me, she'd have never hooked up with Nicky in the first place. Would have saved all of us a whole lot of heartache.

I had no one to blame but myself.

"Knock, knock," Mama said through the screen door. "You mind if I come in a spell?"

"Sure thing." I kept my focus on winding the computer cord. Time to switch gears.

"What're you doing?"

I glanced at her and caught the worry in her eyes. "Mark and me made a deal with Charlie for office space. I'm just packing things up to transport."

"Office space?" She frowned. "Whatever for? Y'all haven't even got a client yet, do you?"

"No, ma'am. There's still some groundwork to do. It'll just be easier with more room."

"I have plenty of that at the house, Derek, and you're welcome to it. There's no need to move over to Charlie's."

I set the computer cord aside and pulled a chair from the table. "Have a seat, Mama. We need to talk." If I wanted honest communication, it would have to start with me.

"I can't say I like the sound of that." She slid into the chair and folded her hands on the table. "This talk have anything to do with why I haven't seen much of you lately?"

"Maybe." I sat across from her and leaned my elbows on the table. "I guess I've been holding on to some resentment, and I'm sorry for that."

Her brow furrowed. "Resentment? Might I ask what for?"

The hurt in her tone cautioned me that I might be treading through a land mine. I scratched my brow as my brain scrambled for the best approach. A military battleground had nothing on tiptoeing through family issues. It was best to begin at the beginning.

"Let's start with Nicky," I said. If we could come out unscathed by that battle, we could survive the war. "I know family's important, Mama, but I don't care to be my brother's keeper."

"Well, goodness sakes, Derek, I didn't mean to put you on the spot. I just thought you might could be a good influence on him. He looks up to you."

"I hate to burst your bubble, but he doesn't look up to me. In fact, just the opposite. He resents me. He sees me butting into his life and judging him, which, to be honest, is what I'm doing. I'm gone twenty years, and when I come home, he's the same spoiled kid he was when I left."

"It's just 'cause he and Charlie are going through a rough patch, Derek. He's taking it out on you."

I shook my head. "Why do you always defend him, Mama? They aren't going through a rough patch. Charlie's fixin' to divorce him."

She *tsk*ed. "I was so hoping they could work things out. I don't know why that boy can't see what's in front of him."

"Thanks to my meddling, he's trying to change her mind."

"Well, that's good, isn't it?" She offered a tentative smile. "So, you see, you are a good influence on him."

"You don't understand, Mama. Charlie doesn't want to be married to him. He's done nothing but hurt her."

"She'll come around, Derek. You'll see."

I rubbed a hand over my face. "I don't think so. And the truth is, I hope she doesn't."

Mama's mouth dropped open, and she let out a little breath. "You have feelings for her?"

"It doesn't matter anymore." But I knew different. It might be the only thing that mattered in the end.

"For how long, Derek?"

"As long as I can remember."

"I don't rightly understand, son. Did she know?"

I shrugged. "When I came home after my first tour, she was too young. Sixteen. I figured I'd give it another four years and see where things landed, but by then, she was with Nicky."

"Well don't that beat all," she said on a sigh, like she was talking to herself. "That poor girl has surely been through it."

"Still going through it, too," I reminded her. "That's the other thing I wanted to talk to you about."

Her gaze flickered from mine, and she moved as if to stand.

"She found her parents' wedding bands."

Mama froze.

"How do you think it makes her feel to know she's been lied to all these years?"

Mama's shoulders drooped as her gaze dropped to her hands. "I wouldn't hurt Charlie for the world, Derek. You know I love her like my own. But it's not my truth to tell."

I slammed my fist on the table and caught her wince. "It's not like her nana's going to come back from the grave and tell her."

"It's best this way, believe me."

"You know what really happened, though. Promise or not, Charlie has a right to know, too. Why are you keeping your word to a woman who wasn't in her right mind near the end? Not only that, you put me smack in the middle of it. Charlie finds out I know, how will that play out for us?"

She stood as if to leave then turned to look at me. "You can pile all the blame on me you want when it comes to Nicky, but what I know about Charlie's parents, I can't rightly share, and you throwing a tantrum about it isn't gonna change anything."

"What about Charlie? What am I supposed to tell her?"

"I'm sorry, Derek. I can't talk to you about this. And if the good Lord determines I should speak up, it won't be to you."

CHAPTER TWENTY-THREE

September 2012
Charlie

Standing at the graveside with her arm hooked into Nana's, Charlie realized death was final. It wasn't as if she hadn't experienced it before, but somehow, with her mama and daddy, it'd been different. Maybe it was because she had no real memory of the days before or after their accident. She hadn't seen their bodies encased in a coffin and lowered into the ground. Nor had they been such an intricate part of her body that she felt the physicality of their absence after they'd passed.

Charlie had always heard that death happened in threes. From her experience, it occurred in twos. Mama and Daddy ten years before. And now, little peanut right on the heels of her sweet pawpaw. The pain of it clawed at her insides, and she wasn't sure if it was she who held Nana up, or the other way around.

The graveside service ended, and people began to disperse,

but Nana refused to move. “A few more minutes, Charlotte.” Her head was bowed, but Charlie could hear the tears in her voice. If Nana wanted to stand by Pawpaw’s grave until sundown, it’s what they’d do.

She sensed the presence of someone standing behind her and turned, hoping it’d be Nicky. Maybe guilt convinced him to do what common goodness couldn’t. But it was Mama G’s eyes that met hers over Nana’s stooped shoulders.

“Let me stay with her a spell,” she said, wrapping an arm around Nana’s shoulders. “You look as if a stiff wind would knock you down, child.”

It was as Charlie stepped away from Nana that she spotted Derek standing on the perimeter of the graveside. His tall, broad form caught her breath, and it took every ounce of energy she had to maintain a steady gait toward him.

“This is a surprise,” she said when he was in earshot. “You fly all the way home for Pawpaw’s funeral?”

“I’m sorry, Charlie.”

Despite the ever-present tears that seemed to lurk in the background, Charlie’s lips twitched with humor. Two words was all it took for her to be transported back ten years, standing in front of Derek while he worked on his daddy’s tractor. “You sound like a tuna commercial.”

His response was a sad smile.

Charlie stopped a mere foot from him and folded her arms to keep from reaching out for a hug. She feared once in his arms, it’d be too hard to let go. His presence brought more peace than any of the trite words Nicky had half-heartedly spouted. “I’m worried about Nana. Can’t imagine being married for near fifty years and then being left alone.”

“I wasn’t only referring to your grandpa.” He tilted his head. “Mama told me about the baby.”

Charlie looked away to hide the sudden swell of tears. His words caused a war between sadness and comfort.

"Where's Nicky?" There was no missing the edge in his tone.

"He's working." Charlie didn't dare meet Derek's eyes—he'd see the lie in them sure as they were standing there.

"How 'bout I take you for an early supper?"

Charlie waved a hand toward her nana. "I can't leave her, Derek."

"Mama's got her. She thought maybe you could use a break. She'll take her home and stay with her a while." He waved her close and, with a gentle hand on her back, guided her toward his daddy's truck. "You going back up to Nashville tonight?"

"No. I have a couple days off work, so I thought I'd stay with Nana. I'm kind of afraid to leave her alone."

"She won't be alone. Mama and Daddy'll make sure of that." He unlocked the passenger door and held it for her.

"When d'you head out again?"

"Day after tomorrow." He waited until she was tucked inside then closed the door.

As Derek rounded the front of the truck, Charlie rolled her window down and breathed deeply. As much as she appreciated Derek's calming force, she almost wished he hadn't come home. Nothing like having a person's poor choices flaunted before them.

"Is Legends okay?" He asked.

"That's fine."

On the drive to the restaurant, they focused on small talk, which was fine with Charlie. As angry as she was with Nicky, and as sick as she was over the loss of the baby, talking about either of them with Derek would feel like a betrayal.

Once seated across from each other in the restaurant,

Charlie dared to take in Derek's clean-shaven face, steel-blue eyes, and the smile that resembled Nicky's when he was at his best.

Derek reached out a hand, and Charlie took it. "What can I do, sweet Charlie?"

The sympathy he communicated with a mere gaze about undid her. Why couldn't Nicky be more like his big brother? "There's nothing to do. Pawpaw had a life insurance policy, and the house is paid for, so Nana will be fine once she gets past the grieving period." If she got past it.

"I'm not as worried about your nana as I am about you." He squeezed her fingers. "Nicky isn't at work, is he?"

She let her gaze slide away. What good would it do to grouse about Nicky when she'd known from the first that he was about as reliable as bucket full of holes.

"Was he at least by your side when you lost his baby?"

Charlie cringed at the judgment she deciphered in Derek's tone and yanked her hand out of his. Nicky wasn't any more to blame for her circumstances than she was. Fact was, she went in with eyes wide open and still stumbled. "I don't want to talk about Nicky."

He sat back and folded his arms. "You gonna stay with him?"

She stared at him like he'd grown two heads. "What're you talking about? Of course, I'm going to stay with him, Derek. He's my husband. Or have you forgotten that?"

A muscle twitched along his jawline. "We both know you married him 'cause you were pregnant. And now that you're not—"

"I'm still married," she said. "Losing the baby doesn't change that." The last thing she was about to do was add the sin of divorce on top of the pile she'd already buried herself in.

"You want to be my friend, you'll refrain from talking bad about my husband."

Derek—2012

The moment Derek saw Charlie standing at her papaw's graveside, stooped shouldered with her nana, he knew he'd never love again to the depths for which he loved her. Didn't matter that she had a lot of growing up to do. Didn't matter that he'd been called to a different life. He wanted a do-over.

It was as clear as a star-studded southern sky that Nicky didn't value what he'd been handed, or he'd be glued to her side in her greatest time of need since they were kids. What could've been more important to his little brother than the slip-of-a-girl who'd grown into a stunning woman? How could he be so casual with the precious gift he'd been given?

Loyal she was, too. When seated in the restaurant, she'd looked him in the eye and declared Nicky as her husband. Didn't appear the pain of losing the baby or the cavalier attitude of a careless husband was going shake that, either.

They moved the food around their plates, neither of them eating much. Derek's mind spun with something to talk about that wouldn't set her off. Nicky was off limits. The baby would only dim the light she had left from her eyes. He didn't want to bore her with the work he was doing—it'd be like rubbing her nose in the choice he'd made.

He took a gulp of sweet tea to clear his throat. "You found a job yet?"

She speared a piece of asparagus on her fork and shrugged. "I've been interviewing for a small interior design firm. I think I have a shot."

"You don't sound all that excited about it."

She grimaced. "There's just been a lot going on, and with Pawpaw's passing, it puts things into perspective. Plus, the owner, a woman named Patrice, reminds me a little of Cruella De Vil."

"Who?" Where had he heard that name before?

For the first time, he saw a spark of humor light her eyes. "*101 Dalmatians*?"

He still had no clue what she was referring to.

"The Disney movie." She shook her head. "I swear, Derek, you're out of touch with reality."

Then it hit him, and he laughed. "*I'm* out of touch? Wasn't that movie made like a gazillion years ago?"

She raised her chin in challenge. "That's a little bit of an exaggeration. More like sixty." She gave him a sad smile. "Pawpaw used to watch it with me when I first came to live with them. I think he bought every Disney movie he could find. We'd spend Sunday evenings watching one or the other." Her eyes filled and she swiped at them.

She straightened her shoulders as if to shake off the gloom and continued. "Anyway, Patrice has that cruel edge to her, but I suppose I have to pay my dues somewhere. If she offers me the job, I'll take it. What about you? Is the military life everything you'd hoped it would be?"

"It has its perks." He shoved his plate aside. "Let's go find us some ice cream."

They left the restaurant, and he drove around using dessert as an excuse. Truth was, he was looking for any reason to stay closed up with her in the cab of his daddy's truck. He didn't have anything dishonorable in mind aside from soaking up as much of her as he could while he had the chance.

"If you really want good ice cream, we need to go over to

Bell Buckle," Charlie said. "There's an antique store there that has a real old fashioned soda fountain."

"Of course, they do." He chuckled. "Might as well go."

Fifteen minutes later, he parked the truck on the main drag of Bell Buckle—all two blocks of it. It was one of those towns that was easy to miss with the blink of an eye. He kept a light hand on Charlie's back as he escorted her to the door.

"What'll you have?"

"Surprise me," Charlie said. "I'm going to look around."

The store was so small, he could keep an eye on her without moving. He ordered them each ice cream in a waffle cone, collected napkins and spoons, and joined her at the back of the shop where she was inspecting some kind of a gewgaw.

"Best eat this quick, it looks like they're closing up."

She put the item back and took the cone. "We can go outside."

He followed her out, and they meandered along the narrow walkway. Eclectic shops boasting antiques, a diner or two, and the ice cream parlor-slash-antique store was all there was to the town.

"Not much here," he said.

"Not on the main drag, but you walk off a ways and there are lots of old Victorian homes and churches. I can only imagine what it was like back in the day."

They continued off the main street, and Charlie pointed out this place and that, sharing what little historic knowledge she had. But it seemed to get her mind off her loss, and he caught more than a few smiles peeking from behind the curtain of gloom she'd carried with her when standing at her pawpaw's graveside.

They finished their ice cream and the tour just as the sun was sinking behind a thicket of trees on the west side of town and had come full circle back to his daddy's truck. They drove in silence to her nana's house, and he parked in the gravel drive.

"Thank you, Derek," she said, her voice just above a whisper.

"It was nothing. You hardly ate a bite."

"I wasn't talking about supper or even the ice cream. You helped me forget for a while, and for that I'm grateful." She leaned across the bench seat and kissed his cheek. "Stay safe, will you?"

And then she was gone.

CHAPTER TWENTY-FOUR

Charlie

If I believed in sci-fis and conspiracy theories, I'd have thought there was a powerful and cruel Oz-like benefactor moving people around the game board of life merely for his amusement. How else could ten years have passed and landed me in the exact same predicament? But I believed in God almighty, even if I'd put distance as wide as the Smokey Mountains between us.

It'd been a long, fitful night of repenting for every sin I could imagine with the hope the good Lord would relent and change the positive sign on the plastic stick to something far more gracious. The hope lingered as light began to dawn in my bedroom window. It was with a prayer on my heart I dragged myself into an upright position and reached for the stick.

Dog popped up from his nightly position beside my bed, and we stared at the evidence of my stupidity. Angry tears filled my eyes while my protector nuzzled my neck in sympathy.

A couple things were now possible, neither of which I could abide. I'd had two pregnancies and suffered two horrid miscarriages. Would this make number three? Or would God finally bless me with a child when I had little to offer it but a history of wrong choices?

Weariness pulled a sigh from me as I climbed out of bed, patted Dog on the head, and stumbled toward the bathroom on shaky legs. There was nothing for it but to take it one day at a time.

A few minutes later, Dog followed me down the stairs, his nails clicking on the hardwood. I could hear Darlene in the kitchen before we entered, grateful for the absence of nauseating scents. Didn't take her for an early-morning person.

"There's the mama-to-be." She slid a plate of saltines onto the kitchen table. "Gotcha some chamomile tea brewing up." She rubbed Dog's ears as she passed.

Somehow her cheerfulness had the opposite effect of what she most likely expected. "Aren't you supposed to be suffering from nicotine withdrawal or something?" I mumbled. "And what's with the crackers?"

"From what I can recollect, they was about all I could keep down when I was pregnant about a hundred years ago. A course, if you want some eggs, I can—"

"Nope." I held up a hand to stop her. Just the mention of eggs had my stomach rebelling the likes of which could rival a band of Confederate soldiers. If this was a normal symptom of pregnancy, it was a wonder mother and child survived birth.

"Eat yourself a cracker or two. It'll settle your belly." She placed a steaming cup on the table in front of me. "Here's you some tea."

"Thanks." I glanced at her own cup as she sat across from me. "You're not drinking coffee?"

"This'll do me for now. Wouldn't want the smell to gag you."

"That's thoughtful of you. But seriously, are you wearing a nicotine patch or sneaking cigarettes on the sly?"

She laughed. "A course not. I told you I ain't never gonna smoke again. God's blessin' my obedience is all."

Maybe Derek was right. Could be, she was mentally unbalanced. "Your house just burned to the ground, and you feel blessed?" I let out a humorless laugh.

She fingered her cup. "God didn't have nothin' to do with my house burnin', Charlie. That's what my mama would a called consequences for my own stupidity. If I hadn't been smokin' in bed in the first place, it ain't never would a happened."

"Consequences, punishment." I waved a hand at her. "Semantics."

Her eyebrows shot up as she lifted her cup. "Punishment? That's a mite harsh, ain't it?"

I picked up a cracker and broke off a corner. "I lost two babies. I did everything right to be sure they were healthy. So, did I lose them as a consequence of my actions?"

"I ain't sayin' bad things don't happen, Charlie." She put her cup down without taking a sip. "Can I meddle for a second?"

"Sure."

"You believe in God?"

I sighed. "Yes."

"But you don't believe He's sovereign?"

"Of course, I do. What would be the point of believing in a God who wasn't?"

She leaned forward. "'Xactly. See, I believe God takes even our screw ups and uses them in a mighty way. I don't rightly know why you lost your babies, Charlie, but I gotta believe He'll use it."

"And how has He used the death of your daughter?" The words were laid down like a gauntlet, and I regretted them the moment they were out. "I'm sorry, Darlene. That was uncalled for."

She frowned. "It don't matter. Was a long time ago. I tol' you it took me to a dark place, an' I admit me and God had some words. But sometimes we don't get to know the answers. That's why it's called faith."

"And you don't blame God for any of it? Not even your daughter's death?"

"Lemme tell you somethin' about Carla." She folded her arms on the table and leaned in like she was preparing to tell a secret. "She was a wild'un, that girl, and I was a single mama with no clue how to tame 'er. She liked them boys, and the parties, and all the 'tention she could git. You know the type?"

I nodded. I'd run across more than a few going to school in Nashville. Nicky had slept with his share, as well.

"It near broke my heart, but I had 'bout as much control as boat with no oars. Didn't matter she was raised in the church and knew right from wrong. She was in the wrong place at the wrong time with the wrong people. That's what got her kilt. You can't rightly blame God for that."

"Consequences," I whispered.

She nodded. "Yes ma'am.

I blew out a breath. "You probably didn't know this, but my mama and daddy were missionaries. I spent the first twelve years of my life in the Congo."

Darlene's eyes widened. "No kiddin'?"

Her shocked tone drew a smile from me. "No kidding."

"So, how'd you end up here?"

"That's kind of where my faith journey took a detour. They

were killed, and I was sent back here to be raised by my nana and pawpaw."

"I'm sorry," Darlene said, reaching for my hand. "How'd they die?"

"If you'd asked me that a couple months ago, I'd have told you they were in a car accident. But lately, I've discovered a few things that don't quite add up."

Her brow furrowed. "How's that?"

"The day I got stuck out at your place without gas?" I waited until she nodded. "I was driving around trying to clear my head. I'd found a cross tucked in the back of one of Nana's desk drawers that'd been hanging in my daddy's Jeep the whole time we were in the Congo."

She tilted her head. "So?"

"I was led to believe that nothing was recovered from the crash site. Even my parents' bodies. Maybe I could reason away the cross, but then last week, I found my parents' wedding rings."

Darlene's mouth dropped open. "Ohh-wee. You got yourself a real head-scratcher there. Any ideas?"

"I'm not sure." I thought again about the night Darlene's house burned down and the dream I'd had. What if it wasn't a dream? And what if Mama and Daddy had been killed in a rebel insurrection, and I'd blocked it from my memory until that so-called dream? Only thing that didn't make sense was why no one would tell me.

"As hard as it may be, Charlie, there's proof of God's hand even in that there cross."

It took a heartbeat or two for her words to register. "I'm not following you."

"If not for the cross, you wouldn't a run outta gas at my house. Now you got yourself a bunch of junk for your shop. And here I am with a place to lay my head in a surely dark time.

It's all part of His plan. There's no such thing as coincidences, Charlie. They're God-incidences."

Derek

The space we'd picked out to set up as an office at Charlie's was about as perfect as could be. There was a glassed-in porch at the side of the house—a remodel Charlie's grandparents added when she was a kid. It was out of the way, so wouldn't interrupt her shop traffic, and had a separate entrance going to the outside, so our clients wouldn't need to walk through the house. We'd need to do some work on the windows and insulation before winter, but it'd be fine for the time being.

I was to meet Mark mid-morning to set up the office and hash out a material's list for the first phase of repairs. When I got to Charlie's, Mark's truck wasn't yet there. I slipped through the outside entrance to our new digs—an empty, wide-open space. We didn't have any furniture except for a wobbly table I'd had set up in Mama's kitchen as a desk.

"Thought I heard your truck pull in."

I spun around at the sound of Charlie's voice to find her leaning in the doorway to the main part of the house. "Was trying not to disturb you," I said.

Hair in a messy pile on top of her head left a clean view of her face. Her eyes seemed bathed in weariness, the same bruising beneath them I'd seen last time. And the time before. Could be this whole mystery surrounding her parents' death was wearing on her. And even though it wasn't my fault Mama was holding onto a secret, guilt sliced through me just the same.

"Y'all have what you need to set up your office?" She gazed around the room as if mentally furnishing it.

"We will in time. Meant to ask if you have Internet. We'll be happy to split the bill with you."

"I don't, actually. That's an expense I couldn't justify yet."

"We'll take care of it." I took a couple steps toward her. She'd put up a wall, as real as brick and mortar, and I itched to know why. Seemed the longer I was around her, the farther she slipped away. "Charlie, you okay?"

Her hand gripped the doorframe, knuckles whitening some with the effort. "I'm good. Just wanted you to know there's plenty of furniture stacked in the basement. You need anything, just take it. We can swap out pieces as I rearrange the rooms."

"What I need is to talk about what's bothering you. Is it your parents? I know there's some questions you want answers to, and if I can help—"

"It's not your concern, Derek. I don't want to trouble you with it." Dog squeezed in beside her and sat like he was preparing to do battle on her behalf. The two of them made quite a pair.

"You're never troubling me, Charlie. I'm asking because I care about you."

"I appreciate it. I really do. It's just..." Her gaze flickered away, but not before I saw the sheen of tears.

"What?"

With a dismissive wave of her hand, she turned to leave. "It's nothing."

"Charlie." Two steps, and I was at her side. With a warning look at Dog, I hooked my hand around her upper arm and smoothed the warm skin with my thumb. "Talk to me."

She kept her face averted but didn't pull away. "I'm a hot

mess, Derek," she whispered. "It seems no matter how hard I fight to get free, the deeper I sink."

"What are you talking about? Is it Nicky?" What I wouldn't give to go back all those years ago and ask her to wait for me. Sure, she'd still have been awful young, but we could have made it work.

She swiped at her cheek with a hand and tugged her arm free. "It's not Mama and Daddy, and it's not Nicky. It's me."

Her red-rimmed eyes met mine, and in that moment, I'd have paid the devil himself to free her from whatever demons she was dealing with. I fingered a strand of wayward hair off her face then caught a tear with my thumb. I kissed her temple and whispered, "Sweet Charlie. I'm sorry I didn't come back for you all those years ago."

She closed her eyes and another tear slid free. "Not nearly as sorry as I am."

Her admission struck me dumb for a few seconds. Surely, I hadn't heard right. What was wrong with me to put Nicky's feelings above all else? Brotherly duty or not, it wasn't fair to Charlie or me. In the long run, it wasn't really even fair to Nicky.

"It's not too late, Charlie." I cupped her cheek and, with breath held, bent down to kiss her. Our lips touched—just a whisper—and she stumbled back.

"I can't." Fingers over her trembling lips, she shook her head. "The fact is, you didn't come back, Derek." Her voice caught on a sob. "And I was reckless with my life. It's too late now."

She wasn't making sense. We could still fix this. "I don't understand. Are you worried about Nicky?" I reached out as she backed away. "He'll get over it. Sure, he'll be upset at first, but he'll get over it."

She hugged herself as if holding her insides together and

continued to back away, Dog whining at her side. "It's not that easy, Derek. Not anymore."

"You're not making any sense."

Her gaze slid from mine. "I'm pregnant." The last word came out on a sob before she turned and fled.

CHAPTER TWENTY-FIVE

Charlie

Channeling Scarlett O'Hara wasn't working for me anymore. All the complications I'd pushed aside to ruminate on later had piled up one atop another until I could think of nothing else. Staying busy didn't necessarily mean anything got accomplished except a whole lot of weary. To make things just a bit more worrisome, according to Jenna and Darlene, my theology was all cattywampus. Not that it came as a shock. Aside from what I remembered as a child, most of my theological education came from Nana, and no one could deny that hers was a little wonky, too.

Whatever was roiling around in my over-wrought brain, life continued. Derek, Mark, and Cal showed up early Wednesday morning to start on the first phase of the repairs on Nana's house. Phase one was the balcony that sat above the front door since it was the most visible and in the worst shape. It was accessible inside at the front end of a long hallway. I hadn't dared step out onto it in years for fear I'd fall straight through the rotting wood.

Ladders and tools were spread all over the porch. It took some maneuvering to cross it without tripping over cords or sawhorses. Harder to evade, however, was Derek's censorious stare. He had questions, but I didn't have any answers. At least none I was ready to share with him. A part of me wanted to go into full Scarlett-mode—all self-centered, romantic gestures—chuck it all and run away with him. Not that he'd bothered to ask. But if he had, and I was weak enough to comply, it would only be another version of evading my real problems or adding to the ever-growing list.

After leaving a pitcher of tea on the front porch, I escaped back into the house to find Darlene rummaging through the kitchen cupboards. She'd taken it upon herself to be chief cook and bottle washer, for which I was grateful.

"What're you looking for?"

She threw a glance at me over her shoulder. "Somethin' we might could offer the fellas for snackin' on."

"I wouldn't worry yourself over it. I'm sure they came prepared."

She slapped a cupboard closed and turned to me. "I ain't sure what kinda arrangements y'all made with your superhero out there"—she flicked a hand toward the porch— "but I'd bet my last dollar he's footin' a mighty big bill to help y'all out."

Maybe I was more like Scarlett than I'd realized, only concerned with what I was getting out of this deal. What was it costing Derek? My face heated at Darlene's reminder. I was no stranger to remodel and repair costs—it'd been my business only a couple short months ago.

"You're right, Darlene," I mumbled. "I'll just take a quick drive to the Piggly Wiggly and pick up some supplies."

"I'll join ya. T'gether, we'll git it figured."

It was just too bad Jesus wasn't here to change fishes and loaves to miraculous proportions, as my bank account was leaking money at an alarming rate.

"I see that there look on your face, Charlie. Don't you be worryin' about nothing. The good Lord always provides."

Said the woman who lived in near poverty for the last ten years. But if I was going to start rethinking my theology, it needed to start now. "Let's go." I snatched my purse off the table and marched toward the back porch, so I wouldn't have to dodge Derek's laser gaze.

As we backed out of the gravel drive, Darlene said, "So, once ya get this place all done up, whatcha gonna call it?"

"I'm not sure. You have any ideas?"

We threw names back and forth but hadn't landed on one by the time I parked at the Piggly Wiggly. A name for the shop wasn't on top of my list of priorities, but, as Darlene pointed out, I couldn't get the paperwork done for a business license without it.

"There's a couple a places a'ready sellin' junk-like stuff on the square," Darlene said as she climbed out of the truck.

"I'm thinking mine'll be quite a bit different." I opened the door to the grocery store so she could go in ahead of me. "I'll already have repurposed things, and each space will be set up like a showroom."

"Should I grab a buggy?"

"Sure."

We wandered down the aisles and picked up whatever we thought the men would like. I tried to ignore pesky details, like cost and my limited bank account, and let the verse *Be still and know that I am God* continually flow through my mind. He was bigger than this, wasn't He?

I was feeling fairly calm as I wheeled the buggy out to my vehicle. As Darlene was too short to transport the grocery bags into the empty toolbox in the bed of the truck, she wandered over to the bulletin board while I attended to that little chore.

"Will ya lookee here," she called out to me as she tapped a flyer.

I shoved the last bag into the box and shut it. "What is it?"

"Come see for y'self."

Sweat trickled down my low back, my stomach was queasy, and I was feeling lightheaded, so I wasn't of a mood to check out some ancient flyer tacked to the wall.

"It's hot as hades out here, Darlene." I sounded like a two-year-old.

"Swear, this here dog is the spittin' image a Dog."

It took my fuzzy brain a moment to connect the picture of the dog to *my* Dog. Once I did, dread turned the queasiness in my belly into summersaults.

My legs were noodles as I made the trek from the truck to Darlene. It was such an innocuous flyer. Plain sheet of copy paper stained by age and weather. LOST was written in black marker with a phone number beneath it. But the photo that took up most of the space was just as Darlene had said—the spitting image of Dog. Only his name was Buster.

"Ain't that a coincidence?" Darlene asked.

I repeated her earlier words to me "There's no such thing as coincidences." I'd been to this same store at least a dozen times since I'd moved back into Nana's house. Since I found Dog lying on the porch beneath the swing. Why had I never noticed this sign? Why couldn't I have seen it before Dog became as much mine as if I'd raised him from a pup?

And how could the God Darlene claimed to be so good, be so cruel?

Derek

Didn't much matter that construction work played havoc with my back, I needed the outlet. Smacking nails was a whole lot better than beating my head against a wall, which was what I wanted to do. How could one skinny, strong-willed, infuriating woman drive a man to such extremes? Love her or hate her, but I surely couldn't be immune to Charlie.

Pregnant. She just dropped that little bomb and ran off like I was expected to accept it without question. And boy howdy, I had questions. Halfway through the night, it occurred to me, though, that I didn't have a right to any answers. That just made me all the madder until I was ready to do some serious damage.

"You a'right?" Mark asked as we were measuring off a two-by-four.

"Fine." I handed him the end of the tape measure.

"You don't act fine. You're stomping around here like someone just stole all your marbles."

I marked the wood with a carpenter's pencil then flicked the end of the tape from Mark's hand. It rattled and rolled back into its case. "I lost my marbles, all right," I muttered, passing off the two-by-four to Cal.

Mark squinted and tilted his head. "Come again."

I waited until Cal was standing at the skill saw he had set up on the front patch of the lawn then leaned toward Mark. "Charlie informed me yesterday that she's pregnant."

"Pregnant?" Mark barked.

With a quick glance at Cal to be sure he didn't hear, I turned to Mark. "Why don't you just take out an ad with the *Tennessean*?" Although it was likely Jenna would've known as soon as Charlie. And what Jenna knew, wouldn't Cal know, too?

Mark grimaced. “Sorry, man. But how’s that possible?”

I pinned him with a stare. “Seriously? Weren’t you just telling me how experienced you are with women?”

He scowled. “You know what I mean.”

“I don’t have the particulars. She won’t talk to me about it, not that I can blame her. When she and Nicky hooked up, I wasn’t exactly supportive.”

“Why would you be? Everyone knows you’ve had a thing for her since she was a kid. Nicky ain’t exactly the most responsible person, neither.”

“Maybe not, but he was smart enough to move in when he had a chance. Lot more ’n I can say for me.”

“There she is now.” Mark pointed behind me.

Daddy’s truck pulled in the drive and passed the other three vehicles parked along the edge of it.

“Let me just go see if she needs any help.” I slapped the tape measure into Mark’s hand before marching across the yard.

“That’s you, all right. Mr. Chivalrous,” Mark called.

Ignoring him, I rounded the house to see Darlene and Charlie climbing out of the truck. “Need any help?”

“We’re fine,” Charlie said, head down as she unloaded bags from the toolbox in the bed of the truck.

“No, we ain’t.” Darlene waved me over. “We got us a load of groceries that need to get inside. Could use the help.”

Charlie threw her a scowl, although Darlene missed it. “We can manage on our own. I’m sure you got more important things to do.” Her voice caught, and she turned her head away.

Was she crying?

“What’s going on?” I’d heard somewhere that women could be emotional when they were pregnant. Probably all it was.

Darlene cradled a couple bags in her arms. “It’s Dog.”

"Dog? I just saw him lying under the cottonwood tree out front. He looked fine to me."

Despite claiming she could unload the groceries just fine, Charlie handed me a bag. "There's a Lost Dog sign up at the Piggly Wiggly." Her voice wavered. "I don't know why I never saw it before, but it looks like it's been there a while."

"I tol' her to just forget it." Darlene headed for the back porch. "But she won't hear of it."

Charlie looked at me with sorrowful eyes. "It wouldn't be right to ignore that stupid sign. I just wish I'd seen it weeks ago. You know how much money I've spent on dog food in the last couple months?"

I knew Charlie didn't give a rip about the dog food. She'd been dismissive of Dog when he first found her, but now they were a pair. Couldn't imagine one without the other.

"Could be a little kid missing him." She hugged a grocery bag to her chest. "Besides, I've made so many wrong choices, it might just be if I started making the right ones, things would go my way."

I took the grocery sack from her and grabbed the two left in the bed, as well. "What's that supposed to mean?"

"I don't know, Derek." She sighed. "Every time I turn around, things go sideways."

"You mean the pregnancy?"

"I mean everything." She leaned against the truck bed and shook her head. "I'm sorry I laid my pregnancy on you like that. I know you want to talk about it, but I need some time. It feels like my whole world is caving in on me, and just when I get one thing kind of figured out, something comes along to knock the wind out of me again."

It was probably a good thing my arms were laden with groceries, or I'd have pulled her in for a hug. I wanted to promise her the moon and the stars and everything in between, but the pregnancy changed things. She might have thought her faith was weak, but I had a suspicion it was a whole lot stronger than she credited it.

She combed fingers through her hair. "And now I got a phone call to make." With a frown, she looked at me. "You think it's a sin to hope the owner died since he put that poster up?" Her attempt at humor failed when her eyes filled with tears.

"It's always possible Dog isn't the one on that poster."

She sighed. "I wouldn't bet the farm on it."

CHAPTER TWENTY-SIX

Charlie

Feeding a crew of men was not my forte, so I was relieved when Darlene offered to take care of lunch. While she laid out bread to assemble sandwiches, I fished the phone number from the store flyer out of my purse. I sat at the kitchen table, cell in hand, and tried to focus on the numbers through the tears that blurred my eyes. I could blame them on hormones, but that'd be a lie. How could I have become so attached to a stray dog in such a short time? It's not like Dog was a baby I'd carried in my womb for four months before being ripped from my body. He was just a dog. And I didn't even like dogs. Or hadn't liked them, until that big, sloppy, shedding canine won me over.

"Dogs is smart." Darlene's voice broke into my pity party. Although her back was to me, I could see she was slapping Duke's onto the slices of bread. "Ain't in them to get lost."

I swiped at the moisture in my eyes. "What's your point?"

"He's happy where he's at. If he weren't, he'd of left." She glanced at me over her shoulder. “I say let sleeping dogs lie.” The pun fell flat.

If only I hadn’t seen that flyer. But I had, and I couldn’t ignore it. I touched my belly to remind me there was a child growing inside, even if I didn’t feel it yet. Maybe God hadn’t taken my babies as punishment for my sins. Maybe, He really didn’t work that way, as Jenna had said. But He certainly wasn’t going to bless me for doing wrong, either. If I let it alone, as Darlene suggested, and I lost another baby, I would always wonder if I’d sacrificed my child’s life for the chance to keep Dog when I knew he wasn’t mine.

That is, if Dog and Buster were actually one and the same. Could Derek be right? Was it possible that Dog and this Buster from the flyer just looked alike?

With an idea in mind, I went outside through the kitchen door. Dog was curled up, snoring, on the bed I’d set up for him on the back porch as if oblivious to the whine of the skill saw and pounding of nails. He was smart, all right. Which meant he wouldn’t have forgotten his name.

I slipped past him and walked out beneath the old magnolia tree, far enough away that he wouldn’t easily hear me, but close enough to observe him. *Please, Lord, don’t let him respond.* I cupped my hands and yelled, “Buster!”

In the time it took me to blink, Dog was out of the bed, his dark eyes searching for me.

Throat closing, I choked out, “Here, Buster.”

Dog scrambled across the porch deck and down the stairs. He didn’t stop until he was planted at my feet, awaiting his next order.

I dropped to my knees and pulled him in for a hug. “You’re such a good boy.” My words got caught up on a sob, and I choked back a wail. When I could find my voice again, I said, “Come inside with me where it’s cooler. We’re going to call your owners. I'm sure they've been missing you." I swiped at my eyes as we went back inside.

Number in hand, I led Dog into the parlor where I'd have some privacy. I sat on the floor, my back resting against Nana's wingback chair, while my trusty companion dropped next to me and laid his big head on my leg. I punched in the phone number, cleared my throat, and waited to connect.

"Yeah," a gruff voice answered. My body twitched with the desire to disconnect the call.

"Um, hi. My name is Charlie, and I saw a poster up at the Piggly Wiggly about a lost dog." The words were rushed so as to get them out before I changed my mind.

"Yeah? You got 'im?"

"Maybe." I rubbed Dog's ear. "I think so."

"It's been so long, didn't think anyone'd find him." He didn't sound as excited as I expected he would.

"He didn't have a collar." It was an accusation, but I didn't care. He had one now, because I'd gotten it for him along with an identification tag. What kind of dog owner doesn't collar his dog? He could've had rabies for all I knew.

"He's a country dog. Don't need one."

I gritted my teeth to hold back my automatic response. I supposed a country dog didn't need immunizations or rabies' shots, either. Of all the irresponsible, fool-headed—

"So, where you at? I'll collect him right now if you don't mind."

I unclenched my jaw and gave him the address.

"Be there right quick."

When Dog, or Buster, and I went back into the kitchen, Darlene had a plate full of sandwiches, a pitcher of sweet tea, and a bag of chips ready to go.

"I'll help you carry those out." Anything to stay too busy to lament over the upcoming loss of Dog.

"I got these," Darlene said, turning slightly to keep me from taking the tray. "Grab you some glasses and fill 'em with ice, will ya?"

"Sure."

She started to pass then stopped. "You called the owner, didn'tcha?"

I nodded. "He's on his way to pick Dog up now."

She shook her head. "Wish you hadn't done that."

A twinge of annoyance turned into a full-blown scowl. "You can't preach doing right one minute and then tell me to do wrong the next. You don't think it's hard enough as it is?"

"You're right princess," she said with a shake of her head. "I'm sorry. Just hate to see you hurt, is all."

I snorted. "You might want to rethink staying here then. Seems I keep walking into situations that leave me worse off in the end." My marriage was a perfect example of that.

What if the real test wasn't what I'd do in the situation with Dog? What if the real test was what I'd do in the situation with Nicky? Just the thought of it snatched the breath clear from my lungs. How was keeping Dog when he wasn't mine to keep any different than divorcing Nicky when I'd married him for better or worse?

My hand touched my belly where our baby grew for the third time. *Why now, Lord?*

Only the sound of hammers slamming on nails met my ears.

Derek

It didn't take a genius to see Charlie was holding on by a razor-thin wire. Didn't rightly know why God saw fit to bring me home at such a time as this when she seemed to be at her lowest. Was it to help her out in some way? Or maybe He wanted to rub it in my face that I'd made the wrong choice more than twenty years ago. Course, that wasn't the God I knew. Sure as I was sitting under the cottonwood in the heat of late summer, He had a plan. Leastways, He always did in the past. Just wish I had a clue what it was.

I leaned against the tree, the bark of it rough even through my t-shirt, and watched Charlie cross the craggy lawn with a glass of tea. Her eyes kept darting to the road, which clued me in that she was expecting someone. My guess was Dog's rightful owner. Couldn't fault her for calling. It was the Christian thing to do. Just made me wonder at the heart of her motivation. She'd admitted that past and present had a way of getting so twisted up, she wasn't sure which end was up.

"How come you're sitting out here all by yourself?" She handed me the glass, wet with condensation.

I glanced up at the porch where Cal and Mark were planted on the steps talking to Darlene before craning my neck to get a look at her looming over me. "Just needed a little space to stretch out my back."

Lines formed between her eyes, and she worried her bottom lip. "I keep forgetting you have an injury." She said it like it was somehow her fault.

"No more'n I do." I took a gulp of tea.

"You shouldn't be out here doing manual labor, Derek. I'm sorry."

"No need to be. I like manual labor." I patted the ground to indicate she should sit . "Besides, it was my idea in the first place."

She kicked off her flip-flops, plopped onto the ground, and crossed her long legs. "Still." Her eyes drifted to the road where an old, rust-on-white truck slowed in front of the house.

"Dog's owner?"

She frowned. "Afraid so."

"You sure about this?"

Pushing up off the ground again, she dusted her bottom and glanced at the porch. "Here Buster," she yelled.

I twisted my body to see what she was looking at and saw Dog bounding down the porch steps, running to her full speed like his life depended on it. He came to a skidding halt at her feet and dropped into a sit.

She buried one hand in the fur between his ears. "He's a smart dog." Her words caught, and she swallowed a couple times.

I stood as the truck parked behind Darlene's van, watching as a man climbed out. He wore a grimy ball cap, ratty jeans and a muscle shirt that showed off wiry arms. My guess was he couldn't take Barney Fife in a fair fight. Might be why Dog, or rather Buster, was so important to him.

"Hey there, Buster."

Dog stayed glued to Charlie's side, her hand still buried in his fur, but his head tilted in recognition, and he let out a low whine.

"Are you the man I talked to on the phone?" Charlie stayed put and yelled the question across the yard.

"Yes, ma'am. The name's Ray." He pointed at Dog. "And that there is my dog, Buster." He leaned forward slightly and clapped his hands. "Come on over 'ere, Buster. We gonna go on home."

Charlie removed her hand from Dog's head and shoved it into the pocket of her shorts. As she marched toward Ray, Dog stayed by her side. Clearly, he'd shifted his loyalty, if he ever had any for this Ray character to begin with.

"He really should have a collar," Charlie said.

Ray scowled at her. "Not that again. I done told you he's a country dog, not some citified guard dog."

His attitude put me on alert, and I moved closer to Charlie.

She crossed her arms. "If he'd had one, I would've known he wasn't a stray. You allow him to wander off, people ought to know if he's had his rabies shot or not."

"Looks like he's got one now, so you can quit your fussin'."

"Mister, I haven't even gotten started yet."

As I hooked an arm around her waist, I glanced at the porch where Darlene, Mark and Cal were watching the interaction like it was a western show down. Only, Charlie's weapon of choice was her mouth, which she was pretty good at wielding. But just in case she decided to lay into him, I thought it best to ready to hold her back.

"Come on, Buster." Ray patted his thigh and headed back to the truck like the matter was finished.

Dog cocked his head to look up at Charlie and whined.

"Go on now, Dog." Charlie swept one hand toward Ray while she swiped at her eyes with the other. "You heard the man." She'd have been more convincing if her voice hadn't wobbled.

Dog stood and took a step forward, but his eyes remained on Charlie as if waiting for a reprieve.

My own throat was suspiciously tight, so I could only imagine what Charlie was going through. Dragging the inevitable out was only making matters worse. I nabbed Dog's collar and gently tugged. "Let's go, boy."

Charlie had one hand covering her mouth as I led Dog to Ray's truck. The man stood by the tailgate glaring at us like we were the enemy. Probably embarrassed by his dog's obvious allegiance to a woman he' d known such a short time.

When we reached the truck, I let loose of Dog. "She took real good care of him."

His beady eyes narrowed. “You sayin’ I ain’t?”

“Just letting you know she has a real affection for him.” I narrowed my eyes. “In case you decide he’s better off with her.”

“Why would I think that?” He dropped the tailgate. “Load up, Buster.”

Dog stared over at Charlie, clearly conflicted, before hopping into the bed of the truck.

I ambled back to Charlie’s side, jaw clenched, and we watched Ray drive off with Buster. The dog didn’t take his eyes off Charlie until he was out of sight.

CHAPTER TWENTY-SEVEN

Charlie

It seemed as if every nook and cranny in Nana's house held reminders of Dog. Half-chewed rubber toys, tennis balls, and bones were scattered every which way. I found them under my bed, behind the sofa, and wedged between the washer and dryer. After Dog had been with me a couple weeks, I'd repurposed old cushions and pillows into makeshift beds, so he had one available wherever we were. There they still sat, as if waiting for his return. Of course, his favorite place to curl up was on my feet. I might've complained a time or two, but truth was, it had been a comfort I sorely missed once he was gone.

Short of finding out where Ray lived and resorting to a life of crime as a dognapper, there was nothing to be done about the loss of Dog. I didn't want to focus too much on the baby growing inside of me, either. I had to protect my heart, because I feared this pregnancy would turn out just like the others, and surviving them was like fighting my way out of quicksand. I filed it all away in my Scarlett-box for thinking on another day.

Instead of bemoaning my precarious future, I was determined to put to rest the questions in my past. I made it a priority to upend every unpacked box in search of evidence that might reveal Mama and Daddy's true cause of death. Dead was dead, so it shouldn't have mattered one way or the other, but it did. The dream or vision or nightmare—whatever it was —I had the night of Darlene's house fire, left me feeling as if I was missing a piece of vital information. If they hadn't been killed in a car accident, there must be some reason everyone felt the need to lie to me.

I'd had enough of deception to last me until the Second Coming.

When I'd had Derek and his friends haul things from the basement, there had been a collection of cardboard file boxes left stacked along one concrete wall. Of course, with Darlene's abundance of goods now housed there, getting to those boxes proved to be a bit of a challenge.

"You sure you don't want no help?" Darlene stood on the last basement tread and watched me squeeze between an iron headboard and an antique barn door. The good Lord willing, I wouldn't be able to do the same in another couple of months.

It didn't escape my notice that random thoughts such as these were starting to resemble praying.

"I'm good."

"Promise you ain't gonna lift any heavy boxes?"

"Yes, ma'am, I promise. I'm sure you have better things to do than act as my nursemaid." I'd reached the first stack of boxes but wasn't sure how I'd manage to go through them and still keep my word to Darlene.

"Sure do, but yell if'n you need anythin' moved."

I waved her away and took a relieved breath when I heard

the basement door close. Aside from Nicky, I'd never lived with anyone past childhood. Darlene was good company, but I was exhausted just from keeping up a cheerful front. God knew she'd had enough tragedy to last three lifetimes, so she didn't need to hear me whining about my own pitiful circumstances.

With a little creative ingenuity and lots of leverage, I cleared an open space. Using my shoulder, I pushed the top box off the pile and let gravity do the rest. It crashed to the concrete floor where its contents spilled out in a cascade of papers loosened from their manila folders.

I'd just gotten my body situated in a somewhat comfortable position when I heard the creak of the basement door. Now what?

"Charlie?"

I bit back a sigh. "Everything's fine, Darlene." I lowered my voice and muttered, "Stop mothering me. Please."

"You got comp'ny."

"Who is it?" Had I forgotten an appointment? Derek had someone scheduled to install Internet, but I could've sworn that was tomorrow.

Murmured voices tripped down the steps as if jostling for position. "No," came Darlene's sharp rebuke that seemed to put an end to their discussion. "Says he's your husband," she called down.

This week just kept getting better and better. It would be easy enough to have Darlene send him away. I had no doubt she was ready to take over Dog's security duties. But he'd only come back another time. Better to rip off the Band-Aid. "I'll be up in a minute." Cramped quarters made standing a tad more laborious than sitting, and it was only accomplished with a few grunts and groans.

As I climbed the steep steps, I practiced the words *I'm pregnant* in my head. It wouldn't be the first time he'd heard them from me, and if he was true to form, he wouldn't receive them well. Then again, my own reaction when I saw the positive sign on that little piece of plastic hadn't been my finest moment, either. However, it would most likely be the catalyst he needed to sign the divorce papers, which was enough to keep me moving.

When I topped the basement stairs, I looked down the long hallway that led to the foyer. Nicky stood just inside the front door, arms crossed and a scowl on his face. No doubt, Darlene warned him not to move from that spot, and Nicky's pride took a hit. Only one of the many reasons he wouldn't have fared well in the service.

As soon as he saw me, Nicky dropped his arms and headed down the hall to meet me halfway. "I know I should've called first, but I was at Mama's and thought I'd stop in and see if you were here."

It took a moment for me to get over my surprise at Nicky's words. He was at his mama's? That was a rare occurrence. And the last time he sounded remotely apologetic was...never.

He hitched a thumb toward the kitchen. "Who's your bodyguard?" There was only the slightest edge to his tone.

"A friend." I tucked my hands into the pockets of my shorts.

"Yeah? What happened to your dog?"

The story was too long and depressing to recount. "What're you doing here, Nicky?"

With a quick twist of his head, he looked toward the kitchen as if expecting Darlene to be lurking in the background. "Can we go outside and talk?"

I shrugged. "Sure. It's cooler out front." Derek and his two-man crew had finished up the balcony in the morning and headed out for lunch. Leftover lumber was stacked against the far railing behind the porch swing which now hung evenly.

Tools were tucked out of the way, so I assumed they wouldn't be back until tomorrow.

I decided the porch swing would hint at an intimacy I didn't want to encourage, so I sat on the top step of the porch instead.

Nicky dropped next to me, but not so close I felt the need to move away. "You doing okay?" He rested his elbows on his knees, hands clasped. He was making an effort, but I was suspicious of his motives. Did Derek tell him I was pregnant? If so, I would have expected him to be running in the other direction.

"What's going on, Nicky? I'm sure you didn't stop by just to see how I was doing?"

He stared out at the yard. "We never finished talking about how you want a divorce, and I don't."

I was so sure once he got over the sting of being dumped, he'd see the divorce as his chance to be free. "I don't get you, Nicky." I pinched the bridge of my nose and drew in a deep breath. "Why the change of heart?"

He shifted so he was facing me. "I don't know. Maybe it took you wanting to leave me to open my eyes."

I wasn't buying it. This may have been the Nicky I knew when we'd first started dating sixteen years before, but he'd morphed real quick into a man-child who wanted the perks of marriage without the responsibility. It only ever made him feel like a trapped animal willing to chew off its leg to get free. Wasn't that what all the sleeping around was about? He all but pushed me out the door.

"Look, Nicky." I licked my suddenly dry lips. "You're going to find out sooner or later, so I may as well tell you now."

He frowned. "Yeah?"

I drew in a deep breath and let it out slowly. Once I told him, I couldn't take it back. "I'm pregnant."

I dared a glance to gauge his reaction. His mouth dropped open then snapped shut. Rubbing his hands along his thighs, he glanced at me. "Is it mine?"

I fisted my hand to keep from smacking him across the face with it. "You don't have the sense God gave dirt." I said through a clenched jaw.

His eyes widened, and his mouth drew into a little boy pout. "It's a fair question."

I barked out a rude laugh and jumped up. "You don't know the meaning of fair."

"I've been out of the picture for two months, and Derek's been hanging around like he's just waiting for the chance to make his move."

I narrowed my eyes. "Seriously? Do you even know me or your brother? Sleeping around is your M.O., not ours."

Nicky slowly stood to face me but moved away from the edge of the step. Maybe he had a little sense after all. If this discussion escalated any further, I might hurl him down the stairs. He raised his hands as if to ward off my ire. "Don't go throwing a hissy fit, Charlie. We both know y'all have had feelings for each other from as far back as I can remember."

I clenched my fists. "That's the difference between you and us, Nicky. We don't *act* on our feelings."

"Okay, calm down. No sense getting all worked up. I just wanted to be sure."

"No doubt you'd rather it be his, so you don't have to be responsible."

He jutted out his chin and crossed his arms. "You forget I came here to see if we couldn't work things out. That ain't exactly avoiding responsibility."

"Why should I trust anything you say? You've been cheating and lying through this whole marriage. I don't think it's me who's forgetful, either. You remember what you said last time I was pregnant?"

Eyes not meeting mine, he combed his fingers through the dark mop of hair. "A course I do, Charlie. But that was a long time ago."

I shook my head. "There is no way you can convince me you're a different person from the one I caught in bed with that...groupie." The image of the two of them would be forever seared in my brain. "I can't go back to that, Nicky, no matter how desperate I become. And if by some miracle I carry this baby to full-term, I'm not going to expose it to the toxic environment you seem to thrive on."

He drew in a deep breath and looked me in the eye. "What if I take that job Derek offered me, and we go to counseling?"

"It's just prolonging the inevitable." Lightheaded, I leaned against the porch post. "Counseling isn't going to fix things, Nicky." And there was no way I'd believe he'd go to work for Derek.

"You don't think people can change?"

I shrugged. "I don't think *you* can change. I think our entire relationship has been built on sibling rivalry on your part and a need for unrequited love on mine."

His mouth thinned and a muscle in his jaw twitched. "Unrequited love, huh? It's always been about Derek."

"No, Nicky. It didn't start with Derek. It started with my parents. I'm not laying all the blame on this mess at your feet, but I wouldn't have left if you'd have stayed faithful. I don't think that was too much to ask."

"So, if you're not rushing off to be with Derek, what harm could a few counseling sessions do?"

"It'd be a waste of money."

He shrugged. "It's mine to waste. Just give me a chance, Charlie."

CHAPTER TWENTY-EIGHT

Charlie

There was a time I prided myself on being clear-headed, disciplined, and resolute. All good qualities for a successful businesswoman. But circumstances have a way of changing things some. I had to wonder if God was altogether sifting that particular sin of pride from my heart, because it seemed some days I didn't have the ability to even find my way out of a paper sack.

One conversation with Nicky and I was more confused than the day I left him. I knew in my heart it was a bad idea to encourage him with even a glimmer of hope. But my head wasn't quite on board. If he could really change his ways—which I knew was a colossal *if*—wasn't our baby better off with two parents rather than just the one? It was only the child growing inside of me that allowed the thought to take shape.

The next morning, my mind was still spinning with doubts as I tucked into the fourth file box. Darlene, bless her heart, had hauled each one upstairs, and stacked them next to the kitchen table, so I no longer needed to squat on the unforgiving concrete floor. If she took so well to mothering me, I could only imagine the kind of nana she'd make. God did work in the most mysterious ways.

Derek and his crew were back at work, this time tackling termite damage along the foundation. I expected the construction noise would grate on nerves already stretched to the breaking point, but instead, I found them to be a comfort. With every hour they clocked in repairs, the less likely the house would crumble around me. That in itself alleviated a bit of stress. It was just a shame relationships couldn't so easily be renovated.

"Hey Charlie," Jenna said from the back porch as she opened the screen door. "I brought us some lunch." She waved a paper sack. "Sandwiches from Coffee Break."

"Was I expecting you?" Forgetfulness was just one more perk of being stuck in that old paper sack. Or maybe it was baby brain. My other two pregnancies suffered from the same malaise.

"Nah." She let the screen door slam and deposited the sack on the counter. "Darlene called and said she was goin' over to her place to sift through ashes. I offered to gather a group of people to help, but she said she needed to do it alone."

"She told me the same when I tried to go with her. I think she's looking for closure. But that doesn't explain why you're here." I laid a thin file folder amid the dozen or so that was spread out on the table.

"Just 'cause." She shrugged. She pulled a chair from under the table and sat.

She wasn't fooling me with the innocent act. "Darlene put you up to this, didn't she?"

She wrinkled her nose. "I don't rightly know what you're talkin' about. Can't a friend come by for a visit?"

I pointed my chin to the bag she'd left on the counter. "What's with the food? I was feeding myself long before Darlene moved in."

"Not so's you'd notice." She sniffed. "You're eatin' for two these days, Charlie. Pop-tarts and any ol' thing you can find sittin' in the Frigidaire won't cut it."

She had a point.

Glancing around the kitchen, she said, "Where's Dog? I didn't see him outside. Figured all the noise the boys are makin' had him skedaddlin' inside."

A knot formed in my throat as tears flooded my eyes. These days, they sat on the fringe just waiting for a reason to spill out. "His owner picked him up the other day."

"What? Oh, Charlie, what happened?"

I waved my hands in the air. "I don't want to talk about it. At least not right now."

Her eyes softened and she nodded. "Okay. We don't have to talk about it." She fingered one of the files. "What're ya doin'?"

I swiped my eyes and sniffled. "The short answer is that I'm looking for a clue about how my parents died. The long answer is a little more convoluted than that."

"Well, when you're ready to let me in on the long answer, I'm here." She jumped up. "Meanwhile, let's eat us some lunch. Got sweet tea in the fridge?"

"Yeah." My eyes locked onto a letter head peeking out from the file I'd just laid on the table. SBMA—South Baptist Missionary Alliance. I slid the paper free and scanned its contents. It was a letter from the director addressed to Pawpaw and Nana—Charles and Florence Van Cleave.

We cannot express the depth of our sympathy for the loss of your son, Charles and his wife, Sarah. They served the mission field with grace and generosity, and their contributions will continue as eternal rewards. We lift their daughter, Charlotte, in daily prayer and know that our Heavenly Father will care for her into eternity.

"Charlie?"

I looked up from the letter, my heart racing like a jack rabbit running for its life. It was just one piece of communication, but it was a start. If nothing else, I had the name of the organization they were affiliated with.

"You okay?" Jenna stood over me with a glass of tea. "You find somethin'?"

I handed her the letter. "I think so." Before I could say more, my phone trilled. I didn't recognize the number, but that didn't mean much. Could be the Internet company letting me know they were on the way out.

"Hello?"

"Is this Charlotte Van Cleave?" The voice was southern sassy in a familiar sort of way.

"This is she?"

"Oh goodness, I can't tell you how relieved I am. I've been trying to track you down for days."

Jenna set my tea down, eyebrows raised in question.

I shrugged at her. "I'm afraid you have me at a disadvantage. Who is this?"

"Oh, I'm sorry." She giggled. "This is Elodie Travers."

It took a heartbeat or two for me to respond as I had to adjust my thinking. "Elodie. I should have recognized your voice."

"That's quite all right. It's been close to a year since we've seen each other. I called Downtown Decor and was told you no longer work there. But I wasn't about to let that inconsequential fact derail me."

Infused with a spark of excitement, I shot out of my chair. Elodie paid well and had a network wider than AT&T. I grinned at Jenna and pointed to the phone just as reality reared its butt-ugly head.

"If this is about a job, Elodie, I'm afraid I can't take it. I have a non-compete clause."

"I'm aware, Charlotte. But just like I told that witch-of-a-woman you used to work for, your hands might be tied when it comes to seeking out clients, but she can't rightly tie mine. I have the right to hire whomever I choose."

That little ol' spark lit up again. "What've you got in mind?"

Derek

Even a day laboring under the hot August sun wasn't enough to smooth out the giant chip that weighed down my shoulder. After talking with Nicky, the idea of re-upping didn't sound so bad. Desk job or not, it had to be better than being a powerless bystander in the farce unfolding between him and Charlie. She told me they were done. But I came to find out Nicky didn't get the memo.

I'd about given up on the notion of getting Charlie alone, what with Mark, Cal, and Jenna hanging around every which way I turned. It wasn't until close to quitting time a van pulled into the drive that I saw my chance. It was the installer from the Internet company. Figured the Wi-Fi was coming out of my pocket, so it made sense I'd involve myself in the decision-making process. Not that I cared a whit one way or the other, except it might afford me the opportunity to talk to Charlie without an audience.

"I'm gonna take a few," I told the boys. "Show this guy where to set everything up."

Cal wiped at the sweat on his forehead with the back of a hand. "It's about time we called it for the day, anyway. If you don't mind, let Jenna know I'm heading out, okay?"

"Sure thing."

I was halfway across the yard when Mark called out. "Need my input?"

"Nah." I waved a hand at him. "See you tomorrow."

As the guys packed up their trucks, I escorted Keith, the installer, through the backdoor and into the kitchen, where I expected to find Charlie and Jenna. But aside from a bunch of file folders spread across the table, it was empty. Charlie had already decided the router should go in the makeshift office we'd set up for Mark and me, so I figured it was best to get him started there.

"This is quite a place," Keith said, taking in the wood-trimmed windows and inset bookshelves. "What year was it built?"

"Around the turn of the century, would be my guess." I stood in the doorway. "Give me a few while I find the owner."

"No problem. I'll go round up the equipment and get to work."

I did a quick survey of the rooms on the first floor, but no Charlie or Jenna. As I neared the stairway, I heard muffled voices from above. "Charlie?" No answer. I climbed the stairs and called out a couple more times.

"In here," came her muffled reply.

I followed the voices down the long hallway until I stood on the threshold of the only other room we considered as office space. It used to be where Charlie's pawpaw would hide out and pretend he was doing paperwork. We all knew he'd had crosswords and old hunting magazines hidden away in his desk. The floor-to-ceiling bookshelves had once been filled to overflowing. I could still see him sitting in the corner in an old, burgundy leather chair, his nose buried in a book.

Now, Charlie sat at his old desk, the late summer sun turning her hair into a golden halo as it poured through the window. She had a laptop opened, and Jenna was standing over her shoulder engrossed in whatever was on the screen.

"Hey, Jenna, Cal asked me to let you know he's on his way home."

Her eyes went wide as she looked at her watch. "How'd it get to be so late? I gotta go." She gave Charlie a quick hug and hustled from around the desk. "See y'all later." She blew past me with a wiggle of her fingers, and all that was left of her was the sound of flip flops on the stair treads.

I turned my attention to Charlie who was closing the laptop. "The guy's here from the Internet company."

"Oh, great." She pushed up from the desk and her eyes caught mine. A spark of something that'd been missing lately was back in her baby blues. Did I really want to snuff it out again?

I pointed to her computer. "Whatcha doing?"

A grin bloomed, the likes of which could compare to one of Mama's peonies. "You're not going to believe it, Derek. I got a call from an old client, and she wants to hire me." She came around the desk, her hands fluttering like a kaleidoscope of butterflies. "Well, it's not technically she who wants to hire me, but a friend of hers, which actually makes it even more perfect, because there's not even a hint of me breaking the non-compete clause in this case. I mean, if Elodie wanted me to do another job for her, it's not really a breach of contract, because she sought me out, not the other way around."

If I didn't know better, I'd have thought she ingested copious amounts of caffeine. I hadn't seen her this animated since she was a kid. "Slow down a minute."

Her cheeks turned a becoming shade of pink. “Sorry, it’s just the first sign of anything good in such a long time. I’m meeting with the client tomorrow, and I was showing Jenna my design ideas.”

Her excitement was as contagious as a yawn, and the last thing I wanted to do was stifle it. How could I broach the subject of Nicky without tromping all over her joy-filled toes?

“That’s great, Charlie. You feel up to another project right now?”

She pressed her folded hands beneath her chin and looked up at me. “I have to, Derek. This could be the first crucial step in making this crazy idea successful. I mean, Elodie and this new client she’s got for me have an endless number of contacts. Word of mouth is the best advertisement, you know.”

I squeezed her upper arm when what I wanted to do was wrap her in a hug. But if what Nicky said was true, I’d not likely have a right to more. “So, I’ve heard. That’s great news.”

“I suppose we’d better get downstairs and see if the installer needs anything.” She started to pass me, but I put out an arm to halt her.

“He’s fine for now, Charlie. I was hoping we could talk a minute.”

“Yeah, sure.” Her eyes shuttered with wariness, which might could have been the answer I was seeking. “What’s on your mind?”

“I don’t want to burst your bubble, but I thought you should know Nicky’s of the mind you two are going to make a go of it.” I surveilled her for any sign of what was to come so I’d not get knocked off kilter.

She folded her arms and chewed on the inside of her cheek for a beat or two—long enough to break my heart. “I agreed to counseling, Derek. That’s it.”

I rubbed my forehead as if doing so would miraculously

bless me with wisdom. Rubbing a bottle and expecting a genie was more likely. "So, it's true. Y'all are giving it another shot."

She dropped her head. "I don't know what to do, Derek. If I'm going to have this baby, it'll need a daddy."

A word jumped out. "What d'you mean *If*? You're not talking about—"

"No!" Her chin shot up. "Of course not. You know better than that. You also know I've miscarried twice, so I'm not getting my hopes up."

I took a deep breath. "Is the baby the only reason you're willing to try?"

"Absolutely."

Talk about history repeating itself. "Does Nicky know that?"

She tilted her head as if giving it some thought. "He ought to since it was his idea."

"Ought to doesn't mean he does, you know. He can twist an idea better 'n a politician."

She shrugged. "I can't help that."

"You don't need him, Charlie."

"Maybe not. But I vowed for better or worse. He's just asking for one more chance at the better. I'm not making any promises, but I told him I'd at least try counseling. You only have yourself to blame for putting that asinine idea into his head." She arched her brows at me. "But we both know he won't last two sessions. And in two shakes, he'll backtrack on that promise to get a real job. I'm just giving him enough rope."

I wasn't so sure about that. I'd underestimated him before, and I wasn't about to stand around and watch while he proved me wrong again.

CHAPTER TWENTY-NINE

March 2016
Charlie

Although Charlie had been stewing in oodles of anger for the last week, she schooled her face and heart to hide it for this one day. It might not have been tucked away as neatly as a pew Bible, but at least it wouldn't be visible to Mama G and Derek. They had enough grief to cloak them in a blanket of sadness without adding Nicky's transgressions and Charlie's surliness to the mix.

Spring was supposed to be the heralding of new birth and promises. Instead, the first day of the season was cold and dreary, as if God ordered it for this particular occasion. Every tree and bloom planted among the cemetery to soften grief and manifest hope was cloaked in sepia tones. The last time Charlie stood at a graveside, Mama G was there to help hold up Nana. Now their roles were reversed.

How strange it was to mingle among mourners without even an iota of memory from her own parents' memorial service. There was no funeral, from what she'd been told, because their bodies were never recovered. Without that closure, it seemed the loss weighed heavier on her heart. If she'd been able to look upon their faces, peaceful in death, then maybe the anguish of loss would have been diluted some.

A hand rested at the low of her back and jolted Charlie from her musings. Every muscle in her body went taut with the need to pull away from Nicky, but she took a couple of deep breaths and stayed put. He might have been a dirty, lying sack of drivel, but he was also a child grieving over the loss of his daddy. That gave him a temporary pass.

As soon as the graveside service was over, Charlie slipped over to Mama G. She and Nana escorted her to the funeral limousine lest she stumble over her despondency. Nicky and Derek followed like two little boys who didn't have a clue how to handle their mama's grief, which came as no surprise to Charlie. Leastways, where Nicky was concerned. Everyone else might think his eyes were bloodshot from crying, but Charlie knew it was from sleepless nights on the couch and too much moonshine. Neither of which had been brought on by sadness.

By the time the funeral entourage arrived at Mama G's house, the church ladies had every conceivable type of cheese, chicken and potato casserole laid out on fold-up tables. Add to it enough Jell-o and congealed fruit salad to feed a third-world country, it was a wonder their hollowed-out metal legs didn't crumble under the weight. Charlie never understood the need to feed grief, but she figured comfort food received its moniker for a reason.

Nicky slipped out the back door with a group of younger cousins, and Charlie drew in a relieved breath. No doubt they had a keg out in the barn, but at this point, she didn't care. At least with him out of the room, she could relax the Stepford-wife smile. She put enough food on her paper plate for show and found a semi-quiet corner. If Nicky wasn't back in an hour, she'd take the car and let him thumb a ride to Nashville.

"You mind a little company?"

She tilted her head back until her eyes connected with Derek's. Aside from a quick greeting earlier, she'd not had an opportunity to catch up with him. A pain she well understood lurked in the depths of his eyes, and unlike Nicky's, they were clear as the Mediterranean Sea.

He didn't wait for an answer but squatted on the floor and leaned his back against the wall. His long body was squished between her chair and Mama G's china hutch.

"I'm so sorry about your daddy, Derek." A knot fisted in her throat. Sure enough, she was hurting over the loss of Sam, too, but attached to that emotion, like a fly caught in a web, was the upset over her memories of Mama and Daddy and the sad state of her marriage. She couldn't be in Derek's presence without being hit, like a pie in the face, with that mockery.

He stretched out his legs and rested a plate-full of food on his thighs. "I was thinking on how hard it must've been for you, Charlie, losing your parents when you did."

How was it that Derek always seemed to have a clear line to Charlie's emotions when they rarely saw each other? Her gaze caught on Mama G being pulled into a back-breaking hug by one of her friends. "At least they went together."

He shook his head and took a deep breath as if to dispel the darkness. "Tell me what's happening in your world, sweet Charlie. How's the career going?"

She knew he was only making small talk to avoid the heavier stuff, but she could play along. "It's good." She moved a glob of cheese around her plate. "My boss is a little tough to take at times." She forced a laugh. "But I figure if I can get along with her, I can get along with anyone. At least I've got my own clients, and if all goes well, I'll be bringing in some decent money."

"Yeah? How's Nicky's music career going?" There was a knife-sharp edge to his tone.

"You should ask him." She shoveled a bite of mac 'n' cheese into her mouth to buy some time. If she started talking about her womanizing husband, there was no telling where the conversation would lead. Knowing Derek, he'd hightail it out to the barn and take off a piece of Nicky's hide.

"Still waiting for his big break, I suppose."

Every conversation about Nicky with Derek was like that old movie, *Groundhog Day*. Wash, rinse, repeat. Would it ever be any different? "What about you?"

Derek's eyebrows shot up. "What *about* me?"

Her irritation with him got all twisted up with her anger at Nicky. "You've been playing soldier boy now for fourteen years. You ready to give it up yet?"

"And do what?"

"I don't know. Maybe come home and help out your mama. Run your daddy's farm." She gave him a pointed look. "Get a life." She was wrong to fuss at him, and she knew it, but there it was.

"You can't be serious, Charlie." A muscle jumped along his jawline. "You want to jump all over someone about being irresponsible, you might start with your husband. Where is he, by the way? Out back drinking with the boys?"

Charlie fisted her hands and drew in a few steady breaths. He was right. She was firing her anger on the wrong target.

She sighed. "Nicky's doing what Nicky does best." Disappointing her. "But good or bad, I've come to expect that from him."

Groundhog Day.

Derek—2016

It was near midnight, and Derek lay in his childhood bed staring up at the ceiling, too edgy to sleep. There was enough moonlight pouring through the open window to catch the glimmer of the slow-moving fan blades. *Whup, whup, whup.* Brought to mind the last helicopter he'd flown in, though not near as much velocity or power. His life was an odd dichotomy of independence and subordination. He'd found a comfort of sorts in the regimented schedule and expectations. It wasn't that he didn't have to think for himself, but that there was someone else accountable besides him and God if things went south.

But it wasn't the kind of life he'd want to foist on a wife and children, both of which he assumed he'd have by now. Thirty-one and no prospects.

The sound of a thud, followed by muttering, broke into his thoughts. Mama had taken to bed as soon as the house emptied of mourners, and Derek had stewed some over it. The idea that he'd never see Daddy again was on par with losing a limb. How much worse it must be for Mama. If there was anything he could do to alleviate her distress some, he'd do it.

He climbed out of the too-small bed and slipped into the jeans he'd flung over his old desk chair. The only room he'd ever known suddenly seemed like it didn't fit anymore. It wasn't the size of it, either. It was the baseball trophies lined up on the shelf Daddy'd built, the odd animal bones he'd found on the farm over the years, and the pictures he'd tucked under a hand-me-down blotter on his desk.

Pictures of Charlie when she was no more than a kid.

If she wanted to know why he didn't give up playing

soldier boy and come on home, all she had to do was look in the mirror. But if Mama needed him, he'd surely find a way to do the right thing. After all, duty was what he was born to.

He maneuvered the stairs like he was avoiding land mines, each creak and squeak ingrained in his memory. How many times had he snuck up after breaking curfew, where one misstep would tattle on him like a whiny five-year-old?

Once downstairs, he looked past the dining room to see a faint glow coming from the kitchen. Mama was either shuffling around, talking to herself, or the house was haunted by a grieving ghost. Either way, Derek thought it best to see for himself. Last thing he wanted to do, though, was cause Mama to have a heart attack by sneaking up on her.

"That you, Mama?" He called out as he passed through the dining room.

"Land sakes, son, who else would it be?" The cutting voice was not Mama talking, but the grief.

He stopped at the kitchen entrance and watched as she filled a kettle with water and put it on the stove to heat. "Can't sleep?"

"Not used to having that big bed all to myself."

Derek couldn't help but smile. The "big bed" was a double. The grinned died, though, with the thought it most likely felt like a king with Daddy's body no longer taking up more than his share.

Mama glanced over her shoulder. "You wanna cup of tea, Derek?"

Tea was as palatable as dirty dishwater, but it would give him an excuse to sit with her a spell. "Sure thing, Mama. Need some help?"

She turned and crossed her arms, a smile flirting at the edge of her mouth. "I think I can manage to pour boiling water over a tea bag. But if you got a hole gnawing at your insides, there's plenty of leftovers in the fridge. Miss Lacy's double chocolate cake might go down good with a cup of tea."

"Better with a glass of milk." Derek moved to the fridge and rummaged around until he found the platter with half a cake wrapped in plastic. He snagged that and the milk. If he was going to be up half the night, might as well enjoy it.

"You wanna slice, Mama?"

"Heavens, no." The kettle began its whistle, and she plucked it off the stove. "I'll be up all night." She poured water into a tall cup, deposited the kettle back on the stove, and carried her tea to the kitchen table.

Derek set his cake and milk across from her and sat. "You must be feeling a little lost right about now."

She blew at the steaming cup before taking a tentative sip. "Never thought a heart attack would get your daddy, that's for sure. Don't rightly know what I'll do with myself."

Mama was only in her mid-fifties—still young by any standard—but not spry enough to work the farm. "You don't have to figure anything out yet. Give it some time."

"I suppose the land will have to go fallow for the time being." She took another sip.

Derek felt as if he was being pulled in two directions, and yet it wasn't a toss-up over which was right. Family over self. He slid the cake aside without taking a bite and leaned his elbows on the table. "Look, Mama, if you want me to come home and take care of things here, I'm more than willing to do that."

She rubbed her thumb over the cup handle, her mouth turned down. "Is that what you want, son? Are you of a mind to leave the service?"

"I don't rightly know what you'll do if I don't. It's not like Nicky will step up and help out." He swallowed back the flood of anger at his brother. Nicky couldn't manage to sacrifice one day in honor of Daddy's life, let alone his cobbled-up dream of becoming the next Luke Bryan.

Mama placed her hand on Derek's and squeezed. "Don't you worry yourself over me, son. Your daddy was smart with the money, and I don't need to work the farm to make ends meet." She pulled back and smiled. "Besides which, I'm a lot stronger than I look."

"I believe that," he said.

Her eyes grew shiny. "Your daddy, he was so proud of you. Every time he shared with friends or relatives about what you were doing, he would grin like a mule eating briars."

Derek swallowed the sudden lump that threatened his airway.

"You take after him, you know." She caught a tear with a finger as shaky as her smile. "You already know this, but the reason he married so late was 'cause he did eight years in the service himself before he was ready to settle down."

Derek nodded. "Yes, ma'am, I sure know it."

"Nothing more important to him than God, family, and country."

Derek picked up his fork and poked at the chocolate frosting. "So, who does Nicky take after? You?" He wanted to get the focus off himself and hoped Mama would catch the humor in his tone.

She laughed. "Lordy, mercy, no. Truth is, I think he's a lot like my older brother, Billy."

"Billy?" The name tugged at some familiar story, but Derek didn't remember it. "Remind me."

"He was actually a friend of your daddy's, which is how we met, you know. The two of them was like two peas in a pod growing up. Can't rightly remember one without the other."

Derek remembered now. Daddy and Uncle Bill were ten

years older than Mama. He died before Derek was ever born. "It was a car accident, wasn't it?"

She nodded, her eyes looking off into the past. "It was a sad day, that's for sure. Billy had a creative streak in him to beat the band. He could play pert near any instrument he set his mind to, but the fiddle was his preference. And boy, howdy, could he sing. Jus' like Nicky."

It might could be Derek's estimation of Nicky's talents were tinged with a layer of bitterness. Putting time in to achieve his dreams suddenly didn't seem so different than Derek's focus on his military career.

CHAPTER THIRTY

Charlie

The medley of a lone mockingbird woke me in the wee hours of the morning, and I laid with my eyes closed as its sad refrain washed over me. Without thought, I turned on my side and reached out for Dog, but my hand connected with nothing more than air. It took a split second to remember he was no longer my faithful companion. It was enough to make a body cry, but I'd done more than my share of shedding tears lately.

The big, red numbers on the digital clock proclaimed it just after three. I flicked on the bedside lamp and squinted at the sudden brightness. No sense trying to go back to sleep, so I pushed off the sheet that covered me and climbed from bed. For the first time in weeks, I craved a cup of coffee, but I'd have to settle for herbal tea. I wasn't taking chances with this pregnancy. It might not stick any better than the others, but it wouldn't be because I didn't follow the rules.

I collected the light robe lying across the end of my bed and padded downstairs with whisper soft steps so as not to wake Darlene. Once I had my tea, I snuck back up to my bedroom with my laptop tucked under one arm. I was supposed to meet the new client Elodie solicited on my behalf the next day, and although I had no idea what her decor style was, it couldn't hurt to do a little research now that I had Wi-Fi again. I'd forgotten how dependent I was on it since living off the grid, so to speak.

Once I got situated on the bed, my tea beside me, and my computer propped with a pillow on my folded legs, I reached into the nightstand drawer for a pad in case I needed to take notes. But it wasn't paper my fingers touched. It took a heartbeat to recognize the smooth hardness as Daddy's leather-bound Bible, which I hadn't thought of since I stuck it there the week before.

I set the computer aside and placed the good book on my lap. The cover was smooth as calfskin and worn shiny in places. The tissue-thin pages crackled when I turned them, and it was a wonder the pen Daddy used to scrawl his notes didn't wear clear through to the other side.

What was that verse that'd gone through my head days before? *Deep calls to deep* or some such. I twisted to get to my laptop and typed the words into Google search engine. A quick scan of the results had me flipping through the Bible until I came to Psalms. It'd have been faster to look at the table of contents, but that would have made me feel like a cheat. It might have been years since I stepped foot into a church, but some things were ingrained.

I flipped the pages until I came to 42:7, and with my voice a shade above a whisper, read the words, "*Deep calls unto deep at the noise of Your waterfalls; All Your waves and billows have gone over me.*" I didn't know what it meant, but Daddy had written *I need to sense Your presence in my affliction* along the margin. What hardships was he referring to? Did they have anything to do with their assignment in the mission field?

Once back in the states, I'd had no desire to delve into the past or reflect on what I'd seen a half a world away. I didn't discuss my childhood in the Congo with friends or teachers, and neither Nana or Pawpaw had ever brought it up. It wasn't until now that it struck me as odd. Unless the idea of it was too painful, or they already knew more than I could have ever told them.

My heart beating like a bass drum, I cleared the search engine and typed *The Congo, 1990-2002*. I hit a goldmine with almost 200,000 results, but I didn't have to look any farther than the first few entries for my brain to make the connection. Second Congo War 1998-2003. Had I been so blind back then that I was unaware, or had I blocked it from my memory, just as I had Mama and Daddy's deaths? Uprisings, displacement, starvation, malnutrition. The words from the article jumped out at me as if screaming accusations to a self-involved little girl.

How many times had I believed my life was unfair, as if I'd been neglected or deemed unimportant? But I had never suffered the likes of which the Congolese had, according to the article. Had the missionaries alongside Mama and Daddy protected the village they served or was my memory faulty? Wouldn't I have known if Mose and those she called family were malnourished?

"Charlie?" Darlene's voice on the other side of my door broke through my thoughts. "You okay?"

Had I woken her? A quick glance at the clock showed it was almost five. I cleared my throat before answering. "Come in, Darlene."

The door swung open, and she stood at the threshold in

striped pajama bottoms and a t-shirt. "Thought I heard you shufflin' 'round and wanted to check up on you."

I pushed the article to the back of my mind and closed the laptop. "Couldn't sleep. Did I wake you?"

"Nah. I was gettin' ready to mosey on down for a cup of coffee and saw the light on under your door. You sure you're all right? You look to be feelin' poorly."

"Nothing new about that lately." I caught the wrinkle between her brows. "This is a little early even for you, isn't it? Are *you* doing okay?"

The fact she didn't answer right off wasn't a good sign. "Been chewin' on a couple things, is all."

I swung my legs over the side of the bed. If she was going to give me bad news, I'd best be prepared. "I'm all ears."

She worked her mouth some as if thinking about the best approach. "It's come to mind I might be gettin' a tad too comfortable 'round here."

If that was the worst she had for me, I was golden. "That's a bad thing?"

She nodded. "I need to find me a place to live permanent like."

Darlene had seemed so at home, I hadn't considered she might not want to stay. "You don't like it here?"

She held up her hands. "Oh, no, ain't that a'tall. But you know the sayin' about comp'ny and fish."

"Where would you go?"

"Don't rightly know." She folded her arms. "But I surely do 'preciate all you done for me, Charlie. Jus' can't keep takin' advantage."

The thought of Darlene leaving was just about as bad as losing Dog. "I think it's been the other way around. You've been a Godsend." The big ol' house would be lonely without her. "But if you would rather live on your own, I get it. I'm not exactly easy to get along with these days, especially with the hormones and such."

"You kiddin' me?" Her eyes went wide. "Ain't got nothin' on me when I was muckin' through my stuff. You've been pure joy."

"Then stay." I sounded like a lost little kid begging for a friend, but I didn't care. I hadn't gotten what I wanted in the past probably because I didn't ask. Wasn't there a Bible verse about that? You receive not because you ask not, or some such thing? "I don't know how I'm going to do everything on my own, Darlene. Jenna's a help, but she's got her own family to tend to."

A smile spread as wide as the Mississippi on Darlene's face. "You mean it? 'Cause I can surely be more help. You bein' pregnant and all. And it ain't gonna get easier once you start takin' on more design jobs."

I pressed a hand to my heart. "That would be amazing, Darlene. You've already made yourself invaluable, and I can't tell you how much it's helped."

"It's decided then." Her mouth hardened. "Only one thing."

I sighed. I knew it was too good to be true. "What's that?"

"You git yourself to a doctor afore too long. With your history, you can't be too careful." She wagged a finger at me as she walked out the door.

Somehow, knowing Darlene was going to be around made it easier to breathe. I might not know anything else, but I knew she was where she belonged. And it was by God's divine grace. He surely worked in the strangest ways.

Derek

For a specially trained, tactical expert it was hard to admit a stump in a Louisiana swamp had a higher IQ than me where Charlie was concerned. While being on mission, it was easy enough to forget the past in order to stay focused on the job at hand— oft-times life and death situations that were part of Special Forces. But home for only a couple months, and my Green Beret buds wouldn't recognize me. Heck, I didn't recognize me.

I always thought God had a plan somewhere down the line for Charlie and me. Isn't that why I was always available to fly home whenever a family crisis occurred? Couldn't rightly chalk it up to coincidence. Didn't believe in them. Only God could've planned for me to be back at headquarters in Fort Bragg, North Carolina every time the call came in that a family member had died. And even if Charlie's grandparents weren't technically my family, I was given leave just the same.

It appeared I had it all wrong. Somehow, I got my spiritual signals crossed. Might be Charlie needed me to be a broad shoulder to cry on, but that didn't mean the good Lord intended it to be anything more. I'd honed patience to an art form, but no one would know it to look at me now. It was time to call it, otherwise I might not survive this present so-called mission. Just wished I'd have seen the light before moving my office space into Charlie's house. That's what I get for jumping in before I got my marching orders.

Didn't know what to do about the situation I created, and God wasn't weighing in. I was halfway to Nashville to meet up with a potential client, lamenting the likes of which would make Jeremiah take notice, when my cell cut in. Didn't recognize the number but talking to anyone was a reprieve.

I connected via Bluetooth. "Derek Daniels."

"Mr. Daniels, this is Guy Richardson from the Billy Graham

group. I'm calling in response to your application. This a good time to talk?" He had a down home twang that felt as comfortable as a pair of old Levi's.

It took a moment to switch gears as I'd all but given up on hearing from them. "Yes, sir. Good a time as any. How are you today?"

"I'm good, Mr. Daniels. And yourself?"

"Can't complain." That wasn't the God's honest truth, but I didn't guess he'd want to hear about my relationship woes.

"I know it's been a while since you've submitted your application. Are you still interested in the program?"

"Yes, sir, I surely am." Traffic was light on the 65, so I decided to continue the drive. Didn't want to make a bad impression by showing up to an appointment late.

"That's great. You want to handle the interview right now, or would you prefer I call back another time?"

"If you have the time, now works for me." I moved to the right lane and put the truck in cruise control. When I'd submitted my application at Mark's urging, I wasn't so sure deployment was something I was ready for. Now, a couple months later, it seemed as if God was opening a door I longed to enter.

"Good. I have to say, your experience is quite impressive. We have a real need for ex-military, especially those with a long career in Special Forces, to be a part of our mission field. I see you were medically discharged."

"I was. Helicopter accident."

"I'm sorry to hear that. Would it limit your ability to perform your duties?"

"Depends." I wasn't going to sugar-coat it. "I'm not a hundred percent when it comes to heavy lifting, but for the most part it doesn't slow me down."

"We can always work around that. Tell me, Mr. Daniels, why do you want to be a chaplain for the Billy Graham Team?"

That was an easy enough question. "I figure if God's allowed me to work in unique circumstances for a number of years, and kept me safe through it all, He expects I'd use it to minister to others. I love the Lord, Mr. Richardson. I just want the opportunity to use my gifts to share that love with those in need."

The conversation continued until I exited onto the 70. By the time I reached my destination, I was accepted into the program. It would mean a trip to Asheville, North Carolina for three-day training, but I was ready to be anywhere but here.

I was ten minutes early. I could go inside and wait or give my little brother one last shot. He hadn't responded to my job offer, and I thought if he was serious about wanting a chance with Charlie, he'd have jumped on it. Daddy always said, "When in doubt, err on the side of grace." Might be futile on my part, but I dialed up Nicky.

I half expected the call to go to voicemail, but he answered on the third ring. "Yeah, bro, what's up?"

"Hey, Nicky. I'm in your neck of the woods."

"Yeah?"

"Yep. Meeting with a potential client and thought we could connect after. You never gave me an answer to my job offer."

No response.

"You there?"

"Oh, man, you shoulda called sooner. I gotta get over to the Honky Tonk for a gig." Which was answer enough.

"Next time, huh?" But I knew better. And although it riled me some, it was also a relief. No way Nicky and I could work together without one of us going off on the other.

"About that, Derek. I just can't see myself working security."

Him and me both "Don't give it another thought." As if he would. I had to about bite my tongue off to keep from grilling him about his plans. Maybe Charlie was right after all. Two shakes was all it took. He didn't want a day job, and Charlie couldn't trust him with the status quo. But it wasn't my business. I was done being put in the middle.

CHAPTER THIRTY-ONE

Charlie

There weren't enough Saltines in Tennessee to quiet the queasiness in my stomach as I drove the hour to Leiper's Fork to meet up with Elodie and her friend. I could have blamed it on the pregnancy, but there was a hefty chance it was nerves. One part excitement to three parts pure fear. I'd gone from design school to working under the tutelage of Patrice, who might have been difficult at times, but she'd also been my safety net. I'd romanticized the endeavor of running my own business in my mind without taking into account the pitfalls.

My knuckles were white from the death-like grip I had on the steering wheel as I drove up 41-A. The constriction in my chest lessened some by the time I got on the 840. Then I passed Thompson's Station, and the only thing that took my breath away was the view out my windshield where thick trees and farmland rivaled only Ireland in its emerald beauty.

Every time I'd been to Leiper's Fork, it felt as if I'd been transported back in time. Of course, every year, that fantasy became a little harder to sink into, what with all the new homes that were continually being built. Still, if I was blessed with a major windfall, I'd find myself a piece of land there and settle in pretty as you please. It wouldn't have to be a big place either—something quaint I could renovate to my liking with enough land to plant an English garden and a few vegetables.

I shook the fantasy loose from my imagination. The fact that Leiper's Fork was just a hop, skip, and a jump from Franklin made it one of the hottest places to buy. Which meant one of the priciest, to boot. Best to pay attention to the map app on my phone if I wanted to land at the right house. I should be thanking my lucky stars for the opportunity to make enough to keep me fed without spinning impossible dreams.

But when I pulled up to the residence where I was to meet Elodie and her friend, that ol' lust made a bit of a comeback. The drive up to the farmhouse-style home must have been close to five hundred feet, bordered by green grass and a grove of maple, poplar, and sugar berry. The house itself sat atop a knoll. Quaint it was not. If my figuring was correct, it was somewhere in the ballpark of six-thousand square feet, and although the property was established, the house looked to be new.

I parked next to Elodie's Mercedes in the spacious drive with more than a twinge of embarrassment. My Lexus would have been low brow for this estate; Derek's daddy's truck looked to be a blight. Even so, as I climbed the pave stone steps leading to the wrap-around porch, I straightened my spine and lifted my chin. There was no need to feel shame for circumstances I couldn't control.

Before I could ring the bell, Elodie appeared on the other side of the glass arched, double doors, a grin splitting her face.

“There you are, Charlotte. Come in, come in.” She threw open the door and stood back so I could enter.

Once inside, the cooler air washed over me as I took in what I could from my limited viewpoint. The wide-plank hardwood floors contrasted nicely with the natural tones of the walls and trim. From the foyer, I could see the open-concept family room, dining area, and kitchen. The windows were narrow, tall, and plentiful. It didn’t appear expense was spared in building this beauty. And what a canvas it would be, too.

“Hey, Charlotte.” The voice echoed in the emptiness.

I swiveled around to meet Elodie’s friend, Karly. She was about as big as a minute and not at all what I’d expected. “Karly, right?” I stuck out my hand. “It’s wonderful to meet you.”

Her dark, curly hair bounced as she pumped my hand, and her eyes sparkled with excitement. “Elodie raved about your work. I was hopin’ you could make this place a real home for me and my husband, Clive.” Her expression was warm and welcoming, with no artifice. She’d probably feel right at home in Derek’s Ford truck.

“It’s gorgeous, that’s for sure. Was it just built?”

“Brand, spankin’ new,” Karly said. “I swear I can still smell the paint.”

I sniffed. “I think you’re right.” We both laughed.

Elodie touched my arm. “I have a phone call to make, if y’all don’t mind. I’ll just step out onto the porch.”

“Sure thing,” Karly said. “I’m goin’ to show Charlotte around, so holler when you come back in if you don’t find us.”

I noticed Karly’s feet were bare, and I moved to slip off my shoes.

She waved her hands as if to stop me. “You don’t need to do that. I’m not particular, it’s just I’m more comfortable barefoot.”

"You and me both." I placed my shoes by the door. I wasn't about to take a chance marring even one square inch of the dark wood. "Where do you want to start?"

Karly took me on a tour through five bedrooms, six bathrooms, a home office, and my ultimate dream kitchen—and I didn't even care for cooking—and ended up on the back patio overlooking the in-ground pool. A smaller building, created in the same style, sat about a half-acre from the main house.

"Can I get y'all some sweet tea?" Karly offered. "Then maybe we could sit out here and talk some about what you got in mind."

"That sounds perfect. Do you need some help?"

She gave me a crooked grin. "No ma'am. If there's one thing I'm good at, it's servin'. You sit a spell, and I'll be right back."

A wrought iron dining set perched beneath the shade of a tongue-and-groove enclosed overhang. Three large ceiling fans circulated the air, making the temperature tolerable. I sank into one of the cushioned chairs and closed my eyes with a sigh. Pregnancy had a way of zapping the energy clear from a body.

"Karly said she'd be right out. She needed to visit the ladies' room."

I opened my eyes as Elodie appeared with a tray laden with drinks and a plate of cookies. She set the tray down and handed me a tall glass of iced tea. "So, what do y'all think of this place?"

"It's stunning but doesn't hold a candle to its owner. When you said you had a friend, I expected someone more—"

"Old, like me," Elodie cut in with a laugh as she sat across from me.

I grinned. "Let's say more established and leave it at that. How'd the two of you meet, anyway?"

"Her mother and mine grew up together. When Mama called and told me Karly and her new husband were moving out here from West Virginia, I offered to take her under my wing."

"What is she, twenty?"

"I'm not quite that young," Karly said from behind me.

Heat crawled up my neck and bloomed on my cheeks as I turned to offer an apology. "I'm sorry, Karly. I didn't mean—"

"Are you kiddin'?" She reached for a glass and sat. "It'd take a whole lot more than that to insult me. Believe me, I feel as if someone plucked me from my one-room apartment in the Appalachians and dropped me here as some kind of psychological experiment."

Elodie laughed. "That's what happens when you marry the hottest thing in country music next to Keith Urban."

The shock of it left me speechless, though I didn't know why. The Nashville area was home to a large number of country artists, including the aforementioned Keith Urban. I suppose it just hit a little too close to home.

As I drove away at the end of our meeting, I couldn't totally tamp down the green-eyed monster that skimmed just beneath the surface. Had things been different, Nicky might've been in the same position as Karly's husband, and I could be living the life. Of course, that'd take a lot of "if'n", as Nana would say. And knowing my husband as I did, it would've just been more opportunity for sleazing around.

Life might not have been perfect, but even in my precarious predicament, it was good enough.

Derek

Whenever someone would tell me they heard the Lord speak directly to them on a regular basis, I'd have to wonder if drink was involved, or maybe they had a touch of schizophrenia. Not that I didn't believe God could do so, but it wasn't likely. Once in a while, yes. Regular-like, not so much. From my experience, it was more a thought laid on my heart, or someone who appeared out of the blue to answer a prayer I'd just uttered.

And so it was when my eyes lit onto Brian in the paint department at the hardware store. Hadn't seen him since I joined up, but I'd have known that red hair and crooked grin if we were eighty.

"Derek Daniels, if you ain't a sight for sore eyes." He gave me a dude hug and slapped me on the back. "What's it been? Twenty years?"

"About that. Summer we graduated if I remember correctly."

"Can you believe it?" Brian shook his head. "You on leave or home for good?"

"I'm officially a free man. Been back a few months. What about you? How's life?"

"Can't complain." He crossed his arms. "Not that anyone'd care if I did. Where you living?"

I grimaced. "For the time being, out back of my mama's house. Haven't had a chance to look for a place of my own."

His eyebrows shot up. "You interested in buying? Tammy and me just had a place built outside of town, and I'm fixin' to sell our old one."

Ask and ye shall receive. "Tammy your wife?"

"Going on seventeen years."

"Seriously?" Hard to imagine anyone being my age and married that long. "Kids?"

"Three." He grinned like a proud papa. "Caleb's near sixteen, Kelsey's thirteen, and then there's Lexie who's only six months. She was our surprise baby, which is why we built us a bigger place."

Couldn't rightly remember the last time I envied someone but didn't mistake that feeling for anything else. Married with three kids. Is that what I gave up staying in the service so long?

"There ain't anything wrong with the house we're selling. Just too small for all them kids."

"I sure need to get out of my mama's place. When's it going on the market?"

"Soon as I get a few repairs done. Course, if you're handy with a hammer, we could do a deal that'd save us both some money."

The idea of bypassing house tours and the usual negotiating was enough to make me jump on the chance. "When can I see it?"

"Now, if you like. I'm just picking up paint to do over a couple of the rooms, but if you're interested, might as well wait and see what you think. Let you pick out your own colors."

The thought of it was enough to paralyze me. As long as it wasn't army green, I'd be thrilled.

Half an hour later, I parked my truck behind Brian's in the driveway of a modest, two-story vinyl and brick house. Looked to be in decent shape, clean and simple landscape, on a half-acre or so lot. If the inside and price was as impressive, I'd be a fool not to jump on it.

"This is it." Brian tucked his hands into the front pockets of his jeans and led the way up the drive. "Two car garage opens up on the side. We got a storage barn out back, built by this Amish guy out in Etheridge, so you don't have to clutter the garage. Three bedrooms, all upstairs, two and a half baths."

He unlocked the front door and pushed it open so I could go in ahead of him. Didn't expect it to feel so spacious what with him needing a bigger place. Hardwood floors throughout and a newly renovated kitchen were also a bonus.

When we finished the tour, I was ready to make an offer. "What's the catch?" There had to be something wrong with it. "You said there's some repairs need doing."

He chewed the inside of his cheek and nodded. "Toilets got a bit of a wobble to them, so they need to be reset. The H-VAC system works, but it's old. Might need to replace that in the next couple a years. Roof's in decent shape, but could use a patch job here and there. And, course, the whole inside could use a coat of paint."

Nothing I couldn't handle. "You know what it would go for in this market?"

"Had a realtor come in and give me an idea. Didn't sign a contract with him, though. Thought I should get the repairs done first. We considered renting it out instead of selling, but truth is, we could use the money more 'n the investment."

"So, what's your 'as is' price?"

Brian quoted a number well below what I'd expected. Then again, what did I know about real estate? "You want, we can have an inspector come through and check her out if you're concerned."

"Seems to me you were upfront about what needs to get done."

He grinned. "It ain't likely I'm gonna try to pull one over on an old friend, and a Green Beret to boot. You could kick my butt from here to Sunday."

I laughed. "Doubtful. You know anyone who could write us up a contract?"

"Yep. What about a mortgage company? I got an in with one of them, too."

"No need. I'll be paying cash."

His eyes shot open. "Maybe I shoulda joined the military instead of slaving away at construction."

"The pay's not all that good, it's just I don't have nothing to spend it on. You got the better end of the deal, trust me." I'd have traded every penny in my bank account for the life he had.

"What's say we grab us some lunch and make a few calls?" He slapped me on the back. "We can work out the details and get the ball rolling."

We stepped outside and a woman standing on the porch next door called out. "Hey, y'all. Is Tammy with you?"

"Hey, Celia. Tammy's not here. Just showing the house to a friend of mine." He lowered his voice. "The neighbors are pretty friendly, too. Celia takes a liking to you, might be you won't stay single all that long."

CHAPTER THIRTY-TWO

Charlie

Families were complicated, most especially when they weren't connected by blood. Mama G had been more mother to me than my own for as long as I could remember. But, with Nicky in the mix, working through the intricacies of those tangled relationships was like trying to unravel a mess of necklaces that'd been sitting on the bottom of a jewelry box. One knot leads to another until I'm tempted to dump the whole lot into the trash. But people aren't so easily dismissed, Mama G especially. She might've claim me as a daughter, but when getting down to the nitty gritty of things, she would side with Nicky every time. It's a what mothers did.

Knowing that, I let the days slip by to avoid the inevitable confrontation. If my own mama were alive, she'd have known about my pregnancy long before now. The line between waiting long enough to talk to Mama G about it, and waiting too long, was more than two weeks past. Each day added to the weight of my uneasiness until the guilt of it was too much.

Since Darlene had proclaimed my activity at home wasn't good for the baby, she'd all but benched me from anything more strenuous than lifting a cup of tea. I needed a brisk walk to clear the cobwebs and tiptoe back into an honest-to-God conversation with...well, God. A thunderstorm blew through Shelbyville mid-day leaving behind a slight coolness to the moist air and the scent no perfumer could ever replicate.

I snuck out before Darlene could ask me where I was going, and the rebellion was refreshing. I'd been cooped up on my computer all morning, creating design ideas for Karly and contacting suppliers in preparation for our next meeting. I couldn't have asked for an easier first client, and I knew I had the good Lord to thank for that, which I did as I neared my destination.

Mama G's house appeared much too soon, and I hesitated at the edge of the brick pathway where a massive maple tree dripped lingering raindrops onto my head. She'd most likely be out back working in her flowerbed if she was even home. I hadn't bothered to check first. It didn't take a session with Freud to know what was behind my lack of planning. It was my out in case I didn't have the gumption to follow through. If she wasn't expecting me, she couldn't be disappointed if I didn't show up.

My stomach knotted up like a mess of worms as I followed the brick pathway around to the back of the house. Riotous blooms from her begonias and impatiens were bursting along the shady side of the house backdropped by coleus and elephant's ear. I might have been skilled with interior design, but Mama G was a master at beautifying a yard.

I caught sight of her bent over a raised bed of zinnias, marigolds and dahlias that bordered the patio, her back to me. Not wanting to alarm her, I cleared my throat before approaching.

Mama G looked over her shoulder at me and rose while pulling off her gardening gloves. “Well, aren’t you a beam of sunshine on a dark and cloudy day.”

The love that shone through her smile was all it took for tears to press at the back of my eyes. Surely, she knew about my pregnancy, and yet there wasn’t a hint of judgment in her welcome. I crossed the patio, and she enveloped me in a warm hug, relieving the knots in my belly in the process.

I pulled back and fingered a strand of hair off my face. “I should have come sooner. I’m sorry.”

“I don’t imagine the distance between your place and mine was easy to cross.” She cupped my cheek. “But you’re here now. Let me get us something to drink, and we’ll sit a spell.” She dropped the gloves on the patio table and led the way inside.

The kitchen window, set above the sink, was wide open, allowing the slight breeze to set the gingham curtains to fluttering. Nothing ever seemed to change here, as if I stepped back in time where the cares of the world washed away like a refreshing summer storm.

“I don’t imagine you’re having anything caffeinated to drink.” She stood in front of the open Frigidaire as if surveying its contents for something safe to offer me.

“Water is just fine, Mama G. Don’t go to any trouble.”

“Never too much trouble for my favorite girl, but since I don’t have decaf-tea around, water will have to do. However, I can make up for it with some homemade chocolate chip cookies.”

She pulled a few from the white ceramic cookie jar that had sat on the counter for as long as I could remember and placed them on a plate. “Looks to me you could use the calories.” She slid the cookies in front of me.

I took a bite from one and closed my eyes. It was sinful how tasty they were. I relished the flavors on my tongue—buttery chocolate goodness—before swallowing. "I suppose you've got a lot of questions."

"I worked out a tidbit here and there by reading between the lines. Nicky's of a mind that the two of you are getting back together, but if that were true, you would've been by a lot sooner."

"I don't know what I'm going to do yet." I picked off a crumb from a cookie and slipped it into my mouth. "I suppose I'm hedging my bets."

She arched a brow. "I'm not sure I understand."

"I just don't want to make another mistake." I laid my hand on my belly. "I've lost two babies, and if I lose another one, it's not going to be on account of me doing things wrong."

She folded her arms on the table and leaned forward. "Just what do y'all think you did wrong with the other two? If memory serves, you were eating healthy and generally taking good care of yourself."

I nodded. "And yet God didn't see fit to let me keep them."

Mama G narrowed her eyes. "We don't always understand the ways of God, Charlie. But I don't rightly know what this has to do with you giving Nicky another chance."

"God hates divorce. It says so right in the Bible." I held up a hand to stop her when she started to speak. "Before you tell me God doesn't work that way, just like everyone else has, let me tell you what I told them. I know it in my head, but my heart's having a difficult time believing it."

She patted my hand. "I gotta say, sweet girl, you sure are a lot harder on yourself than the good Lord would ever be. And at the risk of coming across disloyal to my own blood, there's also a loophole, so to speak, in the Good Word. I believe you'll find it in the gospel of Matthew. A person's got a right to divorce and remarry in the case of sexual immorality." She shook her head. "God knows I love my boy, but he'll never earn rewards for being faithful."

I remembered some such verse but hadn't given it much consideration. Could be Mama G was right about the grace of God. After all, He did send down a Savior, didn't He?

"It's been right hard on you, Charlie, hasn't it?"

"What's that?

She shrugged. "All of it, I suppose. But I was thinking how hard it must be not having your own mama here. Might be if they were alive, things'd been different."

"Funny you should bring them up." Had Derek told her about me finding the cross and wedding bands? "There's some mystery surrounding their deaths that've come about lately."

"Oh?" She broke a cookie in half, her eyes not meeting mine.

"I don't believe they were killed in a car accident." If I told her I'd always had a sense I was at fault for their deaths, she'd think I was certifiable.

"Oh, goodness, Charlie, will you look at the time." She jumped up like her seat was on fire. "I have a Master Gardner's meeting I plumb forgot about. It wouldn't much matter, but I'm leading it today. Do you mind if we finish up this conversation at a later time?"

She had me out the door before I could utter much of a response. If Mama G hoped to avoid raising suspicion by dismissing me, she did a poor job of it. What did she know that had her as nervous as a cat in a roomful of rocking chairs?

Derek

When I showed up at Charlie's to meet Mark at our new—and temporary—office, relief washed over me when I noted Daddy's truck was missing. It meant Charlie wasn't home, and I didn't have to slink around like I was on a reconnaissance mission to avoid running into her. My resolution to separate myself from her was too raw to survive a testing at this point. My new place was scheduled to close in a couple weeks, but Brian gave me the keys as soon as I signed the papers and said I could move in anytime.

"I swear, Derek, it's easier to keep up with my three-year-old than with you. First you move the office here, now you wanna move the office someplace else." Mark threw his hands in the air. "Didn't we tell Charlie we'd pay for Internet?"

"Don't you worry about that. I got it covered. We got other things to tend to right now. Like this new client I signed on. You figure out what needs to get ordered?"

"I'm on it." He pulled up information on his tablet. "We're doing an alarm system, video surveillance, and remote monitoring." He sat on the edge of my desk. "Now how 'bout you tell me what's going on with you and Charlie."

"Nothing's going on. I didn't expect to buy myself a house so soon, but it was too good a deal to pass up. Makes sense to set up shop there rather than stay here. Besides, it'll be closer for you, too."

"We both know you didn't move us out here in the first place on account of your mama's place being too small. Thought we was getting rent in place of the repairs. What're you gonna do about that?"

"That's between me and Charlie."

He snorted. "Yeah, whatever. No skin off my nose you wanna spend your hard-earned money fixin' up Charlie's house only to end up moving us hither and yon. Just let me know where and when I'm supposed to land."

Movement from outside caught my attention, and for a heartbeat, I thought it was Charlie home from wherever she'd gone off to. But it wasn't her. It was Nicky approaching the outside door of our office.

"What's he doing here?" Mark grumbled. "Thought you said he didn't want to work with us."

I moved across the room to open the door. "Didn't think he was. Maybe he changed his mind."

"Must be a hereditary trait."

"You're hilarious," I said before greeting Nicky. "You looking for me?"

He hitched his chin at Mark as he stepped inside. "I came by to see if I could talk to Charlie, but then I saw your truck here. You know if she's around?"

Mark snorted. "I've a suspicion if she was, we wouldn't be."

I shot him a glare as Nicky asked, "What's he talking about?"

"Don't mind him," I said. "He just doesn't take too kindly to change."

"A revolving door's more like it," Mark mumbled then looked to Nicky. "You decide to accept Derek's generous job offer?"

"Nah." Nicky backed out the door. "Security ain't my thing. You see Charlie, let her know I came by, will you?"

"Hold up," I said. "I'll walk you out."

Nicky made a beeline for his truck like I hadn't said a word, so I nabbed his arm to slow him down.

He pulled out of my grasp but turned to look at me. "What's up?"

Even though I promised to butt out, I had to ask. "How's it going with the contingencies Charlie asked for?"

He twisted his mouth in a grimace. "Contingencies? You make it sound like a contract."

I shrugged. "Kind of is at this point, wouldn't you say?"

"Don't take this wrong, Derek, but it's none of your business." He turned his back on me and headed once again for his truck.

A heat missile of anger struck my core. "You made it my business when you asked me to help."

He waved a dismissive hand without breaking stride. "I got it covered, big brother."

"Yeah?" Disgust at his blasé attitude loosened my tongue, the likes of which I'd later repent for. "How's that job search going for you? And a counselor? You find one yet?"

He whirled on me like I'd insulted his mama. "What d'you care anyway? Hoping I mess it all up so's you can come swooping in to save the day? Always ready to play the hero."

Teeth gritted, I shook my head. "Boy, you are dumber than you look. How many chances you think God's going to give you, huh?"

"God ain't got nothing to do with this." He spewed the words at me.

"The heck He don't. He's the only reason I haven't 'swooped in' like you said and taken every opportunity to win Charlie for myself. You're way too casual with her and that baby she's carrying. Your baby." I emphasized by pointing a finger at him. "And I'd bet my military pension that Charlie's fear of God is the only reason she's giving you any kind of chance. You might want to reconsider your position, not to mention your attitude."

"What're you talking about? Charlie don't even bother to go to church no more."

"Thanks to you."

He planted his hands on his hips. "I never said she couldn't go."

"That's right generous of you." Even he couldn't miss the

sarcasm. Where'd everything with him go south? There was a time he played worship for the church we grew up in, now he acted like God was something he had to scrape off his boots.

"You don't know what you're talking about, Derek. Whatever Charlie's issues with God or religion or whatever you wanna call, it's got nothing to do with me. And it's got nothing to do with you, either. From the moment she lost the first baby, she was done with God." This time, when he turned to leave, I didn't stop him.

Could what Nicky said be true? Did Charlie blame God for her miscarriages? She'd said almost as much herself a time or two, but I'd not taken it too seriously. But Nicky was right about one thing—it wasn't any of my business. Only thing was, the harder I tried to disconnect myself, the more I got sucked back in.

CHAPTER THIRTY-THREE

Charlie

Life was a wonder. I was beginning to see that if I viewed it through the eyes of a loving God, which I'd done little of late, there was a tapestry of beauty on the one side, even if the other was a tangled mess of knots. If someone had told me three months ago I'd lose my job, be living at Nana and Pawpaw's rundown house, separated from Nicky, and going on nine weeks pregnant, I'd have thought they were plumb crazy. Add to that a new business venture, my first design client, and a middle-aged homeless woman living with me...well, there was no way of knowing what direction the day might take.

I woke feeling hopeful for the first time in ages. I'd dreamt of Mama and Daddy holding their brand-new granddaughter, and though I knew it wasn't to come true, it brought me comfort just the same. Maybe it was God's way of speaking to my heart, letting me know that everything would be just fine in the end.

The first thing I noticed when I stepped into the kitchen was that Dog's bed was missing from where I'd tucked it in the alcove between the pantry and Nana's buffet. It was a safe bet to assume it didn't walk off on its own. And even though he wasn't around anymore to make use of it, I liked to imagine him curled up there, nonetheless. Darlene, busy as a beaver at the sink, was the most likely culprit.

"Hey, Darlene. Did you move Dog's bed?"

She twisted to look at me over her shoulder. "Mornin' sunshine. You sleep okay?"

"Just fine. So, did you?"

"Rounded up all his beds and toys, 'ceptin' for the ones in your room, and put them in the basement. Don't want you trippin' over nothin' in your condition."

"That was thoughtful, but if it's all the same to you, I'd rather you put them back." I crossed to the pantry to scrounge up a Pop-Tart before heading out.

"Got rid of all your junk food, too," Darlene said, wiping her hands on a towel. "There's some of that healthy bread in the freezer, apples in the fridge, and fresh eggs, too."

"Fresh eggs? Since when?"

"Since I realized God plopped me at this here house to be your keeper. You certainly ain't doin' the job. Ain't even had the sense to see a doctor yet. Besides, a friend of mine has more eggs than she can sell."

"Well, Ms. Smarty Pants, it just so happens I got an appointment later this morning." I fought the urge to stick out my tongue at her and add, *so there!*

"You need me to go with you?"

"I appreciate the offer, but Jenna's coming by to pick me up. Then we're going to run up to Leiper's Fork so I can run some design ideas by Karly." I plucked an apple out of the bowl in the fridge. "We got any peanut butter I can dip this in?" The question was simple enough, but with it came a thought that wrapped me in warmth from the inside out. I had someone taking care of me for the first time since childhood. My independent self would have rebelled against it only months before, but not now. Not when I felt as vulnerable as the baby I carried inside of me.

"In the pantry," Darlene said.

It took a moment for me to realize she was answering my question. I prepared a simple breakfast under Darlene's watchful eye before gathering all I needed for Jenna's arrival.

An hour later, I sat in the front seat of Jenna's van, the air conditioning blasting me full in the face. It was going to be a hot one.

"Nervous about your appointment?" Jenna asked.

I laid my hands across my belly, just now starting to show a slight baby bump. It was a fair question, but for some reason, the lingering warmth from my dream brought me comfort. "I'm fine. I got to thinking."

"Yeah?" Jenna pulled up to a stop sign and glanced at me. "'Bout what?"

"The babies that didn't make it. I've tried to imagine what it'd have been like had even one of them survived. I could have a nine-year-old right now, or a two-year-old. Can't imagine Nicky as a daddy."

Jenna kept her eyes on the road as she turned. "You and me both. I don't imagine he jumped at the chance to bring you to see the doctor himself."

"I didn't bother to let him know. If he wasn't all that keen on being there when we were together, I didn't guess he'd care one way or the other now that we're on shaky ground."

"How're things goin' with him, anyway?"

"I'd rather not discuss him. I've got more important things to focus on right now. Like fulfilling Karly's decor dreams."

"Okay. Change of subject. How's the search into your mama and daddy's past comin' along. Makin' headway?"

I dug into my purse to find my sunglasses. "I told you that missionary place they worked under closed down, right?"

"Yeah. You said you plan to search for the guy in charge, the director or some such, on the Internet."

Shoving my sunglasses onto my nose, I peered at her. "Arthur Kemp. You know how many of them popped up in Google? About a million. I narrowed it some by adding in the missionary he was affiliated with, but still."

"You could hire an investigator." Her mouth popped open, and she turned wide eyes on me. "Or, better yet, ask Derek."

"Derek? Why?"

Jenna was quiet for the time it took her to merge onto the highway. "With his background in the military, he's got to be right smart about that kind of thing. Security, snoopin', whatever."

I'd never even considered it, but Jenna was right. There was just one problem. "I'm not so sure I want him involved in this. He's told me more than once to let it go, like he thinks I'm making up ghosts where none exists."

Jenna clucked her tongue. "You know, Charlie, that man'd do anything for you. Just say the word, and he'd walk through fire."

"I think *you're* the one seeing things that don't exist."

"We'll agree to disagree for now."

I closed my eyes, the cool of the air and movement of the car lulling me sleep. Even sleeping a solid eight hours, I was ready to nap anytime, anywhere. I remembered that from my other pregnancies.

"We're here."

I fought to open my eyes. I must have drifted off because we were now in Franklin.

Jenna turned into the medical plaza lot and parked. "You ready to go in?"

I yawned. "Let's do it."

It'd been two years since I'd last been to see Dr. Greenbriar, and it was with mixed feelings that I entered the familiar waiting room. There was a smattering of other women seated around the perimeter, a couple with male partners, a couple alone. One young woman appeared to be with her mother.

Hope warred with dread, and I drew in a deep cleansing breath as I approached the partition to sign in. I'd had moments of clarity the last few days as I'd thought about my lost babies. They were only lost because God allowed them to be, but He didn't take them from me. I had to hold onto that truth that just birthed in me. It was like the mustard-sized seed of faith I'd read about in the gospel of Luke. Time in Daddy's Bible reminded me how every breath of life was God's grace. He loved me, plain and simple. He wanted the best for me.

I could only pray that whatever else happened, God deemed this baby be the best.

I left the exam room buoyed by hope. I was nearing fourteen weeks, by Dr. Greenbriar's estimation—further along than I'd expected. It didn't matter that I was into my third trimester when I lost the babies before, I chose to cling to the here and now.

"So?" Jenna latched onto my arm the minute we were out the door. "What'd she say? How's the baby?"

"Everything's fine." It was all I could do to tamp down the squeal wriggling up my throat. "She says I'm fourteen weeks along." I didn't tack on that I had another twenty-six to go. One week at a time was going to be my motto.

"That's good. When's your next appointment? Will she do an ultrasound, tell you what the sex is?"

I laughed. "Slow down, would you? You'd think you're the one who's pregnant."

"Bite your tongue," she said, a look of horror crossing her features. "Four youngun's is enough. Don't mean I can't be excited for you."

We'd reached her van, and I rounded it to get to the passenger door. "My next appointment is in four weeks, and she will do an ultrasound. But I'm not sure I want to know the baby's gender." One week at a time or not, I couldn't help but protect my heart.

Jenna spent the twenty-minute drive to Karly's regaling me with the benefits of knowing the gender ahead of time, as if I didn't already know. It was with relief that I directed her up Karly's long, sweeping driveway. It had her changing subjects quick as a lick.

"Will ya get a look at this place?" Jenna said in a breathy voice as she parked in the circular drive. She'd likely have her own battle with the green-eyed monster. "Country artist, huh?"

"That's the rumor. I haven't met him myself, but this is Clive Wynn's home."

"Y'all are joshin' me." She grinned and nudged me with an elbow. "He's all of twenty-seven if he's a day. Must make a right bundle with a place this size."

"Tell me about it. Karly doesn't even look like she isn't old enough to vote." I retrieved my computer. It was an exaggeration, but I'd bet every cent I didn't have that it wasn't much of one.

Jenna oohed and aahed with every step we took toward the front porch. Wait until she laid her eyes on the inside. Unlike the first time I was at the house, Karly answered the door herself. There was no Elodie to run interference, not that we needed it.

"Charlotte," she greeted with a smile as big as Texas. "It's so good to see you again." Before I could introduce Jenna, Karly turned to her with an outstretched hand. "Hey there. I'm Karly Wynn."

"Jenna Carpenter," Jenna said, taking Karly's hand. "Your house is amazin'. You ever get lost in this place?"

Karly laughed. "I know you're kiddin', but I have to admit it's a little intimidatin'." She turned to me. "Why don't y'all come out back, unless it's too warm?" Her smile wavered as if she was undecided. "We could sit at the kitchen counter, if you'd rather."

"Outside's fine, Karly. You have it set up so nice, I'm sure we'll be comfortable."

Smile back in place, she sighed. "Perfect." We followed her out to the back patio. "Let me just get y'all some sweet tea. I made some brownies, too, so I'll bring them out as well."

"If it's all the same to you, Karly"—I halted her before she could disappear— "water's just fine for me."

"I'll help." Jenna followed her inside.

I sunk into one of the cushions, pulled my computer from its bag, and got it set up on the table. I'd compiled several ideas for Karly based on our previous discussion, and I was excited to see her reaction. She was a country girl at heart, which played well with the architectural design of their house.

"One glass of water with lemon coming up," Jenna said as she joined me with a tray of drinks. She divvied out the tall, icy glasses while Karly placed a plate of scrumptious-looking brownies in the middle of the wrought-iron table.

The next two hours, we poured over design ideas, walked through the house a few more times, and put a plan in motion. My excitement over the project matched that of Karly's. She signed the contract then handed me a deposit for more than I'd made on the last job I'd completed working for Patrice. Of course, a large portion of it would go toward materials, but it was a thrill nonetheless.

"I was thinkin'," Karly said as Jenna and I packed up to go. "Maybe you and your husband could come over in a couple weeks before Clive leaves on tour. Have supper with us." She offered a tentative smile, while crossing and uncrossing her arms. "You could talk to him about fixin' up his music studio, maybe."

I'd never told Karly I was married, and I wasn't wearing my wedding ring, so Elodie must have told her. She struck me as a little lost and in need of a friend, and I didn't have the heart to turn her down. It might just be I could use a friend, too. It wouldn't take much to convince Nicky to accompany me—meeting Clive Wynn would be all the incentive he'd need.

"Sounds good, Karly." I gave her a hug. "Of course, we'll be in constant touch as things move forward."

Once out into the van, Jenna and I waved at Karly, who stood on the porch like a lost little girl. Reminded me of myself at twelve. It didn't matter that she had a beautiful home, a famous husband, and likely more money than she'd knew what to do with. She was as alone as Darlene had been before her house burned down.

"You might a just stepped in it," Jenna said as she put the van into gear.

"What d'you mean?"

"You bring Nicky here, he'll never give up the idea of makin' it into the big time. It'd be like dangling a big ol' steak in front of a scrawny, starved dog."

"You might be right, Jenna, but better the devil I know than the one I don't."

She snorted. "You got that right."

CHAPTER THIRTY-FOUR

Derek

Being in the service for more than half my life, I'd never collected much stuff, so packing up what I had at Mama's took no time. The harder part was the office on account I hadn't seen Charlie or made any attempt to contact her. Truth was, I'd done everything I could to avoid it. Chalk it up to a keen sense of survival. But only a yellow-bellied coward slunk away without so much as an explanation.

I lugged in the empty boxes acquired behind the Piggly Wiggly to cart away what little office supplies we had. Mark flat-out refused to help, not that I blamed him. It'd make it a tad easier to confront Charlie without an audience to my humiliation anyway.

The desk drawers had been emptied before anyone made an appearance. I'd assumed Darlene would show since she took to watching over Charlie personal-like. That was good. Unexpected, but good. Charlie needed a keeper of sorts since she was in the family way. Someone who'd make sure she ate, didn't work too hard, and stayed clear of paint fumes. So, when Charlie stuck her head in the door, it shook me up some.

"What're you doing?" Her gaze flitted over the taped boxes and empty shelves.

I waved toward the two chairs facing my desk. Or rather, Charlie's desk. Charlie's chairs, for that matter. "We need to talk."

Her tongue flicked out to lick her lips, and she stared at the chairs as if I was laying a trap. "Nothing ever good starts with those words." Even so, she slid into one of them and crossed her legs.

Rather than taking the other, I sat on the edge of the desk. It put a little distance between us with the added psychological benefit of looking down on her. I needed all the help I could get.

"You're boxing up all your things," she said. "Why?" Wariness shadowed her eyes.

I ignored the heavy thump of my heart. What did I have to be nervous about, anyway? "I bought a house." The enthusiasm I attempted fell flat. "Isn't that great?"

"I didn't know you were in the market. Thought maybe you were happy staying at Mama G's."

"A grown man can only live with his mama for so long before people start to gossip."

Her gaze lit on the boxes again. "I'm happy for you, but why are you packing up your things?"

"Just figured if I was going to have a home office, it ought to be my own home." I shrugged. "Don't you agree?" How could she not see the logic in that?

She picked at a cuticle. "Yes, of course. Only thing"—her eyes caught mine— "I was paying you back for all those repairs with free office space. That's not going to work now."

I held my hands up. "Don't you worry about that. We had a

deal, and the fact I'm changing things up doesn't relieve me of that."

Her mouth dropped open. "I can't do that." She jumped up and put more distance between us. "We'll work a payment plan. If things take off like expected, I can afford it."

"How 'bout this? You furnish our office, and we'll call it good."

She barked out a laugh. "It would take considerable furniture to make that a fair bargain. I have a better idea. I'll furnish your office *and* do a complete home decor makeover on the house. Even that isn't enough, but it'd make me feel like things were a little more even."

And put me right back in close proximity with her, when the whole point of moving was the opposite. At least it'd be temporary. "Deal."

She sighed. "Good. Because it'll make it a smidge easier to ask for another favor." She scrunched up her nose, which warned me I might not like what was to come. "I was hoping you could find someone for me."

I folded my arms. "You mean like an investigator would do?"

"Kind of." She slid back into the chair. "I found a letter to my grandparents from the administrator of the Southern Baptist Missionary Alliance. That's who my parents served through. Only thing is, they closed down a few years back. I thought if I could talk to this man, maybe he could tell me something about my parents."

I'd figured since she hadn't brought it up in a while, she'd let it go. Hoped she'd let it go. I was torn for sure. What if Mama was right and the knowing of these secrets did more harm than good? How could I be a party to that? Then again, it was Charlie's life we were talking about. Didn't she have a right to know what happened to her parents?

"Are you sure, Charlie? I mean, it seems to me things have been kept in the dark to protect you."

She slumped in the chair and looked up at me. "You can't know the things I've been imagining. Dreams I wake from that seem more real than not." She jumped up and paced the small room. "The knowing can't be worse than that. Don't you see?"

I blew out a breath. "I make no promises, but you get me whatever information you have, and I'll see what I can do. Only thing is, it'll have to wait until next week. I'm heading over to Asheville for a few days."

A wrinkle formed between her eyebrows. "Asheville? North Carolina?"

"Yep."

"Are you taking a vacation or something?"

"Something." I thought about the issues she'd always had with her parents' missionary work and even my time in the service. Then again, why should what I chose to do matter to her anymore? Wasn't quite sure why it ever did. "I'm doing some chaplaincy training for a rapid response team."

I could see the gears spinning as her face took on different expressions. "Missionary work?" Was there a slight edge to her tone?

"Missionary, ministry. Whatever you want to call it. I'd be deployed in the aftermath of emergencies to help out with the Billy Graham group."

"In the aftermath." She crossed her arms. "Not, like, in the middle of catastrophic events?"

"Right."

She offered a tentative smile. "Seems like you've been a busy boy lately. New house. New ministry. You're moving on. That's good."

I couldn't be moved by the sadness I saw lurking in her eyes. It *was* good. She had her life, and I had mine. I needed to move on. Stop waiting on the sidelines for something that was never going to happen.

Charlie

A few days after my impromptu meeting with Derek, I was still reeling from all the changes he was making. I didn't like being on the outskirts of his life, but then whose fault was that? Mine. All mine. The reminder was made all too clear when Nicky called to let me know he'd set up a counseling session. To say I was shocked was an understatement. Then after giving it some consideration, I thought maybe he figured if he met me halfway, I'd give the other demand a pass. There wasn't even a hint that he was looking for regular work. But like he'd pointed out when I told him counseling would be a waste of money—it was his money to waste. I had to give him a little credit for finding someone in Murfreesboro, which was equal distance for both of us.

Our appointment was set for 2:00, which gave me ample time to work in the morning. Once Derek left, I contacted a couple vendors, ordered material swatches, and gave some thought to which repurposed pieces from the house might add charm and authenticity to the theme Karly wanted. It wasn't until I was driving north on US 231 that butterflies took root in my stomach and set it to fluttering. What I had to be nervous about, I couldn't say.

I arrived a few minutes early and spotted Nicky's truck at the other end of the parking lot. Over the years, Murfreesboro had grown to near the size of Nashville, which pushed people further and further out. There'd come a time in the not-so-distant future that Tennessee would be wall-to-wall with people. When I was little, this neighborhood was a quiet, two-lane road, lined with quaint businesses. Now it was more like a highway with traffic going every which way.

I stepped into the waiting room to see Nicky seated on a cozy sofa on the far side of the room flipping through a magazine. There was no one else about, and no window to check in like there'd been at Dr. Greenbriar's.

"Hey, Nicky."

"Hey, yourself. How're you doing?" His glanced dropped to my belly.

"Good." I slid into an empty chair. "Went to see the doctor. I'm fourteen weeks along, and everything's fine."

The fact that he didn't respond, other than a head nod, said more than words could. Agreeing to counseling was a mistake. "They know you're here?" Might be I could slip out and forget the whole thing.

"Said it'd just be a minute. I guess the guy's finishing up with another patient."

"You mean the woman." I'd Googled the therapist, and though her first name was masculine, she was a woman. Since Nicky made the appointment, shouldn't he have known that?

I riffled through the magazines stacked on a small side table, not focused on what they were. I should definitely leave.

Nicky's grunt drew my gaze. "How's the name 'Lee' a woman?"

"I don't know. How is the name Charlie a woman?"

"That's different. It's a nickname."

"Okay, what about Taylor or Kennedy or Jordon? Those could go either way."

He glared at me. "Are you trying to start something?"

As if that would take much effort. His attention to detail was unimpressive. "Tell me, Nicky, how'd you find this counselor? Eenie, meenie, miney, mo?"

"Give me some credit, will you?"

Before I could respond, the door opened and an attractive, middle-aged woman appeared. "You must be Charlie and Nick?"

There was no way our sniping hadn't reach her ears. Way to make a first impression. At least she knew what she was getting into. I stood and held out my hand. "Charlie Van Cleave. Sorry if you heard us bickering."

She smiled as she accepted my handshake. "It's the hazard of the job, I'm afraid. Conflict isn't always a bad thing. I'm Lee, by the way." She offered her hand to Nicky. "And you must be Nick."

He nodded once, his eyes not quite meeting hers. If he was uncomfortable now, wait until he found out she was a Christian counselor. God did work in mysterious ways.

"Let's go into my office, shall we."

I'd never been in a counseling office before, but it didn't look much different than Nana's parlor, minus the hot-pink velvet loveseat. Bookshelves lined two of the walls, the austerity of them broken up by the large window overlooking a courtyard.

"Have a seat, won't you?" She indicated two cushy chairs, side by side. She sat in another facing them and waited until we got settled.

Nicky hadn't said a word since Lee appeared, and I wondered if my assessment of him making it through two sessions was generous.

After a few minutes of chit-chat, she asked, "If you had to choose only one thing central to the discourse in your marriage, what would it be?"

I glanced over at Nicky, wanting to give him a chance to respond. When he didn't, I cleared my throat. "Unfaithfulness."

Lee nodded and turned her focus on Nicky. "Would you agree with your wife?"

"I suppose from her viewpoint, that'd be true."

One eyebrow arched. "And what about your viewpoint?"

He shrugged. "It's true I've stepped out a time or two. But you got to understand, Charlie only married me 'cause she got pregnant."

Lee crossed her legs. "I'm not sure I understand the connection."

I waited for Nicky to make his usual accusations. I didn't love him. I'd never loved him. But instead, he stayed silent.

We weren't going to get anywhere at this rate. "Nicky believes I've always loved his older brother, Derek. I won't deny there's been affection between us. But until recently, Derek's been in the service since we were kids. I can't seem to make Nicky understand that it was him I chose, even if we started off doing things backwards. I truly care about him. Every time he has an affair, he throws Derek in my face, as if I'm to blame for his unfaithfulness."

Lee turned her focus to Nicky. "Is that true?"

"The only reason she ever even went out with me was 'cause she was getting back at Derek for leaving." Although Nicky sounded like a pouty child who wasn't getting his way, his accusation had merit.

The dialogue went back and forth, rehashing our history and laying blame. After nearly an hour, it felt as if we'd slogged through quicksand with no idea how to extricate ourselves from the downward pull.

"I don't see how this can work," I said. "I wouldn't even consider reconciling if I weren't pregnant, and I made that clear to Nicky. He's the one pushing it, which I don't understand at all since he never wanted to have kids to begin with. If he resents me now, how much worse will it get a year down the road, or five or ten? That's if, by some miracle, we can even reconcile."

"How do you feel about what Charlie's saying, Nick?" Lee asked.

A muscled pulsed along his jawline—a sure sign he was holding back.

"Here's how I see things," Lee said in response to the silence. "You two need to be on the same page if there is any chance for success. Marriage is hard, even in the best of circumstances. There's a wonderful book by Gary Thomas that's been around for years called *Sacred Marriage*. His theory is that God created marriage as a means of making us holy, rather than happy. I suggest you get yourself a copy and read it. We can meet back here in a week and see where things sit."

Once out in the parking lot, I was at a loss for words. I had little hope that we could make a go of our marriage, and yet, to walk away without trying didn't sit well with me, either.

We stood in the shade of a big oak in the parking lot. He'd made no move toward his truck, so I figured he wanted to talk. "What d'you think, Nicky?"

He blew out a breath. "I'm not much into reading."

I fought the urge to roll my eyes. That was his entire take-away? "Be honest. Why do you want to stay married to me? You clammed up in there, but I know you're stewing about something."

"We been together a long time, Charlie, and even if I never gave much thought to being a daddy, you're pregnant."

It sounded like we were of the same mind there, at least. "There's got to be more, Nicky."

"Let's just see where this takes us." He squeezed my hand, kissed me on the cheek, and walked away.

CHAPTER THIRTY-FIVE

February 2020
Charlie

Charlie thought it peculiar that she'd had a double loss when Pawpaw died, and now again with Nana. To lose two babies within a week of her grandparents. What were the odds? She remembered Daddy saying there was no such thing as coincidence, because God controlled every detail of their lives. Charlie drew no comfort in knowing the Good Lord planned the death of her babies to occur simultaneously with that of her grandparents in such a way. It seemed downright cruel to her. Where was the love in that?

There wasn't much to planning Nana's funeral, since Nana'd had every detail worked out the week after Pawpaw's. "There's no way on God's green earth I'm gonna saddle you with that task," she'd told Charlie. It wasn't until Charlie retrieved the mess of papers Nana filed under "Funeral

Arrangements" that she even knew Nana wanted a church service. Or a viewing.

Mere days after Charlie lost baby number two, Nana died in her sleep. No muss. No fuss.

"Wish I could say the same," Charlie muttered to her splotchy-complexioned self in the mirror. Grief had a way of sucking the very life from a person's features. It would take lots of fuss to paint her face so well, no one would see the soul-deep pain that made it near impossible to stand straight. It had been all she could do to stomach the viewing the day before. But now a church service?

"You about ready?" Nicky called from the other side of the closed bathroom door. "You wanna be there early, we should've left ten minutes ago."

Good ol' Nicky. Always one to offer comfort when it was most needed.

The drive from Nashville to Shelbyville would take an hour, and Charlie didn't know if she could survive being alone with her husband for that long without anyone to run interference. Maybe if they didn't speak, they could get through it in once piece. Things went according to plan for the first ten minutes.

"How long you gonna give me the cold shoulder?" Nicky's death-like grip on the steering wheel was the only hint he cared one whit.

So much for silence. "I need time to process, Nicky. I can't just shove all my emotions into a little box and forget about them."

"You saying that's what I do?"

Charlie barked out a laugh that turned into a sob, and she had to swallow it down before she could answer him. "Of course not. I don't think you care enough to have emotions. Not about Nana, and not about the baby." She pressed her hand against her belly where she'd carried that little one for four solid months before she died.

Nicky groaned as if she was getting on his last nerve. "You don't mean that, Charlie. You know I cared about your nana. But for crying out loud, you make it sound like her death was a tragedy. She was near eighty-six."

Just like Nicky to sweep it all away as if Nana's death didn't leave a gaping hole in her heart. Charlie would miss her on so many levels, not the least of which she was her last real connection to Mama and Daddy. And she and Pawpaw had filled in for the both of them for the last eighteen years.

"And the baby?" Nicky clucked his tongue. "It wasn't even born yet. How was I supposed to get attached to a baby I never even met?"

Nerve endings so raw, the pain ripped through Charlie like a jolt of electricity, leaving her fingertips tingling. She couldn't even look at him. "A baby you wanted me to abort."

"Here we go again. How long you going to throw that back in my face?" His anger could be measured by the pressure he put on the gas pedal. The only thing containing him was the traffic on 65.

"I suppose it doesn't much matter anymore, does it? We lost her just the same. Now you don't have to worry about a child interfering with your aspirations of becoming some hotshot country singer. As if that's ever going to happen anyway." The minute the words were out, Charlie could feel the heat of shame rise to her cheeks. God knew she was fighting mad, but she had no need to stoop to Nicky's level. Nana always used to say, *Rise above, child.* She was tired clear to the bone of taking the high road where he was concerned.

"Let's go back to you giving me the cold shoulder," he said.

The only way she could rise above was to keep her mouth

clamped shut, which is what she did for the duration of the drive.

When they finally reached the church, Charlie bolted from the car without waiting for Nicky. It was a clear day, but the temperature hovered just above freezing. In her haste to leave the apartment, she hadn't bothered to grab a coat. Everyone would think she was rushing toward the warmth of the sanctuary, and she'd let them.

"Oh, Charlie." Myra Johnson hooked her arm in Charlie's as she entered the church. "I'm so terribly sorry about the loss of your grandmother. I had lunch with her just last week, and she seemed so very tired, with her face kind of sagging and bags under her eyes. She was looking so much better yesterday."

Charlie must've surely missed a vital part of Myra's monologue. "Yesterday?"

"Yes, dear." She patted her arm. "At the viewing."

A bubble of laughter rose unbidden up Charlie's throat, and she clapped a hand over her mouth to hold it in. Turning away so Myra wouldn't see her mirth, she saw Derek leaning against the far wall of the foyer. It was as if everyone in the room dissipated when their eyes met, and she got lost in the comfort of his steel-blue gaze.

Without so much as a word to Myra, Charlie broke away from the old woman and moved through the crowd to reach Derek's side. They only saw each other in the midst of tragedy, her own wedding included. She might not have thought it as such at the time, but in retrospect, committing herself to Nicky was the beginning of her downfall.

Unable to abide the intensity of Derek's gaze for long, she let her own drop before closing the gap between them while her mind grasped for something to say. It had been near four years since she'd seen him, yet time didn't seem to exist.

"We have to stop meeting like this." He slipped an arm around her shoulder, enveloping her with his warmth.

Charlie closed her eyes and sighed. "I was just thinking the very same thing."

Derek—2020

The moment Charlie entered the church foyer, Derek felt her presence like a heat-seeking missile tracking its target. Her pale features and golden blond hair were stark against the traditional head-to-toe black she wore. But as she moved closer, he could see the lines of strain around her mouth and eyes. It aged her some. The girl had borne more tragedy than a body should in one lifetime, and it was a wonder the weight of it didn't crush her.

He felt his own lips twitch when her eyes lit up with something an older woman said to her. No matter how bad things got, Charlie hadn't lost the ability to laugh. And when their eyes caught, it was as if the last several years hadn't existed. There'd been no space or time between them. It was always like that with her, and it was the main reason he'd kept his distance. No good could come of them being thrown together, not with Nicky wedged in the mix.

Still, when he saw her moving across the church foyer toward him, his heart kicked up a notch or two, and he straightened his shoulders as if to brace for the impact. Best way to deflect heightened awareness was humor, leastways, that was his go-to strategy. When she sidled up to him as if she belonged, he wrapped an arm around her shoulders.

"We have to stop meeting like this." The quip fell flat.

She rested her head on his shoulder, shielding her face from his eyes. “I was just thinking the very same thing.”

“Your nana was a special woman, Charlie. She will surely be missed.”

“She certainly was one of a kind.” Humor laced her tone, and he smiled in response. She pulled back to look at him, but not so far away that his arm fell away from her shoulders. “I was just thinking on the drive here how her belief system was an odd combination of loving the Lord and a hefty dose of Southern superstition.”

Nicky walked into the foyer and gave Derek a glacial glare as if he caught him doing something inappropriate with Charlie. Derek had no call to feel guilty, but out of respect for Charlie, he removed his arm from her shoulders. No need to fuel the fire of jealousy, warranted or not.

“Look, Charlie, I’m sure you have things to attend to. I just want you to know I’m sorry as I can be about you losing the baby. I’m sure that’s been just as hard as losing your nana.”

Her shoulders slumped, and a cloud crossed her features.

He reached across the distance and tilted her chin up so he could see into her eyes, and if it riled Nicky, so be it. “I’m praying for you, sweet Charlie. I know that probably doesn’t mean much to you, but I hope you can feel the Lord’s hand on your life. And if there’s anything else I can do—”

“How long are you staying this time?”

He sighed. “I leave in the morning.” He tried to get more time, but it wasn’t possible. “You heading back to Nashville after the service?”

Her mouth twisted as if she tasted something sour, but she nodded. “I don’t think I can face Nana’s house quite yet.”

“How ’bout I drive up later? We might could have a little time to talk.”

She glanced over to where Nicky stood, still shooting daggers their way. "I'd like that."

"It'd give me a chance to spend some time with Nicky, too."

"If he's even there."

"That's a chance I'm willing to take. See you then." He planted a kiss on her forehead and slipped away.

Derek and Mama sat several pews behind Charlie and Nicky throughout the service. There was trouble between them, and he didn't need to rely on Nicky's glare when he'd come into the church to tell him that. There was a wall between he and Charlie—they sat next to each other but with as much distance as possible given the length of the pew.

On the drive up to Nashville that evening, Derek thought it was a true miracle Charlie and Nicky were still married. He knew his baby brother, and though he might could change some, Derek found it near impossible without the saving work of Jesus. There was a time Nicky played worship music on the rare occasion the church allowed anything other than the white-robed choir to sing God's praises, but Derek suspected it had more to do with him than with Jesus. For whatever reason, Nicky never did take to the relationship between the music and the reason for it.

He often wondered why the two of them were so different, but realized it'd been that way since Cain and Abel. There just was no telling. Nicky wasn't going to talk about it, that was for darn sure.

Derek had never been to Nicky and Charlie's place. He had the address, and that's all he needed. As he pulled onto their street, he noted cars parked bumper-to-bumper alongside the road. Being raised on a farm made it near impossible for him to picture himself living in a big city. Just finding parking was a nightmare.

The sounds of a party assaulted Derek's ears the moment

he entered the atrium to Nicky and Charlie's apartment building. Country music blasted from the second floor, and it didn't take him but a few moments to find it was coming from their place.

"What the heck?" He muttered as he drew close to their door. Was this supposed to be a wake? If so, they got it all wrong. No way anyone would hear him knock. Instead, he tried the knob, which was unlocked. He pushed the door open just enough to see inside and was assaulted by the pungent smell of cigarette smoke and wall-to-wall people.

He didn't see Charlie in the crowd and figured she couldn't stomach the noise any better than him. He slipped out without even talking to his brother. Whatever was going on with her and Nicky was best left alone.

CHAPTER THIRTY-SIX

Charlie

Although Karly told me at our last meeting, and the two phone conversations after, that she wanted Nicky and me to for supper, it was still a shock when I received the official invite. I had two options—tell her that my marriage was hanging by a web-thin thread, or play along and hope Nicky didn't embarrass me. There was no doubt in my mind he'd have jumped at the chance to meet Clive Wynn. But I wanted him to come because I asked, not because it'd benefit him.

I could've made some excuse to Karly and bypassed him completely, but there was a part of me that wanted to rub Nicky's nose in my recent success. That attitude wouldn't win me any points with Jesus, but I was willing to take the risk. Of course, I didn't reveal who the client's husband was when I asked if he'd come along. I was of a mind to test his commitment, not that there was a doubt he was more talk than action. It took a little cajoling and a reminder that he was the one who wanted a second chance, but he finally agreed. It wasn't until he picked me up at Nana's house with a chip the size of Texas sitting on his shoulder that I fessed up.

"This would've been a whole lot easier if you just told me where we was going from the git go." He could act all high and mighty, but I knew his righteous indignation couldn't hold a candle to the intoxication of meeting a bona fide country-western star. Even from the passenger seat, I could see the gears spinning. Probably trying to figure out how to work one of his songs into the dinner conversation.

I adjusted my seatbelt so it wouldn't wrinkle my blouse. "That's funny. I was thinking it would've been easier if you just did something nice for the sake of being nice." It's not like I hadn't spent hours hanging out in honky tonks to support his piddly music career. And how many times had I cleaned up the apartment after one of his so-called creative sessions with his band? Just thinking about it was enough to get my knickers in a knot, as Nana would've said.

But I didn't want that attitude hanging over me like a cloud of doom, so I stuffed it—a move I'd perfected before our first wedding anniversary.

"I heard just last week that he's looking for a new opening act for his next tour."

"Too bad you're planning on putting all that behind you." Anyone else would have heard the sarcasm in my tone, but not Nicky.

"What d'you mean?"

"You know?" I patted my belly. "For the baby. I believe when you came begging for another chance, you swore you'd give up music and get a day job. Along with counseling, of course." It was small of me to bait him, but he made it so easy. I knew from the moment the promises were out of his mouth, he'd been searching for a loophole. Truth be told, it didn't even bother me anymore. Not much, anyway. Dealing with Nicky was enough to wear me out.

"You ain't serious, Charlie." He tossed a wide-eyed glance my way. "It'd be like you passing up an interview for, I don't know, *Ladies Home Magazine*, or something."

"*Ladies Home Magazine*? I don't believe there's any such thing. *Architectural Digest* maybe, or *Traditional Home*."

"Whatever. You know what I mean."

I absolutely did. I certainly couldn't fault him for being true to form.

"Turn at the next street," I said. "Their place is the second on the right."

The sun was beginning to dip behind the house, leaving the sweeping, uphill driveway in shadows beneath the towering trees.

"This is what I'm talking about," Nicky said as he parked in front of the garage. "I bet this set 'em back an arm and a leg."

Sadly, I thought Nicky would sell his soul for the opportunity to make the kind of money necessary to live like the Wynns did. I just hoped for Karly's sake that Clive was more grounded than that. As much as wealth and position looked to be attractive, I doubted the payoff was worth it. Sometimes, it took a world of hurt before people figured that out for themselves.

I rounded the car and met Nicky, who offered me his arm. I would have been moved by the gesture, but I suspected he wanted to make a good impression in case Karly or Clive were watching from inside. Still, it meant Nicky was going to be on his best behavior, which would make this whole ordeal tolerable.

Before we reached the porch, the front door flew open. Karly, all five-foot-nothing, stood at the entrance with Clive. They looked so young and fresh-faced, holding hands and grinning as if welcoming guests was their greatest pleasure. I had to admit, they made quite a couple—like they'd just stepped off the cover of *Country Music News*.

"I'm so excited you could come," Karly said, dropping Clive's hand to give me a hug. "This here is my husband, Clive." She touched his arm. "Clive, this is Charlotte."

"Charlie." I accepted his handshake. "And this is Nicky." I wasn't optimistic enough to add "my husband."

Once the introductions were done, Karly wrapped her hands around my arm and pulled me across the foyer. "Come look at what I'm fixin' for supper, Charlie. Maybe you can give it a taste and see if it's passable."

"You could serve steamed hot dogs, and I'd give it a rave review. I think of Pop-tarts as fine cuisine."

Karly laughed and turned to the men. "What can I get y'all to drink?"

"I'll handle that, babe," Clive said. "What'll it be, Charlie? We've got wine, beer, sweet tea."

"Water's fine, thanks." It was a little surreal to have the hottest thing in country music taking my drink order. If I was a touch starstruck, I could only imagine how Nicky was feeling.

Clive's brown eyes went wide. "Well, I think we can do a sight better 'n that."

"Charlie's caffeine and alcohol-free these days," Nicky blurted as if he'd been searching for something of significance to say. "Course, she's always alcohol-free, ain't that right?" He directed the question at me, a reminder that I was the designated driver.

"How 'bout Perrier, then?"

"That'll be fine, Clive." Tap water would've sufficed, but he seemed so eager to please, I didn't want to disappoint.

"Are you expectin'?" Karly's eyes lit up.

I let the question hang in the air. "Let's go check on your

supper, why don't we?" Something tantalizing was wafting through the air, and I had no doubt whatever Karly was making would be phenomenal. Then again, as long as I wasn't the one cooking, I was golden.

There was a flurry of activity as Clive got drinks for everyone, then the men disappeared out the patio door. No doubt, Nicky'd have Clive giving him a tour of his music studio. Although criticism toward Nicky was my default lately, I couldn't rightly blame him for being a little enamored. I figured things would go one of two ways—he'd see the futility of chasing after the dream or be inspired to try harder. The fact that I didn't care which way it went didn't bode well for our future.

If I'd been partial to cooking, Karly's kitchen would've had me lusting. Ceiling-tall white cabinetry with glass doors, gray on white quartz countertops, and high-end appliances. And of course, a deep farmhouse sink big enough I could've bathed Dog in it.

"Y'all are gonna be my guinea pigs," Karly said, opening the top double-oven door. "Clive just loves his mama's mac and cheese. It's doubtful mine can compare, but I'm givin' it my best. I used gruyere, fontina, and gouda."

"It smells heavenly." And it did. "But I suspect you could serve squirrel on a bed of turnip greens and Clive would love it. The two of you are adorable together."

"That's sweet of you to say, Charlie." She set the hot dish on a trivet and lifted the lid. Steam wafted up along with the mouth-watering scent of comfort food at its best. She handed me a fork. "Will you taste it for me? And be honest."

I tucked the fork into the creamy casserole just browning on the edges and pulled up a small bite-sized portion, twirling it until the string of melted cheese broke off. The moment I put it in my mouth, the flavors burst on my tongue.

"Oh my gosh," I said, even before swallowing. "This is to die for."

"Really?" Her grin wavered until I nodded vigorously. "Phew." She ran her hand over her brow as if to wipe away imaginary perspiration. "I guess I should've asked y'all if you're allergic to dairy before makin' it."

I nabbed another forkful before she replaced the lid. "Even if I was, I'd suffer before turning this down."

After putting the casserole back in the oven, she adjusted the time. "We'll just keep it on warm until we're ready to eat." Then she opened the Frigidaire and began pulling items from it. By the looks of it, she was making a salad.

"Can I help?"

"I won't have it. You're my guest. This'll be ready in no time. You never did tell me. Are y'all havin' a baby?" When I didn't answer right away, her face appeared to deflate quick as a pricked balloon. "I've stuck my nose in where it don't belong." She gave her head a quick shake. "Gotta stop doin' that."

I reached across the counter and touched her hand. "You're not at all, Karly. Most women would fall all over themselves to share their excitement over a pregnancy."

"But not you?" Her eyes softened and she frowned.

"It's not that." It was going to be near impossible to keep things on a business level with Karly. She was all heart and soul. The world could use more of her kind. "To be honest, I've miscarried twice before, and both times I was well into my second trimester. I'm a little gun-shy and a lot scared."

"Oh, Charlie." Karly rounded the counter and pulled me in for a hug. "That must be so hard. I'm sorry."

Her kindness melted the last of the wall I'd tried to erect between us, but I couldn't bear to tell her my marriage was a sham, as well. It might just give her cause to worry about her own situation. After all, Clive was put in a much more precarious position when it came to groupies than Nicky was. What if it made her question his faithfulness?

Before I could respond, the men reappeared. Nicky's eyes held a glimmer of excitement I hadn't seen in years. "You ain't gonna believe it, Charlie," he said like a kid wanting to show off his Christmas presents.

Even with all the baggage between us, I couldn't help but smile in response. This was the Nicky who'd wooed me all those years ago. "Try me."

"Clive leaves on a two-month tour next week, and he's giving me and my band an audition for his opening act."

Derek

A few days encamped with a group of God-fearing people was all I needed to put things to rights in my heart and mind. Chaplaincy training with the Billy Graham group was more than an answer to prayer—it was a recalibration of my spiritual compass. I'd come to realize maneuvering the dos and don'ts in my relationship with Charlie was like strategizing a war zone without benefit of command leader.

When your CO tells you to wait, you wait. You don't move or fall back until he gives the order. And you certainly don't make those decisions on your own. Not much different than listening to the voice of God. Once I had that figured out, I was able to let go of my expectations. Made life a whole lot easier.

I had all this running through my mind as I drove to Charlie's place. I'd called to let her know I was on my way, but I didn't tell her about my success at tracking down Arthur Kemp, the administrator with the missionary alliance she'd asked me to look into. I'd rather she dropped the whole thing, but it wasn't my call.

I pulled into the gravel drive and spotted Darlene kneeling in a patch of soil that ran from the left side of the house to the steps going to the porch. Appeared they were starting phase two of the renovation project. Mama said she'd been over recently giving advice and direction. If they were wanting to spruce up their curb appeal, she was the one to call on.

"Hey, Darlene." I crossed the newly mown lawn which seemed lusher than the last time I'd come around. Thing were looking a might better for sure.

Darlene twisted to get a look at me. She had a streak of dirt across one cheek mixed with the sweat that poured down her face. "Hey, yourself." She pushed herself up off the ground with a grunt and appeared as unbalanced as a new-born calf. "Charlie's inside. Prob'ly in the kitchen."

"You all right? It's kind of warm to be out in the sun." We hadn't had rain all week, and the temperature was in the high eighties.

She swiped the back of her hand across her forehead, leaving another swath of dirt. "I'm 'bout done. Your mama's bringin' some plants end of the week. Jus' wanna be ready. Think I'll take me a cold shower and stick to inside work rest of the day."

"Wise choice." I climbed the porch steps and peered through the screen door. "Charlie? You here?"

"In the kitchen."

I stepped inside where the air was a bit cooler and crossed the foyer. Charlie stood at the sink, rinsing out a paint brush and threw me a smile over her shoulder.

I pointed at the brush. "Hope you aren't subjecting yourself to fumes."

"It's just latex. And I left all the windows open." She shook the brush out and set it in the sink. "How was your time in Asheville?"

"Enlightening." I hitched a thumb to the kitchen table. "Can you sit a minute? I got something to talk to you about." We didn't really need to sit, but she looked almost as tuckered as Darlene.

"Okay. You want anything to drink?"

"I'll get it. What'll you have?"

It was telling that she didn't argue with me. "I brewed up some herbal iced tea. If you don't mind, I'll take a glass of that."

"You got it." I collected a couple glasses and snagged ice from the freezer. "Darlene appears to be working enough for ten people."

Charlie plopped into one of the chairs and folded her arms on the table. "I gotta say, Derek. She's a peach. I'm not sure what I'd do without her."

After depositing her tea in front of her, I sat across from her. "She got a plan? I mean, is she going to rebuild or what?"

She took a gulp of tea before answering. "Can't. She didn't have insurance. I've asked her to stay on here. There's plenty of room, and she carries her own weight and then some. Besides, once I get the shop open, I'll need help running it while I focus on the design aspect."

I nodded. Sometimes God works in ways so simple, it boggles the mind. "I did some checking on that name you gave me. Arthur Kemp."

She set the glass down and perked up. "Yeah? Any luck?"

I nodded once. "He's living over in McMinnville with his daughter. I gave her a call to see if you might be able to visit."

Her eyes widened and she leaned forward as if the closer she got, the faster she'd have her answer. "And?"

"She's fine with it, but—"

"You're amazing, Derek. When can I go?" She looked at me like I'd just handed her the keys to the Kingdom.

I held up a hand. "Slow down some, Charlie. Let me finish."

Eyebrows drawn together, she frowned. "Is there something wrong?"

I shifted in my seat. "He's got dementia. His daughter says there're days his memory is clear as can be and others he doesn't know which end is up. His good days aren't as often as his bad anymore."

"Oh." She twisted her mouth. "McMinnville isn't all that far to go. Worst case, he doesn't remember anything, and I try again another time."

"Only about an hour drive," I agreed. "If you wanna go tomorrow, I can take you." We both knew she was more than capable of going by herself, but I didn't want her to. No telling what she'd find out, and if she needed a shoulder to cry on, mine were broad enough to handle it.

"Tomorrow? You think we could be back before two?"

"Depends on how early Mr. Kemp's available. I'll give her a call." I started to ask why she needed to be back by two, but it was none of my business. Might have a client she needed to meet, or maybe a date with Nicky.

"Thank you. I'd appreciate it." She took a sip of tea then slammed the glass back down as if she just remembered something. "I didn't tell you who my new client is, did I?"

No point reminding her we hadn't talked in some time. "Didn't even know you had a new client."

"You're never going to believe it, Derek. Not in a million years." She stared at me wide-eyed as if I was supposed to take her up on the challenge. It seemed she was on the brink of exploding with the news.

I threw my hands in the air. "I give up. Who?"

"Clive Wynn." She squealed. "Actually, his wife Karly hired me, but it's for their house."

"That's great, Charlie." I chuckled. "Better keep Nicky away from him. He'll be attaching himself to the man's coat strings like a blood-sucking leech."

She grimaced. "I'm afraid that ship's sailed."

"Oh? How so?"

"We had dinner with them the other night. Let's just say Nicky's been inspired and leave it at that."

Sounded a little cryptic, but again, none of my business.

CHAPTER THIRTY-SEVEN

Charlie

I'd never been a fan of television and couldn't understand the attraction for reality T.V., but my life could surely be a contender if anyone was interested in producing it. Drama, mystery, grief. Only thing missing was romance. Being the main character of this reality show, I was hesitant to play the side characters against one another. That was why I didn't share with Derek that I needed to be back by two for my counseling session with Nicky.

Arthur Kemp's daughter, Sophie, told Derek we'd have a much better chance of her daddy being coherent first thing in the morning. She said the longer the day dragged on, the less his brain functioned. I didn't need Derek to take me out to McMinnville, but there was a comfort in not having to do it myself. Jenna or Darlene would have tagged along, but Derek was more likely to be a better emotional balance. If I was going to fall apart, I needed someone stoic to hold me up, not wallow with me.

Movement of Derek's truck and the warmth on my face through the window lulled me in a dream state. Whenever Derek was quiet for a few minutes, my eyelids would drift closed, weighed down by exhaustion. I'd spent the entire night fighting ghosts. Somehow, I'd slept better when Dog was lying beside me and said as much to Derek.

"You could always get another one, you know," he said as he turned onto 64 East.

"I don't really care much for dogs. They shed all over the house and smell like something dead whenever they get wet."

"That why you still have all Dog's beds and toys littering your house?"

I didn't bother to answer.

"There're plenty of dogs needing a home down at the shelter," Derek continued. "If you could fall in love with Dog, I'm sure you can fall in love with another."

"Who said anything about me loving Dog?"

He snorted. "You aren't nearly as tough as you pretend, Charlie. Never have been."

It was time to change the subject. "When're you moving into your new house?"

Derek chuckled as if he found me amusing. "Fine. I can take a hint." He flicked his blinker on and passed a truck that looked older than his daddy's. "Already moved in. It closed last week."

"That sure was fast." Knowing he wouldn't be down the street anymore left me as bereft as losing Dog. I often thought of how Derek snuck across our property that first night I was in Nana's house to check on things. It made me feel safe to know he was so close—and armed.

"Didn't need a loan, so it simplified things some."

I kept my focus on the scenery outside the window. "Can't wait to see it." Could I have sounded less enthusiastic?

Derek didn't say anything more about it, and I drifted off to sleep. It wasn't until I felt the truck stop that I opened my eyes. "Where are we?"

Derek pointed across the street. "Mr. Kemp's place."

I must've been going through something, because one look at the beautifully maintained, historic two-story home had me lusting as much as with Karly's place. It was a cheerful yellow with white trim, and its three dormer windows stood like sentinels over the wide front porch. I could see myself sitting on a swing watching the neighbors go by or enjoying the flowers that bloomed below. The yard was straight out of a gardening magazine with its lush lawns and curved beds. Of course, with a little more work, Nana's yard could look just as inviting.

"You ready?" Derek sat motionless waiting for my response.

"Let's do it."

As we climbed the wide porch steps, I caught a whiff of something floral-sweet. The house must've faced east because the sun left nothing of the porch in shadows. I was sweating, or as Nana would've said, perspiring, but from the heat or nerves I couldn't have said.

The screen was ornate wood, and since the door was wide open, it was the only thing between us and the foyer. Through the mesh, I could make out pristine oak floors and a curved stairway.

Derek rang the bell, and it wasn't more than a few seconds before a woman appeared. "Are you Derek?" she asked before making a move to open the screen.

"Yes, ma'am. And this is Charlie Van Cleave, the friend I told you about."

She smiled, flicked what I assumed was a hook closure, and pushed the door open. "It's nice to meet you, Charlie. I'm Sophia. Won't you come in? Daddy's in the parlor waiting on you. He had a good night, so you're in luck." She had mid-length blonde hair and kind eyes. Her mouth was bracketed by lines that looked like parentheses. I'd have guessed she was more than ten years older than me, which would put her in her early to mid-forties.

"I appreciate you letting us visit," I said. "You have a beautiful home." What a cliché thing to say, however true it was. It felt as if my mind stopped functioning, and I could only retrieve trite words. Was it nervousness, fear, or baby brain? I could only hope I'd get over it before I had to articulate intelligent questions for Mr. Kemp.

"Why thank you." Sophia smiled. "I grew up here, so I don't give it a whole lot of thought." She looked around as if trying to see it through a new perspective. "It's always just been home. Let me show you the way. Can I get you coffee or tea or anything?"

"Nothing for me," Derek said.

I thought about the doctor telling me I wasn't drinking enough liquids. Maybe that was part of my problem. "Water would be appreciated."

To the left of the foyer was a large parlor filled with traditional furnishings—dark woods, wing back chairs, and a sturdy sofa. Sunlight poured through a large picture window taking the edge off an otherwise austere decor. In the corner sat Mr. Kemp in a well-worn leather chair. A lamp glowed from a side table along with a half-filled glass of what appeared to be water. He wasn't as old as I'd expected, given he was suffering from dementia. Maybe late seventies.

"Mr. Kemp." Derek crossed the room, hand outstretched. "I'm Derek Daniels."

Mr. Kemp struggled to stand, and I expected Derek to wave him down, but he didn't. When Mr. Kemp reached his full height, which was quite impressive, he offered his hand in return. "Derek. It's kind of you to stop by." He turned and offered me a smile. "And who do we have here?"

Sophia stepped up with a glass of iced water with lemon and handed it to me. I hadn't even realized she'd been gone. "Please, you and Derek should sit." She then looked at her father. "This is the young woman I was telling you about, Daddy. Do you remember? Her parents worked with the same missionary alliance as you."

Confusion clouded his eyes, and he raised a finger to his mouth. "Missionary alliance?"

It felt as if my heart dropped clear to my toes as I next to Derek on the sofa. If he didn't remember the ministry he worked with for years, how could I expect him to remember Daddy and Mama? And even less likely, how could I expect him to remember me?

Sophia took his arm and guided him back to his chair. "First Baptist Missionary Alliance." She enunciated each word. "F.B.M.A."

His eyes widened, and a smile lit his face. "Yes, of course. We served in Africa. The Congo, mostly."

My heart fluttered with relief. "My mama and daddy served there through your ministry, Mr. Kemp."

"Oh?" He leaned forward. "You wouldn't happen to know when, would you?"

"I believe from 1992 until 2002. That's when they were killed over there." I felt Derek's hand squeeze mine, but I kept my gaze on Mr. Kemp. I prayed there would be recognition in his eyes.

His bushy brows drew together, and he frowned. "What did you say your name was, child?"

"I'm Charlie"—he wouldn't know that name— "Charlotte Van Cleave. My daddy was Charles, and my mama was Sarah."

He shook his head, a jerky side to side movement. "During

the 2nd Congolese Revolution." His shoulders slumped and his eyes glazed over.

"Yes, sir."

Lifting his head, he looked at me as if just remembering I was there. "Your mama and daddy were there during the uprising."

"So it would seem." I'd read some about it years later but assumed the village where we were hadn't been affected.

"How old were you? Ten? Eleven?"

"Twelve. That's when Mama and Daddy died, and I was sent back here." Maybe he'd remember the accident. "They were driving along a steep embankment and were hit head on. Their Jeep went off the edge."

"No." He dropped his head into his hands. "No." The one word held a depth of grief.

Sophia jumped up from her chair and rushed to his side. "Daddy?"

Derek stood and waved me to do the same. "Maybe we should leave. This is too much for him."

I was torn. So close to having the answers I needed, and yet to make this poor old man suffer for my sake was too much.

Mr. Kemp looked up at us. His eyes were shimmering with tears, yet they were clear and keen. "I don't know what they told you, child, but Charles and Sarah were killed in the insurrection." He waved us back down. "A peace treaty had been signed, but there were insurrectionists that were bent to kill everyone they could, regardless."

"I don't understand." I settled back next to Derek. "Why would my grandparents tell me it was a car accident then?"

"It was brutal what they did to that village. Not many survived. Their daughter—" His mouth dropped open, and he covered it with a wrinkled hand, staring at me. Then he pointed. "You and another little Congolese girl were unaccounted for."

"Mose," I said through stiff lips.

Derek shifted to look at me. "Do you remember, Charlie?"

"I thought it was just a dream. We were hiding in the trees and there were screams and gunfire, and we were terrified." Tears I was unaware of dripped onto my hand. "What happened to Mose, Mr. Kemp? Do you know?"

"Afraid not. To be honest, the fact you're sitting here now is a blessed miracle. The villagers were evacuated, but from what I was told, your parents stayed behind to find you. They didn't —" He shook his head. "They weren't able to get away."

I thought my brain was going to explode from the images that flitted in and out, never able to land on one. All these years, I'd been so wrong about Mama and Daddy.

"We should be going," Derek said, wrapping his hand around my arm and helping me stand. "We appreciate you taking the time to talk to us."

The obligatory thank yous were said, and I was back in the cab of Derek's truck without remembering how I'd gotten there.

We were back at Nana's in time for lunch, but I wasn't feeling inclined to eat. My stomach was a knotted mess, but I wasn't sure if it was latent morning sickness or the images Mr. Kemp painted for me about how Mama and Daddy had died, and why their bodies hadn't been recovered. He could've been wrong, right? I mean, he had dementia, so wasn't it possible he had his timeline mixed up?

I'd offered this theory to Derek on the way home, but his silence was answer enough. A quick Google search would've been all the confirmation necessary. I didn't bother with it, though, because I knew in my heart everything lined up. The repressed memories that revealed themselves in my dreams, the lies about how my parents died, the resurrection of the cross and wedding rings.

I told Darlene a little white lie about eating on the way home with Derek and excused myself for a nap. One of the many benefits of being pregnant was how everyone encouraged rest. Although I was bone weary, I didn't expect to fall asleep. One minute I was pulling the shade against the early afternoon sun and the next I checked the clock to find I'd lost two hours. It'd been my intention to reschedule the counseling session. After all, what was the point? But the hour had gotten too late, and one of my pet peeves were people who cancelled at the last minute. It had happened to me too numerous times to count, and unless I was at death's door, I wouldn't be one of *those* kind.

A splash of cold water on my face, and I was back on the road, my mind racing with the events of the morning.

Nicky's truck wasn't in the parking lot, which didn't come as a surprise. I'd called him on the drive to Murfreesboro but only got voicemail. What was I supposed to do if he didn't show? I snatched my purse and locked the truck. Better to cool my temper in the office than let it escalate in the heat of the cab.

After ten minutes of aimlessly flipping through a magazine in the waiting room, Lee stepped out. "Hi, Charlie." She did a quick survey of the room. "Is Nick with you?"

"I couldn't reach him. I think he forgot." I laid the magazine back where I'd found it and shrugged. "Now what?"

She folded her arms. "That's up to you. I'm going to charge him for it regardless, so if you'd like to take this session alone, I'm happy to oblige."

After the morning I had, God knew I could use a little therapy. It might be it was His plan all along. The more I looked for those God-incidences, the more they materialized.

"Why not?" I followed her into the office and slid into the same chair as the last time, while she did the same.

She folded her hands in her lap. "How've you been since we met last?"

"Honestly?" And just like that, tears fisted in my throat and pierced the back of my eyes. What had gotten into me? "Sorry." I sniffled. "Hormones." Another perk to being pregnant—I got a pass for crying any ol' time.

Lee crossed the room to retrieve a box of tissues and put them on the coffee table in front of me. "This is an apology-free zone, Charlie. Whatever you say, whatever you feel. It's all good."

I plucked a tissue from the box and dabbed at my eyes. "I met with a man today who told me something that I'm trying to process."

"Do you want to talk about it?" It sounded like a pat therapy line, but Lee's compassion-filled eyes were sincere.

I half laughed, half sobbed. "You have a couple weeks?" I drew in a deep breath and let it out slowly. "I don't imagine you got much from the bits and pieces Nicky and I spewed all over you last week. But my parents served as missionaries in the Congo for ten years. I was two when they started."

"And where were you during this time?"

I twisted the tissue. "With them."

Her eyebrows disappeared behind her bangs. "I'm only guessing your age, but you must've been there sometime during the Congolese wars."

I nodded. "Funny you should mention that. We were there, however, I was oblivious to what was happening politically or how much it affected the village where my parents served. I was told my parents were killed in a car accident, which is when I was sent back here to live with my grandparents."

"I...I'm sorry. What a tragedy to lose both of your parents so young."

"The thing is, I had no memory of it."

"That's not unusual. It was a traumatic event which will often cause dissociative amnesia."

The tissue was now mangled, and I shoved it into my purse. "I had a hard time buying the whole car accident thing."

"Lack of closure—"

"No." I shook my head. "I mean, yes. But the last several months I've been having nightmares, and then today I was told they were actually killed by insurrectionists." My voice cracked and sobs built up in my chest until I thought they'd suffocate me. "It's my fault, and a part of me has always known that."

Lee leaned forward. "Charlie, look at me."

She was a blur through the tears swimming in my eyes.

"What happened to your parents had nothing to do with you."

"You don't understand." I plucked a fresh tissue from the box on the table. "They stayed behind because they couldn't find me. Had I been there—"

"Then you would have likely been killed as well."

It took a moment for Lee's words to penetrate my foggy brain, and I could regain control over my emotions. In that time, I replayed her words. *You would have likely been killed as well.* All these years, I'd felt slighted by my parents because they chose to serve others over me. The truth was, they died trying to *save* me. I'd do the same for my own baby if it came to that.

"You may be right, Lee. I had no control back then." Still don't. I drew in a shaky breath and blew it out again. "But I've made such foolish decisions since, and other people have gotten hurt by them. I'm always quick to criticize Nicky for being irresponsible, but when he told you last week that I only dated him to spite Derek, he was right." I swiped my eyes with a grimace. "That little rebellion was the start of all the failures we've suffered through over the last ten years."

Lee dipped her head until her eyes caught mine. "You can't go back and change the past, Charlie. The question is, what're you going to do about the future?"

Thirty-five minutes later I pondered Lee's question as I sat in the cab of the truck. What *could* I do about my future? Was I supposed to go back to Nicky, even though he'd cheated on me time and again? Was he right? Had I pushed him into it because I was dissatisfied with him and the life we'd made together? The questions swirled around in my mind until I was too dizzy to think straight.

I gripped the top of the steering wheel, rested my forehead on my hands, and closed my eyes, still puffy from crying. I was wrung out. *Oh, Lord, I know You've watched me fumble through the last ten years, waiting for me to make my way back to You. I've made such a mess of things, Father.* Tears trickled down my cheeks. Was there no end to them? *I knew when I decided to be with Nicky it was the wrong thing to do, but You allowed it to happen. Now here I am, separated from him, and we're both miserable. What do I do now?*

My cell phone startled me upright, and despite the tears, my lips twitched with the thought it might be God calling with an answer. The smile turned to a sigh when I spotted the caller I.D. Good thing I'd cried all the mad right out of me.

"Hey, Nicky."

"You're probably ticked, and I don't blame you. I missed our counseling session, but something came up and I plumb forgot about it." He was talking so fast, it took a moment for his words to register.

"Everything okay?"

"Better than okay. Clive Wynn auditioned me and the guys, and we're in."

"In where? What does that mean?"

"We're gonna be opening for him on tour, Charlie. Ain't that amazing?"

"Yeah. Amazing." But it wasn't Nicky going on tour I was referring to. It was that God really did call me on the cell with an answer.

Who could've predicted He'd use Nicky to be His mouthpiece?

CHAPTER THIRTY-EIGHT

Derek

If I could count all the time I'd spent with Charlie since we'd met, it wouldn't amount to much. A few hours throughout the summer when she'd moved in with her grandparents more than twenty years before. The conversation the night of Nicky's high school graduation and another the night before they got married. A couple hours here and there over the course of a few funerals. And yet, the connection I felt with her was so powerful, it took all the discipline I'd learned in my military training to walk away after our meeting with Arthur Kemp. I had to keep reminding myself it wasn't my place to be a comfort. That privilege belonged to her husband.

So, when Nicky called wanting to meet up, I was a tad short tempered. Practically snarled at him like a grizzly, which he'd have been better off facing. Told him I was too busy working on a project at my new place and had no time to spare. Didn't deter him any. Said he'd be over right quick, and we could talk while I worked. Nicky never was one to take a hint.

I'd just carried a stack of roof shingles up the ladder when his truck pulled to the curb at the front of the house. I was being plain ornery not coming back down, but I didn't care enough to remedy the situation. He wanted to talk he could meet on my terms. If that meant sitting on a hot roof, so be it.

"Hey, Derek." Nicky was wearing a ball cap, but even so had to squint against the sun to see me.

"Hey, yourself." I laid out a shingle and pulled a couple roofing nails from the pouch on my tool belt. There wasn't a lot of patching necessary, but rain was predicted in the late afternoon, and I wanted it done beforehand.

"You gonna come down from there?"

I peered over the roofline to see Nicky with his hands shading the sun. "I need to get this done. You wanna talk, you'll have to come on up here."

He muttered something, but I drowned it out with my hammering. A few minutes later, his head popped up over the gutters. "You can't stop for a spell, Derek?"

I gazed at the clouds for a moment then shook my head. "Rain don't follow your time schedule."

Arms wrapped tight around the top rung of the ladder, he looked a little green around the gills. Nicky didn't care much for heights. Probably the only kid I knew who never climbed a tree.

"Give me a break, Derek. I can't rightly talk to you hanging on a ladder like this."

"So, get up here. There's plenty of room to sit on the roof." I wasn't about to give him an inch. Charlie'd been doing that for him way too long, and it hadn't gotten her anywhere but alone and pregnant.

Wide-eyed, Nicky stepped up another rung, his face about white as his knuckles with the way he gripped the side rails. The rate he was going, he'd end up taking a tumble.

"Never mind," I barked. "I'll come down."

It didn't take him near as long to get to the bottom as it had to get to the top, and within moments, I joined him on the lawn. I noticed Celia lingering on her front porch, as she seemed to do more often than was comfortable.

"Looks like a fine place to live." Nicky's gaze had tracked mine, and he gave Celia a grin and a wave. Always working an angle.

"Let's go inside." I led the way up the porch steps and into the front door. Aside from a couple chairs, the house was near empty of furniture, but much cooler. And there weren't any prying eyes. "You want a bottle of water?"

"Nah. I'm good."

I went into the kitchen and snagged a bottle from the fridge. Wasn't much else in it, which reminded me I needed to get to the grocery store if I didn't want to live on take out for the next couple days.

Nicky was sitting in one of the chairs when I returned, and I dropped onto the other.

"What's so all fired important you couldn't tell me on the phone?" I twisted the cap off the water and took a swig.

"I'm leaving for a spell." A grin spread across his face. "Going on tour with Clive Wynn." When I didn't respond, the smile wavered, and he dropped his eyes. "It's everything I've been hoping for, Derek."

There was a war happening inside of me. Righteous indignation on Charlie's behalf and more than a smattering of hope on mine. Indignation won out. "All you been hoping for? You got a wife who's waiting on you to grow up and a baby on the way. They supposed to just get by on your hope?"

He jumped up from the chair like he'd been stuck with a cattle prod and paced the wood floor. "You and me both know the truth of things, Derek, and there ain't no reason for me to stay."

"You're talking in riddles, boy." Rather than crane my neck to get a look at him, I stood and planted my hands on my hips. "Isn't Charlie enough to make you wanna stay? Don't you think, after all you put her through, you owe her what you promised?"

He threw his hands in the air. "You don't think she deserves more 'n this? You and me both know this ain't what she ever wanted."

I hit him with a scowl. "Don't start on that again, Nicky. It's getting old. You're just making excuses to not step up and do the right thing."

"It's not an excuse!" He swiped the cap off his head and slapped it against his leg. "It's the God's honest truth." He dropped back onto the chair and hung his head. "You don't think I know what a colossal failure I've been to Charlie?"

"You don't always have to do things the hard way, Nicky. Making the right choice is just as easy as making the wrong one."

He tilted his head and met my gaze. "This is the right choice. Not just for me, but for Charlie, too. I'm not trying to play the martyr here—"

"Good." I snorted. "'Cause no one's going buy it."

With a sigh he sat up straight and spread his hands out. "Let's just get it all out in the open. Take your best shot so I can finish what I was fixin' to say." There was no sneer, or even a hint of irritation, marring his face.

I waved a hand at him. "Go on. I'll let you have your piece without interruption."

"That'd be 'preciated." He nodded. "Ever since I can remember, you were the perfect son."

I opened my mouth to argue but snapped it shut when he gave me the stink eye.

"I admit, I been more than a little jealous of you. It was clear right from day one Charlie had a crush on you, and it riled me up. Even after you left for the service, it was all 'Derek this' and 'Derek that'. It was enough to make a person sick."

"She was all of twelve, Nicky."

"Didn't matter." He shrugged. "Then you came home for my high school graduation and broke her heart. All the time you were gone, she expected you to leave the service and come home. You made it pretty clear it wasn't gonna happen."

I had to clench my jaw to keep from responding. He wasn't saying anything I didn't already know, and it was painful to have it recounted once again. Hadn't I been beating myself up over it for the last sixteen years?

"I knew from the get-go Charlie only went out with me to get under your skin, but I didn't care. Truth was, I wanted to get back at you for being the favorite son. I've always been quick to lay the blame of it all on Charlie, but it was as much my fault as it was hers."

I searched Nicky's expression for signs of insincerity but could find none. If memory served, it was the first time he'd ever humbled himself enough in my presence to be completely honest.

"That it?" I asked when he didn't continue.

"One more thing." Clearing his throat, he shifted in his seat. "I'd bet the chance to tour with Clive Wynn that Charlie's in love with you. Nothing's changed in all these years, even if she says different."

I held up my hands. "We aren't going there, Nicky. The past is the past, and it's best if we leave it there."

He gave me a lopsided grin. "You blow it with Charlie again, Derek, then you ain't as smart as we all thought you were. And as far as I know, there's only one screw up in this family."

Charlie

Dark clouds scudded across the sky and brought with them a reprieve from the afternoon sun. What a perfect day to plant new life into the reworked flowerbeds at the front of the house. It wouldn't be the worst thing to get rained on, either, since the air was still sticky hot. The grass was growing in again, the porch swing sturdy and straight, and vibrant color would soon adorn the walkway. What a difference a little time made. It didn't look near the same as it did when I arrived here to lick my wounds a couple months before, but there was still plenty to do.

Darlene, Jenna, and Mama G carried armfuls of plants from the back of Mama G's truck. They wouldn't let me lift anything heavier than a gallon of milk, so it was my job to line up the pots on the walkway leading to the front porch alongside bags of mulch and gardening tools.

"This isn't exactly the perfect time to be planting," Mama G said as I set the last of the gallon-sized pots in the meticulous row I'd created. "But I'm not so sure waiting another month would be advisable in your condition, Charlie."

"Ain't that what I'm here for?" Darlene said. "If it woulda been better to wait, I'd a planted them myself. Ain't no need to put Charlie or the baby at risk."

I patted Darlene's arm. "I know you would have, Darlene, but I really wanted to get my hands dirty." Besides, I needed the distraction, still not knowing what direction my life was going to take. Nicky was stopping by to sign the divorce papers

I still had tucked away in my desk drawer. Even though it was for the best, it wasn't easy to end a marriage. Or to wrap my head around raising a baby on my own.

"Is this one verbena?" Jenna lifted a pot and eyed the dark green leaves spilling over the sides.

"You know your plants," Mama G said. "Once it's blooming, it'll be quite showy with purple flowers." She handed her a sheet of paper. "I sketched out a plan for y'all to follow. Yesterday I dropped off some azaleas, a couple hydrangeas, and some Hosta. They're sitting against the back porch outta the sun. Didn't want them wilting before we could get 'em in the ground."

"I'm going to get us some water and sweet tea." I dusted my hands off. "Y'all need anything else?"

Jenna barked out a laugh. "You're kiddin', right? After the spread Darlene laid out this mornin'?" She patted her stomach. "I'm 'bout full as a tick."

"I'll help you." Mama G followed me up the steps. "Best if you don't carry a tray loaded with drinks."

Why did I get the feeling Mama G had more on her mind than being helpful? She'd seemed a bit keyed up all morning long, giving me sideways glances and being generally more attentive than usual. Could be she was just worried about my pregnancy, but I sensed it was more.

We entered the kitchen, and I turned to her. "You got something on your mind, Mama G?"

"Whatever do you mean?" She stepped past me to retrieve four tall acrylic glasses from the cabinet.

I wasn't buying the innocent act, not after the day she rushed out on me like I'd lit her tail on fire to get to a gardening meeting. Surely, Derek told her about what I was up to. "It's about me talking to Mr. Kemp yesterday, isn't it?"

She hugged the glasses to her chest and shook her head.

"Land sakes, Charlie, it's a wonder Nicky could ever pull the wool over your eyes."

"He couldn't. Why do you think our marriage is over?"

She set the glasses on the table with a sigh and sat. "Derek told me y'all went over to McMinnville to see that man."

I slid into the chair across from her. "What do you know about it, Mama G? Did Nana tell you something?"

She kept her eyes down and nodded. "Near the time she passed, she was worried about you."

"Me?" I rubbed my chest with a fist as if it would lessen the ache of grief that pierced my heart. "Whatever for?"

Her mouth twisted, and she reached across for my hand. "She figured you'd come to find the truth of your mama and daddy's deaths eventually, but she wanted to protect you from it long as she could. Asked me to keep it to myself, so I felt I had no other choice."

Which part of it? "You mean how they died? Or that it was my fault?"

She looked into my eyes. "That right there, Charlie. You have an uncanny way of taking on the sins of the world. Like how you blamed yourself for losing the babies, as if it was somehow your fault."

I pulled my hand from hers and rubbed my temple where a headache was starting to thrum. "I'm beginning to understand that God allows things to happen for a reason, including losing the babies. And I also know what happened to my parents isn't my fault, although I'm still wrestling with that some." I leaned toward her as a horrifying thought occurred to me. "Did Nana and Pawpaw feel I was to blame?"

"Goodness, Charlie, of course not. In fact, they were dealing with a few struggles of their own."

"What d'you mean?"

She twisted her mouth while formulating her words. "They

were a might angry with your parents. Your grandparents understood their passion for ministry, but they argued with your mama and daddy about putting you in danger." She tilted her head and gave me a sad smile. "They just couldn't abandon their ministry, but they also couldn't abide leaving you behind. They did what they thought was best. Your nana and pawpaw didn't approve."

"They never let on." I couldn't remember a cross word ever said about Mama or Daddy.

"Oh, Charlie, they were grieving the loss every bit as much as you. But your nana especially feared you'd be traumatized if you knew how they died."

And maybe they'd been right. It was hard enough to make sense of it as an adult. "Did Derek tell you I've had nightmares for some time about it?"

"He hasn't told me much, child. He's a little peeved with me over the matter."

"Why ever for?" I couldn't imagine Derek angry with his mama. They'd always been so close.

She patted my hand and stood. "Because of his feelings for you, of course."

"But—"

"Charlie!" Jenna stumbled into the kitchen, eyes wide and a grin splitting her face. "You gotta come out here."

What on Earth...? I jumped out of the chair and headed for the front door, Mama G right on my heels. When I stepped out onto the porch, I gazed around trying to decipher what had Jenna all worked up. And then I saw him.

Ears perked and tongue lolling out of his doggie-grinning mouth, Dog stood at the bottom of the steps.

If I ever doubted there was a God who saw into the very recesses of my heart and soul, the reappearance of Dog would've been enough to shatter my unbelief. A shedding, smelly canine of all things. The Creator of heaven and earth cared enough about little ol' me to return something I'd not even admitted out loud that I'd missed.

"Dog?" I skipped down the steps and dropped to my knees in front of him, not minding the dirt and pebbles that scuffed my bare knees. With my arms wrapped around his neck, he squirmed until he could bathe my face in kisses. He smelled of dirt and dead critter with a hint of skunk to raise the rankness enough to gag a maggot, but I didn't care.

"Goodness," Mama G said as she took the stairs at a more sedate pace, hand skimming the railing. "Where did he come from?"

Jenna reached over and patted his head, setting a plume of dust to rise. "We looked up from diggin' holes, and there he was."

I sat back on my heels and rubbed his shepherd ears then slicked my hands down the scruff of his neck. "No collar." I nearly spit out the accusation. Dog's rightful owner didn't have the sense God gave a goose.

Darlene knelt beside me to rub the underside of his chin. "You ain't gonna call that good-for-nothing again and tell him you got Dog, are ya? You shoulda left things as they was to begin with."

My first instinct was to forget all about Dog's owner. After all, he didn't see fit to get a collar after he ran off the first time. But if I got myself all comfortable with the idea of Dog being mine again, and Ray showed up looking for him, it would be too much. Best to be upfront about the whole thing and trust that God would handle the details.

I started to rise from the ground, and Darlene latched onto

my arm as if afraid I'd take a tumble. "I don't have much choice."

Darlene dropped my arm with a scowl. "Dog wouldn't've run of like he done if he was happy."

"Charlie's right," Mama G said. "Things have a way of working out."

"You still got that guy's number?" Jenna asked.

Scratching Dog's ear, I nodded. "Thought about calling a time or two to check and see how Dog was doing, but I lost my nerve. Better go in and get that unpleasantness done before I change my mind." I caught Dog's face in my hands and touched my nose to his. "You, mister, better stay outside for now. Don't need you stinking up the house."

I could feel four pairs of eyes burning into my back until I got inside. Ray didn't deserve Dog, and Darlene was right—he wouldn't have run off if he was happy. Last time I made this call, my motivation came from a place of fear. Fear of God's judgment being passed down on my unborn baby. Now it was different. I was doing the right thing knowing that God would bless it somehow. Same thing, different heart. Trust was a whole new concept for me. And with it came a peace unlike anything I'd ever felt before.

Ray's number was right where I left it—tucked into the front cover of Daddy's Bible. My Bible, now. I pulled my cell from the back pocket of my shorts and sat on my bed. Right thing or not, my heart was pounding like a jack hammer. *You got this, Lord.* I thumbed the number and took a couple deep breaths waiting for it to connect.

"Yeah?"

"Is this Ray?"

"Who wants to know?" He could use a lesson or two on charm.

"This is Charlie. I was the one who found Dog when he ran off a couple months ago."

He grunted. "He show up at your place agin?"

"Sure did. Good thing, too, because he still doesn't have any tags. Of course, how could he when he doesn't have a collar to hang them from?"

His snort came across the line clear as could be. "The dang dog's more hassle than he's worth. You want him, he's yours." Then the phone went dead.

It didn't matter one bit that Ray was rude and obnoxious. He was my hero. *Thank You, Jesus.* I tore up the scratch paper with his number and tossed it in the trash can by my nightstand before heading back outside. Guess Dog was going to be getting a bath before the day was over. Good thing I saved all his stuff.

I all but skipped out the front door and stopped short when I saw Nicky standing in the yard with Mama G.

"Hey, Charlie."

"Nicky." I waved him up the steps. "You come to sign the papers?"

Hands jammed into the front pockets of his jeans, he shrugged and glanced over at Jenna and Darlene as if fearful they might bean him with a dirt clod. Instead, they continued digging in the flowerbed and merely glared at his backside. They wouldn't dare accost him in front of his mama.

"Y'all can stop fretting now. Appears Dog found his way home after all." I didn't wait for their response before leading Nicky inside.

"What's this about Dog?"

"Long story." My tongue was tied in knots, and my hand shook when I reached for the screen door. Why, after all this time, would I feel awkward around Nicky? "I have the papers in my desk." We walked through the house to the office I'd set up at the back.

"You've sure made this place look nice, Charlie." He sounded so formal it was as if we hadn't spent the last twenty years in each other's lives.

"Thanks." I slipped around the back end of my desk, pulled open the file drawer, and riffled through the folders until I found the right one.

Nicky dropped into the chair facing my desk. "You ain't on your own with the baby, Charlie. I want you to know that."

I slid the folder toward him and retrieved a pen from a mug sitting next to my desk lamp. "I appreciate that, Nicky, but we'll be just fine. I got Darlene and Mama G to help out, and Jenna, too for that matter."

"I mean financially." He took the pen from me. "I ain't been much of a provider." He snorted. "Heck, you've been more that than me. But no matter if things work out with this tour or not...I won't abandon you."

Leaning my arms on the desk, I watched him flip through the document and sign where I'd placed signature tabs. He was every bit as handsome as Derek—just in a different way. I thought about that young boy I first met twenty years ago and how he'd pursued me endlessly. Until he had me.

"What d'you think went wrong, Nicky?"

His raised his head and gave me a crooked grin. "You already forgetting my bad behavior?"

"Something must have caused it in the first place. You can't put all the blame on my feelings for Derek."

He shrugged then lowered his head. "Don't know, Charlie."

"We're ending our marriage, Nicky. I need to know why." I thought about all the times I talked down to him or responded to him with sarcasm. "Was it because I disrespected you?"

"It wasn't you, Charlie. And it wasn't Derek." He slid the

packet of papers across the desk. "It was me. Daddy used to say I sometimes had only one oar in the water, and I 'spect he was right. I knew how you felt about my brother, but more 'n' that, I knew how he felt about you. Seemed I was hell bent on getting the upper hand. I wanted to show him up." He shook his head with a grimace. "I'm sorry as I can be, Charlie."

I'd never heard him contrite before. He was always blustering and pointing a finger. Never owning up to his mistakes. Maybe I wasn't the only one who'd changed.

CHAPTER THIRTY-NINE

Derek

General repairs around a house played havoc with my back, most especially hauling shingles to the roof. Didn't help none that I had to twist my body into awkward positions to get the job done. So, it wasn't a surprise that sleep was hard in coming the night before, although Nicky's visit had as much to do with it as the pain.

He gave his blessing for me to act on my feelings for Charlie, but that was just one part of the equation. I didn't want her feeling like a chess piece being moved at the whim of Nicky and me. She wasn't an impressionable young girl anymore—she was an intelligent, talented, beautiful, independent, capable, stubborn woman. And now she was going to be a mama, too. She didn't need the likes of me coming into her life like a self-appointed knight in shining armor.

But that didn't mean I couldn't make myself useful as a future uncle and see how things evolved.

After a trip into Murfreesboro the next morning, I lit over to

Charlie's with a gift. It was a small step, but it was a step, nonetheless. First thing I noticed when I pulled into the gravel drive were the flowerbeds on each side of the stairs leading to the front porch. Looked as if Mama had used her gardening talents to beautify the place some. Darlene was sweeping the walkway around a wheelbarrow that looked to hold garbage from their project and stopped long enough to wave.

The next thing I noticed was Dog stretched out beneath the porch swing.

"Well, I'll be," I muttered. Climbing out of the truck, I took a quick survey in the back to be sure everything looked to be stable before crossing the grass. "Hey, Darlene." I gestured to Dog who now sat at attention and watched me with keen eyes. "Appears Dog found his way home again."

"Sure 'nough." She leaned on the broom handle and swiped her forehead with the back of her hand. "Showed up yesterday."

"Think he's here for good?" Last thing Charlie needed was to have something else she loved taken from her.

"Yes, sir. She done called that lowlife owner, and he tol' her to keep him. Said Dog's not worth the bother."

I let out the breath I'd been holding. That was good news. "Great. She here?"

"Workin' in her office. Ya know the way." She took the broom in hand again and slid it into the wheelbarrow.

When I reached the porch, Dog meandered over to greet me. His fur was soft and smelled faintly of coconut. "You wanna come inside, boy?"

Dog was smart enough to take me up on the invitation, and as soon as I opened the screen door, he darted inside and headed to the kitchen where his food and water had been kept before.

Not wanting to startle Charlie, I called out to her as I made my way to the back of the house. "You in here?"

I poked my head into her office. She sat at her desk, fingers flying over the keyboard, so engrossed in what she was doing, she didn't see me. But how could she have not heard me? Then I spotted the earbuds. Must be listening to music.

I rapped on the door frame and waved.

Her eyes shifted, and she jumped a couple inches off the chair. Yanking out the earbuds, she drew in a deep breath. "You scared the best years of my life off me, sneaking in like that."

I chuckled at her exaggeration. "That's what you get for blasting music in your ears. Might could end up deaf if you aren't careful."

"Maybe if I was listening to hard rock or metal, but God wouldn't likely strike me deaf when listening to worship songs."

I'd never known Charlie to be into Christian music before. "Who is it?"

"Streaming K-LOVE radio, so it's a mixture." She pushed her chair away from the desk and stood.

"I see Dog's returned. Not sure if I should congratulate you or give my condolences."

A wrinkle formed between her eyebrows. "What d'you mean?"

"I know how you feel about all the shedding and wet-dog stench," I teased.

She gave me a crooked grin. "I'll manage somehow. He'll just have to suffer through baths. I have to say, the goofy doggie grin that greeted me was the sweetest thing I've seen in a while."

"Yeah? Somehow, I'm not surprised. I'm thrilled he's now home."

"Me, too. What brings you out here? Are you heading over to see your mama?"

"Came to see you." For some strange reason, the admission had heat shooting up my neck. There wasn't the barrier of her age or marriage standing between us now, and it made the situation a little tense. Could be it wouldn't change things between us, but I prayed the opposite.

"Me?" She pressed a hand to her chest. "If you're worried about that business with Mr. Kemp, you don't have to be. I'm working through it. Even made another appointment with that counselor Nicky found."

"It's not that. Nicky came to see me yesterday." I watched her eyes to gauge a reaction. "He told me he's leaving."

Her mouth twisted in a grimace. "Yeah, he came by here, too. Signed the divorce papers."

I tapped a knuckle on the desk. "How're you feeling about it?"

"Honestly?" She drew in a deep breath then blew it out. "Relieved." Crossing her arms, she moved from behind the desk. "Does that sound awful?"

"Not at all. It's like you've been fighting a battle for years, and you've done all you could."

She shrugged. "I don't think he's going to be much of a daddy. But you never know."

I waved her to follow me. "Brought you a gift."

Her eyes softened as her mouth dropped open. "A gift?" You'd think she'd never heard the word before. "For me?"

How easy it would be to please this woman if only the good Lord gave me the opportunity. I'd shower her with every good thing I could think of. "There is some assembly required, so I want to be sure you like it before I tackle that job."

Confusion knit her brows. "I'm too old for a swing set, Derek."

"You're too old for a crib, too, but that's what I brought you."

Her hands dropped to her belly, but I doubt she was even aware of the way she caressed it. "But, what if—"

"It's time you live like your prayers have already been answered, sweet Charlie. No more expecting the worst so your heart'll be prepared for disappointment." I ran a finger down her cheek.

Her breath caught, and she looked up at me with complete trust shining in her eyes. "Let's go see what you picked out."

Charlie

A spark of awareness shot through me the moment I saw Derek's face, as if my entire body had been charged with a jolt of electricity. It'd been that way for years, but it was the first time I could recall it not being accompanied by guilt. Who knew signing a little ol' piece of paper could spin things the other way? What was the appropriate time between grieving a divorce and acting on feelings for another man? I didn't think Ms. Manners ever tackled the issue. With the added glitch of affections shifting from one brother to the other...sounded like one of those family squabbles you'd see on a daytime talk show.

But Derek brought me a crib.

I dared not read too much into the gift for fear my hope would be met with disappointment. He'd always had a chivalrous side, and now with Nicky basically abandoning his child, Derek might feel stepping in to care for his future niece or nephew was the honorable thing to do. However, it didn't change the tinge of giddiness that touched every nerve ending as I followed him out to the truck.

"All you got here is the picture," Derek said as he leaned against the bed of the truck and peered into it. "But it gives you a basic idea. At least until I have it assembled."

I stepped up beside him, my bare arm brushing his, sending warmth to my face despite my determination to remain detached. A large flat box filled the back, picture-side up. It appeared the crib had curved rails, fluted posts, and two drawers.

"It's one of them convertible jobs." Derek's eyes slid away as if fearful of my response. "The gal in the store told me once the baby gets to be bigger, it can be a toddler bed. Then when he or she gets even bigger, a daybed." He wriggled a hand toward the box. "Although this shows it in dark wood, I got it in gray. Thought since you don't know if it's a boy or girl, that'd work best. But you can always exchange it, Charlie. Fact, if you don't like this one, you can get whatever you want, and I'll pay for it."

I'd never heard Derek string so many words together at one time, but my throat had closed up, and I couldn't speak to save my life. Had he brought me every conceivable present, none would be more precious than this.

I laid my hand on his arm until I could find my voice. "It's perfect, Derek." The words croaked out of my mouth as my eyes misted. I tried to picture his Green Beret-muscled self in the children's section of a furniture store, and joy bubbled up and exploded into giggles.

"What's so funny?" His gaze flew from me to the boxed crib then back to me again as if trying to see what set me off.

I shook my head. "Nothing's funny." But laughter gurgled up again, and I couldn't contain it.

"Could've fooled me." He stepped back, breaking our connection. "It's fine, Charlie. I can take it back."

I bit my lip and searched his face for anger or indignation, which is what I'd have seen on Nicky's given the same situation. But all I saw was confusion in his furrowed brow and a slight frown. "It's not the crib, Derek. I love it. It's beautiful and thoughtful and sweet."

He threw his hands up. "Then what're you laughing at?"

My lips twitched again. "You, all big and muscular, picking out baby furniture."

A slow grin split his face. "Big and muscular, huh?"

My cheeks heated, but I held his gaze. "We're heading into new territory here, Derek." I wanted to sound confident, but instead, my voice came out whisper soft.

He stepped so close, my breath hitched, and I wanted to sink into his arms. To feel their weight pulling me like I'd dreamt years ago. Without thought to his family loyalty or my marital status.

"I'm not going anywhere, Charlie," he murmured against my temple. "I've waited a long time to stand in this here place with you, so you just take all the time you need to figure out your life. And when you do, and if you still have feelings for me after all these years, I'll be here."

I dropped my head onto his chest and breathed in the scent of Clorox and laundry detergent and Derek as he put his arms around me. "I think I've been in love with you since I was sixteen," I said against his shirt. "Maybe longer. I don't want to wait anymore to start our life together. Not if you feel the same way."

"I do." He kissed my temple then made his way slowly down my face until his lips met mine.

An ache started in the pit of my stomach and warmth spread through every nerve ending in my body as Derek's kiss reached to my very soul. Just like I'd always imagined. After a few minutes, I stepped away and put my hands on his muscled chest while I regained my balance.

"Just one thing, Derek," I said when I could speak again.

"What's that?"

"I'm not doing things backwards again." The announcement seemed ludicrous with Nicky's baby literally nestled between us. I tilted my head so I could see his face. "I'm going to do things God's way this time around."

He gave me a crooked grin. "I wouldn't have it any other way. "

EPILOGUE

One Year Later
Charlie

The eight-foot-long banner—burgundy font on a cream background—hung from the balcony of the house-turned-business and riffled in the late summer breeze. GRAND OPENING—VINTAGE DECOR & MORE. The transformation of Nana and Pawpaw's place was a wonder with all the repairs that'd been done, and the landscape grown in. Jenna, Darlene, and I stood on the freshly cleaned brick walkway just far enough back to get a decent view.

Jenna tilted her head and frowned. "Wha'd'ya think?"

"It's high on the left," I said. Not that anyone other than me would notice.

"I'll be. How'd I miss that?" She marched toward Cal and Mark who were standing by two extension ladders waiting for further instructions. "Y'all need to lift it some on the right or lower it on the left. It ain't quite right."

Darlene nudged me. “Is it ever’ thin’ you hoped it’d be, Charlie?”

I wrapped an arm around her shoulders and smiled. “Thanks to you. I swear, there’s no way we could have done this without you. You’ve been a true Godsend, Darlene.”

Her face turned pink as she shuffled her feet and harrumphed. “It weren’t nothin’, Charlie. You’re like a daughter to me, and now with Derek and Sarah Grace...”

“Speaking of which, I better go see if he needs help getting her down for a nap, then we’ll be ready to get this party started.” I gave her a quick hug to hide the emotion that appeared like an unexpected guest.

I passed between the two ladders where Jenna was henpecking the men and climbed the steps to the house. Somehow, it still took my breath away every time I entered. Hard to believe that a little over a year ago, the place was one step from being condemned. With a little ingenuity, a creative eye or two, and a whole lot of elbow grease, it was now a showplace. All that was missing was Mama, Daddy, Nana, and Pawpaw. But a girl couldn’t have it all. At least not this side of heaven.

“You looking for me?” Derek was halfway down the steps with Sarah Grace in his arms, and my heart fluttered so that all coherent thought slipped right out of my brain. How was it he still had the same effect on me after being married nearly eight months? But then, there wasn’t anything sexier than a strong man cradling a beautiful baby girl.

He was at the bottom of the steps before I found my voice. “Couldn’t get her to go down?”

He grimaced. “She knows this is a big day for her mama and didn’t wanna miss out.” He kissed Sarah Grace’s pink cheek as she waved her arms and gurgled. “This one’s going to be a handful.”

"Your mama's going to be here in a few minutes and will have her asleep in no time. Don't know how she does it." I sighed. "We only got another thirty minutes, and hopefully this place'll be swarming with customers."

Derek wrapped an arm around me and pulled me in for a family hug. "You sure you're up to going out tonight? I'm sure Nicky would understand."

I laughed. "Sure, he would. First time ever playing the Grand Ol' Opry, and we bail out. After signing away his parental rights, the least we can do is support him."

He fingered a strand of hair off my face. "Don't take this the wrong way, Charlie, but you look tired. You've put every ounce of energy into this opening, and there's only so much you can do."

Sarah Grace cooed her agreement as I melted into Derek's one-armed embrace. I laid my head on his chest and offered a finger to the baby. Was there anything more beautiful than this child?

"There's a reason I'm so worn out, Derek," I said, keeping my gaze on Sarah Grace.

"I know." I could feel the rumble of his voice as much as hear it. "You work too hard. Karly's got you running around like a headless chicken with all the clients she's brought in. It's a good thing you got Darlene and Jenna running the shop, or I don't know what all you'd do."

I touched the baby's nose and smiled. "What d'you think, Sarah Grace? Wouldn't your daddy make a cute store clerk?"

Derek snorted. "I'd double my deployments before I'd let that happen," he grumbled. "You're going to have to learn to pace yourself, Charlie. I'm serious."

I pulled back so I could gaze into his steel-blue eyes. "I know you are, babe. And I will. Don't want to take any chances with Sarah Grace's baby brother or sister." I waited, breath held, and watched for his reaction.

Derek's eyes widened and his mouth dropped open. "What're you saying, Charlie?"

I grinned "Looks like you're going to have another mouth to feed. Hope you're up for it."

"Are you kidding?" He threw back his head and laughed. "You just made me the happiest man in Bedford County." He shook his head. "Of course, Mark won't be too happy about it."

Were we even having the same conversation? "Mark? What's he got to do with it?"

He chuckled. "We'll have to relocate the office again to make way for another nursery, and you know how much he hates change."

"Hmm," I said. "Maybe I ought to have a little talk with him. Let him know how powerful change can be, if you just let the Lord lead the way."

ACKNOWLEDGMENTS

First off, I want to thank my Lord and Savior, Jesus Christ for putting this dream on my heart and being my Pilot. I couldn't write a decent story without Your Spirit working in me.

I want to thank my critique group: Joanne Kraft, Wendy Cunningham, and Katie Shands. You make me better than I could otherwise be on my own. Thank you for all your edits, encouragement and support. I'd like to give a special shout out to Katie Shands, the only Tennessee born-and-raised member in the group. You have certainly helped me hone my Southern voice, for which I'm seriously grateful.

ABOUT THE AUTHOR

Jennifer Sienes holds a bachelor's in psychology and a master's in education but discovered life-experience is the best teacher. She loves Jesus, romance and writing—and puts it altogether in inspirational contemporary fiction. Her daughter's TBI and brother's suicide inspired two of her three novels. Although fiction writing is her real love, she's had several non-fiction pieces published in anthologies including two in *Chicken Soup for the Soul.* She has two grown children and one very spoiled Maltese. California born and raised, she recently took a step of faith with her real-life hero and relocated to Tennessee.

Visit her at https://www.jennifersienes.com/

facebook.com/Jennifer-Sienes-Writer-186643172596
instagram.com/Jennifer_Sienes
goodreads.com/Jennifer_Sienes

ALSO BY JENNIFER SIENES

APPLE HILL SERIES

Surrendered (Book One)

Illusions (Book Two)

All That Glitters (Novella)

Providence (Book Three)

Saving Faith (Novella)

Wish Upon a Star (Novella)

BEDFORD COUNTY SERIES

Night Songs (Book One)

A Sojourner's Solace (Novella)

THE ROAD LESS TRAVELED

NIGHT SONGS BONUS STORY

JENNIFER SIENES

CHAPTER ONE

T*wo roads diverged in a yellow wood*...Karly Butler lost herself in the memorization of Robert Frost's poem. Best technique she had to push aside the ugly that wandered into Mama and Daddy's grocery store. Jenna Hastings and Sophie Long—the mean girls. Leastways, that was the nickname she'd pinned on them sophomore year of high school. She reminded herself that their subtle, but cruel, jabs weren't nothing but a pathetic attempt to feel better about themselves. One would think that near ten years later, they'd have the sense God gave a goat and grow up. Daddy often said, "The greatest test of a man's character is his tongue." Course, in this here situation, it applied to spiteful young women.

"You about got that case of corn stocked on the shelf, Karly?" Mama said as she poked her head down the aisle where Karly was hiding out. Or was doing her best before Mama gave her up.

"Yes, ma'am." She lined up two more cans, labels faced outward. "Thought I'd pop over next door and see if Daddy needs a hand with unloading the supplies that were delivered this morning." It was convenient that their hardware and grocery stores were slapped up against each other on Main Street. Mannington might've been a small town, but they had the necessities as long as you didn't need anything fancy like organic produce or name-brand clothing.

Hands planted on her wide hips, Mama said, "You know that's your brother's job. Trent don't need you underfoot."

Mama talked as if Karly was a pesky ten-year-old rather than a full-grown woman. One who should've forged a life of her own by now. Love of God and family ran deep in the Appalachians, but Karly could use a good dose of life outside this Podunk West Virginia town. She was far too old to have her head stuck in the clouds, dreaming of a happily-ever-after that wasn't gonna happen.

She fumbled the last few cans in a rush to sneak into the storeroom to hide but wasn't quick enough. Jenna and Sophie stopped where Mama had stood not thirty seconds before. Was bad enough to face the two of them without being stuck in a position that made her appear to be groveling. Standing, she brushed the dust from her jeans.

Karly held her head high and looked Jenna square in the eye. Only way to deal with a bully. "Can I help y'all find something?"

Jenna snatched a can of Margaret Holmes okra from the shelf and peered at the label. "Fixin' supper for my boyfriend tonight and thought I'd find me something special for dessert."

Karly smirked. "Sure. You drizzle a little chocolate sauce on that, and you got yourself something worthy of Wolfgang Puck?"

Sophie wrinkled her nose. "Who?"

Jenna shut her up with a quick shake of her head and put

the okra back on the shelf. "You happen to listen to the Grand Ole Opry last night, Karly?" That explained their sudden interest in groceries.

Karly picked up the empty cardboard box, careful to keep her face averted. Never could tell a lie without her cheeks turning red. "Can't say I did." Her fingers shook so bad, it made it hard to break the box down. Didn't help her stomach was set to quivering, and a knot big as a baseball stuck in her throat.

"Your old boyfriend was on," Sophie said. "They announced it was his first time. Imagine that, Karly. Clive Witt on the radio."

"It's too bad the two of you didn't work out." Jenna was anything but sorry. Karly didn't have to see her face to know she was lying.

"I'd love to stick around and rehash old times." Karly tucked the folded box under one arm, "but I have a mess of cases to unload. Y'all have yourselves a nice day, ya hear." Without glancing back, she waved and walked away. Tears blurred her vision as she slammed into the storeroom and flung the box like an oversized frisbee. It skittered across the floor and landed at Mama's feet.

"Land sakes, child, what's gotten into you?" She picked up the cardboard and added it to the stack in the corner. "I saw those two catty girls sniffin' around. Hope you're not takin' anything they said to heart."

"No, ma'am." Karly swiped the moisture from her eyes and blew out a breath. "They just like to spread a little sunshine wherever they go."

Mama chuckled. "Winter storm's more like it." She crossed her arms. "Heard them say something about Clive. You're not still nursin' that pain, are you?"

"Course not, Mama." *Liar, liar, pants on fire.* "Y'all forget I'm the one that broke it off, not the other way 'round." Last thing a man needed was the anchor of a hometown girl when he was born to fly the world.

CHAPTER TWO

The days blended into one another in such a way, Karly didn't need to keep a calendar—she knew where she'd be at all times. Working at the grocery store Monday through Saturday, eight in the morning until six at night. Sundays were for church and the family supper at Mama and Daddy's along with Trent. Only change there was her sister Laura was away at nursing school. Thursday nights were spent with Sadie at Big Momma's Pizzeria.

"What're you gonna have, Karly?" Sadie plucked a paper menu from the holder on the table while they waited for the server. She stared at it like she hadn't seen it a hundred times before. Why'd she even bother? They had the same thing every single Thursday night. A Big Momma square pizza and sweet tea. Karly was all of twenty-four, and her life was as dull as day-old dishwater.

"I'm gonna get me the chicken alfredo." That'll shake things up some. "And a Coke."

Sadie's head snapped up, eyes wide as cow pies. "But we always get the Big Momma."

"Then why'd you ask?" Karly winced the moment the words spewed from her lips. There was no need to be ugly with Sadie; it wasn't her fault Karly was living out that old movie *Groundhog Day*.

Sadie's eyes went soft, and she patted Karly's hand where it rested on the table. "It's on account Clive played at the Opry you got yourself all worked up, isn't it?"

Karly swallowed a groan. Not this again. "I'm sorry I was short with you, but Clive hasn't got a thing to do with it." She pulled her hands off the table and rested them in her lap. "Why's everyone making such a fuss over him, anyway?"

Beth appeared with two glasses of sweet tea before Sadie could answer. They all went to high school together. And middle school. And elementary school. There wasn't a person in the place Karly hadn't known since she could walk and talk. Nothing changed for her, but Clive Witt was living the dream. His dream. Wasn't it about time she got herself one of her own?

Beth plopped a glass in front of each of them. "Hey girls. Already got your order ready for you."

Karly slid her glass toward the edge of the table. "Well, I'm afraid you'll have to take this back and bring me a Coke."

Beth frowned. "Since when?"

"Since now," Karly said. "And I'd like to have the chicken alfredo tonight." She glanced at Sadie. "You gonna want that whole Big Momma's to yourself?"

Sadie shrugged. "Sure. I'll just give the extra to Jimmy."

Beth took Karly's glass. "If that's what you want." She looked at her as if she'd gone plumb crazy. "I'll get you your Coke then."

As Beth walked away, Sadie giggled. "I bet she thinks you got but one oar in the water, changing things up like you did." Her smiled faded as she slipped the wrapper from a straw.

"What'd you mean earlier when you said everyone's makin' a fuss? Something happen today?"

Karly scowled. "It wasn't anything. Just ol' Jenna and Sophie spreading a little love the way they do. Had to come into the store today and rub it in they heard Clive on the Opry."

She grimaced. "Guess I stepped into it then, didn't I?"

"Forget about it," Karly said. "It's more about me than him. I'm bored sick with my life, is all, while he's off living his."

Sadie arched a brow. "You coulda been off living it with him, sweetie. Instead, you let everyone think he dumped you."

"We've been over this before, Sadie. I wasn't about to travel around with him when we weren't married, and he didn't ask."

"All you had to do was let him know what you wanted." She plucked a few napkins from the dispenser against the wall. "He's not a mind reader."

Karly snorted. "Doesn't take a mind reader to know I'm not about to disrespect myself or my family by traveling with a man I wasn't married to."

"You know, Jimmy and I had a pre-marital counseling meetin' with Brother Davis last night."

It was the perfect moment for Beth to appear with their order. It gave Karly the few minutes needed to consider her response. Sadie'd never intentionally be insensitive, so there was no call for Karly to be irritated with her. Mama was always reminding her that it was the heart behind a thing the Lord cared about. And Sadie had the sweetest heart in the whole of Marion County.

"Here's you your Coke," Beth said, placing Karly's drink in front of her along with a huge plate of chicken alfredo. Might be the Big Momma's pizza would've been a better choice, after all. Beth handed Sadie a to-go pizza box. "For the extra."

Sadie blew out a breath. "There's enough here to feed all of South Sudan."

Karly rolled her eyes. "That's an exaggeration."

"No," Sadie said, "it's hyperbole. Trust me, it's one of the vocab words I gave to my students this week."

"Whatever." Why did everything Sadie said tonight point a spotlight on the chasm between her life and Karly's? Sadie was getting married, had a career, and wasn't mooning over the one who got away. Course, if Karly hadn't chased Clive off, things would've been different as a tadpole to a toad, like Sadie'd pointed out.

"Anyway, I was sayin' that Jimmy and I met with Brother Davis. One of the things he made clear was that a person can't hardly meet your expectations if they don't know what they are."

Karly forked a bite of chicken and pointed it at Sadie. "And you're telling me this why?"

Sadie shook her head. "I gotta say, Karly, for a smart girl you sure can be obtuse."

"That another vocab word?" She slipped the cream-covered pasta into her mouth.

"I'm saying you gotta ask for what you want in life, otherwise you'll end up with nothing." Sadie put a square of pizza onto her plate, plucked a slice of pepperoni from the top, and popped it into her mouth. "I know for a fact, Clive's still in love with you."

Karly held up a hand. "Don't wanna hear it, Sadie. We been over this. Whatever is between Clive and Jimmy needs to stay between Clive and Jimmy. I don't need your boyfriend—"

"Fiancé," Sadie corrected. Maybe she didn't have the sweetest heart after all.

"Sorry. Fiancé. I don't want him in the middle of this. Clive made his decision, and I made mine."

"So, you're gonna tell me that if Clive Witt walked in that

door right now," Sadie pointed to the door in question, "and told you he loved you, you'd send him away again?"

"It doesn't matter now, does it?" Karly shoved her plate aside. "He's been gone near two years, and I don't think he's coming back." Her voice broke. She'd sent him away for all the right reasons. She'd put his wants and needs above her own. So, why'd she still hurt as much now as she had the day he left?

CHAPTER THREE

Unmet expectations. Karly mulled over Sadie's words from the night before as she checked the order sheet against the inventory that'd been delivered. The storeroom was the perfect place to think—private and quiet. Sure, Sadie'd been referring to Karly's relationship with Clive, but wasn't that true of every aspect in life? If Karly wanted something different than what she had, she'd need to first know what that was.

She did well enough in school, but she had no desire to tackle college, like Laura had. Her sister was smart, driven, and organized. And Karly did fine working in the grocery store, but she didn't have a head for business like her brother Trent. He was taking online courses with an eye on earning himself an MBA eventually.

But Karly never wanted more than to be a wife and mother. If that made her weak and uninspired, so be it. Might not be PC (as some would say) to aspire to nothing more than having a family, but there it was. She loved working with the little ones in Sunday school, and nothing tickled her more than the joy she saw on their faces with each new discovery.

"What's got your head in the clouds, child?"

Karly spun around to find Mama standing between the swinging doors of the storeroom. "Oh, Mama. I didn't see you there?"

"Didn't hear me, neither. You okay?"

"Yes, ma'am." Karly tucked the clipboard under her arm. "Just thinking about the meaning of life."

Mama's eyebrows shot up. "Jesus is always the answer. Don't you know that by now?"

Karly bit back a smile. "It'd be real nice if He'd give me a road map."

"I hear you. You've been in a funk lately. Wanna talk about it?" Mama stepped further inside and let the doors swing closed.

"Just seems like everyone knows where their lives are headed, and I'm stuck here." When Mama frowned, Karly added, "That didn't sound so ugly in my head. You know I love working with you and Daddy, but this is your dream, not mine."

"I have a feeling your dream is touring the countryside. What're you gonna do about it?"

Karly sighed. "I don't rightly know, Mama. I suppose I just need to be patient and continue to pray that the Lord will direct me." She held up the clipboard. "Until then, I best get the inventory done."

Mama rested her hip on stack of boxes that hadn't been unpacked. "Maybe you need a change of scenery."

That sounded good to her. "You mean like a vacation?"

Mama pursed her lips and folded her arms. "I was thinking more along the lines of giving Stewart Miller a chance to court you."

Karly wrinkled her nose. “No one calls it courting anymore, Mama. It’s just dating now.”

“Courting sounds more sophisticated,” Mama said with a sniff. “And proper. He’s been working up the courage to ask you out for some time, you know.”

“No, I didn’t.” Karly narrowed her eyes. “And where’d you come by this fascinating piece of information?”“His own mama,” she said with a grin. “Where else?”

“Doesn’t say much for a man when his mama has to do his speaking for him, now does it?”

“Following in the footsteps of a local legend like Clive isn’t an easy thing, child,” Mama said. “If you aren’t opposed to the idea, might be a start to you washing that man outta your hair, if you know what I mean.”

Karly didn’t take kindly to Mama fixing her up with anyone, let alone Stewart. Then again, it wasn’t like she had men beating down her door. Was it because she didn’t appeal to the local boys, or was Mama right? Was following in Clive Witt’s footsteps a little intimidating? They’d been together all through high school and four years past. Everyone expected they’d get married one day, including Karly.

There was an Einstein quote Karly learned in school that came to mind at that moment: “Insanity was doing the same thing over and over and expecting different results.” Stewart wasn’t a bad sort, although Karly couldn’t see herself marrying the guy. But maybe if she accepted a date from him, people would see that she wasn’t waiting around for the likes of Clive Witt, local legend or not.

CHAPTER FOUR

"You're gonna do what?" Sadie's face puckered up like she'd sucked a lemon clean dry.

"It's just a date." Karly readjusted the strap of her purse on her shoulder and squinted against the bright sunlight. Early April and it felt more like June. Might be a scorcher of a summer.

"But you don't even like Stewart, do you?" Sadie speeded up to match Karly's steps as they crossed the church parking lot.

"I don't know. Haven't hardly talked to him since we were in high school. Have you?"

"Suppose not." Sadie clucked her tongue. "But still, what's the attraction?"

"Don't make a big deal out of this, Sadie. Mama asked would I be willing to go out with him, and I said yes."

"But it's Sunday." Sometimes the girl made about as much sense as a screen door in a submarine.

"So?"

She rolled her eyes. "So, you're missing supper with your

family to go out with a guy you're not even sure you like. First, you order chicken alfredo instead of Big Momma's pizza and now you're ditching family supper. What's gotten into you, Karly?"

They'd reached Karly's Toyota. She pulled the key fob from her purse and hit the button to unlock it. "You kinda just made my point for me, Sadie." She opened the door and tossed her bag onto the passenger seat. "I'm twenty-four years old, and I'm as predictable as my nana. Same thing day in and day out. Next thing you know, I'll be watching *Wheel of Fortune* and going to bed before the sun goes down. I can't take it anymore."

"But Stewart Miller? He ain't nothing like Clive."

"That's a mark in his favor." Karly blew out a breath. "I haven't seen Clive in almost two years, and y'all act like I'm going out on him. I guarantee you, he's not thinking of me these days. Probably has women hanging on him everywhere he goes." And why wouldn't he? He had the sweetest voice this side of the Mississippi and was a cross between Jake Owen and Tim McGraw. A girl would have to be out of her mind to walk away from that.

Karly swiped the bead of sweat off her upper lip and fought the tears that bit at the back of her eyes. Maybe she was crazy, but unless Jesus Himself appeared to her and told her to wait on Clive Witt, she had to do something different. Anything different.

"I gotta go, Sadie. Stewart's picking me up in an hour."

Sadie took a few steps back, arms spread wide. "You sure you know what you're doin'?"

"No," Karly choked out. "But I can't just do nothing anymore."

It didn't take Karly but ten minutes to know she'd made a mistake. If she was dull as dishwater, then Stewart was the dingy rag used to wipe down the counters. From the moment she'd stepped out of her apartment, he'd been tongue-tied as a pimply-faced teen. The drive to Muriale's Italian Kitchen was awkward as Stewart was so focused on keeping to the speed limit, he couldn't hold a conversation—even if he'd been able to loosen his tongue.

"So, Stewart, Mama tells me you work at the First Exchange Bank. You been there long?"

Hands wrapped so tight around the steering wheel, his knuckles were white, he dared to take his eyes off the road for a split second. "Yeah."

Karly glanced out her window and rolled her eyes. She got more conversation out of her cat, Winston. "How long?"

"It'll be five years next month." Wow. A complete sentence. She snuck a look at him. He wasn't bad looking. Dark hair, brown eyes, trim build. In fact, if someone could give him a dose of personality, he'd be quite a catch.

"I imagine since you've stayed that long, you must like it."

"Where else am I gonna go?"

Karly could fault him for his lack of ambition, but her attitude hadn't been much better. Is this how she appeared to others? Apathetic, indifferent, uninspired? What a terrifying thought.

They pulled into a parking space as Karly scrambled for something encouraging to say to Stewart, but nothing came to mind. She let him open her door then followed him across the crowded parking lot and into the low-lit restaurant. If she'd been with Clive, she'd have said it was romantic. With Stewart, it was just awkward.

Once seated at the table, Karly was able to get lost in the menu. It gave her something to focus on, even if eating seemed an impossibility. Her stomach was in knots, and if she had more nerve and less class, she'd ditch Stewart and take an Uber home.

"The salmon is good here," Stewart said.

It took Karly a full five seconds to realize he'd spoken to her. "Do you eat here often?"

"Used to." His shoulders sagged, and he swiped a hand across his mouth. She recognized defeat when she saw it. Could be there was more to this man than he let on.

Karly set her menu aside. "Look, Stewart." She waited until his eyes met hers. "If I didn't know better, I'd think you were forced into takin' me out. Mama said you'd been building up the courage for some time."

He closed his menu with a sigh. "That's not exactly the truth of it." His gaze caught hers for a beat before slipping away again. "I was goin' out with Lindy Miner for a long time. You remember her from school?"

Karly nodded. "Course. I see her around town all the time."

"We broke things off last year. She wanted to get married, and I wasn't ready for something that permanent. Thought we were too young. When Mama nagged at me about finding a nice girl, I kinda lied to her so she'd let up some."

"I don't understand. You lied about what, exactly?"

"About wanting to go out with you." His face went all shades of red, and he stammered. "I didn't mean that the way it sounded. I just figured you were a safe bet, 'cause you'd never agree to it." He shrugged. "Guess I was wrong."

Karly wasn't sure if she'd just been insulted or complimented. "So, what you're sayin' is I'm your dupe?" Sadie should slap that vocab word onto her students.

"Dupe?" Stewart's eyebrows shot up.

"Yeah, your patsy. You're using me to keep your mama happy."

He wrinkled his nose. "Never thought about it like that, but I suppose. I'm sorry, Karly. You must think I'm a real dog, huh?"

Karly's motive for going out with Stewart wasn't much better. "You're fine." She leaned her elbows on the table. "Is there someone you are interested in seeing? Because it'd make a whole lot more sense to ask her out instead."

"Only one I care to see is Lindy. Breaking things off with her was a real jerk thing to do. Didn't realize how much I loved her until it was too late."

Karly didn't want to think too hard about the parallel between her and Stewart's predicament. Sadie's words came back to bite her. "Can't get what you want in life if you don't ask for it, Stewart."

CHAPTER FIVE

For almost two years, Karly had avoided every bit of gossip and news that had anything to do with Clive Witt—aside from the night he played the Opry. Hearing his sweet voice again was like bein' hit with a sugar addiction. She figured if she could pretend he didn't exist, then losing him wouldn't hurt so bad. One so-called date with the likes of Stewart Miller, and she saw herself for the fool she was.

She didn't rightly know what to do, so she did what she'd been taught from the first day of Sunday school. She prayed. Every night and every morning, she kneeled on the floor of her bedroom with only a thin rug between her and the hardwood. *I reckon You hear me, Lord. I've not come to Your throne room of grace as I should, and for that, and so much more, I'm truly sorry. I'd like to believe Clive is the man You intend for my husband, but maybe I'm just being a fool. Y'all have every minute of my days mapped out, if I'll only listen to Your direction. You know the plans You have for me, and if my future includes Clive, I trust You'll bring him back. If not, please, Lord, guide me in the way I should go.*

Then she waited. Six weeks went by, and she didn't tell a

soul until she was sure as the sun would come up in the morning that Sadie's nagging was gonna be the death of her.

"You mean you're not gonna call Clive yourself?" Sadie sat across from her on another Thursday night at Big Momma's Pizzeria, picking the pepperoni off her pieces as usual. Some things never changed.

"I'm doing what I shoulda done all along." Karly bit into the thick crust and chewed for a few moments. "I'm trusting the Lord."

Sadie scowled.

"Don't you believe in the power of prayer?" Karly wasn't feeling nearly as confident as her words let on. Not because God wouldn't answer her prayer, but because He might not answer it the way she'd hoped.

"Jimmy says Clive's playing Fayetteville this weekend. It's only a couple hours south of here."

Karly's heart nearly dropped to her toes. "I know where Fayetteville is."

"So, call him." Sadie appeared ready to have an apoplectic fit, face all red, words accompanied by spittle. "How's he gonna know you've had a change of heart if you don't? Maybe the fact he's gonna be close by is answer enough."

Karly's mouth went dry, and she took a gulp of her sweet tea. This is where the rubber would meet the road. "I can't be sure God intends for Clive and me to be together unless I step back and let Him work out the particulars."

"You tend to go about things the hard way, Karly." Sadie shook her head. "I hope you know what you're doin'."

Karly's tongue was so thick, she couldn't respond. *Be still and know that I am God.* She'd been meditating on that short scripture verse for days. If God could part the Red Sea, He could surely answer one little ol' prayer for the likes of Karly Dean Butler.

"Oh, my word," Sadie said, grabbing Karly's wrist.

"Let it rest, Sadie, will you? You're gonna make Jimmy a fine nag of a wife if this is the way you respond when someone doesn't agree with you."

"Not that." Sadie smacked Karly's hand, her eyes fixated near the door. "Look at what just walked in."

Karly closed her eyes and sighed. "If it's Jenna and Sophie come to spread doom and gloom, I'd rather not."

"Karly?"

The deep, sweet drawl had Karly spinning so fast she nearly tumbled from her chair. Sapphire blue eyes locked onto hers as the air whooshed from her lungs. Her mouth dropped open, but she couldn't seem to form a word.

Sadie squealed. "What took you so long, Clive?"

Clive cut a glance at Sadie. "You mind if I steal her away for a bit?"

His question cut through the fog in Karly's brain. "How... how'd you know where to find me?"

He turned his crooked grin on her. "It's Thursday night. Where else would you be?" He tilted his head toward the door. "It's a perfect night for a walk. What d'you say?"

"Um, yeah." She glanced at Sadie. "Do you mind?"

Sadie's mouth dropped open. "Are you kiddin' me? I'd like to bury you alive if you turn him down."

Karly's face heated when she realized everyone in the place was staring at her and Clive. Why wouldn't they? He was a celebrity. But she was no one, and he had to have figured that out while he was away. Just because he was here, didn't mean anything. Maybe God brought him back to her long enough to say goodbye.

Although the sun had started its decent, it was still light outside. And warm. Or maybe that was Karly reacting to seeing the man she'd loved since freshman year of high school again after all this time. *Whatever he came to say, Lord, please don't let me make a fool of myself. I need Your strength and Your wisdom.*

"You look real pretty, Karly." Clive moved so he was on the street side of the sidewalk. Since the time she could remember, he'd had a chivalrous streak. His daddy taught him well.

Karly folded her arms, head down. If she looked at him, she'd surely melt. "Nothing compared to the women you've been around, I'm sure. I'm never gonna be anything more than a hometown girl, Clive."

He slipped his hand around her elbow and eased her to a stop. "Look at me, Karly. Please."

She raised her head until their eyes met. The time apart hadn't done a darn thing to ease her feelings for him. How could she have thought it would?

"I get why you pushed me away when things started happening for me." He twisted his mouth. "Can't say I cared for it none, but I get it. You seem to have it in your head that makin' music and traveling around is gonna change me. And maybe it will some. But my feelings for you won't."

Karly's heartbeat quickened like the flutter of a hummingbird's wings. Didn't sound to her like he was saying goodbye at all. "It wasn't just that, Clive." If she was going to trust in God, she had to lay it all out. "You and me, we were together since we were just kids. Growing up in the Appalachians like we did, we've been isolated."

Clive ran a knuckle down Karly's cheek spreading heat clear to her toes. "You think I can find anything better out there than what I got right here, girl?" He shook his head real slow. "You're a pure treasure, Karly. It didn't take me touring around to know that. But unless you believe it, we don't stand a chance."

"A chance at what?" Karly held her breath while she waited on his answer.

"Marriage. Babies. Life." His grin was wide as the Smokey Mountains. "I hear June weddin's are all the rage."

Indignation was the only thing that kept her from falling all over him. "You're awful sure of yourself, Clive Witt. What makes you think I've been waitin' on you all this time?"

He barked out a laugh, his eyes bright as the stars in heaven. "I got my ways. You can't think I'd let you chase me off like you did without a backup plan, did ya?"

Sadie and Jimmy. She didn't know whether to kick 'em or kiss 'em.

"What d'you say, Karly? You gonna make an honest man of me or send me away 'til I grow me a couple more gray hairs?"

Lord, when You go to work, You sure do it up right. "Aren't you forgetting something?"

Clive grinned. "Got it right here." He reached into the pocket of his baggy shorts and pulled out a ring box. "They got this jewelry store in New York called Tiffany's. Ever heard of it?"

Before he could open the lid, Karly put her hand over the blue velvet box. All reason would be gone the moment she laid eyes on the ring. "First things first, Clive."

He slapped his forehead. "What was I thinking?" He started to drop onto one knee, but she grabbed hold of his arm.

"You gotta talk to Daddy, Clive. It may be backwoods to those you been hanging with lately, but if he doesn't give his blessing—"

"Already done, darlin'. Stopped by the hardware store first thing. Took every bit of charm I got to keep him and your mama from followin' me to the pizza place."

This couldn't truly be happening, could it?

Clive opened the lid of the box. A square-cut, vintage diamond ring twinkled beneath the street light. "I love you more than life, Karly. Always have. Will you please take me outta my misery and marry me?"

Tears pooled in Karly's eyes as she gazed into his. "Are you sure, Clive?"

He blew out a breath, his own eyes suspiciously moist. "Babe, I've known you were the only one for me from the time I slipped you that first note in our freshman English class. I was just waitin' on you to figure it out."

Karly couldn't find her voice to save her life, so she wrapped her arms around his neck as their mouths met. He lifted her off the ground and deepened the kiss until she was sure her heart had melted into a puddle at their feet. It could have been seconds, minutes, or hours. It didn't matter. This was exactly where she was meant to be.